a kindred spirit

a novel by

ej Morgan

ZiaLink Ink

an Imprint of

CogDisCo, LLC

a kindred spirit

by

ej Morgan

www.AKSbook.com

ZiaLink Ink Publishing / CogDisCo, LLC

Any resemblance to reality is purely coincidental.
Credits, Copyright and Legal Disclaimers, and other Acknowledgments in back matter of this book

Trade Paperback ISBN: 978-0-9827619-0-8
eBook ISBN: 978-0-9827619-2-2
Library of Congress Control Number
LCCN: 2010934357

Printed in the United States of America

Yiroglyphic font on papyrus
Dan Zadorozny info@iconian.com

Cover by Jonathan Cartland/CogDisCo
Interior illustrations by mmgray

Final Revisions: July 6, 2011

dedicated to

my friends
for their years of support!

and to

Philip K. Dick

who for 53 years, through more than 40 novels,

asked

What is Real? What is Human?

May the Search continue...

Important Disclaimer—

It's fiction. Any resemblance to reality is coincidental.

That said, some of the characters are "really real." **Philip K. Dick** (1928-1982) the Prince of Pulp. Many claim he will be remembered as the greatest fictionalizing philosopher of the 20th Century. Writing about him was highly encouraged by Paul Williams, former Literary Executor of the Philip K. Dick Estate. And, by Phil, too ;)

Bishop James "Jim" Pike (1913-1969) Episcopalian Bishop of California, 1958–1966. He *was* a friend of Phil's and did appear on the cover of *Time* magazine. His controversial story was followed by the news media before and after he died.

Dr. John R. Gribbin is a British astrophysicist (still living and writing.) He wrote *The Jupiter Effect, Time Warps* and one hundred (yes, 100!) scientific and literary works, plus some fiction. He graciously agreed to be a character in this story with a fictionalized 1982 U.S. appearance. Thank you, John. You're still my idol, you sexy thing.

Use of the Los Angeles Griffith Observatory, and all the alleged events that took place there, was encouraged by **Dr. E.C. Krupp**, for whom the G.O. is his raison d'être. He's been keeping watch over the stars from the famed Hollywood hills observatory for nearly forty years. You're the Dogon best, Dr. Krupp—I am Sirius!

Benjamin Crème, of Share International, speaks of peace and the arrival of Maitreya. He has been doing so for 28 years and asks us to "share the information with as many people as possible." I am. He discusses his beliefs on radio broadcasts, including the one that aired in January 1982 with **KNX News Director Tom McKay**. Tom, consenting to be in this novel, sent an email of his recollections of that interview being "fascinating/ridiculous/scary/Twilight Zone-y/ all at once." Full-page newspaper ads, in 1982, announced that the Maitreya would appear that spring. He didn't.

Remarkably, on January 14, 2010, Crème claimed the Maitreya finally did appear on U.S. network television. Did He? Has the time come? PKD was fascinated by this idea. Perhaps you will be, too.

-- ej Morgan, Albuquerque, NM

Table of Contents

Back Matter:

Warning: Yes, I used web emoticons ;) and some web speak (LOL, but only in author commentary or when Phil speaks from the future), questionable punctuation (!?#@!), odd diagrams, sketches formatted in varying methods, and there will be authorial intrusion (mostly from PKD.) Get over it, old school grammarians!

Web Speak and Emoticon Lexicon:

;) winky smiley face = amusement
:(frown = disappointment
(jk) = just kidding!
LOL = Laughing Out Loud
ROFLOL = Rolling on Floor, LOL
TEOTWAWKI = the End of the World, as we know it
!?#@! = e-Cursing
... something was omitted (for a variety of reasons ;)
FDO = For Dickheads Only
R U = Are you (RU into PKD?)
PKD = Philip K. Dick
AKS = A Kindred Spirit (U R holding it!)
Tweet = microblogging on Twitter site, as in:
"FDOs, let's trend up on AKS!"

The Big Bang

"Suppose a man died with the dearest wish of his heart unfulfilled. Do you believe that his spirit might have the power to return to Earth and complete the interrupted work?"

-- *Jerome K. Jerome "Ghost Story"*

November 17, 1971 - Santa Venetia, California

It was an ordinary ranch-style house on a quiet cul-de-sac; a dark, starry night—until the explosion. Even that was muffled and neighbors would later claim they didn't hear a thing. If they had been watching, they would have seen a firestorm roll through the house and crack the front picture window.

An hour or so later, a big, red 1963 Pontiac convertible rumbled around the corner onto Hacienda Way heading toward the house. The couple inside the car giggled like teenagers. The girl driving was only eighteen, but the man pawing at her was old enough to be her father. He was also a semi-famous science fiction author, but that meant nothing to her. She had other interests in Philip K. Dick.

"Stop it," she said as she pushed him away. "You smell like greasy burger and onions. You know that stuff'll give you bad dreams."

"Not tonight, baby," he whispered in her ear as Sharon parked the car in front of Phil's place. "I'm only dreaming of you." Phil was swaying to Carole King's light and breezy voice on the radio. "Let's do it here."

"Nooo," she whined. "Let's go in and do it on the floor."

Phil's girlfriend-of-the-moment hopped out of the car and pulled him from the passenger seat. He playfully tugged at the buttons on her blouse as they staggered up the walkway to the front door. Phil had never actually "done it" with this girl, but liked the idea. Since his last divorce, he hadn't technically been dating anyone. Sharon was one of several young druggies he let crash at his house.

In the Bay Area in 1971, everyone was scoring or selling some kind of dope. Phil didn't care much for hash or coke, but was a considerable consumer of white cross tabs—amphetamines. Writing fuel. His need for speed was also a way to keep Sharon around, and keep an eye on her. Phil fancied himself her savior. Actually, Sharon was the one taking care of Phil. Someone had to.

Phil was prone to terrible bouts of depression and paranoia. He was also agoraphobic, and needed someone to drive him places, even to the grocery store or burger joint. But on such a starry night, Phil was happy for a change and focused on the possibility of making it with this young dark-haired girl.

"Vincent," he slobbered in Sharon's ear while fumbling with the key to unlock the front door.

"Man, you are stoned," she frowned. "Are you a homo?"

Phil chuckled. "It's a song. Fabulous, brand new album. Wait 'til you hear—" He pushed the door open with his hip and was about to give another push toward Sharon. Before he could finish his thought, she shrieked, "Jesus, Phil, look!"

For a moment, Phil couldn't comprehend the devastation.

"What the…"

A million tiny pieces of white debris covered everything, the carpet, furniture, drapes—it was even sticking to the walls. His eyes darted toward the adjoining room, his writing room, where chunks of metal were strewn among the bits of white. Phil pushed past Sharon, who was frozen in place, and entered the study. That's when he saw the mangled remains of his fireproof file cabinet.

"Shit, I knew it!" Phil rubbed his eyes and temples. The force of the explosion had blown slivers of steel into the side of his oak desk. Bits of canceled checks, and other unrecognizable paper and plastic swirled together into a sickening stew of debris.

Phil allowed friends to come and go, smoke pot and make a mess of his house, but no one was allowed in the writing room. It was his only safe haven, strictly off limits. He kept that room neat and tidy. It was the only way he could organize his thoughts and have any privacy to work on his novels. Now, his mind was as cluttered and confused as the mess around him. He knew one thing for sure—his latest and most important manuscript was gone.

Sharon followed Phil into the den and found him staring off blankly. Then he erupted into a crazy, maniacal laugh that scared her.

"Thank God I'm not crazy!"

"I'm calling the cops," Sharon said looking for his phone.

Phil grabbed her forcefully. "No you're not." The wild look in his eyes scared her. "No fucking cops, you hear?"

She began to shake and cry.

"I'll deal with this. You need to leave." Phil practically shoved Sharon out the door and then felt bad. It wasn't like him to be mean, especially to a crying woman. But he was about to cry himself, and didn't want anyone to see that.

Phil collapsed in a heap on the living room floor, in the middle of the mess. "Damn," he sputtered. "I knew the sons of bitches were after me."

He sat on the floor for hours, rocking back and forth, playing over in his mind theory after theory of who would go to such extremes to steal his writing. It was a carefully crafted, professionally executed explosion. Whoever did it knew to use heavy wet bath towels to muffle the sound and contain the contents.

The bastards. He hoped they got a soggy, illegible manuscript, and that maybe one of them had blown off a hand in the process. Eventually, he drifted off to sleep in his half-sitting, half-fetal position.

In the light of day, the scene was even more disturbing. It hadn't been a dream. The mess was real.

Stiff and foggy, Phil got up and stumbled to the phone, which remarkably was still intact. He found the number of a guy who had been a demolitions expert in the Special Forces. Carl knew all about explosives. Once he was on the line, Phil identified himself and mumbled some cryptic, code talk. He had no trouble conveying the point. In less than an hour there was a knock on his door.

Phil cautiously peeked through the peep-hole. Standing there was a mountain of muscle; six-foot-five, at least two hundred and fifty pounds of it, still sporting a marine-style buzz cut.

Phil opened the door and the ex-marine had the same reaction that Phil had the night before.

"Shit!" Carl cursed as he carefully stepped inside.

Carl instantly began surveying the scene. He reached down and ran his fingers through some of the white debris.

"Asbestos. Your safe was blown, eh?"

Phil shushed him, finger to his lips, and turned on the TV for background noise. Amazingly, it still worked. His stereo, an expensive quadraphonic, was gone. Suspecting the place was bugged, Phil spoke in a hushed voice.

"An eleven hundred pound Mosler Class D fireproof file cabinet." He pointed toward his den.

As they walked through the mess, Carl bent down, picked up a bit of metal debris and sniffed it.

"Plastic explosive. C3, even C4. This stuff ain't on the street. Very suspicious." He offered it to Phil who took a whiff and shuddered. Carl also pointed out something else Phil had missed.

"Check out that print. Combat boots." Sure enough, several tracks were visible where the white powder was crushed into the thick green carpet.

The two men stood together surveying the remains of Phil's den. In comparison to the tall, muscular jarhead, Phil was hunched over, and for the first time he could ever remember, felt old.

At forty-two, Phil's beard was streaked with gray and an emerging pot-belly was in competition with his barrel chest. His once luminous blue-gray eyes were tired and underscored with dark circles. His head ached, actually his brain hurt. He had always worked too much, writing into the wee hours, sometimes all night, so he could continue to pump out pulp after pulp fiction.

Phil had been known to crank out a novel in less than two weeks, especially when he needed money. He'd written over twenty just in the past ten years. The hours and speed were taking a toll. This break-in might be the proverbial "final straw" for Phil.

"Who's after you, man?" Carl asked, snapping Phil back to reality.

"Everyone—religious fanatics, the CIA—maybe both. They got my manuscript."

"Manuscript? What the hell kind of stuff are you writing?" Carl looked confused as he pulled his pack of Camels from his shirt pocket.

"Guess you don't mind if I smoke in this mess, do you?"

"Actually, I'll take one myself."

Carl lit both cigarettes and handed one off to Phil, who took a deep drag and immediately coughed and choked as if his lungs might be the next thing to explode.

"Prefer snuff, myself."

"So, what are you writing that would justify this?" Carl asked again. "Does sci-fi pay that well?"

"No, not hardly. This is something else. If I tried to explain it, you'd think I was certifiable." Phil took a small drag this time, and blew the smoke right back out.

Carl reached down and picked up another piece of the metal casing and studied it. "I recognized this shit because a buddy from my unit showed me how to detonate it. In fact, he claimed it was used in a political hit back in D.C. just a couple of months ago. Even said Nixon was behind it."

"Wouldn't surprise me," Phil responded. "Nothing would after this."

Carl took a long drag and studied Phil. "You're right, this took some military expertise. Why would the Feds or Special Forces hit your place?"

Phil was formulating an idea, but aloud he simply said, "Um, not sure."

"You're gettin' in way over your head if you're taking on Nixon," Carl warned. "Next time you might not be so lucky. Could be you, not a book."

"I know," Phil sighed. "Let's go to the kitchen and I'll make some coffee."

Phil was buying time, debating how much to reveal to Carl. After all, as an ex-Marine, Carl was still loyal to the U.S. government. Phil felt no loyalty to these Nixon-led, fascist pigs that were running the country. He had openly criticized Nixon in several of his novels, so that was nothing new. Why would government operatives break in and steal a manuscript that had nothing to do with Nixon? No, this was definitely about Pike.

His good friend Bishop James Pike, of the Episcopal Diocese of California, survived a heresy trial, but then died mysteriously in the Judean desert. Authorities claimed it was an accident. Phil suspected something far more sinister. The timing was too ironic.

Less than a week before the Bishop died, he had sent Phil a telegram. Pike said his findings were too controversial to wire, but he wanted Phil to help him write the story as soon as he returned. Phil was the only one Pike had contacted.

Phil's own life was in danger now, or so it seemed. This professional hit proved it. Pike warned that taking on the Church was dangerous, that they could be more diabolical than the Feds. Most of the serious bloodshed in the world is over religion, especially in the Middle East. Phil knew that, but didn't have the energy or inclination to explain all this to Carl.

So, they drank coffee while Carl chain-smoked and rambled on about explosives. Phil let him go on believing the break-in was probably the communist-obsessed Minutemen and even muddied the water further telling him about Black Panthers who lived in the neighborhood. He didn't say a word about Bishop Pike. Instead he said, "Listen, I know how you feel about deserters, but I'm way beyond draft age. I may have to leave. You know, get out of the country for a while."

"Mexico?" Carl asked, blowing a smoke ring into the air.

"No, Canada. I've got an invitation to speak at a sci-fi convention in Vancouver. I could just stay on awhile."

"Yeah, can't say I blame you."

Carl stubbed out his cigarette and stood up, towering over Phil. "You should stick to outer space and stay out of politics, man."

With that, ol' Carl flashed the peace—or victory sign—Phil wasn't sure which, and said, "You know how to reach me."

Phil didn't call him again. He just packed a few things and left for Vancouver, leaving Sharon and the mess on Hacienda Way behind. He didn't even bother to clean up the place. Sometime after he left, looters broke in the back door and stole everything else of value. Phil never returned to Santa Venetia, California.

Who would go to such lengths to steal Philip K. Dick's files? Did he really have evidence that could destroy the Church?

Before the *Da Vinci Code*, or holy bloodline theories, there was Bishop Pike—the original heretic and clerical bad boy. What did the Bishop discover back in 1969 that could be so controversial?

It was enough to drive Phil out of Marin County and the Bay Area to Canada and over the edge. Luckily his suicide attempts failed, but the raid on his home remained a life-long obsession.

Eventually Phil returned to California, but to Orange County, where he made new friends. One was a young writer and long-time fan, Paul Williams (the rock music historian, not the song writer) who convinced Phil to "go public" with the facts of the break-in.

A lengthy article in *Rolling Stone* magazine (11/1975; Issue #199) explored five theories about the 1971 break-in. Not one of those mentioned that church officials might have wanted to silence Phil. There was nothing about Phil's most important piece of writing or his relationship with Bishop Pike. And no discussion of the "really heavy shit"—as Phil called it.

The *Rolling Stone* spread did wonders, though, in terms of publicity for Phil and his novels. But by that time, his life had become much more complicated. There was a new kind of "break-in" to worry about.

Something had infiltrated Phil's mind. A presence—a pink light—that he said beamed information to him. Mental illness? Had Phil finally flipped out? When you claim that an info-firing pink beam is after you, your friends and fans get really worried. But in true Phil-form he could describe his fantastic vision in exquisite detail. He called it VALIS—the Vast Active Living Intelligence System—and wrote a novel about it.

One novel was not enough to explore his mysterious, mystical experiences. Philip K. Dick spent eight years and eight thousand pages of Exegesis (his private ponderings and speculations) about the events that began in the early 1970s. Phil obsessively searched for the source and true meaning of the revelations. Were Russians beaming secret signals into space that Phil somehow intercepted? Did he receive alien transmissions? Was he channeling Bishop Pike? Or—was VALIS actually *God?*

∞

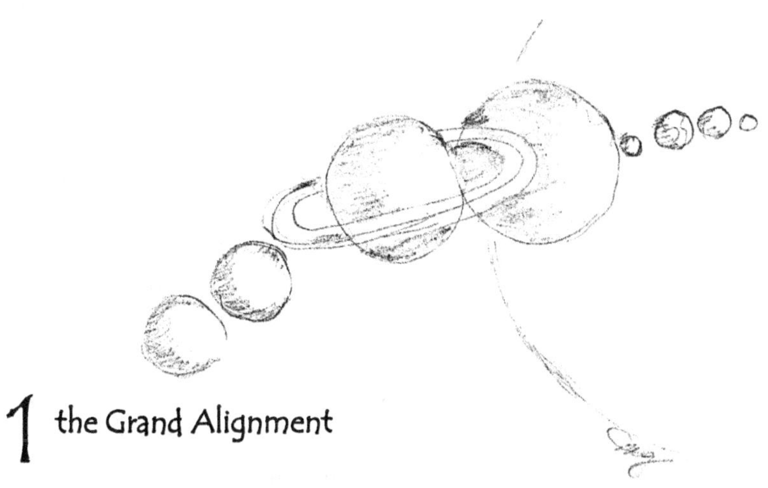

1 the Grand Alignment

The world was supposed to end March 10, 1982–obviously it didn't.

"You can't go to L.A. Don't be ridiculous. What makes you think the guy will give you an interview?" Frank said as he stubbed out his unfiltered cigarette in the over-flowing ashtray. He leaned back in his ratty desk chair, his glare as harsh as his raspy voice. Niki knew he didn't really want an answer. She stood in front of his desk, arms folded across her chest, waiting for the last word. It came, right on cue.

"The *Courier* won't pay for it."

"I'll pay for it myself, then. I'm going Frank, even if I have to take vacation."

It was the first time the young reporter had ever looked down on her boss, literally and figuratively. Frank wasn't just her editor, he was her mentor, the one who discovered her "nose for news." How could he not understand that she had to go after this story? This wasn't just any story, this was *her* story.

On her way out the door, Niki turned and called back, "Just schedule my time off. It's less than a month away." She held her breath until she was outside the Editor's office, then slumped against the wall and finally exhaled.

It's worse out here, she thought as she choked her way through the haze hanging over the heavy wooden desks in the open newsroom. What constituted reporters for the *Courier* were mostly chain-smoking, middle-aged men with yellow stained shirts and teeth the same shade. She hated the stale stench and the way it clung to her clothes and thick auburn hair.

When she got to the spot designated as her "desk," she could hardly hear herself think. There was no cubicle or partition to separate her from the clattering of old manual typewriters and the teletype machine racket bouncing off the walls. Some loud-mouth sports jock sat about a foot away yucking it up on the phone. She slumped in her own creaky desk chair and stared at the calendar she had taped to the wall.

Two dates on her 1982 Year-at-a-Glance wall calendar were circled in heavy red ink and were inextricably linked; February 3rd, the day John Gribbin would speak in Los Angeles, and March 10th, the day the world was supposed to end.

From the moment she learned that European astrophysicist Dr. John Gribbin would make his first U.S. appearance, there was no doubt she was going—she had to meet him, write the story, perhaps have his child.

For Niki, the sexy, controversial author was a rock star. Gribbin was crossing the Pond (as the Brits say) to speak at the prestigious Los Angeles Griffith Observatory. He was promoting his latest book and doomsday theory by the same name: *The Jupiter Effect.*

Niki had discovered Gribbin several years earlier when she was still in college. He didn't write dry science, far from it. He delved into time travel, paranormal paradoxes and metaphysical mysteries—the type of stuff she used to discuss late at night with her mom. The fact that he was coming to the States on what would have been her mom's 60th birthday was a gift, if not an omen.

Niki was still flush-faced over the run-in with Frank. She would find a way to get to Gribbin, interview him, and prove to Frank, and the world, that she too could explain the inexplicable.

In a nutshell, *The Jupiter Effect* was John Gribbin's theory that on March 10, 1982, a rare planetary alignment could create such an intense gravitational pull that it might spawn world-wide tsunamis and devastating earthquakes.

Book promoters made it worse claiming the California coast could slip into the ocean. There were other cataclysmic claims, too. Horrific graphics portraying Earth engulfed in flames and speculation that the events might rock the planet right off its axis. With the alignment just weeks away, there was increasing buzz about the Big One and Californians were getting nervous.

Niki was getting nervous, too. Few knew that Gribbin had agreed to speak in Los Angeles. Once that word got out, all hell might really break loose. Network TV reporters and doomsayers would hype his hypothesis. Latter-day lunatics would turn the event into a true end-time epidemic. Niki wasn't sure if the End was truly at hand, but felt her fate hinged on putting her own spin on the cosmic collision. But how? She was working for the Ottumwa *Courier*.

A grand alignment of seven planets in our solar system is the kind of thing that draws people to a planetarium. But staff and astronomers at the famous Los Angeles observatory were wary of the Cambridge scholar and his claims. The Griffith gang called Gribbin a "sleek, gaudy paperback tale spinner" and tried to suppress news coverage of his appearance. They didn't want a riot on their hands.

If only she could reveal the truth about Gribbin, rather than these ridiculous publicity stunts—that's it! Niki realized she could write a promotional piece to set the record straight. Her thoughts ran wild. Maybe she could syndicate the story and even meet Gribbin when his plane landed.

The Jupiter Effect would be headline news, and when it was, it would carry Niki Perceval's by-line.

Her heart pounded faster than her fingers could fly over the old manual Olivetti keys. Soon she had a list of descriptive phrases: astronomical acrobatics, a celestial circus, maybe even a cosmic Conga line. Some of these were probably too corny, even for Iowans. After all, she was reaching for a national, or even international audience. If she played her cards right, covering the end of the world would be her ticket out of this god-forsaken rat hole.

Niki stopped typing and stared off into space. Maybe she should start with an analogy about the Persian stargazers and how throughout the centuries, eclipses and planetary conjunctions had always been harbingers of doom. More importantly, she needed to explain that even though planetary alignments are not that unusual, it's only once every two thousand years that we enter into a new constellation. And on March 10, 1982, the world would see both: the transition to the New Age of Aquarius, and a rare planetary configuration—truly making this a Grand Alignment.

She yanked the paper with the cornball phrases from her typewriter and started over:

"Those who search for signs will find them."

Late January, 1982

Phil could hardly wait for the late night radio program *Insight Out* to air. He was going to record it. He had a new cassette tape all cued up in his stereo system. If friends, or anyone showed up, he didn't want to miss a word—this one was extra special.

The excitement had begun that morning when Philip K. Dick was washing a few dishes while listening to his favorite mellow rock station KNX-FM out of Los Angeles. The DJ promised a real treat. He said News Director Tom McKay would be speaking that night with a man who claimed Christ had already returned.

"Don't miss this one," the announcer said in his deepest promotional tones. "Benjamin Crème, of Share International, claims to be in telepathic contact with Christ, who will be known to the world as the Maitreya."

Phil dropped and nearly broke his favorite coffee mug.

"What?" he blurted, and for a moment worried it might be the *voices* again.

Phil had heard auditory hallucinations in the form of warnings over the radio back in the 1970s. Sometimes hateful messages that felt like bad acid-trip flashbacks. There were also religious epiphanies. But that stuff hadn't happened for years. He was sure this was real. The announcer actually said telepathic contact with Christ. Phil repeated the words under his breath while he searched for the phone book. He looked up the number of KNX and called the radio station. A perky, young female receptionist, who identified herself as Pat, answered the phone.

"I just heard the announcement for tonight's talk show," Phil said. "*Insight Out.* Can you tell me who the guest is?"

"Hang on," the girl said as she chomped what sounded like an enormous wad of gum.

"That's the Tom McKay show. On at ten tonight."

"And, his guest will be Benjamin Crème?" Phil asked.

"Yep, that's what the card says," Perky Pat confirmed.

Phil wanted to ask more, but knew the girl wouldn't know. "Well, thank you then," was all he said and hung up. He felt like a kid at Christmas. "Could it be possible?" he wondered. "This Crème is really a teep?"

Phil was amazed that someone else might be receiving telepathic religious transmissions. He always called telepaths teeps or precogs in his old sci-fi novels. If this guy was truly having epiphanies and speaking with God, it would change everything. This might be the missing piece of the puzzle—what he'd been waiting for!

Phil could not recall the last time he taped an interview or talk show. He had quite a few tapes of himself being interviewed; some from past sci-fi conventions like the Canada Con in Montréal, or his famous "If You Find This World Bad" speech from the Metz fest in France. It took a lot of willpower to travel that far, agoraphobic that he was. But even in SoCal—the name hip locals called southern California—Phil had become hip too, now that the *Blade Runner* movie promo had been released. His 1968 book *Do Androids Dream of Electric Sheep?* was about to premiere as a Hollywood movie. It was no longer just young fans that wanted to interview him. Now even a few mainstream journalists had come to call. Phil could not recall the last time he wanted to tape someone else being interviewed.

The first thing to do was clean the heads on the recorder deck. In fact, better double check the entire system and verify it can still tape from the radio, he decided. He did not tape music from the radio because the quality was never good enough. Tapes of radio broadcasts had too much static and were basically crap. As a full-fledged audiophile and former record shop manager from the early days, Phil was picky. He would make an exception tonight, though.

After hours of anticipation and testing audio equipment, it was finally time for the program.

Phil had a bottle of Laphroaig single malt whisky ready. He poured two fingers full into his highball glass, added a splash of water, and then raised it into the air as a symbolic toast to his late friend Bishop James Pike. This would have been a night to remember, sharing this program, and the Scotch, too—something neither of them could afford back in the 1960s.

"A fine spirit, for a fine Spirit," Phil toasted aloud. "Jim, old pal," he wiped a tear away. "I sure wish you were here for this."

Immediately, Phil realized Pike might very well be listening in. In fact, he thought, maybe Pike had a hand in this—orchestrating the events, making sure he heard the promo.

Of course, if this Crème guy really is a teep he'd know I've been waiting for this type of revelation for years. Before Phil could concoct further scenarios, he heard the show's theme music begin. He quickly put down the whisky glass, pressed the record button and exhaled.

Philip Kindred Dick, who had spent the last eight years of his life pondering all things spiritual, metaphysical and religious, sank into his recliner chair anxious to hear a kindred spirit who communicated telepathically with God.

∞

February 3, 1982

On the first Wednesday of February, Niki was not trudging through mounds of snow to cover the boring Ottumwa City Council meeting. She was driving a rental car up the steep hill that led to the Los Angeles Griffith Observatory. It was a balmy 70 degrees and Niki was in hog heaven, as they would say back in Iowa. Before she left, Frank had convinced the managing editorial board to pay her expenses. There wasn't much choice once the Associated Press wire service picked up her story and cast Gribbin and his *Jupiter Effect* into the national spotlight. Ted Koppel had mentioned the *Courier* and her story on the network news. The boys in the newsroom had quit laughing then.

Other than a glimpse from the plane, it was the first time Niki had seen the ocean. From high in the Hollywood hills she saw water merging with the horizon. The curvature of the earth—such an awesome sight—disturbing and beautiful at the same time.

"I wish you could see this," Niki said to her mom who had always wanted to see the ocean, but never did. "Maybe you can. If so, Happy Birthday!"

As she snaked up the narrow observatory road, ever closer to the crest of the foothill, she saw the iconic "Hollywood" letters on a nearby hill. She was really here!

Niki also saw a glint of the greenish copper dome of the observatory straight ahead. Then she saw something even more daunting—

a never-ending snarl of bumper-to-bumper traffic ahead. TV trucks and even bigger rigs with satellite dishes were honking.

Maybe the promotional piece wasn't such a great idea. Niki glanced in the rearview mirror. There were cars and more trucks behind her. She was trapped. She had never had a panic attack, but felt this could be one. She was perspiring and felt dizzy. There was no way off the hill. She had to sit and wait with nothing to do but ruminate on the mess she had created. What was I thinking? I should have known it would turn into a huge media circus. She wiped drops of perspiration from her forehead.

"Good God!" Even the foreign press was there. Niki had not anticipated being in competition with big media like the BBC or other network television crews. Frank was right, she thought. I'll never be able to get an interview in this mess.

Finally, a parking attendant waved her forward and Niki flashed her press pass. He directed her to a special area for the media. She clipped the pass on her shirt, grabbed her bag with her camera, tape recorder and notebooks, took a deep breath, and got out of the car. The cool air against the back of her sopping wet shirt gave Niki goose bumps as she headed toward the incredible white marble tri-domed compound that was the Griffith Observatory.

She took in the incredible panorama of the Los Angeles basin one last time before stepping through the heavy ornate doors.

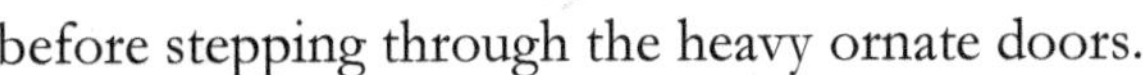

One way or another, she knew what she had to do—find Gribbin and convey to him that she was his most avid long-time admirer, and the reporter who promoted his U.S. appearance.

Inside, other news crews were heading toward the Planetarium for the lecture. Niki decided to explore, heading down the hall in the opposite direction until a security guard stopped her.

"Miss, the Planetarium is back this way."

"Oh, I know," Niki replied. She flashed a smile at the guard and continued on. "I'm looking for a friend who works here." She lowered her voice, "and I need to use the restroom first."

"Okay, I guess," the guard shrugged and smiled back at her. "As long as you know where you're going."

"I do." She nodded and kept moving. Yes sir, she thought. I know exactly where I'm going—off to find my elusive, dreamy Dr. Gribbin. After rounding a bend in the circular hallway, she spotted a geeky guy wearing a large access card around his neck.

"Excuse me," she said waving to get his attention. "You wouldn't happen to know where the computer room is, would you?"

The guy pushed up his glasses and without making eye contact muttered, "We don't have a computer room."

"Oh, come on. You can't fool me." Niki moved a little closer and whispered, "I work with computers and I would just love to see the stuff that runs this place."

"Honestly, we don't have anything but an Apple that runs some trajectory calculations."

Niki leaned over to look at his badge, and saw his name was Marvin. "May I call you Marv?" She continued talking before he could answer. "You have no idea how much it would mean to me. I've been programming for ten years."

"Nah, that can't be true. We just got the Apple II here a couple of years ago and Jobs had just released it at the West Coast Computer Faire. What would you have been using?"

"Well, first of all I interviewed Wozniak, the other Apple inventor, when he came to Des Moines. But I programmed cards on a Honeywell and later a VAX in college."

"A VAX, no kidding? You really are a programmer!"

"Yep, and I cannot leave here without seeing that telescope, because I'm also a gadget geek," Niki paused. "Please? Just a peek?"

"I'm the A/V guy. I don't really work on the telescope. Dr. Krupp is really picky about his gear. The Zeiss is super cool, if you like gadgets. It's the ultimate multi-media projection system." Marvin checked his watch, which featured a certain little alien by the same name. "Anyway, I gotta run."

"Wait," Niki said as she grabbed his arm and admired his wristwatch. "That's my favorite cartoon, too. I must see your space *mod-u-lator*." She attempted a bit of Martian speak which made them both laugh.

"I really do have to go," Marvin said. "Our guest lecturer needs a quick lesson on how to run the system."

"You mean Gribbin?"

"Uh huh."

"That's even better! I would love to watch."

Marvin motioned as though he was going to protest again, but then just sighed and said, "Okay, this way."

Niki suppressed a giggle of delight and followed the geeky guy down the hall.

"Have you met him yet?" she asked.

"No, but he's down this hall in the break room with the other techs. They're going over the special effects stuff he wants for the show."

Niki spotted a restroom just across the hall from where the briefing was underway. She really did need it, plus wanted to freshen up before seeing her dream brainiac.

"Sorry, Marvin," she apologized. "I've got to dash in here. Go on. I'll catch up."

Despite the huge crowd at the observatory, the restroom was basically empty. Not many women here, she realized as she washed her hands and surveyed herself in the mirror.

What a mess, she thought surveying her crumpled cotton shirt. She tried to smooth it while tucking it into her too-tight jeans. Should have worn that stupid pantsuit, she thought about the navy blue polyester "set" she bought just for this occasion. It wouldn't be wrinkled. That fake fabric never is, and that's exactly why she couldn't force herself into it this morning at the motel. She had convinced herself that her best indigo jeans and white cotton shirt looked just fine for a newspaper reporter. But now she reconsidered as she glanced at a perfectly coifed small Asian woman standing next to her. TV reporter, Niki knew without even reading the press badge clipped on the expensive lapel of the tiny silk suit.

The contrast in the mirror between the sleek black Asian hair and her own frizzy auburn mop was startling. After the woman clicked her way across the tile floor and out the door, Niki waged war on her thick, shoulder-length waves. No amount of brushing helped. Still looks like Janis Joplin, she sighed and dabbed a dash of powder over her freckled face, then turned to finish checking herself in the mirror.

At five-five, she wasn't tiny like the Asian woman, but she was slim and athletic. Niki knew she could never work in TV and click around a crime scene in heels. She dusted off her Doc Martens and tossed her duffel bag over her shoulder.

Leaving the restroom, she was still adjusting her bag when she collided head-on with someone coming around the curved wall. She started to apologize, then gasped as she glanced up. "Oh my god! Dr. Gribbin, is it really you?"

The man stepped back and began to smooth his wool jacket. He eyed the young woman who had just crumpled it. Before he could speak, her girlish gush began.

"I recognize you from the cover of your *Time Warps* book. You look even better in person. You are the reason I studied both science and religion in college," she went on. "Transcendental physics, parallel universes—that stuff changed my life!"

"Well, what can I say to that?" Gribbin responded as he pulled a pair of spectacles out of his jacket pocket to have a look at her press badge. Perhaps he also wanted a closer look at the gregarious redhead who knew so much about him.

"Ah, a news reporter," he said and stepped closer to read her badge. "Autumn wah?" he mispronounced her hometown with his distinctive British accent.

"Oh TUM wah," she corrected him. "It's a small town in Iowa, the Midwest." She stopped, realizing that none of these places meant anything to him.

"I wrote the promotional piece about you coming to the States, your bio and why you wrote *The Jupiter Effect*." Niki reached into her bag and quickly produced a copy of the newspaper with the alignment article, and offered it to the suave scholar.

As he glanced at the *Courier*, Niki blushed, embarrassed that it was just her small town paper. She quickly added, "My story was syndicated and ran in the major U.S. markets. It was quoted on *Nightline*—a network news program."

Gribbin took the paper, stepped back, and rubbed a hand over his bearded chin. His only response was, "Ah."

"I came a long way to be here," Niki said. "To be honest I was hoping for a private interview. You know, an exclusive, since I'm so familiar with your work." In a final breathless rush she added, "I've read everything you've written. I'm a huge admirer."

"It certainly seems so," Gribbin said glancing up from reading.

"Nicole Perceval," he tapped the folded newspaper and tucked it under his arm. "Entirely my pleasure." The scientist reached for her hand and as he clasped his fingers around hers, his dark eyes locked onto hers. She was surprised by the rush of sensations. Not only did she feel a warmth creep through her that she hadn't felt for awhile, she also sensed things. Intelligence, intensity, but maybe a sinister side. Could that be? She also wondered, given his unusual angle on science, if he too could read energy fields. If so, wouldn't there be a feedback loop? She felt something exciting—like electricity passing between them. It also gave Niki a boost of confidence.

"Is there any chance I could get a special interview? Just a few minutes of your time after the lecture, that's all I would need."

He gently released her hand. "Anything is possible. May I keep this?" He waved the *Courier* with her article.

"Please do."

Niki blushed as Gribbin walked away. That is one sexy scientist, she thought, and definitely her lucky day. She had not forgotten that it was her mother's birthday. She looked up and whispered, "Thanks."

The security guard appeared out of nowhere, took her by the arm and led her toward the planetarium. Niki couldn't care less. She'd made a connection that might pay off.

The planetarium was full, actually overflowing. No seats were left. Niki didn't mind standing, or leaning against the back wall. She had a clear view of the elevated lectern where Gribbin would soon speak. Being close to the door would make it easy to leave and get a prime position on the lawn for the press conference afterwards. An energetic, wiry man, who reminded her of a young version of her editor Frank, stepped up to the lectern.

"Hello. I'm Ed Krupp, the director here," he began. "We are thrilled to have such a large crowd and so many photographers and reporters. I must ask, though, that you do not use flash bulbs or..." Niki wished she could fast-forward through the inevitable housekeeping rules and get to the all-important introduction of her man. Finally, it came.

"So, to the reason you've all gathered here today. It is my honor to introduce, for this special one-time-only event, a young but extensively published man of letters who has traveled from Sussex, England to join us. With a doctorate in astrophysics from Cambridge University, making his first appearance in the United States, I present the distinguished Dr. John Gribbin."

Loud applause broke into Krupp's introduction as Gribbin appeared from the darkness. The handsome scientist walked toward the center of the round room, and Krupp motioned for Gribbin to step up on the platform.

Applause died down, creating a brief awkward transition while Gribbin manipulated the dials and switches of the elaborate Zeiss projector. Soon, "oohs" and "ahs" replaced the silence when the dark dome came to life displaying stunning graphics of the now famous planetary configuration known as the Grand Alignment.

Niki was thrilled to be standing where she could see Gribbin, at least his dark figure, surrealistically surrounded by the planets. She snapped off a couple of shots with her 35mm camera on wide-open aperture, no flash, and then stuffed it into her bag. After that she remained mesmerized, watching and listening to the man who had just held her hand in the hallway.

After thanking Krupp and the City of Los Angeles, Gribbin explained, "For the planetarium show, I'm not going to address any of the controversies or concerns that have brought so many reporters and TV crews here. We'll confine that discussion to the press conference afterwards. So, those of you who are only here for that might give up your seat to some of the children or others waiting in the hall who are more interested in cosmic rays, solar flares and what the Alignment will look like when all the major planets converge on one side of the sun."

This caused an unexpected disruption as some reporters left, allowing more spectators to sit in the planetarium. Niki had no intention of sitting or leaving. While the last few people came and went, Gribbin resumed. "Actually, I was in California once before, eight years ago, to finalize research for the book. I spent time at the Old Mission San Juan Bautista, anyone familiar with that area?" Several hands went up.

"So, you know about the illumination of the altar during Equinox and Solstice cycles?" There was a low murmur.

Soon he was discussing the main topic. "Solar tides and flares are affected by four planets–Mercury, Venus, Earth and Jupiter. The first three, due to their proximity to the sun, and Jupiter, because of its size. That is why the theory is called the Jupiter Effect."

Niki loved hearing him speak, both his debonair accent and his dynamic presentation. The multi-media effects of the solar flares and realistic movement of the planets was spectacular—unlike anything she had ever seen, other than the *Star Wars* movie.

As the forty-five minute presentation appeared to be winding down, Niki inched closer to the door. She wanted to be sure to find a prime spot for the press conference. The same security guard who rather roughly escorted her into the planetarium had his eye on her.

When the moment came, Niki dashed outside but it took her eyes a minute to adjust from darkness to bright sunlight. When they did, she was surprised at the crowd that had formed on the lawn.

Protestors were waving signs that read: "Armageddon is Here" and "the End is Near." Niki squeezed through the crowd, past police, showing her press badge, and found a spot between two TV crews.

Gribbin finally emerged through the big brass doors of the Observatory to take his place at the podium. Niki was practically front and center. He made eye contact with her.

"Did you enjoy the show?" He asked everyone, but Niki felt like the question was just for her and nodded enthusiastically.

"I must address concerns raised by the director and his staff," Gribbin said. "Calling my theory 'pseudoscience' and a 'gigantic deception' is a bit harsh." This caused a roar from the crowd and reaction from the cops.

After a few questions from the BBC and U.S. television crews, Niki waved her hand. Gribbin called on her.

"Yes, Miss Ottumwa, here in front." Nearby reporters craned their necks to see who she was.

"Dr. Gribbin, you spoke today about sunspots and atmospheric particles, but what about the real concern here in the U.S.—the affect on the tectonic plates underlying the California coast. What is the possibility the gravitational pull will compromise the fault line?"

It seemed to Niki that Gribbin's eyes sparkled as she spoke, but he did not answer her question. Instead he said, "Perhaps Dr. Krupp would honor us with his Earthquake Hoax presentation. I hear it's quite a show."

The media crowd laughed, and protestors jeered. Niki took it personally, as if they were making fun of her.

"Excuse me," she interrupted. "I'm more interested in *your* response. The media continues to report that the San Andreas fault line may shift, causing a devastating earthquake. Is that possible?"

"Well, Nicole," Gribbin said standing a bit taller, his eyes dark and intense. "As I said before, anything is possible, but in this case, let's say it's not probable." Calling her by name generated a hum of interest from other reporters.

Gribbin took a few final questions, and thanked the crowd, signaling the end of the press conference. Krupp, the observatory director, took the microphone and began giving instructions on how the crowd should disperse.

Niki took a step toward Gribbin. This was her last chance to broach the subject of an exclusive interview. Before she said a word, Gribbin reached out and pulled her toward him.

"You have been studying," he said. In a hushed voice he added, "Perhaps I could elaborate a bit more on gravitational pull and tectonic tension if you'd join me for a steak dinner."

Niki felt weak in the knees.

"Sure," was all she managed to squeak before Gribbin whisked her away to the back seat of his chauffeured Town Car. A traffic officer waved his baton, parting the crowd of reporters and onlookers like the Red Sea, as Niki and her Lord Britannia drifted off into the twilight and twinkling lights of the City of Angels.

There is no route out of the maze.
The maze shifts as you move through it, because it is alive.
-- Philip K. Dick, "VALIS"

2 End Times

February 17, 1982

Phil frantically fast-forwarded and rewound the stereo tape player, trying to locate a specific passage to play for his reporter/biographer friend Rick Gregory, who was there to hear about Phil's most recent mystical experience.

"If I can just find what I'm looking for, you'll see. This proves I'm not crazy, or at least not alone in my anamnesis."

"Your what?" Rick asked.

Phil didn't even look up. "Our immortal recollection. True knowledge. Just hang on, you can hear it yourself," Phil said as he punched the play button. A wavery, almost ghostly, stilted English voice wafted from the tape recorder.

"... it was as if a beam of light or energy had been focused at my head and my consciousness was raised by several notches. And there was created a kind of inner tranquil space. All my own thoughts disappeared, and into that space was placed a message as clear as your voice over the air waves now. It said, 'Go to—' Crème paused.

"If you know London—Blackfriar's Bridge, south side, Blackheath side—I was given a date, about three weeks ahead, and I wrote this down so I wouldn't forget it. On that designated date and time I went out there with quite a thrilling expectation. I didn't know what I was going to find."

Rick's eyes widened and Phil raised his eyebrows and nodded. They continued listening to the tape.

"There was a car waiting at the far end of the bridge, and I sidled up and sort of looked inside it, and there were some people in it that I didn't know, but it seemed they knew me."

"And one of them was Jesus? I mean the Maitreya?" talk show host McKay interjected.

"No, no. Not yet," Crème corrected. "One of them was the man I'd seen earlier who told me I was receiving communications from the Wisdom Masters. It was later, some months later, I began receiving dictation from the Masters. My vibratory level was stepped up—"

Both Phil's friend, and McKay on the tape, seemed to hang on for the explanation. After a purposeful pause, Crème continued.

"Then I had the most extraordinary experience of my life. I was overshadowed, as it's called, by the Maitreya. Probably some minuscule fragment of his consciousness entered into mine, and I was filled with love, for all the world. An extraordinary experience of total identification with everything and everybody in the world! A kind of universal experience such as I had never felt before. I was filled with tremendous energy, and he gave me a vision of how the Masters see reality."

"A vision. Oh, my," McKay responded and noticed the clock. "Well, to be honest we were supposed to end here. If you can stay on after the break, Mr. Crème, I'd like to hear more about your Vision." A commercial began, and Phil stopped the tape.

"See Rick, we both saw a beam of light and then had the same type of experiences," Phil exclaimed. "We could *see.* Crème is describing the same exact experiences I had."

Gregory scratched his head. "Yeah, I gotta admit, he sounds a lot like you."

Phil was already forwarding and searching the tape for another part to play. Again, he talked over his shoulder to Rick.

"Wait 'til you hear this part about the beggar. This happened to me, too, when I was just a little kid. I saw an old blind man with a tin cup, back when we still lived in Chicago. I knew the old guy wasn't a bum. I *knew* he was special. My dad gave me a few cents to put in the cup. The old man whispered *I will repay you one day.*" Phil almost choked up while telling the story. "He did, you know—repay me. Listen." He punched the play button again on the recorder.

"He changes form," Crème said ominously. "If the Maitreya wishes to appear as a beggar man, as he often does, hundreds of people have such experiences encountering him, yet never know it."

"I have to ask the obvious," McKay said. "Are you sure you weren't suffering some sort of, um, psychological breakdown when all of this occurred?"

Phil punched the stop button before Crème answered. "See, poor guy. Reporters, even nice ones like you, ask me that same thing over and over."

Gregory grinned. "Phil, I never said you had a breakdown— that was those other guys. I'm your friend, remember?"

"Yeah, I know," Phil said calming down. "After listening to this program, I'm convinced the voices and messages I heard were the Maitreya. I actually wrote it myself in my Tractate, entry #12." Phil grabbed a worn copy of *VALIS* and flipped to a passage in the back of the book.

"Let me read it to you: 'the Immortal One known to the Greeks as Dionysus; to the Jews as Elijah and to Christians as Jesus. He moves on when each human host dies.' Exactly what Crème said. That the Immortal One, Maitreya, overshadowed Jesus during the last three years of his life. That is when he became Christ. You see?"

Rick tried to follow along as Phil pulled out other reference books and a huge stack of papers from what he called his Exegesis. As always, Phil was passionate and quite convincing. At one point Phil proclaimed, "The Maitreya is the new World Teacher, just as Crème says. He told me this himself."

"He speaks to you, too, Phil?"

"That's what I'm telling you. He has for eight years. I just didn't know the name Maitreya until now. I knew it was the Immortal One."

Rick put down his pen and turned off his own small tape recorder. "Phil, just for the sake of argument, why would God, or this Immortal One, select you, a science fiction writer, to reveal these Truths to? Why not someone powerful or well known?"

Phil smiled. "That's exactly why he always picks the least likely person—a blind beggar, an unknown carpenter, or like Crème, an obscure artist from Scotland. He wants people with no authority whatsoever. So when the average person hears the message they will accept it on its own authenticity, not on the basis of power or position, or through some organization, especially the Church."

"Have you called or spoken with this Crème guy?"

"Not yet," Phil said. "I wrote to him, though, and sent him a copy of the Tagore letter, which provides a detailed account of my vision of the burned and crippled Messiah. I'm sure now that Tagore *is* the Maitreya. That letter explains the transubstantiation. I sent along a copy of *VALIS* so Crème can read the Tractates Cryptica Scriptura. I'm sure once he sees that we've been receiving the same information he will want to meet. Then I will share my secret." Phil's eyes darted around, surveying the room. In a hushed tone he added, "the revelations from Pike."

Phil unexpectedly jumped up from his chair, clutched his head, and seemed to "go off." Something about the Church and "religious junk." It appeared another two or three-hour wild speculation session was about to ensue.

"Okay, why don't I just stay here tonight and we can work through all of this," Rick offered.

Phil shook his head, "Those bastards got my idealism." He looked tired, beyond tired, and upset. He claimed he wanted to jot off a few letters and maybe even turn in early, for once.

Rick nodded, gathered his things, and gave Phil a quick hug. On his way out, he promised to call as soon as he got home.

It was after eleven when the phone rang. Rick reported he had made it back to the coast. Phil sounded much better, alert and in good spirits. Apparently, he was not.

Soon after Rick left, Phil had called his therapist and made an appointment for the following day, February 18. When he mentioned vision problems, the psychologist said it could be something serious and he shouldn't wait—he should immediately go to a hospital. Phil said he would, but he didn't. Instead, he pulled another all-nighter, scribbling more theories and notes in his Exegesis.

Neighbors claimed they saw Phil pick up his newspaper early Thursday morning, but no one saw him leave. When he didn't show up, for his appointment or answer his telephone, the therapist was concerned and began making calls. Philip K. Dick was not registered in any local hospital, so he called Phil's emergency contact (a friend from the condominium.)

Phil's car was parked in the usual place, but he did not answer the door. Neighbors finally entered the condo and found the author unconscious on the floor.

Frantic calls for an ambulance came too late to help Phil. He had suffered a paralyzing stroke—one that silenced him but did not kill him. Was there any difference, Phil wondered. If he could not move or speak, he certainly couldn't write. If he couldn't communicate, how could he go on? This was the ultimate Black Iron Prison. No one knew, but his mind raced while lying there in the emergency room. He recalled another passage from Crème:

"The Maitreya will present a choice: either we continue as we are now, in the old, greedy, selfish, complacent ways of the past, and destroy ourselves, or we accept the principle of sharing, accept that we are one, and begin the creation of a civilization such as this world has never yet seen."

A tear rolled down Phil's face.

∞

March 2, 1982

Back in Ottumwa, Niki was driving home after having dinner at her friend Linda's house. Every beer-guzzling bozo like Bob, Linda's husband, is stocking up on ammo and cleaning out his bomb shelter, preparing for the End. This is crazy, she thought. Guys like that will probably kill each other over supplies before we even see the Alignment.

In a few days, all hell would really break loose. Gribbin was scheduled to be on the cover of *Time* magazine. Niki wasn't sure if she felt guilty or excited over fueling the frenzy. She never mentioned a thing to Bob and Linda, but thanks to her syndication agreement, she would get a nice chunk of change. Yeah, life was good, even if the world was about to end.

Niki smiled to herself as she parked her car and hurried through the night sleet into her apartment.

Once inside, she shook off her cold, damp parka and hoped that soon she would shake off Ottumwa, too. As she unraveled the wool scarf from her neck, Schroeder, her big yellow tomcat, strolled around the corner. He stretched and batted at the fringe on her scarf with his huge paw. She let him play with it for a few seconds then reached down and scooped him up in her arms.

"You and I are getting out of Hicksville, baby. Moving someplace fun," she said cradling the heavy tomcat like a baby. "And warm," she added, still feeling damp and cold. The cat jumped down, landing with a plop and strolled toward his dish, demanding his dinner.

After feeding him, Niki glanced at her watch. It was already ten o'clock. She flipped on the TV just in time to catch the late news.

As the picture came into focus, there on the screen was none other than the man of the hour—Dr. John Gribbin—surrounded by a crush of reporters and flashing camera lights. A deep crease formed on Niki's freckled forehead as she fell back onto her sofa.

"What? Another press conference?" she sputtered aloud, in disbelief. "Why didn't I know about this?"

Disappointment and frustration quickly gave way to curiosity as Niki studied the man she had spent time with in LA. The suave scientist looked particularly scholarly in his herringbone tweed jacket with a brown wool scarf wound loosely around his neck. Such a sexy egghead, she smiled as she studied his dark brown, deep-set eyes. He wasn't wearing his glasses, she realized.

She sank into the sofa cushion and reached up to turn off the lamp on the end table. With only the flickering light of the TV, it seemed intimate, like being back in the Town Car. She wanted to reach out and touch him.

Gribbin had the rugged looks of an outdoorsman, someone who should tackle a marlin instead of a science problem. She thought of the firm body hidden beneath that professional veneer and suddenly felt warm. She piled her hair on top of her head with one hand and reached for the newspaper lying on the coffee table with the other. She fanned herself as he stepped toward the microphone and then tenderly clutched the paper to her chest—her only link to the distant, inaccessible dark-haired hunk. His beard was perfectly trimmed, accentuating his high cheekbones. A soft, dreamy glow came over Niki's face as she thought of those whiskers touching her cheek.

"I'm afraid I have bad news for the doomsayers out there." Gribbin began. "I must make it perfectly clear that there is absolutely no reason to expect any unusual seismic activity next week. No reason for anyone to panic—not even those living on the coastlines."

"What!?!" Niki shrieked at the television.

"I am completely retracting my prior predictions about the Jupiter Effect," Gribbin announced. "Don't believe those media forecasts of doom."

His once-sophisticated sounding accent now seemed like a stuffy staccato drone. She jumped up and began pacing frantically in front of the TV set waving her newspaper and cursing at him.

"Next Wednesday will be no more dangerous than any other day for Californians. There is no specific threat to the San Andreas fault line…"

"That's just great. I'll be the laughing stock of the whole damn newsroom." She tossed the newspaper on the floor and stomped out of the living room.

The *Courier*, now lying crumpled on the floor, featured Niki's original article:

Dies Irae: The Day of Wrath
By Nicole J. Perceval

"When Jupiter aligns with Mars…

***Peace** will guide the planets and **Love** will steer the stars."*

Whether you believe it's the dawning of a new age, or the end of the world as we know it, you *can* expect a spectacular celestial show in the coming days.

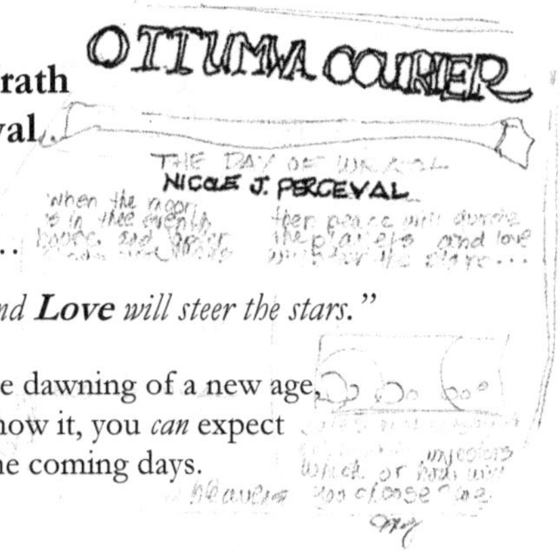

Radio stations had dusted off old copies of *Aquarius* and began playing it as the dreaded day approached. *Time* was going to quote her lead. Why was Gribbin ruining everything?

"The Jupiter Effect was always based on a series of hypothetical 'ifs' and was never intended to be taken as a dogmatic assertion of cataclysmic events—"

"Oh, shut up!" Niki yelled from the kitchen, where she was creating her own seismic disturbance rattling pots and pans as she searched for her teakettle. She flung a frying pan across the room. It breezed past Schroeder, barely missing him and creating a nerve-rattling crash as it landed on the tile floor. The cat hissed and screeched out of the room, leaving Niki alone with her troubles.

"There's an important lesson here," Gribbin continued. "Don't open the door for half-baked cults to latch on to your ideas—" Niki stomped back into the living room and punched off the TV.

"Bastard," she said under her breath and then stood in the dark with the full impact of Gribbin's words ringing in her head.

“It’s over,” she exhaled, envisioning a collective sigh of relief being breathed around the world. She felt so alone.

Am I the only person on the planet who isn’t relieved? Meaning what, she wondered. That I *wanted* the world to end? Her head was throbbing.

Back in the kitchen, she grabbed the teakettle and filled it with an angry burst of water from the tap. “Damn you, John Gribbin.” With the kettle on the stove, Niki slumped into a kitchen chair and rested face down against her folded arms on the table. Her thoughts drifted back to that magical day in L.A.

She really had felt like Cinderella, a princess far from home in a carriage with her Prince Charming. Niki had hoped some TV reporter had footage of her being whisked off to her fantasy night with her European idol. She especially hoped it would air back in Iowa to the jaw-dropping amazement of her friends and newspaper colleagues.

She had found herself sitting in plush, luxurious black leather just inches from the man who had long ago captured her imagination. The faint fragrance of some unknown but expensive after shave, mixed with a hint of leather, filled the close quarters, where the sleeve of his tweed jacket brushed against her bare arm.

She would never forget the sound of the glass panel sliding open and hearing Gribbin’s husky, English accent when he spoke to the driver. “Brown Derby, please.” He must have noticed her reaction because he had patted her hand.

Riding down the Hollywood hills with the last traces of sun setting over the ocean, and the twinkling lights of Los Angeles below, was certainly the most surreal experience of her young life. She had to get a grip on herself and get past her groupie-like gawking at this gorgeous man.

Gribbin-groupie. The thought made her smile, and relax. After all, she wasn't going to rip the man's clothes off there in the limo.

As the driver pulled up to the famous Brown Derby at Hollywood and Vine, Niki panicked. She wasn't dressed for dinner. She was still in her crumpled cotton shirt and jeans.

"I can't go in there, look how I'm dressed," she confessed to Gribbin feeling embarrassed.

"Not a worry," Gribbin assured her. "It's a casual diner."

As they entered the iconic restaurant, she couldn't imagine calling it casual. Movie stars and tons of famous people ate here. It wasn't like the *Canteen* back in Ottumwa. That was her idea of casual. No one in Ottumwa would believe that she ate at such a famous Hollywood spot with John Gribbin who had just commanded an international press conference. And Frank thought I couldn't even get an interview. Of course, if the world ends, they'll never know anyway, she mused.

After their intimate dinner of steak and lobster with all the trimmings, Niki knew it was time to make her move. She reached under the table and pulled a small tape recorder from her bag.

"May I ask a few questions now?"

Gribbin laughed. "Perhaps over an after-dinner drink?" He summoned the waiter and ordered two Cognacs. Niki wondered what angle to take to assure her story would get national ink.

"The doomsday aspect," she began.

After answering a few questions, and several sips of brandy, Gribbin took her hand, holding it like a precious artifact. He even lightly kissed the back of her hand. He cleared his throat. The moment felt like an eternity.

"Nicole, you are a delightful, attractive young woman and I sense we share, well, a certain chemistry." He stopped as if to assess her reaction. Niki was hanging on every word.

"Perhaps I am—how do you Americans phrase this—leaping to conclusions, but I am a married man."

Niki wanted to say "who cares," but instead she felt tears well-up in her eyes. She pulled her hand away and turned her head. He gently turned her chin back toward him and wiped a tear away with the back of his hand.

"You are bright, a star in your own right, and special," Gribbin told her. "I'll do whatever I can to help with your story. In fact, I'll ring you up immediately when I return to Sussex and provide you with the very latest developments."

∞

The sound of the whistling tea kettle snapped Niki back to the present moment. She had believed him—that he would call. But the cruel bastard never kept his promise. They never do, she thought.

She had let her physicist fantasy go way too far, she decided as she took the kettle from the stove. Niki had pictured the two of them on the *Phil Donahue Show*, discussing *The Jupiter Effect* and inevitably creating their own alignment. Crazy? Probably, but after all, it was *her* fantasy.

As she dunked the tea bag into her cup, she realized that if the world really had ended, none of this would have mattered. Maybe that's why she felt so upset. She had wanted her final fling to be with the dark-haired, world-famous scientist who would take her far away from reality and Ottumwa, Iowa. Now what, she wondered. Stupid-ass men ruin everything.

Before going to bed, Niki decided she had to have one last look at the night sky. She threw on her parka and stepped out into the bitter cold, moonless night. The stars were still her friends, even if her guide to them was not. And they were particularly dense and beautiful. The major planets that would soon form the much-awaited Grand Alignment were already moving into place. She shivered in the cold night air. Just as she was about to turn and go back inside she saw a spectacular shooting star.

"Wow!" Someone special is rocketing to heaven. That's what her mom had told her when she was a kid, and she knew it was true when she saw a brilliant meteor, like this one, the night her mom passed away.

It's her way of letting me know that things will work out—a sign—just like before.

Niki looked up again but everything was blurry now that tears had formed in her eyes. One ran down her cheek and this time she wiped it away herself.

That same night, March 2, 1982, as John Gribbin recanted his Jupiter Effect theory before an international audience, there had been a major disturbance in California. A great light faded.

Phil's eyes were fixed and dilated. He was in a coma and hadn't so much as twitched for the past eighteen hours. A few close friends paced the third floor corridor at Western Medical Center in Santa Ana, California, each praying to his or her god for a miracle that none believed was likely. It was only a matter of time.

A massive stroke followed by a severe heart attack, all in less than two weeks, was more than any physical body could endure, especially one as wracked by wear and tear as Phil's.

Philip K. Dick was only fifty-three years old, but you'd never guess that to see him lying there. His face and body were contorted and he certainly wouldn't want anyone to see him like this. His compelling blue-grey eyes were empty and hollow; his trademark hairy barrel chest was sunken and frail-looking.

Like Gribbin, Phil dealt in cosmic matters, but his were events of his own creation. Phil wrote science fiction, not scientific fact. In some ways, he had never been good at physicality, spending most of his life behind a typewriter living in the alien worlds he created. The bennies and booze he had used to fuel his creative life had finally ended it.

Suddenly, a rose-colored glow came over the stark hospital room. At first it was faint, but it intensified into a brilliant pink beam of light that focused directly onto Phil's face.

The heart monitor flat-lined and buzzed with urgency. A nurse rushed in, followed by an intern, who quickly grabbed the defibrillator paddles and tried to save him. It was too late. Phil had already left—his body that is.

His spirit hovered over the bed, and without any effort Phil found he was still aware. For a moment he thought his body had been replaced by an index card labeled PKD, a gimmick he used in one of his early novels. In that story things would phase out of reality leaving behind only a scrap of paper describing what had been there. The idea of a PKD card made Phil laugh. Of course, no one could see or hear him laughing. His view widened and he could see his friends. They looked so sad, and a couple of them were crying.

"No," he said, "don't cry. I'm fine." More than fine he thought. I'm my old self again. And he was. Phil had reverted to a younger, healthier version of himself—strong and vibrant.

Damn, this is hard. Surely there must be a way to let them know what's really going on.

"Hey, I'm still here," he whispered into the ear of one of the crying women. No reaction.

"I've just phased out of your reality," Phil said as he touched his best friend's shoulder. Again there was no reaction. His friend could not see or feel him.

Then a glimmer of light caught Phil's ethereal eye. The light was coming from an old, crippled Hispanic woman sitting in a wheelchair in the hospital hallway. She looked right at him and waved.

She sees me! Phil waved back. The real adventure is just beginning, Phil chuckled to himself.

3 Black Iron Prison or Palm Tree Garden

Niki lingered longer than usual in the parking lot, organizing cassette tapes in her car, smoothing her hair in the mirror, anything to avoid walking into the newsroom. She was not ready to deal with the embarrassing fallout from the Gribbin fiasco.

How could she explain that he hadn't told her about this latest press conference? All that bragging about the Brown Derby and Hollywood. These guys thought she was practically dating the guy. Yet Gribbin goes on international television to recant *everything* and doesn't even bother to tell her. How could he?

Niki ran her hand over the dashboard of her prized possession, a 1979 limited edition, metallic silver 280ZX. It was a Nissan Datsun, but she never called it anything but the Z car or just the Z.

It wasn't just any old Z, either. It was a ZXR Silver Mist Limited Edition Coupe, to be exact, with dark blue racing stripes. She loved the way the control panel curved around with all the dials and gadgets within easy reach. Even more, she loved the powerful engine and the way she could blow past the guys in their souped-up Chevys on the downtown loop.

Blood money bought this baby, she thought. It had taken time, and a considerable toll on her, to settle things after her mom died. Selling the house was the worst. After paying off the last of the bills and her college loan, she knew she should invest the rest of the money, but instead she bought the Z-car.

Sometimes she felt guilty about it, because her mom never bought anything extravagant. Her mom believed in saving for a rainy day. Niki had seen plenty of those. First, watching her dad's deterioration and death from a rare lung disease, and then the shock of learning her mom had cancer. But she couldn't dwell on any of that now. She was already late and she had a new problem to deal with. She would have to face the jeers from the jerks in the newsroom, or worse—their looks of pity.

"I'll punch Bruce in the face if he says a word," she muttered and slammed the car door.

Luckily, Bruce was on the phone as she snuck in the back door and stepped quietly behind his desk. She avoided making eye contact with the other guys, trying to get to her corner spot before anyone said anything.

Niki sank into her chair and pulled a thermos out of her big leather bag. She was twisting the cap off when suddenly her old wooden swivel desk chair also spun around. She was now facing Bruce, still holding her thermos. The temptation to douse him with the hot contents was overwhelming, but Bruce prevented that by grabbing her thermos.

"You know I hate it when you do that."

"Do what? Steal your coffee?" he smirked.

"No. Twist my chair around." She snatched the thermos, and swiveled back around.

"Hey, what about *my* cup of joe?"

"It's hot water, not joe, you dork. You're lucky you didn't find out the hard way."

Bruce Kauffman had worked for the *Courier* about a year and covered the "red eye" early morning cop beat, an assignment that was always given to the rookie reporters. That had been Niki's beat almost five years ago, but now she was considered one of the senior reporters. She had shown Bruce around town, introducing him to local officials and good sources when he first moved to Ottumwa fresh from college. She liked him, even though he was a spoiled Ivy-league loafer-type from Purdue who called the local guys hicks and hayseeds.

He came from money, so doors opened and things came easy for him, unlike Niki and her friends who struggled to pay for school or didn't go at all. Despite his comfortable station in life, or maybe because of it, Bruce was naïve and immature. His boyish, cherub face and wide toothy grin always gave the impression he was contemplating some silly prank. But he was cute and likable, in a goofy "Barney Fife" sort of way.

Bruce was also younger than Niki, but still closer to her age than anyone else that worked in the newsroom. So they often confided in each other about their dates and personal problems. But on this morning, she couldn't bear the thought of his idiotic antics.

"What's up with you? Man trouble?" he asked, batting his long black eyelashes in an exaggerated manner.

"Come on Bruce, you know exactly what's wrong with me. Don't play coy. I'm not up for it this morning."

His face took on a dark look that matched his complexion. Then, just like a cartoon where the light bulb flashes over the character's head, his eyes opened wide and the goofy expression returned.

"Oh, the big press conference last night. Everyone here was talking about it early this morning. Why didn't your boyfriend call and tip you off?"

Niki waved the thermos ominously at him, then spit out the first stupid thing she could think of.

"Why don't you make like a tree and leave. I told you I'm not in the mood for this today."

"Sorry, Nik," Bruce appeared serious now. "You must want to talk about it. Is the doomsday thing really over? What do *you* think will happen now?"

"I think I'm gonna look for another job," she snapped.

"Reeeally?" Bruce raised an eyebrow. "You mean really leave, like get in your car and—" He paused and then under his breath started singing. "Bye, bye Miss American Pie. Drove her Z-car to the levee cause she thought she might die." He burst into giggles.

"Ok, that's it. I'm going to the library." Niki grabbed her coat and a file of papers off the desk and pushed past Bruce, ignoring him. Then suddenly turned around and glared.

"Don't you dare tell Frank what I said."

He smiled and pulled his fingers across his lips, indicating he was zipping them. What a goofball, Niki thought as she headed for the door. The public library was just a few blocks from the *Courier* and she was glad to get out of there. The cold, fresh air felt heavenly as she stepped out of the smoky newsroom.

March is often bitterly cold in Iowa, and there were still mounds of snow outlining the circular downtown park that surrounded the local government buildings. So Niki quickly zig-zagged her way through the snow maze of Central Park.

The name made Niki laugh because this park was tiny, basically a round patch of grass with a gazebo-style bandstand, a few wooden benches, and a couple of big oak trees for shade. The trees were bare with spidery branches that made the overcast day seem even bleaker.

In contrast, though, nearby city hall and the county courthouse, were massive stone buildings that sat high on the Des Moines River bluffs, an impressive, if not ostentatious, sight for a town of its size. Just across the river sat the huge Ottumwa Coliseum, with monumental columns. But the domed and porticoed, two-story, limestone Carnegie-built public library was the crème de la crème.

The once-beautiful structures were falling into disrepair, though, since the declining tax base could barely support the upkeep. Ottumwa was shrinking from its World War II hey-day and could no longer support projects built by philanthropic railroad money or the Roosevelt-era "New Deal" WPA (Work Projects Administration.)

Niki was seeing the town, and her life for that matter, with a fresh perspective. She had never thought about leaving until her adventure in California. Now, she couldn't think of a reason to stay. No family, no kids. I could get a job anywhere, she thought as she climbed the stone steps of the library. My clips and AP awards would look good on a resume, especially the syndicated article, even if the Alignment was a bust.

Niki was now charging up the library steps two at a time, gaining resolve with each upward bound. Someplace warm, she thought pulling her parka tight to keep out the biting wind.

Just as she reached the top step, she felt light-headed, dizzy, and braced herself against one of the big columns. The traffic noise and voices of a couple passing by faded out. All she could hear was a high-pitched whine in her left ear. Everything looked gray and her field of vision narrowed.

She blinked slowly, but when her eyelids lifted, something was wrong.

The familiar Ottumwa landscape was gone—
replaced by something that looked
like ancient Rome.
People wore robes,
and sandals, and walked
on dusty roads.
The coliseum was,
well, the *real Coliseum*
with chariots,
instead of cars
in the
parking lot.

Niki squeezed her eyes shut for a moment hoping things would return to normal the next time she looked. The buzzing sound persisted for a few more seconds and then ended. She held her head, still leaning against the column. When she opened her eyes a well-dressed elderly man was standing in front of her.

"Miss, are you all right?" he asked.

Niki startled and surveyed the surroundings. The old man, surprised by her sudden moves, almost fell backwards off the step. Niki reached out to steady him. They both looked confused.

"I guess I just ran up the stairs too fast," she said still feeling very disoriented.

"You better sit down on that ledge and rest a minute," the man said as he patted her shoulder. "In fact, I think I'll join you."

The two sat in silence for a few moments, but Niki could feel the ice-cold concrete through her jeans and knew the frail man must feel even colder in his thin dress pants.

"I'm fine now," she said. "We better get off this cold ledge."

The man rose shakily, then steadied himself on his cane, gave a polite tip of his hat, and headed toward the library door. Niki stood up, brushed off her frozen behind and headed right back down the stairs, forgetting about the library research.

That was crazy. She shook her head as if to knock a fly from her ear. Food, she thought. Nothing a cinnamon roll can't fix.

∞

Phil smiled. Well, he didn't actually smile, since he no longer had a body or mouth, but he felt a smiling sensation.

Time, what a concept. If only they knew it really doesn't exist at all. The Universe is information—a hologram. Phil recalled his own experiences with time anomalies.

Once he was walking along and suddenly Sonoma County became ancient Palestine. Of course, no one believed him so he used his visions in his science fiction stories. Now he could see this girl was experiencing the same thing—seeing first century Rome; the time of the Essenes and the Gnostics.

Who is she? Phil wondered as he watched the young red-head walking down the street. The experience was fascinating, like watching a movie. She's not even a dark-haired girl, he thought reaching to scratch his head. He didn't have any hair, or even a head. "Where am I? How did I get here?" he must have asked aloud.

"You can help her," an authoritative voice boomed.

Instantly Phil's landscape changed. He wasn't seeing the girl or Essenes. He was standing at what appeared to be the Pearly Gates. Then it came back to him: Western Medical Center, the old Hispanic woman waving at him— "I'm..."

"Yes, son, you have slipped the surly bonds," a fatherly, white-haired figure spoke to him.

"And, danced the skies on laughter-silvered wings," Phil finished the line for the old man. It was one of his favorite poems. He shuddered recalling the next line. *Put out my hand and touched the face of God.*[1]

"Are you—" Phil couldn't finish the question.

The old man chuckled. "No, no. I'm just the gate-keeper. But we've got some business to attend to, if you want to pass on." He pointed at the massive, jeweled gates behind them.

Pass on. Phil shuddered. I thought I had already passed on. Then it came to him how this might explain apparitions and spirits who linger behind, those who can't, or don't pass on, and hover around—Earthbound. Just as he turned to address the Father-Thing it vanished, along with the radiant celestial light. Then there was nothing. Phil was free-floating in space and he worried that he would find himself on the banks of the River Styx, in some terrible scene from Dante's Inferno.

I'd rather be a ghost than end up there, he shuddered. Instantly he was in a thick fog and heard a raspy female voice.

"Your decision?"

Then he saw her. She was a composite of all his ex-wives, schoolmarms, and his mother. A plump, authoritarian—angel? What next, a Faustian pact with the devil?

"I can arrange that," she said having read his thoughts. "You have exactly three minutes."

"Three minutes for what?" Phil yelped.

The Administrative Angel shrugged her wing-laden shoulders and clicked an oversized gold stopwatch she had been swinging around.

---

[1] Quote from John Gillespie Magree's poem "High Flight." Other author citations and references are included in end notes on page 334.

"Your decision on your fate," she said, tapping a satin covered toe.

The hefty angel pointed to a pearly entrance with a tall, solid gold pole and two gilded signs. One of the gold-leafs read Rebirths. The other sign pointed to Eternity.

"So, what will it be?" she asked still tapping her toe.

Phil's mind—or what used to be his mind—raced.

Chubby demanding cherubs, my ass. Who conjured up this crazy concept? The stopwatch was ticking loudly. He had to make a choice. If he went back, would he be a writer again? Could he finish his work? Record all these new revelations, he wondered. Do we have a choice? What if we don't?

Phil couldn't imagine being trapped in a routine day-to-day grind. He had lived life as a free spirit. That was more important to him than the unnecessary luxuries money could buy. You can't take it with you, they say, and now he knew that for sure.

Phil also knew he couldn't live another life of barely existing. He had spent most of his time behind the typewriter. Days would pass and he would never notice whether it was light or dark outside. Now he could see that he'd been living in the alien worlds he created. Often the lines between his meager physical existence and his alternate other worlds became so blurred that it hardly mattered that he had a flesh-and-blood body to feed.

In fact, not having a physical body and the mundane chores associated with it might be preferable.

He could just float around and truly experience all the realities his demented half-mind could conjure up. More importantly he would have access to—well, everything! All the philosophical and metaphysical quandaries would be revealed.

That's the great thing about being dead, Phil realized. No restrictions. He would finally know the truth about what happened to his friend Bishop Pike in that Judean desert. He'd be able to mingle with the great creative geniuses of all time.

And, even find out what happened to my twin sister Jane, who died in our crib. A tear formed in his etheric eye.

No more endless speculation. He could finally know the meaning of everything, exactly what's what.

He also realized he could not know *everything* unless he stayed. He was in a preliminary phase, like limbo to Catholics, or Bardo to Buddhists. If he stayed, he would become part of VALIS—the Vast Active Living Intelligence System—all pervasive, all-knowing!

Phil became excited at the prospects. He could think of only one problem with such an omniscient existence. What enjoyment would there be if he couldn't share the experience? That's why he wrote, to share his speculations and quest for truth with others. Now he would have all the answers he always longed for, but no way to share it—maybe that is hell.

The sound of a chime startled him.

"Your time is up," the Admin Angel said as she pointed to an infinite line of souls waiting behind him. "If you don't choose," she explained, "you'll automatically be sent back."

"No!" he cried out. "Eternity. I choose Eternity."

And, with that Phil started down the Never-ending Path.

Floating forward, he felt pleased with his decision. People, especially wives and women, had come and gone from his life. Would it be any different if he tried again?

Probably not. Just as he was about to enter Eternal Bliss, a burst of brilliant white light appeared before him. Now what?

It was old Saint Pete, the guard keeper, again. Phil knew this now, being omniscient and all.

"There's one more business matter to resolve, son," Pete said. "Your Akashic Record."

"My what?"

"Your Book of Life. No one can proceed without a review of your deeds and contributions."

"I'll never get past this." Phil hung his head. "Can't fool the Big Guy. I should have taken rebirth," he sighed.

The old man smiled. "Well, let's just take a peek."

Saint Peter pulled out a pair of 24K gold spectacles, and opened an enormous white book with gilded edges. As he scanned a few pages his eyes widened. "Five ex-wives?"

"Oh, there's much worse in there, I'm sure. Does this mean I'll be sent to—," clearing his throat and casting his eyes downward, "the other place?"

"You mean Earth?" St Pete raised a brow.

"The important question is: *Did you complete your Mission?*"

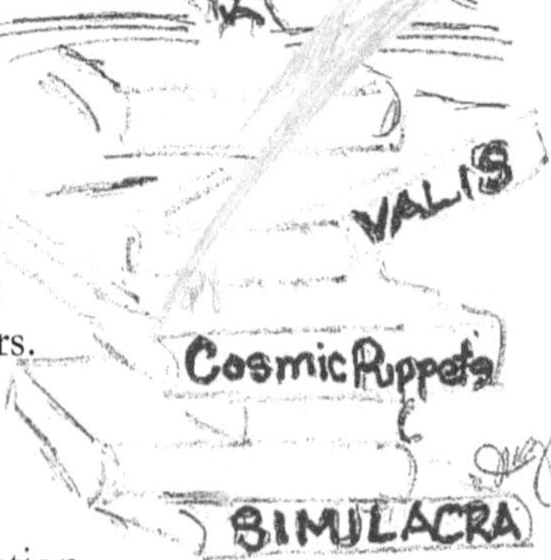

A deep crease formed on Phil's former forehead.

"Uh, what was it?" he asked.

A loud clap of thunder exploded. Phil jumped. Then a golden bolt of lightning crashed right in front of him. When the luminiferous aether cleared he saw a huge stack of trashy-looking pulp fiction books with lurid covers.

"In all that," Saint Pete pointed to the books. "Did you answer the question?"

Phil winced. He knew the question.

"You mean what's real—really human?" Phil squirmed under the Gatekeeper's gaze. "I guess not, but you gotta admit, I sure found a lot of ways to ask the question."

The Heavenly Host did not seem amused. Stroking his long beard he said, "There is only one other option then."

Phil waited anxiously to hear his fate.

"You must take on a pupil." Saint Pete paused, then pulled back the gossamer Veil to reveal a scene on Earth. It was the young redhead Phil had seen earlier.

Phil looked confused. "Me, a teacher?"

"Not a teacher. Her Guardian."

"An angel? That's even more ludicrous."

"That's the way it works here," Pete said. "She's a writer, but needs encouragement. She's lost her way. You can inspire her. Be her muse, just as others were for you. If you succeed and she completes the Mission, you can stay. Otherwise it's Rebirth for both of you."

"Both of us? You mean she will—"

"The D word?" Saint Peter said looking amused.

Phil shuddered, shocked at the angel's devilish humor.

"Depressed," Peter said, as he shook his head disapprovingly. "You shouldn't jump to conclusions, and if you stay here, you must learn to read minds better. You will be on probation," the angelic gate-keep began swinging the keys to the Kingdom for effect. "The Ultimate Reward awaits."

"It's a lot of responsibility," Phil said. "I wasn't very good with women on Earth. I was hoping to get some rest here."

"You have promises to keep and miles to go before you sleep. And I have an infinite number of other clients waiting," Pete smiled at his paraphrased quote from one of his best clients. "Here are your instructions—just a few *Guide*-lines." He handed Phil the paper and a scroll. Then, in another blinding flash of light, disappeared.

The instruction sheet had only one Law, two sub-clauses and no exemptions:

1) The Law of Non-Interference: work within her frame of reference and abide by rules of Earth physics.
    a. No physical contact – antimatter clashing with matter causes explosions and annihilation.
    b. Do not materialize – it scares them.

Just as suddenly as the heavenly episode began, it had ended. Phil found himself back on Earth, hovering around the young woman with no idea what to do. He read the instructions and nodded. Then he pulled open the scroll. To his amazement it read:

"For a writer, that wasn't very imaginative. People see whatever they expect to see in the afterlife. You could have conjured up something really creative, but harps, jewels, Saint Peter?

Really, Phil, not your best work. But the girl, and your Mission—that's *really real.*

I still have faith in you. You'll find a way."

It was signed exactly as Phil expected.

∞

4 Precession of the Equinoxes

The Jupiter Effect fizzled out right on cue. March 10th came and went with the California coastline still intact—there was not a quake or even a quiver. End-time excitement ended and all thoughts of Gribbin were gone. The final blow came when Niki's editor, Frank, handed her a clip from the London Times:

I Do Not Believe Anything

This remark was made, in these very words, by **Dr. John Gribbin**, physics editor of *New Scientist* magazine, during a BBC interview on the failed Jupiter Effect. The comment provoked incredulity on the part of most viewers. Gribbin clarified, "It seems to be a hangover of the medieval Catholic era that causes most people, even the educated, to think that everybody must 'believe' something or the other." Gribbin added, "My own opinion is that belief is the death of intelligence."

The article was longer, but Niki didn't read it. She shoved the clip into her Jupiter Effect file, then in front of Frank tossed the entire folder into the trash bin.

"I don't believe anything either, John." Frank gave her a fatherly pat on the shoulder and handed her a new case of local corruption to investigate.

March 20, 1982

A few days later, it was the Spring Equinox. Niki was alone in her apartment with piles of files, research she had amassed on the Case of the Slimy Supervisor, as she called it—probably the result of watching too many reruns of *Perry Mason.*

Niki had tried to regain interest in her work at the *Courier*, more to please Frank than because she cared. Recently, he had been more than the Managing Editor of the paper. He had cut her a lot of slack hoping she would "get her bearings" as he said. He knew how upset she was over missing her big break with the Gribbin situation. Since then there had been none of their usual arguing over copy or her passionate pleas about what she wanted to work on next. She was aware of his worried looks, but no one was more worried than Niki. She had to pull herself together.

She brought the Remke file home with her but hadn't looked at it once all weekend. Sunday night, before going to bed, she was determined to review the clips and be prepared for the Monday morning editorial meeting.

Carl Remke was the Chairman of the County Board of Supervisors, a low-life scum in her opinion, who had been ripping off the taxpayers for years. It was practically common knowledge in the community. The new, young county attorney was willing to consider an indictment for fraud, but only if someone could turn up some hard evidence. If the *Courier* could dig up some dirt, they might get old Carl thrown out of office and into the county jail—maybe even the state pen.

At one time the case, or at least the handsome young attorney, might have intrigued Niki, but now she couldn't care less about either. She had been reading for over an hour but not retaining a word of it. She would catch herself just staring off in space. Suddenly, she jumped up.

"I can't do this. I just can't do this." Niki paced the floor, talking to herself. "What possible reason is there to stay here?"

Niki meant Iowa, but Phil, who had been enjoying time on the Other Side chatting with a couple of his favorite dead authors, Jonathan Swift and A.E. van Vogt, had lost track of the girl's situation. Her current distress was like a buzzing alarm. As her newly appointed Guardian, Phil felt he should intervene. This could be tricky, he thought looking for his guidelines and instructions. Can't be overt. Can't manifest...

An old Cream tune came on the stereo. She turned up the volume and began dancing and singing along.

"I'll be with you darling, soon... when stars start falling."

Stars start falling. Niki remembered the shooting star she had seen the night of the Gribbin fiasco.

The heavy beat of the music was mesmerizing. She continued singing along.

"I've been waiting so long," Niki sang and swayed to the rhythm as she gathered up the research papers from the sofa and put them back into the file folder. "I'm with you now—"

Suddenly a high-pitched whine in her left ear was louder than the music. The music faded out and the only thing she could hear was the buzzing sound in her ear. A flurry of notes and papers fanned through the air as she let go of them to grab her head. When the buzzing stopped, a moment later, she heard words with crystal clarity: *the time is now.*

Niki stood frozen in eerie silence until the buzzing returned. It wasn't loud or painful, more like a soft electrical hum but very distinct. It too faded and the music and other sounds returned. The episode only lasted a minute or so. She turned off the stereo and listened for anything unusual in the apartment, but the only remaining sounds were the ticking of her mother's mantle clock and the pounding of her own heart.

She definitely heard something—not just something, but words. *The time is now.*

Niki knew it wasn't a real voice, not someone in her apartment. She checked anyway. Schroeder was curled up at the foot of her bed. He was sensitive to the slightest sounds and would have been alert and hissing if there had been an actual voice. It was in her head, and that was not comforting. She hadn't heard anything like this for years, not since her dad died.

Niki sighed and walked toward the kitchen. She stopped, just before she reached to flip on the overhead light. She had a weird sensation that someone was in there. Niki had never been afraid living alone, but now she was spooked. She forced herself to turn on the light. Nothing. She still felt uneasy—as if someone were watching her. The sensation was so strong that she turned around expecting to see something behind her. The air felt electrified.

"Shit, this is ridiculous," she mumbled aloud as she picked up the tea kettle and filled it with water. "My nerves are shot."

Niki turned on the gas burner under the kettle. While the water boiled she paced in the kitchen tilting her head back and forth trying to crack her neck and loosen her stiff muscles.

Screeeeeech! She heard a terrifying sound behind her, like something ripping apart.

"Jesus!" Niki blurted and turned around in one quick jump. Again, the ripping sound tore through the silence of the kitchen. This sound was real and it was coming from the back porch.

She stared at the back door. What to do? She surveyed the kitchen and saw the block of knives on the counter. She reached for the biggest butcher knife, never taking her eyes off the back door. Niki wondered if she had the courage to open it.

With her back against the kitchen wall, she switched the knife to her left hand and slid close to the door. She paused, barely breathing, and listened. Then, as fast as she could, she flipped the dead bolt and flung open the door. The porch light reflected two tiny, glistening yellow eyes. The little body they belonged to had been clinging to the screen. In the light, Niki saw a tiny kitten scramble away into the sleet.

"Shit!" Niki slammed the back door. When she turned around, there was Schroeder with his back arched and hair on end.

"You?" she said to the cat. "How do you think I feel?" She imagined her nerve endings all spiked up like the hair on Schroeder's back.

"What else can happen tonight?" Instantly Niki wished she had not asked that. Once again she felt nervous and uneasy. She flipped on her bedroom light. Nothing unusual—at least nothing she could see.

Niki jumped into bed with her sweat suit on, pulled the covers tight around her and still shivered. She stayed awake for a long time playing the events over in her mind: the buzzing sound, the message, the way the air felt electrified, the unnerving episode with the kitten. She wondered if there had been an intruder, could she have plunged a knife into him?

∞

Shit is right, Phil thought. Scared me and I'm a ghost. A ghost? Is that what I am now? How depressing. I don't want to haunt the girl—I want to help her, but it seems impossible. Can't even sigh. No breath; heck, no lungs.

The Cream song on the radio, stars falling, great stuff. Phil felt amused at his private joke from *VALIS,* his novel where fictional rock star Eric Lampton was contacted by an unearthly presence.

Fun as it is for me, they're inside jokes. She hasn't read *VALIS* or any of my stuff. So, even if she is a teep, or semi-teep, she won't be able to make sense of my cryptic connections. This only depressed Phil further and he decided being dead is a drag.

Niki woke up the next morning from a vivid dream. A man had been trying to convey something about a religious text. She couldn't remember the details, just a glimpse of an old scroll. It must be very important. The man in her dream was not her dad, but the urgency of his message and hearing *the time is now* reminded her of a dramatic deathbed experience that still haunted her.

Niki was nineteen when her dad died and nothing prepared her for the loss. It didn't matter that he was always too old—late sixties when she was born—or that he had been sick for months. None of that mattered. She was not ready to hear the news the day she drove up to University Hospital in Iowa City to see him.

Niki had a unique relationship with her dad, James Perceval, who was already retired before she was even born. It was the reverse of all her friends—her mom worked and her dad took care of her.

One of her earliest memories was of walking to the doughnut shop with him. She never realized until many years later how special it was for him to have a daughter so late in life. He doted on her, brushed her long, wavy hair and made hot chocolate for her in the mornings. Later he took care of her little friends as well, walking them to school and meeting them afterwards to see their finger paintings or coloring projects. He had nothing but time and it was well spent on Niki.

Things turned rough, though, during her teen years. She blasted the stereo, paraded boyfriends through the house and wore him to a frazzle with her increasing lack of respect. Niki felt embarrassed that he was so much older than her friends' parents. She even began to resent her mom for marrying an old man. "What were you thinking of?" she would yell, or "He's older than grandpa!" (meaning her mom's dad.)

He was eighty-four when she graduated from high school, and amazingly could still ride a motorcycle. Her friends, especially guys, thought that was pretty cool. By then, she had come to terms with his age.

But once he developed a lung disease, he aged quickly. By the time he turned eighty-seven his condition was critical and he was in treatment at University Hospital in Iowa City. It was her turn to take care of him, to bring him hot chocolate and goodies. They talked a lot during his last few weeks about things they had never discussed before, like religion. That had become a taboo subject in the Perceval house when she dropped out of the holy rolling Pentecostal family in favor of Buddhism. Her Irish dad had even called her a heathen.

"How would you even know what went on there?" Niki fired back at him. "I never saw you go to church one day in my whole life. I went with Mom and Grandpa."

Her mom stopped those heated discussions, fearing her dad might have a heart attack, or stroke. Now that he was in the hospital, facing mortality, he professed to be a believer.

Then one day, after he had been in and out of a coma, Niki got the shock of her young life. Her dad was quoting what sounded like bible verses—something about getting rid of all your earthly possessions. It sent a shiver down her spine.

"Dad, who are you talking to?" she asked.

"Niki, come here," he whispered. "Listen to me." She sat beside him and took his hand. He opened his eyes and looked into hers. His voice was shaky, but urgent.

"You will write a peace 'treaty.' Something important." He paused and gasped for breath. Niki had no idea what to say or do. She wanted to hear more, but he was struggling just to breathe. After what seemed an eternity, he added, "We must have peace on earth."

"Dad, you should rest now. You can tell me more about this later." Niki doubted there would be another opportunity, but she couldn't bear to see him struggle to speak.

He pulled on her shoulder to draw her closer. His voice was barely audible.

"It's your mission. You'll know when the time is right." He squeezed her hand and drifted off, someplace far away. By then, her mom had walked in and started to cry. They stepped out into the hallway. Niki explained what he had said and how he had quoted the Bible before that.

"He was talking to Joe this afternoon," her mom confided as she wiped tears from her eyes. That was his dead brother.

Just a few days later James E. Perceval joined Joe. His ominous message to Niki about her "mission" turned out to be his last words.

As remarkable as it was, what happened *after* he died had an even more profound affect on her.

On Easter Sunday that year, 1974, about a week after the funeral, Niki and her best friend Sheri took a late afternoon car ride, on Iowa back roads, to Mars Hill Church. It had been one of her Dad's favorite spots.

It was an old log cabin church that pre-dated the Civil War. Niki had begged her family to bury him in the cemetery there, but for some reason her mom had said they couldn't. It was a beautiful high hilly area offering a panoramic view of the Iowa farmland and a covered bridge below.

She and Sheri had gotten out of the car and walked around. It wasn't morbid. They reminisced about a picnic long ago on the church grounds.

"Remember when we were little and your dad brought us here?" Sheri asked. "He told us that story about how organ music mysteriously played in the old church on full moon nights?"

As they laughed and talked, the sky turned twilight. Just for effect Niki said, "I think it's a full moon tonight."

"We should get out of here now," Sheri said. "It's freezing." Niki was sure that Sheri was shivering more from the story than the weather. March in Iowa was biting cold, though, when the sun began to set.

"Yeah, plus I'll have a nervous breakdown if that organ music starts," Niki confessed.

They laughed and got in the car. Sheri hadn't even started the engine on her T-bird when they looked at each other. Something was happening. They both felt it at the same time.

"Nik, I don't want to freak you out, but—"

Niki interrupted her, "It's my Dad, isn't it?"

"Yeah," Sheri swallowed hard. "You know that picture of him—"

"The one hanging in Mom's hallway?" Niki finished.

They sat in silence, just looking at each other.

"He's here, Sheri," Niki said, glancing around.

In that instance, Niki began to feel a strange sensation—like floating away. It was more than her body floating, it was as if every molecule in her body was drifting apart and she was expanding into, actually merging with, the universe.

Somehow she understood that this was a glimpse of what happens when you die. Only she felt more alive than she had ever felt before. She *knew* she was merged with the cosmos, part of some universal intelligence. It was an absolute rush of knowledge—a true knowing—about the nature of things.

In a flash, Niki felt she understood what happens before we are born and after we pass on. We don't die, we just change form. We literally "pass on" to another reality. Our energy, our life force, merges back into the Universe and we truly become One with everything. She felt she had merged with her dad's mind, his thoughts. That he was conveying this information. Not just him—he was part of a vast pool of knowledge, Universal Consciousness, now. That idea seemed emblazoned in her mind. She was tapping into universal knowledge.

Just as abruptly as it began, it had ended. Niki became aware of being back in the car, the feel of the cold car seat, and of Sheri's wide eyes staring at her. It felt as though she had been slammed back into her body and physical reality.

"Are you all right?" Sheri asked, her voice trembling.

Niki felt fantastic, but her body wasn't cooperating. She was shaking, actually vibrating, and couldn't seem to move her muscles, or even speak. After a couple of minutes, which seemed much longer, she finally managed a slight shrug.

"You were gone," Sheri said. "I mean your body was here, but *you* were someplace else. Like a trance. It scared the shit out of me," she paused. When Niki still didn't respond Sheri continued, "You're still scaring me. Say something."

"I'm trying," Niki finally spoke. After another moment or two, she added, "You're right. I was definitely someplace else."

Sheri could see Niki's breath as she spoke and realized how cold it was in the car. She started the engine and while the car was warming up said, "You said some stra-a-a-nge things." Sheri intentionally drew out her words, trying to imitate the way Niki spoke while in the trance-like state. "Like *U-ni-ver-sal knowledge.* That's just how you said it, real slow like that."

"I know. I mean I *really know.* I felt it. I experienced what it's like to merge with the One—as the Buddhists say." Her expression confirmed it. She had a new look of confidence.

They sat in silence for another couple of minutes. Then Sheri pulled away from the church-yard onto the gravel road.

"That's the weirdest thing I've ever been through," Sheri said, as she looked nervously back and forth from the road to Niki.

"You?" Niki said. "I was with Dad. Not physically, I mean I didn't see him. He conveyed information to me," she paused, still trying to assimilate it all. "Sheri, I know what happens, or can happen to some people. It's possible to merge into the cosmos. I did it," she continued. "It was bliss. Better than pot—better than sex. Better than anything you can possibly imagine." Niki was becoming more animated as her physical sensations returned.

"It was a spiritual encounter. I remember that term. Dad wanted to show me what he was experiencing. He wanted me to know that I'm not a heathen. The Buddhists are on to something. Satori, enlightenment. It's possible! And, he wanted me to know what he's experiencing, that he's fine. More than fine. That we continue on. Wow!"

"Wow, is right," Sheri agreed. "Who will ever believe this?"

"Who cares? I know what happened. I understand now. And I'm certainly not afraid of dying anymore."

Sheri looked frightened. "You're scaring me again."

"Don't worry. I won't kill myself," Niki assured her. "I'm just saying I don't have to be afraid of death or the afterlife. I had a glimpse of it. Some souls merge with the universe, and others come back to learn, or because they have unfinished business. Dad is done. He won't be coming back and I won't see him again. That was it. He wanted me to understand and now I do."

That had been ten years ago. Niki had not remembered it in such vivid detail for a long time. But the dream, and her recent experiences, brought the memories into sharp focus. *Unfinished business.* She shuddered. And, what about the peace treaty, her mission? Was it finally time?

5 Unfinished Business

Unfinished Business! As soon as the girl thought it, Phil agreed. That was it—exactly.

I'm dead, but I'm not done. How can I be dead, when I feel so alive? Phil felt more alive now than he had for years. No physical constraints, no aches or pains—okay, no body, but that means anything is possible. He hadn't really missed his body. He felt more sensations and awareness, not less, and he knew so much. So enlightened.

I understand everything now, just like the girl described. It's great. It's way more than great—it's fucking fantastic!

After all those years of struggling with multiple view-points, the occasional faux pas of authorial intrusion, and of course the ghastly violation of limited omniscience, now I have the answer. I know who's telling the story. I am! Phil was ecstatic.

It always bothered him. Stories told by some all-knowing, yet unknown narrator. Who was the person spinning the yarn? Only God could have such powers of omnipotence and omniscience, right? Wrong.

Apparently dead authors are also granted this privilege. We can swoop down and see into people's minds, then report what they are thinking and feeling. *At least I can.*

In case you feel disoriented, *I should introduce myself.* I am the disembodied spirit of Philip K. Dick, a novelist whose mainstream work was never appreciated—at least not while I was alive. The only stuff I could ever get published was science fiction, SF as it's called in the trade. So I became a crap artist, a creator of pulp fiction. I used to crank out those SF pulps so fast it would make your head spin. I had to if I wanted to eat. It's how I made a living, barely.

Back then, in the 1950s and 60s, only kids and nerds read that stuff. I'm not so obscure now that "sci-fi" is considered cool. There's a whole new generation of techno-geeks and science fiction aficionados. They surf the World Wide Web of confusion and use gadgets that look just like homeopapes. That was my invention—computerized ultra-thin newspapers that read the news to you.

Of course, they didn't exist in 1982. Al Gore hadn't invented the internet yet (j/k as you say. ;) There were no "e" or "i" things, and none of my stories had been made into movies, yet. Just before I croaked I did see a reel of *Blade Runner*, what movie guys call the dailies. *Blade Runner* is the movie version of my novel *Do Androids Dream of Electric Sheep?* I actually liked what I saw of it. I hated the screen play initially, but the special effects and atmosphere of the movie looked great.

A lot of movies are being made from my stories now that I'm dead and can't benefit from the royalties. Money. I have a lot of thoughts on that, but enough for now.

This isn't about what I did, it's about what didn't get done. I spent my entire life searching for answers to the hard questions: What is real? What is human?

Now that I'm dead, I have all the answers and no way to tell the story. Well, that's not exactly true. You wouldn't be reading this if I hadn't found a way.

I am the friggin' Omniscient Voice and I want to tell the story. I can show you some scenes and let you watch the events unfold. I know a little something about what readers like. I hope so after forty flippin' novels. (I'm trying not to curse. They don't care for it much over here.)

It may seem obvious. Just plant some ideas in the girl's head and let her solve all my troubles. She can find my manuscript, the one that allegedly was stolen during the break-in, the one with Bishop Pike's revelations. She can figure out how his telegram to me was intercepted. Why he was killed and my safe was blown.

Too much, too fast? Did you read the Big Bang at the beginning? (tsk, tsk! better do that.) There's a lot of shit to clear up. You, dear reader, are a captive audience—but with the girl it's not that easy.

I never really knew for sure if Pike was contacting me, or if I was going crazy, or if God—VALIS—was directing me. I spent eight years trying to figure it out, and never really did. Now I have access to everything, the accumulated wisdom of the ages. But what good is it?

With so much going on, over here, it's impossible to focus. That's definitely some dead humor. *Unable to focus.*

Phil laughed at his own joke. Knowing everything, as he does now, Phil could see he was confusing things by speaking directly to the reader. It was getting pretty boring, too. Just a long monologue. Clearly this was not going to work.

"My novels were always lively. That's what readers like," Phil started again. Without time, he was experiencing chaos and confusion. How could he tell a story without past and present? "What year is it?" Phil intruded yet again.

That's enough! a disembodied Voice boomed back at Phil.

To be the omniscient narrator, a spirit—even a dead author—must follow the Rules. The instruction sheet applies to story telling, too.

Work within their frame of reference and do not manifest—not even on the page, the real Omniscient One concluded. Phil had been warned. And, now he was on probation.

March 22, 1982

Niki took a deep breath and stepped into the conference room for the Monday morning editorial meeting. It was hard to focus. She felt distant and removed like she didn't belong there, even though she had sat through these sessions every week for what seemed like an eternity.

Frank Simmons sat at the head of the huge, pretentious mahogany table. He was like a caricature of a small town newspaper man—a skinny, wiry guy in his fifties who lived on caffeine and nicotine. The other old farts were droning on about ad space and how many column inches they had left for local news. Their voices faded into the background and the clicking of the second hand on the big Wessex wall clock became loud. Niki feared she might have another "episode." What if she started hearing messages now, right in the middle of the meeting?

The time *is* now, she realized. With each tick of the clock she felt her life draining out. She had to restrain herself from jumping up and running out of the room. There just isn't time for this any more, she thought. I've got to do something meaningful with my life, get on with my mission—write whatever it is I'm supposed to write. She became aware of eyes turning toward her and wondered if she had said that out loud. Bruce gave her a nudge. Frank looked disappointed and sad.

"Niki, the Remke story." Frank cleared his throat. "Is it ready?" he asked.

Leaning forward against the big conference table, Niki regained her composure and responded.

"It won't be ready this week. I've still got more research and I need to get both Carl and the County Attorney on the record."

"Next week, then." Frank turned to Bruce for the weekend crime update.

When the meeting broke up, Frank shot a look toward Niki, but before he could call her over one of the big-money bosses, a publisher, walked in and Frank was detained. Bruce bumped Niki intentionally and guided her out of the room. Acting more like twelve than twenty-four, he started singing a childish chant under his breath.

"Someone's gonna be in trouble."

"Oh, for Christ's sake Bruce, knock it off." This time Niki did not give him a chance to tease her. She just grabbed her coat, the files, and headed straight for her car. This is as good a time as any to confront Remke, she decided.

Why waste energy on Bruce and his bullshit, when she could put the hostility to good use and nail that Remke bastard. She would try and catch him off guard at his construction site. The county supervisors were only part-time officials and she knew she could find him at his regular job on a Monday morning.

Niki rehearsed what she would say as she drove north on Court Street toward Remke Construction. She would start by asking innocent questions about expenditures, and then whip out copies of the invoices. She would tape record whatever he said. Damn. She had forgotten her small recorder in her rush to escape bonehead Bruce. She'd left it on her desk.

Niki was debating whether to turn and go back for it when the now familiar ear-buzz began. The surprise sound caused her to jerk the steering wheel, swerving dangerously toward an on-coming car. Perspiring inside her heavy parka, she pulled over to the curb.

Just like before, outside noises—music from the car radio and street sounds—seemed to fade as the humming in her ear became louder. When that stopped, in the strange silence she heard the words, *the Empire never ended.*

It sounded like a man's voice, kind of a whisper. The buzzing sound returned briefly, but within a moment that also ended and she heard traffic noise and someone yelling at her to move her car. She understood and even expected the various phenomena when her parents died, but why now? Who would be trying to contact her now?

Niki looked up and down Court Street, then pulled a U-turn. She was not going to Carl's construction site and couldn't go back to the *Courier.* She needed to—she had no idea what she needed to do, but decided she wanted to go home and lie down.

She drove too fast in her little silver sports car. The radio was playing one of her favorite songs, *Radar Love.* She started to sing along: *There's a voice in my head that drives my heel...* Those lyrics were disturbing, "Voice in my head."

By the time she got home it was mid morning and Schroeder didn't even bother to get up to greet her. He just stretched and yawned and settled back down on the bed. Niki lay down beside him. Sleep. Her way of dealing with stress, a technique that had worked well getting through the ordeal when her parents died, and also when her boyfriend had moved out. That asshole.

She recalled they had lived in the apartment together, originally. But things became strained between them when times got tough. Soon after her dad died, and when she first learned her mom had cancer, she had come home one night to discover he had moved out. He had left a note that said they never had fun anymore. Right, Niki thought then and again now. It's hard to have fun when everyone around you is dying.

Dying—that got Phil's attention. He had been engrossed in a game of poker with Einstein, Nietzsche and Tesla, but that could wait. It's pretty boring when everything is gold and you can have as many poker chips as you want.

"You manifested it," Phil heard Tesla say as he focused his attention back to the girl.

"What did she say about dying?" Phil asked.

Death had always been one of his favorite subjects.

Been there, done that—isn't that what you say nowadays? *I wrote all about the afterlife* and metaphysical stuff in my… Phil hesitated, recalling the guidelines he was supposed to follow.

Editors and fans didn't like it when I strayed away from SF when I was alive. Now what—I'm edited for Eternity?

His thoughts drifted to *Ubik*. He wrote that one in the 1960s, but used 1950s-era product ads at the beginning of each chapter. Now he was thinking of ads for this book:

Death, can't get enough? Don't worry. We have it in every form and flavor imaginable. Half-lifers who communicate from cold-pac (already used that one in *Ubik*), dead that grow young (nope, that was *Counter-clock World*.) *A Maze of Death*, another good one.

Phil recalled how most of that information and story came from Bishop Pike.

Salvation in a spray can. That was another *Ubik* product ad. Phil realized if he was writing that stuff forty years ago, it might be a bit stale now. *My fans still love it, don't you?*

Phil felt a twitch, a strong telepathic warning. He would have to find another way to communicate. He was not going to get away with speaking directly to the reader. Even if he could, he did not want to ruin yet another mainstream novel.

∞

Niki tossed and turned for awhile. It was the middle of the day and hard to sleep. The Empire, Rome, the Coliseum. What could it mean? She finally drifted into a fitful sleep and another bizarre dream.

She was with her friend Linda in a public building. A sign said it was "The Marina del Rey Community Center." They were attending some kind of workshop or lecture. Everyone, both guys and girls, were dressed in low-rise jeans with floppy bell bottoms, or beach wear. Their clothes looked like 1960s, but something was wrong. Instead of long hair, the kids had shaved heads or short, spiked-up hair. It could not be the 60s, it must be a future time or parallel universe. Some had little tuffs of hair in strange bright colors. She couldn't tell if they were guys or girls, except for one older man, with pale blue-gray eyes and a salt and pepper beard. He walked over and sat beside her. He was holding a book. Niki wanted to see it. She knew it was her book, the one she was supposed to write, but the man shook his head. "Soon, but not yet," he said.

Niki heard a faint chime in the distance, like a doorbell. Wait. She wasn't ready to leave. She had so many questions. Who was he? What did he want? The chiming sound grew much louder and forced her awake. It was the doorbell, she realized, as she glanced at the clock. Three in the afternoon.

"Wow, I was really out," she said stumbling to the front room. She peered through the peephole and saw Bruce outside the door. Niki sighed and unlocked the door. He had something cupped in his hands. That kitten—the one that scared the bejesus out of her during the storm.

Bruce extended the small furball toward her.

"It was sitting here on your doorstep."

"Put it down. I don't want another cat."

"But it's so tiny and alone," he pleaded, petting the fluff of fur.

"I said I don't want another damn cat," her green eyes flared. Bruce put it in the grass and came inside. Niki slammed the door.

"Still mad, I see," Bruce said as he rubbed his face and looked down. "I got worried when Frank said you went home. I felt kind of guilty. You know—" Before he could finish Niki said, "Bruce, you don't know what's really going on. It's complicated."

"Okay, if you don't want to talk about it I understand. I guess I shouldn't have come over here." He had the hurt little boy look. Niki bit her lower lip wondering what to say.

"I'm sorry," she began. "It's not just the Gribbin thing. It's other stuff. If I told you, it wouldn't make any sense. It would just sound crazy."

Niki wanted to talk about the dream, and the book, but couldn't imagine telling him about the voices and visions. That would mean revealing that she'd been dealing with strange stuff all her life. Did she really want to tell him about Aunt Lorene, the carnival queen, who really was psychic? This kind of thing was rampant in her family—fortune-tellers, magicians, Masonic rituals, but how could she share all that with Mr. Ivy League? She had worked hard to be a reporter and have a respectable job. Remembering some of their past discussions about weird phenomena, it had seemed like two worlds colliding.

Bruce was raised in a conservative Methodist family. Nothing wrong with that, but he only knew how to deal in the tangible—if you can't see it, it's not there. Niki knew otherwise. She was certain that we only see a small part of reality.

To avoid eye contact she had walked into the kitchen and called back, "Want some instant coffee?"

"I've had ten cups today. How about some of your tea?" Bruce paced in her living room, still wearing his heavy blue peacoat. Over the sound of running water, Niki shouted, "Take off your jacket."

Bruce started to look for a coat rack, but seemed sidetracked by so many strange books and unusual artifacts. Weird stuff was everywhere: an odd mix of religious icons, little Buddha statues, tarot cards, and many other occult-looking objects. He grimaced as he picked up a gourd rattle and then quickly put it down when it made a hissing noise.

Schroeder, the tomcat, was rubbing against his legs now and purring. He didn't want cat hair on his navy blue jacket but he couldn't figure out where to put it, so he was just standing there holding it up in the air, away from the cat.

When Niki emerged from the kitchen her face appeared pale and drawn. She took the coat, handed Bruce a cup of tea and hung the coat on a hook by the door without saying a word.

"Jeez, Nik, what's wrong with you? You look like someone who's seen a ghost."

Without hesitation or humor she said, "No, I don't see them, I just hear them."

"What?" Bruce chuckled nervously as his dark eyebrows formed a Spock-like V shape.

"Nothing. Never mind," she frowned. "Sit down, for God's sake. You're making me nervous."

Niki was already sitting, actually rocking in her mom's old Kennedy rocker—one of the few pieces of furniture she had kept when she sold her mom's house. It had been her mom's favorite chair.

Bruce sat stiffly on the edge of the sofa while Schroeder continued to rub against his legs. Niki yelled at the cat.

"You call it Schroeder like that kid on Peanuts, the one that likes classical music, huh?" Bruce speculated.

"No, it was a quantum physics paradox about a cat. Something I learned in a Gribbin book."

"That's why you said you might leave town and quit your job, isn't it?" Bruce winked. "You were going to run off with that physics guy."

"Forget Gribbin, that's over." Niki continued rocking and thinking. Bruce looked uncomfortable, as if afraid to crack another joke. Finally, Niki broke the silence.

"Remember when we talked about the news story, those kids in Yugoslavia who saw apparitions of the Virgin Mary?"

Bruce pointed to one of Niki's many icons of the Blessed Mother, which were scattered around the room. "Like that?"

"Yeah," Niki nodded. "It's something like that—"

His eyes widened, "You're seeing the Virgin Mary?"

"Not her," Niki laughed. "But strange things, kind of like that, have been happening," she paused, "for a long time."

The tea kettle whistled loudly and they both jumped. Niki forgot she had refilled it, but it gave her extra time to collect her thoughts.

It seemed like she had been gone too long. Bruce stepped into the kitchen to see what was going on. He found Niki sitting at the table staring off into space. When she realized Bruce was in the kitchen, she looked up at him and blurted out, "I hear voices."

"Voices? What does that mean?"

"I've heard them on and off all my life. But recently I've been hearing them more often. "

Bruce sat down at the table as Niki described her current and past experiences with ear buzzing, and the recent dreams.

She did not mention seeing Rome at the library. That seemed too weird, even for her. She had never been a seer, just a "hear-er."

"Everyone has strange dreams now and then. But what about the voices?" Bruce asked. "What did you hear?"

"On Sunday night, the Equinox, I heard: *the time is now.* It's especially strange because my dad's final words to me were that I would write... well, something important, and I would know when the time came." She searched Bruce's face for a reaction, and saw a side of him she hadn't seen before. He seemed serious, even kind of attractive when he wasn't making stupid faces. His dark wavy hair set off his big brown eyes, and his face didn't look as round when he wasn't smiling from ear to ear. His attentive look gave her enough confidence to continue.

"Then, just awhile ago, I was in the car on my way to Remke's site, and I heard a man's voice very clearly," Niki stopped deciding not to reveal the phrase about the empire ending, "and lyrics on the radio were also about voices."

"The voice comes through the radio?" Bruce asked.

"No!" she barked causing Bruce to bounce backwards. "I hear the voice in my head." She paused and then stood up and began pacing. She did think she was hearing messages in song lyrics, but no way would she admit that to Bruce. To him she said, "I knew I couldn't explain it. It sounds crazy."

Niki jumped up to check the tea kettle. Why in the world had she told Bruce? Bruce of all people. She felt angry at her own stupidity. My mom was the only person who understood this kind of thing. Even though Bruce hadn't said a word, Niki reacted. "Go ahead, laugh at me. I know you want to."

Bruce did not respond. He watched as she poured water from the kettle into mugs. Then he calmly said, "When we first met you said you were psychic. So, what's the big deal?"

Niki did not recall telling him that, and she did not think of herself as psychic, just sensitive. Her mom always said she had the family "gift" but she had never been able to actually read anyone's thoughts. Spirits seemed to like her, though.

Even before the experiences with her dad, there had been other signs, and now this. She felt like some kind of speaker for the dead. Bruce was still talking.

"I saw that stuff in your living room," he continued. "All your occult books and weird fortune-telling things. I bet you know exactly what's going on. Who do *you* think it is? You said it's a guy. "

"I'm not sure," she responded, still avoiding eye contact. "An older man with a beard and distinctive blue-gray eyes. He showed me a book and said *not now, but soon.*" She looked up at Bruce. "I think it's time to write a book. I just don't know who the guy is, or what I'm supposed to write."

"Why can't you try some of that stuff?" Bruce asked pointing toward her shelves. "You know, ask that *I Ching* who it is, and what you're supposed to write about." Niki laughed at Bruce's slow Midwest drawl when he said eye ching.

"E-sching," she corrected. "That's not a bad idea, but you can't get very specific answers from tossing coins." She recalled her mom and aunt using the Ouija board to contact her grandmother, their mom, who had died before she was even born. Niki and her friends had used it at slumber parties. The Oracle would spell out words and names of their future boyfriends. After her mom died she put the board away.

As open-minded as she was, Niki had never tried contacting her parents with the Ouija board—that was too much. Not to mention, she had a pretty strong ongoing connection to them anyway. It might be just the ticket for this situation, though. As she poured more hot water into the cups and dropped in the tea bags, she looked at Bruce and suggested it.

"You know, we could try the Ouija board."

"We? Not me," he said recoiling. "I don't want any part of that. I said *you* should try one of those things." Bruce's brow was now a big black question mark.

"That board is the Devil's plaything."

"Come on, Bruce, you started this," she pleaded handing him a cup of tea. "I can't work the board alone. It takes two and you're the only one who knows anything about this. You have to help me."

Niki didn't wait for an answer. She hurried off toward her spare bedroom closet to search for her mom's old Ouija set. Bruce paced the living room. He paused in front of a large iconic painting of the Virgin Mary.

"Can't you put a stop to this?" he asked, half joking, but shivered as Mary's eyes seemed to look right through him.

If I had a body, I would roll on the floor laughing, Phil thought. ROFLOL. Rolling on Floor Laughing Out Loud.

Isn't that what you web heads type on your homeopapes? What do you call them? Eye Tabs? Raspberries? Kindlers? What kind of names are those? Like I said, I called future newspapers homeopapes. I saw that coming years ago. Fans of mine call themselves Dick-heads now. Sorry, I digress.

I understand it's hard to listen to a disembodied spirit. Believe me, I spent eight long years trying to understand what was happening to me. And I must say it wasn't a damn bit funny, either. I never tried the Ouija board, though. I used to consult the *I Ching* and even used it to plot a couple of my novels. In fact, I won a Hugo Award for *Man in the High Castle* and almost all of those ideas came from the coins and the *I Ching: Book of Changes.*

Speaking of books, who published *Radio Free Albemuth*? That was a draft. I spent three years revising it and then scrapped it. I wrote *VALIS* instead, you know just used the best parts of RFA in there. It was much better. Even so, people claimed I was nuts. I remember reading a review of *VALIS* that went something like this:

> Philip K. Dick is no longer making any effort to conceal his obsession with metaphysical matters. Protagonists have epiphanies, talk to the dead, and now he actually used himself as a character.

That hurt. I think my friend Disch said it, too. Fans complained I'd gone off the deep end. That I was insane—that my last novels weren't even science fiction and made no sense. No sense? Well guess what—I was right! Pike was communicating with me, just like I'm communicating with you—all of you!

Even though his rant was an obvious violation of the "rules," no one stopped Phil that time, perhaps because his next point was valuable.

How can I convince the girl of who I am and where to find the information she needs? You wonder why I gave her such cryptic clues. Well, sometimes it wasn't intentional.

Being a teep, she was able to pick up on my thoughts and memories. I didn't mean to convey *Black Iron Prison* or *the Empire never ended.* Those were my obsessions.

And, then there's the problem of Pike; Bishop Pike and his unfinished business. He's the one who showed her that ancient scroll in the dream. I tried to straighten things out. I thought I could show her the book—her book. But that was unacceptable. I can't believe there are so many damn rules here in the afterlife. Who knew?

Phil felt the strongest reprimand yet, but was determined to make one last point.

Now that she's off to get the Ouija board, I have a great opportunity to give her a solid clue. But what? I could spell out my name, but what would that mean to her. Dick? She would just toss the board into the trash.

∞

6 Ouija Words

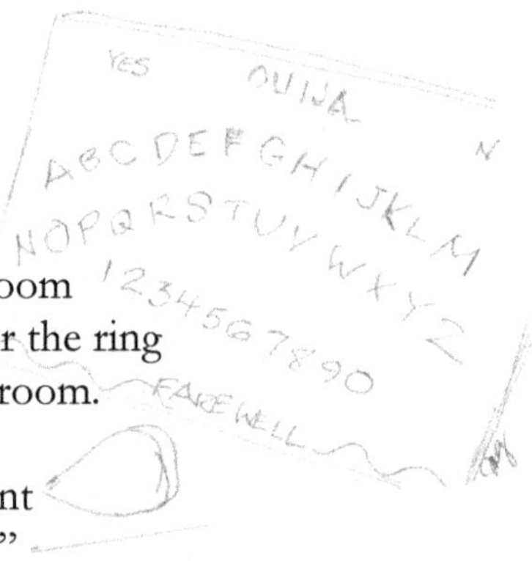

Niki emerged from the back room waving the board and reaching for the ring on a window shade to darken the room.

"Do you have to do that?" Bruce asked shuddering. "You want to make this as creepy as possible."

"Oh, lighten up," Niki said. "This could be fun." She plopped down cross-legged on the floor in the middle of the darkened living room.

"Sit right here," Niki pointed to the spot across from her, "and relax."

"Relax?" Bruce rolled his eyes, then asked. "How do you work this thing?" He was fidgeting with the heart-shaped piece of wood that was part of *Ouija; the Mystifying Oracle.*

"It's called a planchette," Niki said as she took the wooden piece from him. "It's the oracle-reader we use on the board, "she explained. The board was about eighteen inches across and a foot from top to bottom. One side was covered with words, symbols, the alphabet, and numbers.

"We place the board on our knees like this," she said.

Niki arranged the thin board between them, then placed the heart-shaped pointer on the table-type surface.

"Real planchettes were used for automatic writing," Niki started to explain, but when she saw Bruce screwing up his face, she decided less information was better. This oracle pointer/planchette had a circular window cut into the wood so inquirents could see through it to the letters and symbols on the board.

Whatever appeared in the window was considered the spirit communication. Niki had decided not to use terms like that with Bruce. She would leave out a lot of ritual, and just silently ask for protection. She'd grabbed one of her mom's silver Kennedy half dollars when she retrieved the board because silver is good protection against evil spirits, and you can't be too careful, she determined.

"We rest our fingers lightly along the edge of the reader like this," Niki said as she demonstrated the technique.

Bruce pushed too hard on his edge and flipped over the light-weight pointer. Niki patiently placed it back on the board.

"Very gently," she prompted. "Don't push it. The spirits will move it for us." Niki wished she hadn't said that, but too late.

Beads of perspiration were visible on Bruce's forehead.

"I *really* don't like this."

"I haven't consulted the Ouija in years," Niki said, ignoring his discomfort. "In fact, I think the last time was when I was about fifteen. Mom and I tried using it after my aunt died. Mom thought her sister, Lorene, might communicate with us."

"Did she?" Bruce jerked his hands away from the board and the planchette.

"I think so," Niki said reaching for Bruce's hands. "Please

keep your fingers on the reader. No laughing."

"Don't worry," Bruce said grimacing. "It doesn't feel a bit funny to me." The room was quiet with only the ticking of the mantle clock. Niki began.

"Are the messages I heard this past week connected to the mission my dad spoke of?"

For a few minutes nothing happened, other than Bruce's constant squirming and sighing. In a soft voice Niki reminded him again, "Please, keep your eyes shut and just relax."

The oracle-reading planchette began to twitch, then move slightly. Suddenly it lurched toward the top of the board and stopped over the word "Yes."

Bruce peeked through one squinted eye. "You pushed it."

Niki shook her head, indicating "no." A drop of sweat fell from his forehead onto the board. Even he felt a change in the air. Something was happening. Bruce started to get up. Niki shot a stern look at him and whispered.

"Sit still. You'll break the connection."

"So, it's time for me to write something?" Niki asked the Oracle as she placed the pointer back in the center of the board. She felt electricity as the heart-shaped reader began moving. It slid smoothly back up and stopped over the word "Yes" again.

"My turn," Bruce whispered. Then as if addressing the board asked, "Can we stop now?"

Niki shook her head disapprovingly and continued.

"What should I write about?"

As she moved the pointer back to the center, she anticipated receiving a "P" for Peace. She was surprised when the oracle slowly moved to the letter "N", then "A", then "G", then a pause and back to the center. Bruce burst out laughing.

"Nag! This thing does work." He couldn't stop giggling.

Niki wanted to slap him. "It's not done. It will move to the top of the board or point to 'good-bye' when it's finished.

She felt frustrated. It had been working. More than ever she wanted to know what the board was trying to tell them. Niki insisted they resume.

It took a couple of minutes for the energy to settle. She felt the oracle twitching and it slowly spelled out H-A-M, then moved away, and came back to M-A-D-I. Then the reader quickly moved to the top of the board and the word Ouija, indicating it had finished.

"What is that? Just gibberish." Bruce shook his head and searched for his handkerchief to wipe perspiration from his forehead.

Niki grabbed her notebook, and wrote the letters in all caps: NAG HAM MADI the way the Ouija board had spelled them

"Could be middle eastern."

"Or, an illiterate spirit," Bruce offered, resuming his usual poor attempt at comedy. "I still think NAG was the answer," he added.

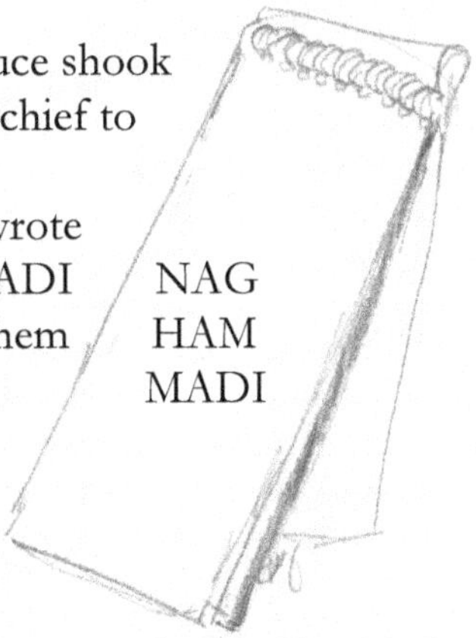

Niki rolled her eyes and studied her notebook. She tried pronouncing the term using various emphasis and intonation. Nag (Bruce's way) ham mad eye. Then she tried: Nog ha mah dee, saying it a couple of times.

"That sound's right, Bruce. I think I've heard of this." She looked at Bruce, then added, "I'm pretty sure it's the name of an evil Middle Eastern jinn."

Bruce jumped up and began shaking his arms as if to cast off evil vibes.

"You were right," she continued. "Tampering with spirits. We're probably doomed."

Bruce's expression was priceless. Niki stepped toward him, got close to his face and whispered, "Boo!" It was her turn to giggle.

"Touché," he smirked, then glanced at his watch. "Jeez, Nik, it's almost five and I have to pick up Sally from work. Gotta go."

Sally was his girlfriend who Niki thought was an air-head.

"Don't tell her about this."

"Yeah, right. Like I would," Bruce said grabbing his coat from the hook. Niki gave him a quick hug and whispered, "Thanks."

When she opened the door, there on her door step was the damn kitten. Bruce pointed at it and said.

"Just like you, won't take no for an answer. You should keep it."

"Take it to Sally. Tell her you got a little pussy," she winked.

Bruce could not rush off fast enough to get into his GTO.

Niki was still chuckling as she made another cup of tea, but got serious quickly. It seemed important to keep a record of the events. So, in her reporter's notebook, she made a list, and dated, her experiences.

3/20/74	Dad died – Equinox (Peace message before dying)
3/28/74	Mars Hill/Spiritual Encounter
3/03/82	Strange Vision at library
3/10/82	Doomsday?
3/20/82	Equinox / Time is Now! (dream of scroll)
3/22/82	Empire Never Ended (car) Radar (radio) "not yet, soon" – my book? NAG HAMMADI (Ouija)

She decided to start with the experiences when her dad died. Looking at the list, something was immediately obvious. All the events occurred in March—specifically around the Equinox! Why? That must be significant. It was like piecing together a puzzle.

Nag Hammadi sounded foreign, but the man in the dream wasn't. He was a middle aged white guy. She looked up, directly at Phil. She couldn't see him, or even sense him, but said. "Why can't you just tell me?"

Phil, who had been hovering around during the Ouija session, was literally right over the table and felt frustrated that he couldn't respond.

"Believe me," he said, but of course was inaudible, "I wish I could manifest and tell you exactly what's going on." He felt like one of his demented *Ubik* "half lifers."

In his novel *Ubik,* half-life meant only the body was in cryogenic stasis. The mind remained active after death. Friends and family could communicate with their loved ones using special headphones.

Phil's story wasn't so far off the mark, especially his concept of psychic invasions, where the newly dead projected stronger signals than the long dead who were fading out.

The former rogue Bishop of California, Phil's friend James Pike, was creating the same kind of confusion. Thoughts were jumping from one spirit mind to another.

"Even if she figures out Nag Hammadi, how will that lead her to my manuscript in California? First the scroll and now this. What are you doing, Jim?"

The remnants of Pike's thoughts were merging with Phil's, making for a muddled mess.

No wonder no one ever communicates with the dead—it's too damn complicated, Phil decided.

∞

Bliss shifted into low gear… melding with the downtown Des Moines traffic.
"You're not going to enjoy the next five years," Joe Chip said.
"Why not? The whole state of Iowa is behind me in what I believe." ***UBIK*** *by PKD*

6½ Lifer

March 23, 1982

Nag Hammadi was real! It was a place in upper Egypt. Niki practically danced her way down main street, back to the paper. She could hardly wait to tell Bruce the Ouija word wasn't mumbo jumbo, or whatever he called it. And it wasn't an evil spirit, which she had made up just to freak him out. Nag Hammadi was an area on the west bank of the Nile, where ancient religious scrolls referred to as Codices were found in the 1940s.

Niki had discovered this Tuesday morning when she went straight to the library, allegedly to search through clips for the Remke case. But as soon as she arrived, she wrote out the letters on a slip of paper and showed it to the librarian.

There was only one minor reference to Nag Hammadi in an archeological digest at the Ottumwa library, but for Niki it was the ultimate confirmation:

> "The Nag Hammadi Codices pre-date the Dead Sea Scrolls and are considered the most valuable original biblical texts ever found."

The librarian ignored Niki's enthusiastic reaction and said, "I believe a complete translation of the scrolls has recently been published. The University would probably have a copy."

Niki was ecstatic. The University of Iowa was her alma mater. She recalled some heated discussions in her comparative religion classes over biblical interpretations.

It had been obvious, to her, that the Bible could not be taken literally. There were at least fifty English versions, and untold numbers in other languages, each slightly different. She could not understand how fundamentalist churches, like the one she was raised in, could take the Word so literally.

"Bibliolatry makes no sense," Niki had argued. "The text had been translated from language to language." She was shocked to learn that it wasn't just poor translations.

Through the centuries, various secular leaders had influenced, and at times forced, clergy and monks to twist translations to fit their particular purposes. One of the worst was the fourth century fiasco. Christianity was essentially "created" by Emperor Constantine who forced a majority of bishops to sign the Nicene Creed. That creed accomplished several things: it declared Jesus divine, but also empowered the Roman government to suppress all rival religions. Christianity became the *only* religion Romans could practice.

In one civil action, religious tolerance was over for Rome. Pagans, and those who professed gnostic enlightenment, were imprisoned or crucified. The Emperor claimed he was giving Roman society what it wanted—its savior Jesus—but he was actually using the new religion to control society.

"And, they made him a saint?," Niki muttered under her breath as she walked back to the *Courier*.

Memories of religious studies were swirling in her mind. Going back to U of I would be great, she thought. She could look for the new translation and maybe gain more insight about what exactly she was supposed to write.

She didn't see Bruce when she walked into the newsroom, so she took the opportunity to review her notes again. She sat at her desk looking at her notebook, not only the notes she had just jotted down at the library, but also the events that had been happening over the past few days.

It's all here, she realized. Like a story unfolding. The man in her dreams had pointed to a scroll. The first message, *the time is now,* was pretty clear. More amazing was the message she heard in the car, that hadn't made sense at the time: *the Empire never ended.* Constantine, Roman Codices, she thought. That empire? Hairs on the back of her neck stood up. New biblical interpretations would affect peace on earth.

The din of the manual typewriters seemed to fade out, and the buzzing began in Niki's left ear. She glanced around the newsroom. The other reporters were still typing and their mouths were moving, but she couldn't hear a thing. *Tractates,* she heard. Then another phrase that she had no idea how to spell: E*xegesis.* It sounded like "exit Jesus." That's what she wrote in her notebook. Her palm felt sweaty against the metal pen.

"Earth to Niki," Bruce was waving his hand in front of her face. He was much too loud. It wasn't just the buzzing ending. The sports jock and another reporter craned their necks to see what was going on.

Niki whispered, "Come on. We've got to get out of here, right now. I just got more information."

"Just now?" Bruce asked frowning. "I just walked in from a press conference. The cops nabbed those two hoods that broke into the—"

"*This* is more important," Niki interrupted. "Trust me."

"Okay, let's go to the *Canteen*," Bruce conceded, "but only for a few minutes." He reached for his jacket avoiding eye contact with the sports guy.

As soon as they were outside, Niki blurted out her news.

"First of all, Nag Hammadi is real! It's a place in Egypt where scrolls were found. That's why it sounded familiar to me. I'm sure I heard of it when I was in college. Walking back from the library I was thinking about Constantinople and the Council of Nicea—"

"The what?" Bruce interrupted.

"Wait. I have a lot of new information. Just now, I got another message: *Tractates on the exit of Jesus*. Something like that."

"Trac-tates?" Bruce emphasized the long 'a' sound. "Exa Jesus. Is that what you heard?" When Niki nodded, he explained. "Exegesis is an explanation of the bible, you should know that."

"Bruce!" Niki stopped in the middle of the sidewalk on Main Street. "Then, I really am receiving revelations!"

A man and woman walking past them began to stare. Bruce smiled at the couple, and took Niki by her elbow.

"C'mon, let's cut over to the alley," he hissed still showing his pearly whites.

Bruce navigated her toward the small diner, the *Canteen Lunch in the Alley*. Once inside, they sat in one of the few booths. Most of the seating was at the counter.

"Now, slow down and keep your voice down, too. What just happened?" he asked.

"It really is time," Niki whispered. "I'm being called to work on the peace treaty, only I think it's a treatise. I can't explain why, I just sense it."

One of the waitresses came to take their order. Bruce ordered two coffees.

"Make mine a hot tea, please." Niki corrected.

"Just drinks?" the young woman wearing the housedress scowled and checked her watch.

The *Canteen* was one of the most popular lunch spots in Ottumwa. Both the restaurant and the hamburger they served were called Canteens, a concept invented during the war in the 1940s.

The small building was in an alley off Main Street. In the middle of the one room was a huge metal vat where women (no man was ever known to work there) steamed ground beef then served it scrambled, and greasy, on a bun. All the women, young or old, wore the same type of loose-fitting floral dress and apron. Niki had no idea why. The place was usually too busy to just sit and talk. But at eleven in the morning, it had just opened. Bruce assured the waitress they'd be gone before the lunch crowed arrived.

"What are you talking about? What treatise?" he asked.

"I'm supposed to write a religious treatise of some sort."

"Nik, I think you're letting this ESP and magical thinking consume you. It's all you think about now."

"Oh, you're just as bad as that Emperor Constantine."

"Why do you keep talking about Rome and emperors?"

"I'm starting to understand the messages, Bruce," she said. "I took a lot of religion classes in college, you know."

"I'm just not used to such weird ways of bible study—Ouija boards and e jing coins."

Niki rolled her eyes. "In fact, we could go to Iowa City, to the University, and look for more information about Nag Hammadi."

"We? Why are you dragging me into this?"

"Dragging *you*? I didn't want to tell you anything, but you showed up at my house and practically begged me to bare my soul."

The waitress appeared with tea and coffee, and started to ask them about pie. She must have felt the tension and disappeared. Niki didn't even touch the tea. She slumped in the booth. Bruce ran his hands through his hair. "So, what's your plan?"

Niki perked up. "I can drive us to the Religious Studies library. I know exactly where it is."

"When?" He took a sip of coffee.

"Now."

Bruce, in mid swallow, choked on his coffee. "Now?" He looked at his watch again. It was 11:11.

"You're almost done for the day. I can take the afternoon off. We could leave by noon or twelve-thirty."

Bruce said nothing, but his dark eyes said no.

"What's the big deal? Just one afternoon out of your life. Are you worried that the Prom Queen will get jealous?"

"Leave Sally out of this," Bruce frowned. "And no more comments like you made yesterday."

"I was just getting even for all your teasing about Gribbin. Come on." She urged. "Let's just go. It'll be fun and we'll be back before dark."

"Well, if I write up the arrest story," Bruce reconsidered. "I guess there's nothing else until the arraignment." He flashed his goofy grin. "Of course, lunch is on you."

∞

Phil watched the young reporters interact with great interest. Cause and effect. Maybe that's all there is. Everyone needs and wants something, and it doesn't end with what people call death. That's the whole point, there is no death.

Things just change form. Water evaporates and becomes steam. People evaporate and become spirits. Our soul lives on. We carry our desires with us. We're not done until we're finished with them. Pike certainly wasn't done, he knew.

The Bishop's passion had been to learn the truth about the entire Christian kerygma—the truth of the Gospels. But his strangest revelations, discoveries he made just before he died, were his unfinished business. His will had been so strong... Phil stopped. It was hard to think with Pike trying to correct his every thought. Some people linger much longer than others. Pike was considered one of the Long Dead, who wouldn't—or couldn't— move on. He was still exerting his influence.

Phil kind of wished that the Pike pieces *would* merge into the Collective, or VALIS as he used to call it. It dawned on him that Pike knew what he had just thought. Not good.

"Listen Jim, I want the girl to look for our manuscript," Phil clarified. "Not go on a wild chase through the Middle East, like you did. You're complicating the communication."

The Pike parts were either ignoring him or were too unfocused to respond. Phil wondered if Pike's interference was real or just another figment of his imagination.

Bruce and Niki left for Iowa City around 12:15. She calculated they could make it to the campus by two, if she pushed it.

It was another bone-chilling, gray, overcast day, but at least the sun was trying to break through. Niki glanced over and saw that Bruce had his arms wrapped around himself to keep from shivering.

"Does this thing have a heater?" he asked.

"This thing?" Niki turned up the heat, literally and verbally. "You mean this superb piece of automotive machinery?

You'll be begging me to turn it down." She peeled out of the parking lot, throwing Bruce back into his seat.

As soon as they pulled onto Highway 63 heading north, a ray of sunlight beamed down on the pavement ahead.

"Good omen," she commented, pointing at the illuminated spot. "I'm really glad you agreed to come with me." She smiled at him. "It will make the research fun." Niki just kept talking without waiting for a response. "I made some calls while you were submitting your copy. The Center for Religious Studies is open 'til 6 o'clock."

"We're not staying that late."

"Have you considered that this could also be a story? I mean, if there are earth-shattering insights from these scrolls. It could be huge." Niki glanced at Bruce raising a perfectly plucked eyebrow. "Pulitzer stuff."

"Pulitzer?" he laughed. "Earth-shattering like end times?"

Niki didn't care for his sarcastic tone. The car warmed up, but she turned icy and drove in silence for a while. When they reached the outskirts of Iowa City, they stopped for a quick lunch at a popular family restaurant and resumed their usual banter.

It only took a few minutes from there to arrive at the home of the Hawkeyes—the University of Iowa.

The sprawling campus was beautiful, even at this desolate time of year. In fact, the stark setting of barren trees against the gray sky added a foreboding look to the Gothic buildings. In a few more weeks the old institution would take on a completely different character when the rolling hills and vast lawns became green and lush with foliage.

"This brings back a lot of memories," Niki sighed. "I used to come up here every Saturday to Johnson Hall, when I was working on my degree."

Niki pointed to one of the massive columned buildings where ivy covered an entire wall. "Seems like ages ago."

Iowa City represented both fun and painful times for her. Those high-speed trips were before the Z car, and often the destination had been University Hospital.

As Dickens said, "the best and worst of times." Mostly hell. Niki had finally managed to piece together a normal life, until a week ago. Now she didn't know what she was doing. Maybe leaving Iowa altogether.

"Knock, knock. Anyone home?" Bruce waved his hand in front of her face. "Wasn't that our turn?"

"Oops, sorry. I was lost in thought." She pulled a quick U-turn and headed toward a massive four-story stone building that resembled the courthouse. She could see that Bruce was admiring the campus.

"It's the old Capitol Building complex," she explained. "The grounds and buildings were converted to the university around 1850—the first public university in the U.S. to give women the same academic standing as men. We're not all hicks here." She nudged him as she parked the car.

It was just after two-thirty when they walked into the quiet study center. Shelves of books, research materials and work tables were scattered throughout the large open area. There were only two other people and they seemed engrossed in their own projects. A middle-aged woman approached them.

"Hi. Are you the students Professor Rodgers sent over?"

"We're here to review recent translations of the religious scrolls found at Nag Hammadi in Egypt," Niki dodged the question. "Do you have those documents?"

The woman peered over the top of her reading glasses. "Are you part of the Egyptology class?"

"Professor Rodgers was one of my advisors. I minored in religious studies." That much was true, but she hadn't spoken to him in years.

"Oh, I thought you were current students," the woman said, but seemed satisfied. "It's a fascinating project. We're probably the only place in the Midwest that has this information. Let me show you how our system works." Niki did a thumbs up sign once the woman turned her back to lead them to the index file.

The listing showed a few sources ranging from texts in the Egyptian Coptic language to the recent English translation of the Codices. The most promising and comprehensible seemed to be a book by James Robinson called *The Nag Hammadi Library*. When the librarian left to retrieve the volume, Bruce whispered the obvious.

"I don't think we're supposed to be here."

"Too late now."

"Why so much secrecy?" Bruce asked. Niki shrugged.

They sat down at the table, and as soon as the librarian handed Niki the thick book, they opened it and scanned the introduction. The first thing to catch her eye was a sentence in the introduction. "The Gospel of Thomas begins with a word to the wise: *Whoever finds the interpretation of these sayings will not experience death.*" She poked Bruce and scribbled that in her notebook. Bruce raised a black eyebrow again.

It didn't take long for Niki to get the gist of the Codices and why they had been suppressed. They were considered heretical teachings. The scrolls had apparently been buried in the Egyptian desert in the 4th Century to keep them from being destroyed by Roman officials after Emperor Constantine banned gnostic beliefs. Gnostics were "knowers" and saw God as Universal—"That Which Is"—not a patriarchal figure in the sky. They saw no need for a formal, structured religion with hierarchy and dogmatic rules—especially rules from a Roman emperor, Niki surmised.

Knowers. It sent a shiver down her spine since this was the same message she received during the spiritual encounter after her father died. Apparently, it was being reinforced now by the messages and dreams. She wanted to inhale the book, but it was slow and tedious reading.

The introduction indicated the books were organized around thirteen Codices and over fifty Tractates. Niki pointed that out to Bruce and whispered, "Tractates!" Even better, there was an Exegesis on the Soul.

Over the next hour, Niki absorbed as much as she could while Bruce yawned and kept getting up and down. These gnostic texts confirmed just what she suspected about the Bible—it was carefully edited for political reasons.

For instance, one of the first Tractates was a letter from James, Jesus' brother:

The Apocryphon of James professes to be a letter written by James, the Lord's brother. The letter introduces a secret writing." The book said this Apocryphon was intended for an elect few—even among the disciples— for James and Peter only, but salvation is promised to those who receive its message.

A code, a secret within a secret, the introductory material called it.

James revealing the Apocryphon given to him and Peter from the Lord who had appeared *again* 550 days after the resurrection.

"Could that be true?" Niki gasped. "Jesus already returned?" She was too loud.

Bruce, who had been at the water fountain, rushed over. The librarian reminded Niki to keep her voice down. As she walked away, Niki showed Bruce that part. He scowled.

"What makes this stuff more authentic than the Bible?"

"I'll explain later."

"You can't read that whole book this afternoon," he pointed to his watch, which indicated it was already three-forty five."

"Just let me figure out which parts I really need," Niki said. She had been scribbling furiously, after learning she could not photocopy any of the materials.

When she finally took the heavy book up to the counter to return it, the librarian asked Niki to sign a disclosure form and provide identification. Niki hesitated. She did not want to give her name. After all, she was a reporter, not a student, and it might cause problems.

Niki always carried a fake ID that she had used on a couple of investigative stories. It was a good one, realistic. She pulled it out of her bag, and signed the paper. The librarian handed the card back to Niki and said. "Thank you, Evelyn. I'll tell Professor Rodgers you were here."

Niki nodded, grabbed her notebook and hurried out of the building. Bruce was right behind her.

"I hope you got everything you wanted, Evelyn," he smirked, "because you can't go back there. Not after lying to them."

Niki had thought the same thing. If writing about these texts was her mission she might need to spend a lot of time there.

"I can always contact Professor Rodgers and explain my way out of it," Niki said and decided she couldn't worry about that now. For now, she was thrilled with what she had found and wanted to enjoy her successful adventure.

"You've got to admit that the whole thing was pretty amazing" she added. "Finding just what I needed about Nag Hammadi."

"Yeah, considering your source was a Ouija board." He gave Niki a suspicious look. "I bet you knew about this the whole time. You pushed that thing around, didn't you?"

"Honestly, Bruce, you never stop." She drove in silence for awhile wondering if she really had known about Nag Hammadi. She remembered studying the Dead Sea Scrolls, and maybe something about fragments from other scrolls. Tractates. Exegesis. Were these things in her subconscious? But what about the man in the dreams? Hearing the words?

Niki thought about the information she had just read. The Gnostics received revelations in the form of inner messages. This Gospel of Thomas claimed that Jesus had preached the importance of direct access to the Divine within us.

Thinking aloud she said, "Those gospels claim everyone can receive messages inwardly. *Inner messages*—like I receive." She paused and looked at Bruce. "Is that hard for you to believe? We can receive direct insights just like the prophets?"

"I don't know," Bruce rubbed his eyes. He had been half asleep. "To be honest, I'm tired of thinking right now. I just want to get home before that storm moves in." He pointed to the darkening sky.

Iowa is famous for sudden weather changes and Ottumwa is part of tornado alley. This appeared to be a severe electrical storm with a lot of thunder and lightning. Each clap was louder and lingered longer, meaning the storm was getting closer. Niki drove faster trying to outrun it.

She had barely dropped Bruce off at his vehicle when heavy rain began. She hurried home to unplug her stereo, TV, and her new Vic 20 computer. She unplugged the phone, too, remembering a news story about some guy whose face was burned off when lightning came through the telephone line.

There was a constant din of rain on the roof, interrupted by the room-shaking booms. Where is Schroeder, she wondered, looking around the apartment. He was curled up, asleep on her bed, oblivious to the racket.

Good idea, she thought, and was about ready to jump in, when between crashing thunder she heard a scratching sound on her back porch.

"It's that damn kitten." She had totally forgotten about it.

When Niki opened the back door, there was the pathetic sight, again. The tiny kitten clinging to the screen, trembling and soaking wet. She dried off the kitten with a towel and gave it a little saucer of milk. It couldn't be more than a few weeks old, she thought, hoping Schroeder wouldn't discover that she had let it in.

Lying in bed, listening to the thunder, she thought of something her dad had told her when she was about five years old. The angels are bowling. That's exactly how it sounded. Like a giant bowling ball rolling down a lane and then, kaboom, a strike.

She thought of the term she heard during the encounter with her dad: *Universal Knowledge.* That's exactly what the Nag Hammadi scrolls and gnostics called *Knowers.* It's true that we have access to God, or the Source, without formal church rituals, she thought. No wonder gnostics hid their insights and writings in caves, though. The Roman government would have destroyed them.

That message, *the Empire never ended,* must mean it's still not safe to speak the truth. The man trying to reach her, must be a gnostic, *a knower,* telling her *the time is now.*

As she dozed off, a light flickered through her closed eyes. Nothing dramatic, just a pleasant pink light. Niki fell asleep.

7 In the Pink

Niki dreamed she was walking through an ancient temple where she heard soft, haunting music. Flute? Comforting, yet eerie. As she explored the stone structure, she heard the echoes of her footsteps, but saw no one. There were huge arches and ornately carved wooden beams overhead. It was peaceful listening to the harmonic sounds. It seemed as if she had been there many times before. She noticed a soft pink glow all around her. It wasn't until she looked outside the temple walls that what she saw jolted her awake. It was an alien landscape, with pink sky and purple rock. Was it really another planet, or another dimension?

Niki looked around at her bedroom and realized she had been dreaming. But it was so vivid, the sounds and sites of that place. She could still hear the mesmerizing music, and a word she couldn't get out of her head, Zadokite. What was it? An alien word? She started to remember all the revelations from the Nag Hammadi texts. Was it an Egyptian temple? Were hieroglyphics an alien language? Maybe it's a sign to dig deeper. Maybe even go to Egypt!

She threw back the covers, ready to jump up, but there was the damn kitten. It had crawled into her bed.

"If Schroeder sees you, you're a goner," she whispered as she put the tiny furball in her bathrobe pocket and quickly tip toed past the sleeping tomcat. On her way out the back door, she grabbed the sack of dry cat food and gave the kitten a few pieces.

Standing outside she admired the huge oak trees with traces of spring buds. Rays of sunlight against the mass of branches cast shadows on the yard. Quiet streets lined with old English Tudor and brick homes. No sign that there had been a big storm last night. Everything was peaceful and normal now—except me, she thought.

Maybe now is the time to leave, or at least take some time off. Why couldn't I take a leave of absence? I made extra money from the syndication. I could go to Egypt. Why not, she defended her own thoughts. It would be a research trip. I could really study the Nag Hammadi Codices.

Niki's heart pumped faster. Just the thought of getting away from Ottumwa and taking off on such an adventure was exciting. I could ask Frank for three or even six months. I don't have a husband or kids to take care of. Schroeder could stay with…"

"Dammit, Jim," Phil cursed. "I warned you about this. Why do you fill her head with dreams of Egypt and Zadokite scrolls. We need to direct her straight to California, to find our manuscript." Phil felt like killing Pike, but of course the Bishop was already dead. "I wrote everything you wanted me to. It's done."

There was no response from Pike. Why? Phil should feel something, he thought. Telepathic contact should be instantaneous, especially in their case. After all, it's hard to say where Pike ends and Phil begins.

Strange as it sounds, the two are merged, cross-bonded into a biomorphic entity—a nebulous blur, as Phil had once referred to a similar schizoid duo in his novel *A Scanner Darkly*. Their merger actually began while Phil was still alive.

After Bishop Pike died in 1969 he tried to "come back" through Phil. Pike had a story that had to be told and he wanted Phil to do the telling.

The Bishop's unfinished business *was* in Egypt, or maybe what used to be Persia or ancient Sumer. He went to Israel to study the Dead Sea Scrolls, but that led to more fascinating findings.

Were ancient Zadok Priests actually Sumerian Shamans? Was Jesus part of that lineage? The Zadokite Fragments were older than any other biblical scrolls. They were part of the Damascus Document, which allegedly pre-dated the birth of Jesus. Why were those documents suppressed and considered heretical? Bishop Pike believed the Church was controlling scroll translations that could be explosive if made public.

The Bishop wanted to stay in the Middle East and find out exactly what the anokhi and Parousia really were. That never happened. He died in the Judean desert, just after he had telegrammed Phil with his suspicions. The Church would not tolerate one of its bishops advocating heretical gnostic gospels. But how far would they go to stop him?

Phil first met Bishop Pike in the mid-1960s through a connection to one of Phil's wives. The Bishop contacted him and requested that Phil attend a séance. The goal was to communicate with Pike's dead son, Jim Junior, who had committed suicide. Phil was stunned that such a high-ranking Church leader would turn to parlor tricks, or want someone he barely knew to participate in such a personal quest. The Bishop assured him he had two good reasons for the request. First, Phil was also Episcopalian, but more importantly, he considered Phil an expert on such matters.

"How so?" Phil had asked.

Pike pointed to the writer's then-recent novels, *The Three Stigmata of Palmer Eldrich* and *Ubik*. Phil found that funny.

"I make up that shit," Phil had confessed. "I'm just a dabbler in metaphysics—a crap artist." He recalled writing *Confessions of a Crap Artist* back in the 50s; a character who just collects a lot of crackpot ideas. As for the séance, Phil assured the Bishop that he had no experience in contacting the dead.

Pike was persistent and Phil, always intrigued by the inexplicable, basically just went along with the weird request for the experience. He and then-wife Nancy attended the séance. Despite dubious results from the charlatan who conducted the session, Phil and James Pike became fast friends.

Phil found that by remembering specific past incidents, like that, or just a clear visual memory of Pike's appearance and habits or mannerisms, it was as if the Bishop came back to life—manifested. Of course, with no linear or sequential time, the Bishop *is* real. That's part of the time paradox and why the Echo Effect is so incredible.

"Oh, I haven't explained the Echo Effect," Phil said. "It's what most people call a ghost—the echo, or imprint, of a person, animal, or any living thing that remains after death.

Generally, the Long Dead, like Pike, blend and assimilate into the Universal Consciousness—the U.C.—which is also called the Collective. It's an amalgamation of everyone and all thoughts—past, present and future.

For instance, the girl's account of what happened with her dad, the Spiritual Encounter, was an example of merging with the U.C. She experienced Universal Consciousness while still living because her dad had already merged with the U.C. and wanted to convey his experience. Pike, on the other hand, may have retained more of his own consciousness due to unfinished business, or perhaps so he could merge with me," Phil speculated.

"Perhaps," Pike conveyed. "It wasn't much of a wait on this side, since no time passes here. And, given your lifestyle, Phil, I knew you would join me rather soon." It was the first time Pike had coalesced enough to communicate.

"Jim, finally!" Phil was thrilled.

"In retrospect," the Bishop continued. "I was a Taoist and simply didn't know it. I thought I was an Episcopalian priest. That's why I was always in trouble, accused of heresy. I was in good company. Jesus was a heretic, too, perhaps something far stranger."

The Pike parts were faint, hard to decipher in the chaos. Everything occurs simultaneously—echo effects, constant din from all the great minds of history (authors, artists, scientists), parallel universes, basically everything, all the time.

"And, it's quite exhausting," Pike conveyed, then faded out.

It takes a lot of energy to convey, especially difficult for the Long Dead, Phil could see. Not to mention the added problem that on this side everything is inexplicable or unfathomable.

"That's why God is fond of saying, '*I am what I am*' or *VALIS,* as I called the Vast Intelligence." That was Phil's final profound thought, for now. He too faded out.

Niki didn't receive any further gnosis or clues about Nag Hammadi, or communication from the U.C. for a few days. That was probably a good thing. She might have gone totally crazy. Mad. With all the telepathic activity between Phil and Pike, and her ability to tune in to it, she could easily have ended up in a mental ward.

There are times when glimpses into other realms—other dimensions—are just too overwhelming. Trying too hard to fathom the incomprehensible can create madness. Perhaps it did for both Phil and Pike.

They both spent too much of their "life time" trying to untangle the Great Cosmic Mysteries. They should have lived more, enjoyed life. Some things must remain occluded. The living get too obsessed with trying to untangle what lies Beyond. It's not possible. Fish cannot comprehend the ocean. Humans cannot comprehend God. *It's like your air—What Is.*

"Hey, who's telling the story now?" Phil phased back in just enough to convey to whoever had taken over the telling.

You can't comprehend that, yet– Human! The Voice boomed.

Our air? Phil couldn't resist. "That would have been great in a science fiction story," he said but knew he must stop talking. This might be the last warning, although he couldn't imagine what the punishment would be. Death?

What those on the "other side" want to convey is this: You have eternity to ponder the cosmic condition, but only on the earth plane can you have sex, write, and smoke. Okay, maybe only Phil wanted to convey that. He still thinks he's omnipotent and narrating the story. He has a lot to learn, Pike decided.

March 28, 1982

Niki actually finished the Case of the Slimy Supervisor, as she called it. Of course, she had probably been watching too many reruns of *Perry Mason.*

On Thursday, three days after her investigative piece ran, the cute County Attorney had called and said he wanted to meet with her; take her to dinner.

"Yeah, he just wants a piece of…" She didn't go.

Sunday morning, she was home listening to Mozart totally engrossed in a stack of books on life-after-death, especially one called *Stigmata,* that described unusual religious manifestations. Phil, of course, was watching and shook what used to be his head. They just can't leave that stuff alone, he thought.

"Inner locutions?" Niki said aloud. That sounded exactly like what was happening to her. Hearing voices inwardly, she read. That's just the same as Gnosis, isn't it? Inner knowing?

Check the I Ching. The thought was so strong it startled her. Niki nearly dropped her tea cup. She thought tossing coins would be too vague. She was never good at reading them, either. She considered herself more of a tarot type. She got up to survey her book shelf and located a copy of the *I Ching: The Book of Changes.* The cover stated:

> The *I Ching* is the oldest divination tool, in continuous use for over five millennia. It consists of 8 trigrams which represent the forces of nature. Trigrams, however, combine to form 64 hexagrams, which are said to reflect everything in the Universe.

The book also claimed that even if you use the *I Ching* for fun, it will lead you along the path toward the Tao.

Niki randomly opened the book and glanced at one of the introductory pages which described the Tai Ch'u hexagram, said to represent the mountain and heaven:

"This symbol represents Heaven within… Man stores in his memory the knowledge of antiquity and deeds of the past."

It went on to say that every object or idea can be represented by a certain hexagram.

And accessed by the reader, she heard as she studied the circular Yin-Yang symbol, as Americans call it. She read on:

Niki was so enthralled with her experience, she did not perceive Phil's commentary. Good thing, because stereograms were not popular yet in 1982.

Phil continued pontificating and occasionally Niki picked up on an errant thought. To her they were like inspiration or insights.

"Solidity is a state of mind. It's no more real than time, air, love or any other incorporeal thing. Everything is comprised of zillions of molecules, and even those aren't solid. No one knows for sure if the smallest *thing* is a particle or wave. So, actually there is no thing." Phil was gaining more knowledge as he transmitted to Niki. "Nothing. No thing. *I am what I am.* God, VALIS, *All That Is* are all the same."

The energy and excitement Phil generated caused Niki to pick up on his last thought. For her, it felt like divine intervention.

"I AM having inner locutions— revelations," she declared. "It is definitely time to write the treatise."

Niki searched for her notebook. She wanted to write down these new thoughts and epiphanies. Her hands were shaking so much she wasn't sure she could make notes.

She sat at the dining room table, flipped to a blank page and scribbled 3-28-82 11:11 a.m. Before she wrote anything else, she heard another message. This one was crystal clear:
It is already written. Find the manuscript.

The manuscript? Her eyes widened, and she wrote down what she heard. Then she felt confusion, and the communication faded out.

"Wait! I have questions. What manuscript? Where is it?" Niki was trembling, "Who are you? What am I supposed to do?" She sat for what felt like an eternity, hoping for some final clarification that she knew wasn't coming.

Phil felt sad and telepathically conveyed his concerns to Pike. "She doesn't know whose manuscript. All we've done is confuse her. How did we get into this mess? All we needed were two words—read *VALIS*. Couldn't we have just said that in the first place, during the Ouija session? She's smart. She would have eventually found my novel. Why did you spell Nag Hammadi, talk tractates, and other cryptic crap? It's too confusing, and it certainly didn't work well for me when I was alive."

"Except for one thing," the Pike particles pronounced.

Phil began to ask, but instantly knew. Pike had created a cipher.

11:11

This would be a sign, a symbol to trigger memories of her Mission. "Actually, it will have widespread ramifications by the year—"

Phil cut him off. "Jim, she already knows that it's time to write, she just doesn't know what." Phil felt more frustrated than ever. "A cipher is just another enigma. What does it accomplish?"

"Soon, but not yet," Pike taunted Phil, as he had Niki.

"I won't see you again in this world,
see you in the next one..."

VooDoo Child

by Jimi Hendrix
as sung by SRV

8 Don't be late

"I'm from Austin," Gene Pool, the new *Courier* clip clerk, introduced himself to Niki. She sensed he was about to flirt with her and wanted to tell him to save his energy. She was focused like a laser beam on wrapping up the Remke series, so she could take a leave of absence and go to Egypt. Niki did everything she could to send body language that said, "forget it." This guy was not discouraged. He was determined to find common ground.

"You like music?" he asked. "Let me tell you, Austin is the blues capital. Better than Kansas City. There's a kid down there that can play the blues guitar like nothin' you've ever heard, and Hendrix stuff, too. Stevie Ray Vaughn. You'd swear it was Jimmy resurrected."

"I'm more interested in Nag Hammadi at the moment," she said, sure this would throw cold water on the guy, but he seemed even more excited.

"Now that is interesting." He slapped the counter with his hand. "I just heard a radio program last night where some guy claimed the second coming was already underway. He was talking about the Gnostic Gospels and how the Maitreya Messiah would reveal himself in May."

Niki's jaw dropped. "Did you just say Gnostic Gospels? Who was this on the radio?"

The research clerk pulled a pad from his pocket.

"Hmmm, I wrote it down. Benjamin Crème, from Scotland. I wanted to check for clips on the guy. Since you're interested, hang on and I'll go get them." The clerk put his cigarette in the ashtray while he went off to find her clips.

Niki, who always hated cigarettes and would normally gag at the smoke, actually thought of taking a puff. What was this? Stress? She paced back and forth in front of the counter. Even the clip clerk knew about the Gnostic Gospels? This seemed crazy insane to her.

In a few minutes he returned with a handful of articles. He spread them across the counter and resumed smoking. The first clip to catch her eye was this:

> "Many now expect the return of their awaited Teacher, whether they call him the Christ, Messiah, the fifth Buddha, Krishna, or the Imam Mahdi. Few know that the Teacher who fulfills all these expectations already lives among us now. It's the Maitreya."

As she continued reading other clips, the clerk said, "This is the reason Crème was giving the radio interview." He pointed to a clip with a large headline, **Day of Declaration**. The clip read:

"Maitreya will be invited by the international media to speak directly to the entire world through the television networks linked together by satellites," says Share International, a non profit religious organization that promotes the return of the Christ as Maitreya.

The organization's founder Benjamin Crème claims, "On the Day of Declaration, which will occur in May or June of this year, Maitreya's face will appear on television screens wherever we have access. The biblical statement, 'All eyes will see him' will be fulfilled, in the only way in which it can be fulfilled. We will see his face, but he will not speak aloud. His thoughts, his ideas, his call to humanity for justice, sharing, right relationships and peace, will take place silently, telepathically. Each of us will hear him inwardly in our own language. In this way, he will re-enact on a worldwide scale the true happenings of Pentecost 2,000 years ago."

Hear him inwardly. This was the third time Niki had heard or seen this term in recent days. First as part of the Gnostic Nag Hammadi scriptures, then as a description of inner locutions, now in the Maitreya material. An ad, placed by the Share International organization, continued:

"The energy which He embodies—the Christ Principle, the energy of love—will flow out in tremendous potency through the hearts of all humanity. He has said: 'It will be as if I embrace the world. People will feel it physically.' This will evoke an intuitive, heartfelt response to his message. Simultaneously, on the outer, physical plane, there will be hundreds of thousands of miracle healings throughout the planet. In these three ways we will know that Maitreya is the World Teacher, come for all groups, religious and non-religious alike."

This is amazing, actually incredible, Niki thought. It's exactly what she had been experiencing, but clearly she wasn't the only one. As she spread the newspaper clips across the counter, yet another one caught her eye. It had a familiar headline:

Those Who Search for Signs Will Find Them

Niki could not believe her eyes. Confused, she scanned for the date: November 8, 1977. That was five years ago. She had used the exact same words three months ago to promote Gribbin's appearance in Los Angeles. She had never seen this article before. In fact, with her syndication on the doomsday series, wouldn't someone at some paper, or the AP guys, have realized that? She grabbed the clip which read:

"In the 10th Message of Maitreya, given through Benjamin Crème, He said His Presence in the world would be accompanied by signs. That He would flood the world with such revelations and happenings that the mind could not comprehend, nor deny it. That Worldwide reports of miracles will increase daily."

The paper slipped through her fingers. Lying on the counter was another incredible sight. A full-page ad with a huge headline:

The CHRIST is Now Here!

Without Sharing there can be No Justice
Without Justice there can be No Peace
Without Peace there will be No Future!

Peace on Earth. That's what Crème is talking about. For Niki there was no doubt what she had to do. If there was the slightest chance this was real, that the Maitreya might appear or even if Benjamin Crème was speaking in L.A. in May, then she had to go back there. *The time is now.* Did she hear it again, or was she just recalling her mission. She glanced at her watch. It was 11:11.

"What do you mean you're leaving?" Bruce asked.

"I'm getting into this Westfalia VW van I bought and I'm hitting the road. That's what I mean," Niki said emphatically into the telephone.

"You quit your job?"

"No. I convinced Frank to let me take a six-month leave of absence so I can get to the bottom of all this."

"I just don't get it. How will being on the road alone help you figure it out? To quote one of your own favorites, how are you going to search for the answer when you don't know what the question is, Socrates?" Bruce said sarcastically.

"Are you reading that off my wall at work?"

"Really, Nik, you can't live in a VW van for six months."

"What makes you think I'm going to? I have places to go."

"Like California?" Bruce hit a sarcastic tone. "To do what? Didn't you learn anything from the Gribbin fiasco?"

That stung. Niki almost slammed down the phone, but instead took a deep breath and in a measured tone said, "Bruce, you can't stop me. It's done. I've already sold the Z, put Mom's things in storage, and given up the apartment. I am leaving tomorrow."

Bruce was silent.

"Good grief!" Niki continued, "It's not like I'm getting on a transport ship to Mars. I'm going back to L.A. on a fact-finding mission. Listen. I'm sorry I can't say good-bye in person, but I'll call and let you know what's happening."

Phil felt perplexed, but the Bishop seemed pleased. He gathered himself together and announced, "I don't mind this at all. The girl should see Crème and learn more about the Maitreya. Why not? The Maitreya is the Future Buddha—the One who is coming. The One who might unite all fractured factions and religions."

Pike paused, as if assessing Phil's reaction. He didn't get a response because Phil was sulking. He continued. "Crème is right, about Christ Consciousness. Call it the Maitreya or the Cosmic Christ. It's the Living Logos. You called it a plasmate, or a living intelligence—VALIS. It has overshadowed many: the Buddha, Zoroaster, and a Jew named Jesus. And, when the final prophecy unfolds—" the Bishop stopped abruptly. "Well, just trust me. Follow truth above all—*Truth is the Way, it is the Tao.* Eventually the truth will emerge."

∞

Niki began a steep downhill descent on the gravel road, winding around to a river bank crossing with a dilapidated, scary-looking covered bridge known as Cry Baby Bridge. The name said it all. The sagging and sighing, as she crossed the rotting wood slats, sounded like crying or wailing and seemed so much worse in this rattle-trap contraption. Oh no, maybe it's too much weight, she worried.

The 1974 Westfalia van was packed, actually crammed full. Her friends could not believe she sold her rare Z car to buy this hippie mobile, but she had to. Niki planned to live in the van while traveling.

It had everything she needed: a sofa/bed, table/desk area, tiny kitchen with a refrigerator full of cheese, cold cuts and cold Cokes. She had lots of non-perishable food, plus emergency supplies, sleeping bag, bedding, memorabilia (photos and special things that had belonged to her mom and dad), several books, her 35mm camera, boombox and all her cassette tapes (Mozart and rock), plenty of writing supplies, and one thing she would not sell or give up: her brand new

Commodore Vic-20 computer. It would hook up to a small portable AC/DC TV. That way she could have a monitor or watch television. She also had a 300-baud modem and a small dot-matrix printer, so she could earn money by doing some writing. In fact, sending Frank some travel copy was part of the bargain for getting an extra month's pay in advance and her six-week non-paid leave.

Six weeks, what a joke. For sure six months, she thought. If she had asked for it all at once Frank would probably have denied it. Niki thought she might never return, but she hadn't dared to say that to anyone, especially blabber mouth Bruce.

One last sharp turn to left, and there it was on the left side of the road, her favorite spot—Mars Hill Church.

The property was surrounded by a wire fence, but the gate was open. Niki pulled in and turned off the engine. She took a deep breath, and quickly jumped out of the van. The fiery red rays of the setting sun framed the church perfectly.

The wood was weathered gray with age, but the white-washed façade under the pitched roof looked like new. Work crews had clearly done some clean up and repair for Easter. They must have just painted the raised wood letters because the words MARS HILL were jet black on fresh white paint.

Some might wonder why come here, instead of visiting her parent's grave. Graves meant nothing to Niki, not with what she *knew* and had recently reconfirmed about the Beyond and other dimensions. Grave-sites were the least of her concern. In fact, the idea of physical remains; bones, biological matter, and bugs, yech. If there was any hope of a one last "encounter" with her dad, or any sort of sign, it would be here.

More than anything, Niki wanted one last confirmation that she was doing the right thing by following these cryptic clues and unseen guides.

Deep down she knew it really was time—time to leave Ottumwa and move on. Most importantly, time to begin her mission. Even though she wasn't sure of the exact message yet, Niki felt certain it would all unfold if she followed her intuition. I just have to go. "That's right, isn't it Dad?" she asked and began to sob.

Phil had developed a soft spot for this girl. There was no way he could stand to see her crying and so confused. This was it. He felt energized, as if he might manifest. He knew it was against the Law of Non-interference, but he had to do something.

Just then Niki heard a rustle in the leaves. Before she could work up a cold sweat, she saw a small fox squirrel scurry out of the dry underbrush. It stopped and looked right at her. This squirrel had the same bushy tail as the one her dad had named Bessie and turned into a pet when she was five years old.

Her mom had snapped a photo once of her dad teaching her how to feed the new little pet, offering it a nut. James Perceval looked as happy in that photo as she could ever remember seeing him. She sobbed remembering how much her Mom had loved that photo.

This *was* clearly an omen—a sign. Niki was certain it was time to leave the newspaper and pursue her true mission.

∞

Phil received another stern warning for interfering. He knew her dad would have done the same thing, but he had already merged with the Collective and couldn't. It's one of the benefits of remaining earthbound. A spirit can project into animals—say cats or squirrels—at critical times.

Pike was right, the truth would emerge. Phil knew that, too. He had to let the girl make her own discoveries, just as Pike had let him arrive at his own conclusions. He chuckled, recalling how many of them there had been. Enough to fill many novels and thousands of pages of what he had called his Exegesis, thanks to Pike's persistent pestering.

∞

Wednesday morning, April 21, 1982, Niki Perceval rolled down Albia Road, headed toward Highway 34 West. On her way out of Ottumwa, she looked at all the familiar sites with new eyes. The Five Corners intersection where her old three-story brick grade school had stood was now a *McDonald's.*

The thought of hamburger made her mouth water for a Canteen. She wished she could stop and get a few for the road. But she glanced at her watch. It was too early. The little diner wasn't even open. But the time made her smile. It was lucky, just like her birthday:

7:11

PART TWO - A Long Strange Trip

"My god,

he thought, she's ready—

she has it all mapped out…
she's answering questions in advance,
questions I haven't even asked. I have to listen to her answers, he thought excitedly. And figure out from them what's what; what the real situation is."

Man Whose Teeth Were All Exactly Alike
-- Philip K. Dick

9 It's about Time

Leaving Iowa was the hardest thing Niki Perceval had ever done. That wasn't really true. Losing her parents was the hardest, but this was also pretty damn difficult. She knew she wouldn't be back—at least not to her job or life as before. She had always hoped and dreamed of leaving, but actually doing it was something else. And alone, with just her cat, was especially hard.

The first four hours were pure escapist fun—listening to tapes and the radio, thinking about all the possibilities, and putting some distance between herself and her hometown. She was bouncing down the highway on bad shocks but good music.

"Yeah, I'm already gone. I will sing my victory song," Niki sang along with the Eagles, sure she had made the right decision to leave. Schroeder was curled up in the passenger seat perfectly content. But she was hungry and needed more than a quick gas-and-snack pit stop this time. She saw a sign.

Carter Lake was just east of Omaha. It advertised gas, food and recreation. Just what she and Schroeder needed. And, it would be her last stop in Iowa. Perfect!

It was too cold and windy to eat at a picnic table. This became obvious when she was blown around just trying to get to the restroom. She was back in her "bus" searching for the cat leash when a real bus, one of those huge RVs, pulled in and parked practically on top of her little Westfalia. Niki was still bent over, looking for the cat leash and muttering under her breath about the whole empty parking lot, when a rap on her window scared the shit out of her.

"How's the fishin' here?" Some old codger asked. Then, before she could respond he winked and continued, "Are we in Iowa or Nebraska?"

She felt like saying, "How the fuck would I know?" but instead took a breath and as politely as possible said, "I'm not really sure. I just pulled in myself for a quick break."

The old guy was anxious to tell her a story about the history of the lake and some land dispute, but Niki was in no mood. She excused herself by saying she only had time for a quick break and moved to the back of the van.

It was a harmless incident, but got her thinking about the danger of trusting people now that she was traveling alone. Next time it could be a serial killer instead of an old timer. She wasn't carrying a weapon, other than knives for cutting food. Maybe she should have used one of her connections to get a gun and training before she left.

Even as a reporter Niki never felt worried about danger or the situations and places she found herself. But now she truly felt alone and vulnerable, and hated it.

When the big rig pulled out, she surveyed the rest stop. A couple of semi-trucks, an elderly couple fussing with a fifth-wheel, and a young couple cuddled up at a picnic table.

It looked safe enough. Niki opened the side door of the van and let Schroeder out on his leash. She locked the van behind her, something she never did in Ottumwa, and let the cat sniff around.

The chilly April air and overcast sky added to her anxiety. Traveling with a pet, especially a cat, was going to be difficult. The thought of traveling alone seemed incomprehensible. Schroeder would be her friend and confidant. As she watched him struggle with the leash she thought, "we're both going to have to make adjustments."

∞

Many hours later…

Niki changed routes sometime after Lincoln, Nebraska and finally managed to get on the Kansas turnpike. She had wasted a lot of time on small highways. The open road sounds better than it is. Kerouac had a way of making a bum's life alluring. Endless hours of bouncing around in the noisy air-cooled VW "bus" made her long for her sleek Z car. This wasn't her dream—driving an old VW van cross country like some hippie. She had long since grown weary of listening to *Born to be Wild* and had tossed the tape out the window somewhere back around Topeka. Miles and miles of flat pavement and boring scenery on the turnpike didn't help.

If there was something new to see—maybe mountains or if a UFO landed in one of those fields—traveling could have been fun. But the endless checkerboard farm landscape was monotonous. Niki thought of every cliché she had ever heard to describe the highway: endless ribbon, open road, asphalt as a black cloak. She even tried counting mile markers.

"I need a catchy title if I'm going to write a travel column," she said to Schroeder, who opened his eyes, stretched and resumed his never-ending cat nap. Kerouac already used

On the Road for his book, and Willie Nelson had done it "again." So all of that was out. After watching several more mile markers pass by she came up with "And Miles to Go…" With her new-found syndication contacts, Niki was pretty certain she could sell the idea of a weekly travel column. No one was doing that. After seeing all these big motor homes, with retirees, the editors would smell money.

Horseshit. The word came into her mind so clearly she startled. That wasn't Maitreya or her *I Ching* entity. It felt the same, except like someone was laughing—at her? A muse? That's the thought that came into her head. Niki swerved the van hard enough to wake up the cat, and pulled off onto the shoulder.

"A muse? Is that what all of this has been about?" She felt foolish, naïve. The prodding, glimpses of books, allusions to her dad's message—from what? Some mischievous muse trying to prompt her to write?

Niki jumped out of the van for some fresh air. Screw the cat leash, she thought and let Schroeder out in the open field. She still sensed the laughing and it made her even madder. Was she a fool leaving on such a whim? She had believed she was on a religious quest. What about the Maitreya clips and seeing the squirrel at Mars Hill?

Unfinished Business. That thought was crystal clear and felt serious again. She felt confused. It wasn't making sense.

Standing there in the middle of a field, far from the highway and any possible traffic, Niki stomped her feet like a child having a temper tantrum, then collapsed into a sitting position holding her head in her hands. "Fuck!" she screamed out loud. Over five hundred miles from Ottumwa, sitting in a friggin' field with no idea what she was doing. She had only two choices—get back in the van and continue west, or turn around and head home.

Niki had vowed that under no circumstances would she go back to Ottumwa without solving this mystery. There was no possible way she could show up empty handed and admit defeat. And returning to the *Courier* meant she could never take a chance like this again. This was her only shot. If she went back now she knew she would have to knuckle down and accept the day to day grind, forever. That simply was not an option.

"Schroeder," she called for the cat. He came bounding toward her. After sitting on the cold ground and petting him for a few minutes, she lay down—her only way of dealing with stress.

Phil had been watching and thought the travel column *was* horseshit. It amused him. He didn't mean to convey those thoughts to Niki, though. Now things were really a mess. Why is she just lying there on the cold ground? He couldn't just let her lie there and go into hypothermic shock. He had to do something.

Good grief, he realized, maybe this was the probability that the gate-keeper, Saint Pete, had seen. This absolutely cannot happen. She is in the middle of nowhere and there will be no one to come and rescue her.

If the situation wasn't so urgent, it would have been funny. A disembodied Philip K. Dick in Kansas, struggling with a girl who actually looked a bit like Dorothy, especially the Dorothy who fell asleep in the poppy field.

The thought of himself as the Wonderful Wizard was amusing. He had always loved Frank Baum, the author of Oz.

In fact, as a kid it was Baum and Jonathan Swift that first inspired him to write. Just as he thought this, Frank Baum manifested and began complaining about how the movie wasn't faithful to his screenplay or children's story.

"Who are you?" Phil asked not recognizing the man with the thick moustache, or realizing that his fleeting thought had animated yet another dead author. Baum didn't seem offended, though. He seemed thankful for the opportunity to elaborate on his many accomplishments.

"I'm L. Frank Baum, son. You thought me back to existence." A chatty guy. He informed Phil that he had written over forty books himself, mostly children's stories. "…and before that I was a reporter for the Chicago Evening Post." Being the good conversationalist that he was, Phil wanted to listen, and have a long discussion with a fellow writer, but he had an emergency to deal with there in the wheat field.

The urgency of the situation was instantly telepathically communicated to Baum, as all things are in the after-life and Oz.

"Just wake her up. Anything you've communicated will be like a dream to her," Baum explained, with a fatherly air.

"Son, there are no problems here that can't be solved. Just remember that." With that, the real Wizard of Oz was gone in a flash, leaving nothing but show tunes playing in Phil's head. It was the scarecrow singing if he only had a brain. Phil wasn't sure how to take that, but realized he could do the same thing. He felt powerful.

Instantly Niki began to wake, with a tune in her head. Not the "rainbow" or "brain" song. She heard the Optimistic Voices singing "You're Out of the Woods!" Just as Baum said, for Niki it was a dream or imagination. She had seen the *Wizard of Oz* movie at least twenty times, herself, and she was waking up just like Dorothy—refreshed and ready to move on.

Phil felt a huge sense of relief. He could not believe how attached he had become to this girl with the red hair. He could see that back in California his friend Paul Williams was already thinking about a tribute book for him called the *Dark Haired Girl.*

If only his friends knew what was happening here in Kansas with a redhead. Wasn't it Leo Bulero (head of Perky Pat Layouts) in "Stigmata" who thought a redhead was sexy? Or was that Palmer Eldritch, Phil couldn't remember his own characters. They were all a blur now. Because Phil had not yet gained control over his transmission process, thoughts and craving for snuff, Niki was receiving all three messages. She wanted to go to California, heard something about a sexy redhead, and wanted a smoke. She searched for the cigarettes feeling as though a tug-of-war was occurring inside of her.

California, still California. She lit a cigarette and felt a sense of relief, even though her lungs still objected to the smoke.

"Who are you?" she blurted. The nicotine-craving cretin was getting on her nerves. She angrily stubbed out the cigarette. "I hate smoking. Are you trying to kill me, or save me?"

Before Phil could think, much less transmit, Pike took over.

We are trying to save you.

"Wow, that was clear," Niki thought. *"We?"* What does that mean? Two of them? A group? She racked her brain thinking back. Had she heard *we* before? During the I Ching insights?

Yes. The thought-answer came back. *We need the manuscript.* Niki felt the internal voice fading as though it had expended all its energy. Before it did, Pike was able to let Phil know that his longevity and afterlife seniority counted for something. Once again Phil had to defer to the Bishop's wisdom. Being omniscient doesn't mean you're always right.

Niki paced around in the field, trying to comprehend the ever-changing phenomenon that had become her life.

Schizophrenic. Isn't that the term for hearing voices or multiple personalities in your head? The fact that she continued to question her sanity was a good sign. She didn't have to explain anything to anyone for now. She was alone. Just her and the cat. The cat! Where was Schroeder? She began calling and searching.

The sun was setting, she was shivering in the cold, and had no idea where to spend the night. Once Niki found and gathered up the cat, she got in the van and drove off. She would just stay at the first decent motel she could find. For now, she just wanted a hot shower and a good night's sleep. She was not out of the woods—far from it. In fact, she had just entered them.

10 the Road of Awe

April 22, 1982

Niki had decided to keep a journal on the road. She bought a cheap, fake-leather "hand-tooled" souvenir daily diary at one of the truck stops. So far, it was basically empty except for one brief line: too much Oz.

She intended to write notes about hearing *horseshit* and the strange dream of being Dorothy, hearing show tunes, and especially that he was "we." She would write more, maybe tonight. But for now, she just wanted to move on. Getting out of Kansas, and the Midwest, was her goal.

Since she had taken a long hot bath when she got to the little motel near Emporia, all she needed to do was splash cold water on her face, pull on jeans and a sweatshirt, and gather up the few items she had brought in from the van. First she needed coffee, and then she wanted to see how Schroeder had fared spending the night alone in the van.

Snapping the leash on his collar, Niki let the tomcat out in the early morning air. They walked around a vacant lot near the Super 8. Sounds of semi-trucks and traffic on the near-by freeway were a constant reminder that she was neither here nor there. Niki wasn't sure where she was or even where she was headed. Thoughts of the stolen manuscripts were very vivid in her mind.

"We just keep heading south and west for now," she told the cat, who was pulling and twisting on his leash. Cat on a leash is crazy, Niki thought, especially a big old tomcat. She noticed a couple loading suitcases into the trunk of their car and heard snippets of what sounded like an argument.

At least I don't have to argue with some dick about what route to take, or when to leave. She was grateful for that.

Some dick? I resent that, Phil thought. I knew I could never try to convey my name. I am going to have to get creative and overpower Pike. After all, she's my ward, and my fate hinges on the success of her efforts. Phil hovered in a binary flutter with Pike, watching Niki and plotting his next move.

Friday, April 23, 1982

Since that crazy episode in Kansas, nothing seemed worth writing about—for the travel series or even in the journal. What? Miles per day? Number of yellow lines on the highway?

The Topeka Turnpike, Wichita linemen, and now the Okies from Muskogee, just didn't excite her. She actually thought of trying to find Muskogee, but decided it was more important to make Amarillo by morning. Maybe she could write some corny piece using all country-western song titles. She needed to come up with something, because she hadn't written anything yet. The travel log, horseshit or not, was her only meal ticket for now.

Luckily, Palo Duro Canyon near Amarillo provided the change of scenery that Niki needed. It's called the "Grand Canyon of Texas." Finally, she felt inspired to write. It could be fun to compare this to the real Grand Canyon, which she would see in a few more days.

"Camping here *is* grand," she began, then realized part of the charm was basically having the place to herself. In April it was still chilly for camping, near freezing at night. The camp hosts let her stay in one of the depression-era cabins, built in the 1930's—maybe because she was the only person there, or because she told them she was writing a travel piece, possibly for national syndication. That was a stretch, since she hadn't even created the proposal yet. But Goodnight Cabin, and its dramatic, deep canyon setting, seemed promising for her first submission.

By the time Niki crossed into New Mexico, she had been on the road three days and traveled over a thousand miles. In some ways it felt longer. Time was becoming vague. She had always faced deadlines: in school, with her parents and their doctor appointments, and certainly at the newspaper. Now her time was her own. No one was looking over her shoulder, and it was becoming harder and harder to keep up this pace. She wasn't even sure if she was still trying to get to California and Maitreya. "Find the manuscript" was the last message she had heard. Wasn't New Mexico the land of mañana? Couldn't she slow down, especially with landscape like this to enjoy?

It was nearly high noon, so Niki decided to treat herself to a real meal, instead of cold cuts, for lunch in Tucumcari. She stopped at a diner on Route 66 for meat loaf, mashed potatoes and gravy, and a piece of apple pie for dessert. When the waitress brought the food, Niki was struck by the fact that even though the landscape was finally changing, the human scenery was much the same. A small town is a small town no matter where it's located. People like to tell the history and little-known facts about their communities. It would be easy to gather up stories from each little town. This was a perfect place to begin.

Tucumcari comes from the Comanche word tukanukaru, one of the locals said. It means to lie in wait for something. Makes sense, she thought having also heard that the lone mountain once served as a lookout post for the Comanches. Speaking of the Wild West, a couple of locals were also quick to brag about Tucumcari being in the opening scene of the famous Clint Eastwood movie, *For A Few Dollars More.* Surely they knew the movie was filmed in Spain, she thought as she pulled out of town. She had loved Clint in those early movies.

Interstate rest stops were just too impersonal. Those people had been friendly. She made notes of their comments in her journal and concluded with: "Spend more time in the small towns."

As Niki drove west on I-40, the scenery became brown, mostly scrub brush. Wheat fields and greenery were long gone. Everything was desolate, like being on the moon, until she came through the mountain ranges that opened up into Albuquerque. It was an optical illusion, but it looked as though the ocean lie ahead. It was actually the way the city was nestled in a massive valley, with the view of mesas and high ground further west, that created the illusion.

She thought Albuquerque would be flat desert, but there were mountains all around. No wonder they call it the Land of Enchantment, she thought, looking at the purple and pink colors of the sunset and how it illuminated the landscape and unique rock formations ahead to the west. Purple and pink, she recalled the dream of the alien landscape. Was it another planet, or was this what I saw? Her ear buzzed as she recalled the flute dream.

"We should stay here tonight," she told Schroeder who was busy in his cat box. "Well, that confirms it. I gotta get out of this van and get rid of that." But before she knew it, she had passed several exits and seemed to be heading out of town. There were billboards for a Stuckeys at Nine Mile Hill. If it didn't work out, she could always turn around and drive back.

"Oh my," Niki exclaimed as she crested the volcano ridge that had looked so dramatic from the other view. Now she saw the sunset over mesas, and rugged rock formations, not to mention the huge open sky which was really indescribable. This is why people paint, she realized. Words can't do this justice. The rest stop and Stuckey's was just ahead. Perfect, if she could spend the night there.

Once she used the restroom and confirmed she could park there overnight, she was able to relax and look at the postcards. These were the same gorgeous scenes she had just seen, each more beautiful than the one before. A rendering of the "Albuquerque Volcano Cliffs" with a spectacular sunset of deep orange and magenta—she had to have that one. And the mountain peak she had admired west of Albuquerque, Mt. Taylor.

After selecting cards, Niki looked at other novelty items.

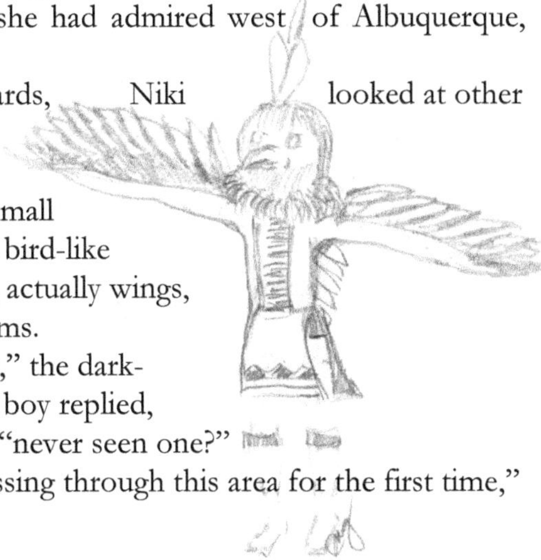

"What is this?"

She was holding a small wooden carving of a bird-like Indian with feathers, actually wings, strapped over his arms.

"Kachina dancer," the dark-haired, dark-skinned boy replied, frowned and added, "never seen one?"

"No, I'm just passing through this area for the first time," Niki explained.

"Maybe you should stop at Sky City. Acoma Reservation. On your way on I-40 heading west," he spoke in a halting, kind of broken English. "Favorite for tourists and locals," he concluded.

Niki thanked him for the tip, and returned the favor with the change, as she bought gas, postcards, the small Kachina called the Protector, candy, cat food, and a few other items. She was thankful to see truckers parked for the night. It made her feel safer and more relaxed about staying.

She was so exhausted that when she crawled into the back of the camper with Schroeder there was no chance of working on her travel piece, or even writing in her journal. Niki barely finished her food before her head hit the pillow.

Phil and Pike, however, were quite active and determined to intrude on Niki's dream time. They were enjoying a lively debate about the meaning of Anu-naki, an ancient Sumerian word for "people from the sky." Phil felt certain this was the source concept of angels. Pike, however, said it was more than that—it was the Sons of Heaven, including Jesus, and certainly Enoch, famous for the seeing wheels in the sky.

For Niki, sky people and Sky City were synonymous in her dream. Wheels, flying kachinas, purple mountains, pink lights, and probably a show tune or two were swirling in her mind. That was not the dream that she awoke with, however.

You will eat, bye and bye,
In that glorious land above the sky;
Work and pray, live on hay
You'll get pie in the sky when you die.

-- Labor Activist, Joe Hill, 1914

11 All Ghost Writers Go to Heaven?

The man with the salt and pepper beard, the one who showed me the book—Niki scribbled wildly in the journal. He had a big black marker and wrote the most stupid graffiti on the side of my lime green Westfalia van:

Jump in the toilet and stand on your head.
I am real. UBIK should be read.

It seemed so real she jumped up, and wrote the words in her journal so she wouldn't forget them. Even when I was sure it was a dream, she wrote, I had to go out and look at the van to be sure there wasn't graffiti on it.

What could it mean? Jump in the toilet. Why had everything turned vulgar? If there were two of them, then one must be an evil entity, or at least a trickster spirit. She had joked about that with Bruce, but now, isolated on the road, it wasn't funny. Maybe they had lulled her into feeling safe with the references to her dad, her mission, and the religious references. Now that she was alone and vulnerable, their real motives seemed to be emerging.

What was the real motive? Why lure her out West—it didn't make sense. Niki jotted more notes, trying to figure out how and when things became so depraved: constantly craves nicotine, makes me smoke, curses—said *horseshit* when I was out in that field, and I even heard him say *fucking bishop* once. It's like having an insane entity in my head. Writing the notes made her even more agitated and nervous. In fact, she felt like smoking and cussing. Instead Niki walked to the camp restroom. By the time she got back to the van, she was freezing.

It was seven a.m. but too cold to stay up. She hunkered back into the sleeping bag thinking about what to do next.

Since Sky City was just a few miles away, Niki decided she would go there and write her first travel piece on Indian culture. It would be fun to see mysterious mesas and red rock, and forget about her problems for the day. Maybe that would help clear her head and give her a fresh perspective.

"Obviously, I am not an evil entity," Phil said indignantly. "nor is my esteemed craniopagal conjoined colleague Bishop Pike. We have, however, made a mess of things—that much is true. And I did say *horseshit* back in Kansas, because frankly this travel log idea is horseshit."

"Writing 'jump in the urinal' on a men's room wall might have worked for your adolescent readers, but I don't see what you hoped to accomplish scrawling it on the girl's van in her dream," Pike conveyed to his counterpart.

"It seemed to work for you, Jim. You once told me that *UBIK* is why you called and convinced me to help you with your séance. That I must know something about communicating with the dead."

"We were alive then," Pike conveyed. "And I had read *UBIK*. It was new and current. We're dead now, the book is a pulp relic, and she has no idea what any of that meant. It was a stupid move."

The two could spend eternity in a telepathic squabble.

∞

Niki must have dozed off again, because when Schroeder woke her up treading on her, it was warmer. Nine am. She could get coffee at the shop, feed the cat and check out the Acoma Pueblo.

Sky City certainly was unique. It was a community of pueblo Indian adobe structures built on a mesa nearly four hundred feet above the horizon.

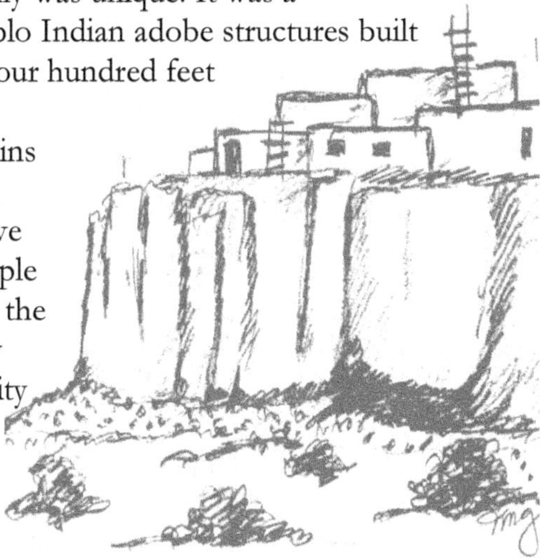

Unlike other ruins in the southwest, Acoma was an active pueblo. Native people still lived there. It's the oldest continuously inhabited community in the Southwest.

There was no need to carry her 35mm camera up the steep, narrow staircase that led to the top of the mesa. Photos were not allowed anywhere on the mesa

Acoma Pueblo was founded around 1100 on the high mesa as a defense against other marauding tribes. The worst offenders—the "white intruders"—had not yet arrived in America, she realized. Niki was beginning to understand the native people's viewpoint. The name Acoma came from the Spaniards, and was considered derogatory by the native people. Niki wished she had an authentic contact, not just a tour guide, so she could get the real story.

As she was leaving, she bought a hand-painted gourd rattle as a souvenir, and wondered what their ceremonials were like. Outsiders were not allowed to view the sacred ceremonies. Niki shook the rattle a couple of times as she headed back to her van, then felt woozy, a little light headed and realized that she hadn't been craving coffee or cigarettes.

"That's a good thing, right?" she said to the cat. Talking to the cat is better than constantly talking to myself, she determined. But if her guides were unreliable, what purpose was there in heading west? How would she know what to do next? For years she had tried to be more logical and not rely so much on intuition. But out here, on the road, it felt as though the rug had been completely pulled out from under her.

"Well, it's not like that is new," she told Schroeder. "I know how to be alone. I'll just focus on writing that travel log piece."

She jotted a few notes on Acoma so she could write later and decided to keep heading west. At her next stop, Grants or maybe Red Rock Park that she just learned of, she would start writing the article. It was the middle of the afternoon as she cruised along I-40 toward Grants.

Niki's head was full of Indian lore, the traditions and sights she had just seen. It seemed odd to grow up in Indian country yet know so little about their beliefs. In just a few hours, she knew more about the Acoma tribe than the Sac and Fox clan that lived in and around Ottumwa and Wapello County.

She would suggest to Frank that she could write a piece contrasting Wild West Indians to the French-Canadian tribes found in the Midwest. In fact, she would start it tonight and send him a sample. She was enjoying the dramatic scenery, too. There were huge rock formations along the interstate. At a rest stop she snapped shots for herself and the article.

For now, solid rock formations were more comforting than inexplicable entities. All of this kept her mind off the obvious—the reason she left Iowa in the first place—the messages, Maitreya, and writing her peace treatise.

∞

Phil felt laughter—the unique airy, light vibration of laughter. It was Pike. "What?" Phil questioned, unamused. The Pike particles began to stir.

"She's back to the 'travelogue' idea, and maybe smoking a peace pipe," the bipolar bishop chuckled. Remind me Phil, how toilet humor is more helpful than my prompts about knowers and Nag Hammadi?"

"If you're such a knower, you should know. I couldn't control some of that. She's a teep, for Christ sake. How many times do we have to go over this." Phil was fed up with being cross-examined by and cross-bonded to the self-righteous bishop.

"So you *did* say 'fucking bishop.' After all I've done for you," Pike scolded.

"I don't know why I have to explain everything to you. Are you my…"

"As a matter of fact, I am your guardian. Why do you think I was showing you all the 'cryptic crap' as you so charmingly called it?" Pike asked.

"I'm sorry, Jim," Phil sighed. "We were doing good as a duo, working together. When you said, *We are trying to save you,* that worked. She believed it. And, you were right about Nag Hammadi, too. After running the probabilities, it was the only way to lead her in the right direction. Now, however, we must get her mind off Egypt and onto California. That's why I was trying to lead her to my writing—*UBIK, VALIS*. I have one more idea. If that doesn't work, you can take charge."

Niki knew nothing of any disagreements or negotiations occurring in the ethereal realm. She had found a secluded spot in Red Rock State Park where she could spend the night. Even though it cost a few dollars for the electric hook-up, it was worth it. She would be warm, and able to stay up late with a light and could even plug in her VIC 20 computer and work on her article.

After fixing food for herself and the cat, Niki had spread out her new Indian culture notes, postcards, artifacts and information on the small sofa in the back of the van. The computer, basically just a thick keyboard, was hooked to her tiny black and white TV.

That's why it was called a VIC, short for Video Interface Chip. Of course, Niki's was "souped-up" with extra memory cartridges. She also knew how to transmit information using the VIC's new technology, a direct-connect modem, but she would need a phone connection for that. Maybe she could find one in Flagstaff.

For now the van was locked, Schroeder was sleeping, and Niki was settled in to write. Sitting quietly at the tiny table in the back of the Westfalia van, it was late at night. She was trying to figure out what angle to take, what her lead should be for the article. She flipped through her notebook, the same reporter's notebook with the Ouija words and log of events that began back in Iowa. Even though she wanted to focus on writing the American Indian feature, she couldn't keep from reading all her notes again. It represented the chain of events that began in March. As she read, the atmosphere inside the camper changed—that feeling of electricity began again, as if the air was charged.

It also felt colder. She rubbed her shoulders and reached for a jacket to put over her sweatshirt. It had to be them, the cosmic odd couple. Looking around the cramped inside space of the van Niki wasn't sure if she was mad or sad. She wanted to throw things and cry at the same time. Maybe she really was crazy. Her mom and aunt might have been. She blamed them for making her crazy, hearing things other people don't and attracting weird spirits.

She heard a sound. Her little portable TV was on. It clicked, then the screen popped and flickered. The sound of the static startled her. The text was gone. The screen lit up with a chaotic flitting of indistinct images—a man's face intermittently flashed amidst the static.

She had not turned on the TV. Her hands felt like ice. It was definitely a man's face. She thought of one of the ads in the L.A. newspaper—*The Maitreya's face will appear on television screens.* The newspaper article actually said that—the clip that clerk pulled back at the *Courier.* "We will see his face, but he will not speak aloud. His call to humanity, for justice, and peace, will take place silently, telepathically."

Niki rubbed her eyes. Could it possibly *be* the Maitreya? No, the face was familiar—

"It's you, isn't it!" she squealed. It *was* the man with the beard from her dreams. He was trying to speak, but Niki couldn't understand anything. It was too garbled. She could see him, though. It was definitely the man with the compelling eyes and beard. She moved closer to TV.

"Come on," she said. "I'm ready. You say the time is now, so let's resolve this. Who are you and what do you want?"

The picture locked in for just a moment and she got a really good look at him. Wide forehead, thinning gray hair with a much thicker salt and pepper beard. Those eyes. Even in black and white, she could see the intensity. He managed to transmit just one word before the image broke up: Valis.

Niki wasn't sure how to spell it, but she knew how to say it now. Obviously, it was very important. And the way he said it, like he was revealing some never before imparted secret: ***VALIS.***

When the student is ready
the teacher will appear.
— Buddhist Proverb

12 Crossroads

Sitting in a booth at a truck stop restaurant in Flagstaff, Arizona, Niki was enjoying scrambled eggs and bacon, totally lost in thought. Did someone really appear through her TV screen last night? It wasn't a dream. She saw the man's face so clearly.

She had spread a road map over the worn Formica table top. Highway 89 north would take her to the Grand Canyon, or she could continue on I-40 west toward California.

Niki ran her finger over the map along the interstate line trying to imagine where she would go if she did end up in California. L.A. to look for Maitreya?

What about the manuscript? That seemed more urgent now. She also needed to make some money and finish the Indian article. The Grand Canyon was one of the most sacred spots for Indians, the original Americans, she'd been told, and it was only about sixty miles—

"Penny for your thoughts," a man's voice interrupted.

When Niki glanced up, she saw a large elaborate silver buckle with chunks of turquoise at eye level. She tilted her head up and that's when her eyes met those of a young man with high cheekbones, flawless copper skin, and shiny pitch-black hair pulled back into a ponytail that hung midway down his back.

"I guess I was a million miles away," Niki responded, still checking out the amazing hunk standing by her booth. He was the best looking guy she had ever seen. He was wearing tight jeans, a flannel shirt, a quilted vest and silver jewelry which glistened against his dark skin.

"Are you real?" Niki couldn't believe she said that, and attempted a quick recovery adding, "I mean, do you work here?"

"Here? At the truck stop? No, I'm a tour guide." He extended his hand to Niki. "My name is Koteen. I take tourists on jeep rides. You look kind of lost, like maybe you could use a guide."

If you only knew, she thought. A real Indian guide—surely that's a sign. "Jeep rides. Really?" she asked. "To the Grand Canyon?"

"Well, I go south mostly." He rubbed his chin. "You know, to Oak Creek Canyon and red rock tours of Sedona."

"Sedona? What's that?" Niki asked.

"You really are lost," he laughed and pointed to the seat across from her. "Mind if I sit down?"

"Please." She couldn't help but notice his slim waist and hips as he slipped into the booth. "May I buy you a cup of coffee?" she asked.

"Sure." He pointed to a spot on her map, between Flagstaff and Phoenix. "Sedona is about 25 miles south of here, but the scenery is different from the Big Hole. Lots of red rock formations."

"Big Hole," Niki laughed and asked, "Is that what the locals call the Grand Canyon?"

"Oh, there are lots of names for the sites. You must be on vacation?"

"Not exactly." Niki paused wondering how much to reveal about her status. "I'm a reporter and I'm writing a piece on Indian country—the monuments, traditions and beliefs. So, it's pretty incredible to run into you. How much are your tours?"

"It's my day off," Koteen hesitated, "but how can I turn down a chance to show a pretty reporter the sights."

Niki blushed.

"Let me grab some flyers from the jeep." The handsome guide jumped up, adding, "I'd consider a trip up to the Canyon, too, if that's what you prefer."

Niki could not believe this good fortune. She wanted to dash to the restroom and check her hair and face, but he was already coming back in with the brochures.

As Koteen tossed one on the table, Niki immediately felt a bolt of energy run up her spine and a slight ear buzz.

"Where is this?" she asked.

"That is Oak Creek Canyon. It's on the way to Sedona." Koteen smiled.

"I have to see that place."

"A lot of people have that reaction." He winked.

"No, I mean I really *have* to see that place. It may be important."

"It is important," Koteen agreed. "I know all the legends, and the ancestral history. By the way, does the reporter have a name?"

"I'm sorry," Niki said realizing she had never introduced herself, "Niki Perceval. I work for a newspaper in Ottumwa, Iowa."

"Iowa? They sent you all the way out here?"

"Trust me, it's a long story." She said as she slid out of the booth to pay the check.

"Well, Niki Perceval, we'll have lots of time while we sight-see."

After paying the bill she went to the van to check on Schroeder and get her tape recorder, camera and backpack bag to put everything in. She locked the van hoping it would be safe at the truck stop.

She turned around and saw the red jeep with white lettering that read, *Take a Ride on the Wild Side.* Oh boy, she hoped it wouldn't get too wild, or maybe wild was just what she needed.

By ten o'clock they were bouncing toward Sedona. The off-road trip through Oak Creek Canyon was something not to be missed, like descending into a visual wonderland. Niki was overwhelmed by the spectacular rock walls, awe-inspiring colors and the thrilling ride over and around the formations.

"Hang on," Koteen warned as he headed off a main trail and what felt like straight up a huge rock.

"Oh my God," Niki screamed certain the jeep would flip over when he came straight down the other side. "That was worse than the run-away mine car at Disneyland!"

"You've been there?"

"Yes, this year, when I covered an astronomy story in Los Angeles."

"That Iowa newspaper must be something." They both laughed.

"Well then, Miss World Traveler," Koteen said with a mischievous glint in his eye, "I better give you the really wild tour. Boynton Canyon is one of the best sites and you're going to get the off-road view."

Niki was just happy to let someone else take control for awhile, especially a real guide instead of the unseen ones she had almost forgotten about.

The jeep bumped along over rocks that felt like boulders, and even through a small waterfall. Wild flowers were blooming and some areas looked like they had never been touched by humans—unspoiled meadows, all kinds of wildlife.

"How do you avoid hitting those little critters?" Niki asked.

"Practice," Koteen said and flashed his beautiful white teeth. He had a soothing voice and she loved when he told little anecdotes about why certain formations were sacred to the Anasazi (Old Ones) that had once inhabited this area. Niki recorded some of his stories.

"Get ready," he warned. "Boynton Canyon is just around this bend." The rock walls formed cathedral spires of gold, red and even purple. Majestic, magical. How would she describe this in her article?

"It's unbelievable!" Niki gasped.

"Told you this was worth the wild ride." He winked. "Want to hike in a ways further?"

"I'd love to, but I didn't bring any water or supplies."

"Hey, I do this for a living," he said tossing her a canteen of water and a bundle with some first aid items, jerky, string, matches and small flashlight, among other things. She crammed them into her backpack.

The weather was perfect, about 65 degrees now that it was midday and just enough cloud cover to make the sky interesting. Koteen noticed a darker cloud bank further north.

"You'd be surprised at how a storm can move in suddenly and cause flash flooding in these steep canyons. I'm always aware of it." He explained.

They hiked and he continued telling stories, then Koteen suggested climbing a ridge that would afford yet another great view and place to rest for awhile.

"Great," Niki responded, "lead the way." At times the rock cliff was so narrow, Niki could barely put one foot in front of the other. She didn't dare look down at the sheer drop off.

"Not much further," Koteen said over his shoulder. But the last few feet were the worst. Niki had to hug the rock wall and scoot around the corner. Koteen had made it to a wider spot and said, "Here," reaching for her hand. Niki couldn't release her grip on the rock wall, so Koteen put his arm around her waist and pulled her around the edge. When they were both on the wider ledge, her palms were scraped and sweaty, and she was shaking.

"Sorry," Koteen confessed, "I didn't remember it being so narrow."

"Or, so high?" Niki asked. "That *Thunder Mountain* is more of a kid's ride. I'm afraid of heights and should have mentioned it."

"I thought you were a brave bellagonna, as us injuns say," Koteen laughed. "I know an easier way back. Look up ahead."

There was a cave with what looked like little rooms and living spaces. Several of them on the rock wall. Niki hadn't seen anything like this.

"Anasazi ruins." He explained. "Where they lived. Hardly anyone sees this. Tourists never make it back here."

Suddenly, Niki felt everything go deathly quiet. Koteen's lips were still moving, but all she heard was the high-pitched whine in her left ear. Koteen grabbed for her.

"Are you faint?" He looked worried. "The color just drained from your face." He eased her toward the cave ruins.

Once Niki was seated, he found the canteen and offered her a drink. She drank almost half of it, then realized they had a limited supply.

"Don't worry, we have another one." Koteen felt her forehead and looked concerned. Niki couldn't help but laugh, an uneasy, nervous one.

"You could have fainted and fallen off the ledge." His forehead was gleaming with perspiration.

"The altitude is probably getting to you. You are a flatlander, right?"

Flatlander. That was a new one. Niki didn't want to tell him about her odd experiences back in the old flat land or the now-familiar "ear buzz." Looking at the cave, she *knew* these ruins must be similar to those caves in Egypt.

"Altitude. I'll be fine," she said. "Didn't I see some jerky and trail mix in one of those supply kits?"

Koteen brought out some trail mix. Niki felt better as she ate and asked him to tell more about the Anasazi ruins.

"You went through New Mexico, but didn't see the Great Kiva at Chaco Canyon, I take it?"

"No," she mumbled with a mouthful of nuts and raisins.

"These ruins are many centuries old," Koteen explained.

"Wait," she said as she dug into her knapsack for the tape recorder. "I want to get this for the article." She turned it on and nodded for him to continue.

"These dwellings were probably built around 900 AD." The Hohokam, he said, meant those who vanished. He told about the Old Ones, Anasazi, and how his people, the Yavapai, lived in communities like this until Spanish marauders destroyed them. He showed her the glyphs—what white people call pictographs on the cave walls.

"So, what do they represent?" Niki asked.

"More than scribbles or art. These symbols are like your bible, to us—lessons and stories handed down to us from our Elders, the Anasazi. It's a language and source of power for our medicine men, our shamans."

"I'm amazed, but thrilled, that you're willing to share this," Niki said. "I feel honored. Are you sure you don't mind if I write about this?"

"My people believe we must continue to sing the ancient songs and tell the legends, otherwise our heritage will die."

"How beautiful." Niki spontaneously reached out to hug him, but Koteen stiffened. She felt foolish, that perhaps such close contact was inappropriate.

"I'm sorry," she said. "I'm just so grateful to you."

Koteen relaxed again, but said nothing.

"Would it be alright to take some pictures here?" Niki asked, recalling that some tribes did not allow photography.

Koteen thought for a moment. "Sure. I don't see why not. As long as there's no map or directions. We just don't want tourists to damage this special place, as they have Chaco and the Grand Canyon."

Niki took some shots of the pictographs, the ruins and a view looking straight down into Boynton Canyon.

"Why did you bring me back here?" she asked. "I'm just another tourist."

"No, I don't think so."

"Oh, I bet you say that to all the flat-lander girls," she joked, but Koteen remained serious.

"I suspected it when I first saw you, but was sure when you reacted so quickly to Oak Creek Canyon. I confirmed my diagnosis—your people's term— when you almost fainted on the ledge." He looked into her eyes and said, "I believe you have ghost sickness."

"Ghost sickness? What is that?"

"I think you know." Koteen held his hand over her forehead, as he had done when she felt faint. "I'm a medicine man, you cannot hide this from me."

"You are a doctor for your people?"

Koteen smiled. "Not a doctor like you think. We see into other realms, beyond ordinary reality. We heal by mending the soul. I know what is happening to you."

Niki began to sob uncontrollably. Finally, someone could understand what she had been going through.

"We can do a Vision Quest," Koteen said, "and learn more about these spirits, but not here." His voice and words were comforting, but he did not touch her. He looked at the sky and continued.

"We need to hike out now. It will take longer getting out if we avoid the cliffs." It was after two o'clock and Koteen explained it gets dark early in the canyon.

On the way out Niki thought about the Vision Quest. She knew a bit about shamanism from her University religious studies. "There is no shame in a shah-mun." She remembered her instructor telling the class so they would remember how to pronounce the term.

Niki had described the spiritual encounter with her dad to the instructor, after class one day, and he had confirmed it was much like the ecstatic experiences of the shamanic trance. She wanted to ask Koteen questions about his "ways" and the Quest, but with such a strenuous uphill climb, and him walking ahead of her, it was difficult to talk. He advised that she conserve her energy, so she wouldn't faint.

At times he had to help her over rocks and with her footing. He was incredibly muscular, in fact as solid as the rocks they were climbing, with big, but well-manicured hands. They were a little rough, but not calloused or scarred. A shaman. It was so intriguing. She couldn't wait to hear how he could help with her ghost sickness.

It took almost two hours to get back to the jeep and then they still had to drive back to Flagstaff. The trip provided an opportunity to learn more about the Vision Quest.

"Do you live there, in Flagstaff?"

"I have a small trailer there for the jeep business. I have to spend time in Flagstaff to get tourists, but it's not my home. All Yavapai are from the Sacred Well, my mother's home."

Niki sensed he meant Great Mother, not his birth mom. Even though she had never heard of these terms before, she knew what he meant. Maybe the effects of the Indian ruins and sacred areas were influencing her. She had felt something back at Acoma, too. Koteen apparently noticed she was lost in thought, or maybe he could read them.

"Do you want to tell me anything about these spirits and how you came into contact with them?" he asked.

"Like I said, it's a long story," she sighed. "It started back in March…"

Niki did her best to summarize not only the recent events, but a bit about her family connections. She told him about the message, *the time is now.*

Almost immediately when she began talking, she felt a slight ear buzz and decided not to reveal much more. She wanted to see what he could discern from his methods.

"So, I took a leave of absence from my day job, the paper, to follow these clues and messages. Incredibly, a shaman showed up at my table—the perfect guide."

"I'm sure you've heard the saying, *When the student is ready the teacher will appear,* right?" Koteen asked.

Niki cocked her head. "I have, but I thought that was a Zen saying."

"The Vision Quest will show you many connections you may not have realized before, like Indra's web." Koteen's eyes twinkled.

Indra's web indeed, Phil thought. A Western Indian linking to East Indian culture. "Fascinating isn't it, Jim?"

There was no response. He expected Pike to comment on his TV appearance, too. PKD on TV was a good one he thought, but the Bishop remained silent.

Well it didn't matter. Phil knew where this was heading and what some of the incredible connections would be.

"It explains so much..." Phil stopped mid-thought remembering to just let the story unfold.

When Niki and Koteen pulled into Flagstaff, the sun was already approaching the horizon. He said twilight time was perfect for beginning the Quest and wanted Niki to get her van and follow him to his trailer.

"We'll do the ceremony in your trailer?" She asked.

"It's not really a ceremony, but yes, that's where I have the drums and crystals and music we need. I have a sweat lodge, too, but I don't think you're ready for that yet, Miss Iowa."

That was the first time he had smiled and joked in hours. Even though she felt a little strange about going to a trailer in Arizona with a "wild Indian," Niki had spent the day with him and believed he was an apprentice shaman. She certainly didn't think he would harm her.

"You know I don't really know much about you, not even your last name."

"I could make up anything," he said frowning. "If we're going to do a Vision Quest you have to trust me or we might as well not do it." He looked at the sky. "We must go now," he said. "It's not that far. Follow me."

Koteen's trailer was on a small piece of land with a clear view of Flagstaff's San Francisco mountain peaks. The sunset cast a yellow-gold light illuminating the side of the closest mountain.

Niki let Schroeder out to play as they admired the view.

"That one is called Mars Hill," he said.

"What?" Niki reacted. "You're kidding! You must be able to read my mind. How do you know Mars Hill?"

"That's the Lowell Observatory up there." He seemed to ignore her reaction, looking at the setting sun again.

"Come on. It's important we begin at twilight to assure the proper assistance from the spirit world."

Niki continued talking about her own Mars Hill in Iowa while Koteen gathered his incense and drums, and spread blankets on the floor. She also assessed his trailer. It was clean, but very little furniture. The walls were covered with native art and rugs, but also drawings of mazes and concentric circular mandalas that looked more like Buddhist art. She also noticed the fragrance of lingering incense when she walked in. Koteen was lighting more and with the glow from a single candle, the room was transforming into a sacred spot. The final touch was the music. Flute, like in her dream, then she heard the soft drumming sound.

She turned around after studying one of the maze drawings to find Koteen sitting cross-legged on the floor with a small bongo-type drum. He had changed into some loose woven pants, but most noticeably he was bare-chested. His skin looked satin smooth and she could see muscles rippling as he maintained a constant rhythmic beat with the small skin-top drum. There was a gourd rattle, larger than the one she'd just bought at Acoma, lying on one of the blankets.

"Try it," Koteen said, tilting his head toward the dried gourd and wood object.

Even though she felt embarrassed at first, once Niki began shaking the rattle, she began to feel a transformation. The sizzling sound of the seeds along with the drums and flute was instantly hypnotic. Koteen was chanting in deep melodic tones. Layers of sounds and scents were mystical, magical and ancient. There was no resisting the power of the mesmerizing music. Niki began dancing and swaying involuntarily. It was like losing consciousness, yet feeling a heightened awareness—a cosmic awareness—like she felt during the encounter with her dad. This was definitely an ecstatic-trance. Soon she was not thinking or analyzing anything, she was simply in the throes of the experience dancing and shaking the rattle with total abandon. When she collapsed on the floor, Koteen checked and confirmed she was in an altered state, but safe.

He was not "out of it." Koteen was very much in control. He had made the tape and used it before. It was like a familiar map to places that could only be accessed in an altered state, what shamans call the SSC—Shamanic State of Consciousness. The flute and rattling had stopped. The remainder of the tape was just a constant drumming sound used to produce a deeper, hypnotic trance.

For a shaman to journey into the other world, drumming is critical. The constant measured rhythm of the drumbeat maintains the trance state, almost a wave that the shaman can ride right into another dimension.

The pre-recorded music and drumming allowed Koteen to participate. He stopped drumming and lay down; not next to Niki but with their heads together, like spokes of a wheel. In this way, he could affect a mind-link of sorts and see what she was experiencing. A shaman can heal a physical or psychological trauma using these techniques.

Koteen had many options. He could travel to the lower realms, especially if there were evil entities creating her ghost sickness. For this journey he chose to explore the celestial realm. He wanted to ride the clouds, become the Goshawk hawk-spirit, and soar over the mountain tops and to the stars beyond. In his previous journeying, he had never experienced anything like this. This was total freedom from all earthly constraints. Boundless, pure energy.

He's experiencing VALIS, Phil thought. Those two have completely lost touch with external reality. I can relate to that. I was always phasing in and out of reality, riding a galactic beam, as someone once claimed. Anyway, here's what was happening: constant drumming actually produces perfect sound frequencies affecting nerve pathways in the brain. Scientists have measured those theta waves and found that the four to seven cycles per second—"

"Stop, Phil," Bishop Pike had mustered enough energy to convey. "This is no time for rational scientific measurements. This is sacred, religious ecstasy. You are the one ruining things this time. I'll intervene—"

"No, you won't." Koteen interrupted the Bishop. In this realm he could easily tune in to the energy of the spirits. He saw them, using his shamanic vision and they did appear as a nebulous blur. Two older white guys entangled, phasing in and out like a single pulsating spirit.

"Why do you inhabit this girl?" he asked them.

"We are not inhabiting her," Phil said indignantly. "I am her appointed guardian."

"Says who?" Koteen asked telepathically.

Phil didn't want to convey St. Peter, but in this realm there is no hiding any thought or idea.

Koteen laughed like the wind. He appeared mostly as a hawk, but he too pulsated with energy. At times his flowing black hair and full lips were visible. His silver soul-arc necklace glinted, like a beam of light.

"I can't believe it!" Phil yelped. "It's the dark-haired girl with the Christian fish necklace."

Koteen conveyed his necklace was not a fish symbol, and that he was certainly not a dark-haired girl. Phil's mind was blown. He had spent the last eight years of his life believing that a young dark-haired Roman girl had appeared at his door in 1974. He swore it was the secret Christian fish symbol on her neck that triggered the pink-beam visions. Now, in a flash, it all made sense. Indra's web indeed!

"What do you want from her?" Koteen's shamanic spirit demanded. His life force was strong. He conveyed he did not believe they wanted to help the girl, but were using her.

Phil focused his own energy enough to convey, "We can help each other. Our unfinished business *is* her Mission."

Koteen knew he could gather more insight, but his time in this realm was restricted. The pace of the drumming had changed. The fast beats were calling him back to ordinary consciousness. The shaman summoned one last powerful psychic vibration and blasted both the Bishop and Phil with a warning. "Protect her."

Niki began to stir as the drumming pace changed and a high-pitched flute sound seemed to pull her back to reality. For her, it was like waking from a dream. She rubbed her eyes and coughed from the pungent incense that had filled the room.

"Penny for your thoughts," Koteen said, propping himself up on one elbow. His face was close to hers.

"Jeez, isn't that how this whole thing started?" Niki asked. She reached up and touched his necklace. "What is that? I saw that symbol in my dream."

"The arc represents the soul. Two arcs are intertwined, like soul mates, or kindred spirits," he explained.

"Do you have a soul mate?"

"Maybe," he smiled at her.

Niki expected Koteen to reach down and kiss her, but instead he took off the necklace and put it around her neck.

"This will protect you," he said. "I saw everything. You will have to tell me more about the peace treatise, though."

"How do you know about that?" she asked, sitting up. "Did you see my dad?"

"Maybe. I saw two older white guys. Their spirits are connected. They cannot be released without your help."

Niki began sobbing uncontrollably. Koteen did reach out and hold her this time. Her tears ran down his smooth hard chest. He ran his hand over her forehead and into her thick wavy hair.

"It's not my dad," she sobbed.

Phil's mind was clicking like a biomorphic computer again. He could see two strong probabilities at play in this scenario. If he was writing the story, he would have forgotten about spirits and even the peace treatise. They should fall into each other's arms and make passionate, unabashed love. The Bishop, who was no prude himself, might do the same. After all, he had with his secretary.

But Koteen was in charge of this scenario, not Phil, and he had more resolve than Niki, Phil, or the Bishop. So he got up to get Niki and himself a glass of water. They compared what she knew and had seen in her dreams to what he had just experienced in the Vision Quest. At some point, Niki checked on Schroeder who was still enjoying the great outdoors. She felt comfortable enough now with Koteen to ask about the necklace. "So, tell me the truth," she said, playing with the chain and totem he had placed around her neck. "Who is the real soul mate?"

If Koteen blushed, Niki could not tell with his dark skin.

"A friend, who makes jewelry, made it for me," he said. "Like I told you, it's good medicine—protection."

"To protect you from evil white women?" Niki laughed.

"Could I please use your shower? I've been out on the road and would love to clean up in a real bathroom."

"Sure, and I'll find something for us to eat," he said. "I am starving and you must be, too."

After a long, hot shower, Niki glanced around his small bathroom and determined it was too clean for a single guy to be living there, yet there were no signs of female belongings. No traces of make-up, jewelry, nothing to indicate a woman used this bathroom. Niki was tempted to just walk out naked and see what would happen, but she couldn't bring herself to do it. Instead, she called out, "Do you have anything I could wear instead of these dirty, dusty clothes?"

He handed her a pair of his loose cotton pants, with draw string top, and a big cotton shirt through the door. She was wrapped in a towel and the room was steamy from the hot water. But any steam between them had dissipated for now.

Koteen had warmed up rice, some type of chili stew, and tortillas. They gobbled up the food.

"I can't stand it any longer," Niki said, "I have to know. Are you involved with someone? You must be. Who cooked this stew?"

"I am betrothed," he confessed. "In our culture our mother picks our wife."

For the first time, perhaps ever, Niki was speechless.

"It's the old way," Koteen continued. "The girl is Bird Clan, and—"

"Don't tell me. You two are saving yourselves for each other." Niki wanted to cry, but her tears were all spent on the rollercoaster experiences of the past twelve hours. She was too exhausted to cry.

"I'll reveal something that I never thought I would say to a white woman." Koteen paused. Niki could not imagine what secret he might impart, especially after just announcing he was engaged. She tried not to appear overly anxious, but could hardly wait to hear what it might be.

"My shamanic name is Dark Chanting Goshawk," he revealed. "The goshawk is a long-tailed, broad-winged hawk. I become that hawk when I journey to the other worlds."

"A hawk. That's really comforting," she said sarcastically. Koteen's expression conveyed disappointment, but not even a shape-shifting shaman could sense how conflicted and ridiculous she felt.

"I'll sleep in the van." Niki scooped up the cat and went out to wrap herself up in the sleeping bag, alone.

Twenty-four hours after first meeting Koteen they were back at the Flagstaff truck stop, sitting in the same booth drinking coffee.

"Déjà vu all over again, huh?" Koteen joked.

"And I've got the same decision to make," Niki thought aloud. "Do I head north to the Grand Canyon or continue west to California?"

"Maybe go back to New Mexico, to Chaco Canyon," Koteen suggested. "You can't write a story about Indian Country without Chaco. It's the hub of all Anasazi legend. My people claim *all roads lead to Chaco.*"

Niki recalled the odd sensations she felt driving through New Mexico, feelings of unfinished business there.

"Maybe I'll go to the Canyon and then back there." Whatever she decided, it was time to say good-bye to Koteen.

As they walked to her van, she asked, "How old are you?"

"Twenty-five, why?"

"Just wanted to know. And your birthday? When is it?"

"November eighth. Why, are you going to run a police check on me?"

"No, but I might want to send you a card." She smiled.

"And yours?" he asked.

"July eleventh. Lucky seven-eleven."

"I knew you had good medicine. People born in July are Flicker People—Bird Clan, too."

Niki felt weepy. "I'll never see you again."

"I'll be right here. You can always take *A Ride on the Wild Side.*" He kissed her forehead.

"I've got your brochure, and this," Niki touched the soul-arc necklace then jumped in the van and drove off, so he wouldn't see her cry.

For a few miles she wasn't sure if she was driving north or south. Then a sign read: Highway 89, Sedona 28 miles. Oh well, she thought, I never did see the town of Sedona and I don't really feel like going to the Grand Canyon alone. She decided she would take more red rock photos for her article. She checked to make sure she had the tape recorder, then punched the play button. There was Koteen's soothing voice describing the Anasazi.

There was something comforting about driving the same road they had taken together the day before. Familiarity. She had so little of it. She savored the ride back through Oak Creek Canyon, absorbing all the sights and sounds of this special place. When she arrived at the spot where Koteen had turned for the off-road trail, she touched the charm on the necklace, and silently said good-bye to him again.

"It's a spontaneous self-monitoring
negentropic vortex...
tending to progressively subsume and
incorporate its environment into
arrangements of information."

-- Philip K. Dick, *VALIS*

13 May Day at the VLA

Continental Divide, the sign ahead read: Elevation 8500 feet. Niki laughed at the thought of Koteen calling her a flatlander. Iowa was actually hilly, with river bluffs and not nearly as flat as people thought, but nothing like this incline. Niki's only idea of New Mexico came from Roadrunner cartoons—a big desert with a few cliffs, or buttes, for the coyote to skid off. This was the continental divide, definitely mountainous terrain, with vast panoramas. The surrounding mesas and rock formations were awesome. Colors ranged from deep reds, through orange and even pinks in the morning light.

Then came a fast descent into the little town of Datil with a dramatic view over the Plains of Saint Augustine. The last gas station guy mentioned a ghost town straight ahead, but Niki never found it. Just tumbleweeds and now a combination gas station, grocery store, and steakhouse in Datil.

She topped off the tank and picked up a few supplies. Mostly she wanted to stretch her legs and walk the cat.

"Cool van," some teenager said. Niki gave him a nod and jumped back in the van. She checked the map. If she continued east on Highway 60 then north at Quemado, it appeared she had a 150-mile stretch back into Albuquerque. She'd hang a left at Socorro and pick up the interstate there. Niki rounded up the cat and prepared for the long trek.

She had barely settled in to the rhythm of the road, when she crested a hill and saw something that wasn't part of the usual high desert scenery. In addition to the flat high plains that opened up for miles ahead, there was something straight out of a science fiction novel; acres of enormous satellite dishes stretching as far as she could see.

"What is *that?* she shrieked and the cat jumped. A military installation?

As she drove closer, she could see that each of the satellite dishes was the size of a building. A sign read: the National Radio Observatory's Very Large Array. Another pointed to a visitor's entrance.

Talk about gadgets, she thought. She had to check it out. A man in the guard booth wore a badge identifying him as Volunteer Bob. Niki rolled down her van window.

"Hi Ma'am," he said. "The visitor center is straight up this road."

"What is a radio observatory?" Niki asked Volunteer Bob.

He happily launched into a stream of mind-numbing techno babble, concluding with, "These radio telescopes are positioned in a Very Large Array. The VLA, as we call it, is just a year old. The scopes track information on the structure of distant galaxies and star formation regions. The high altitude and clear air here minimizes problems caused by the earth's atmosphere. There's lots more information about the project at the visitor center."

He handed Niki a brochure. Immediately the high-pitched whine began in her ear. She tried to ignore it and looked down at the brochure. A pinkish-purple beam of light burst from the paper up into her face. She yelped and dropped the brochure.

"What's the matter?" Volunteer Bob asked.

"What was that?"

"What was what Ma'am?"

"That beam of light." Niki felt nauseated. "I think I'm going to be sick," she said, jumping out of her camper and rushing toward a grassy spot.

Just as fast, Bob was out of the guard station and trying to see if he could help. Niki was retching and motioned him away. He backed off and watched her from several feet away. Within a couple of minutes she felt better but still had a nasty headache.

"Would you like some water?" Bob called to her.

"Yes, please."

After emptying a small paper cup he provided, she said, "Something—a beam of light—shot up at me from that brochure. Didn't you see it?" Before he could respond, Niki felt a chill.

"*This array system could be used to validate the super temporal abreaction of the Dogon star. Psionic transmissions from Sirius.*" The words came from her mouth.

It's hard to say who was more shocked. Niki's eyes were completely dilated. Combined with her wild wind-whipped hair, she looked like a drug-crazed hippie.

"I better get my supervisor," he said and broke into a run for the guard booth.

Niki noticed that Volunteer Bob had a walkie-talkie. Her head had cleared enough that she realized she should jump in the van and leave before government officials showed up. They might arrest her, she thought. But her body felt heavy, sluggish. And in her mind she heard, *this technology could help us.*

"No!" Niki screamed.

Of course, Bob must have thought she wanted him to drop his radio handset, but he had already called for back-up.

"I'm sorry," she said and smiled. "Really, I'm okay now."

Bob looked confused as he headed back to his booth, no doubt to hide until help came.

Niki turned her head away from his direction and under her breath began scolding her unseen accomplice.

"How dare you make a complete fool of me! I don't care if you were an engineer or scientist, this is a government facility. Do not use me to talk to them. I mean it."

Bob stayed in the guard shack watching Niki until a jeep pulled up next to her van.

An older man in a uniform got out and asked, "Is there a problem here?"

"No Sir. Everything is fine now," Niki said. "I just got sick." She mustered her most helpless, innocent expression. "Maybe from driving or something I ate."

"You are very pale," the official said skeptically. "Have you been doing drugs? Do I need to search the van?"

"You're welcome to search the van," Niki responded. "I don't have any drugs, not even a prescription. I'm sure it was that truck stop food."

The older man looked at Volunteer Bob, who shrugged.

"Turn your van around and leave then," he said.

"Thank you. I'm sorry for the disruption," Niki replied. She walked calmly to the van and jumped in. She could hardly wait to drive away from the place, but smiled and waved one last time for good measure.

Glancing in the rearview mirror as she drove off, she saw the official was writing down her plate number.

Niki drove for several miles, her hands shaking on the wheel. Once she was a few miles away from the observatory, Niki pulled the van off to the side of the road.

"Will you please just tell me, who are you and what do you want?" She rubbed the necklace totem. "Koteen, the medicine man, saw you and gave me this to protect me. He also said I could use it to invoke you. Speak now."

We're a unified tutelary spirit, she heard.

"What the hell does that mean? Say something I can understand," Niki demanded. Her cigarette craving was over powering. She stepped out of the van and lit up. "See what you've done to me. You've turned me into a smoker. I hate you."

There was no further communication, just a sense of disappointment. Smoking brought back feelings of nausea. She threw the cigarette on the ground, stomped it out and got back in the van. She would have cried, but she was too angry.

"I refuse to drive all over the country with lunatics for guides. Smokers and snuff addicts, my ass." She longed for Koteen. He would know what to do. Niki hit the accelerator and headed for Albuquerque.

14 Déjà Vu in ABQ

Driving into Albuquerque, this time northbound on I-25, Niki could not have cared less about the view. She was exhausted and just wanted to find a motel.

She spotted a Super 8 midway into town and was anxious to get out of the van and take a shower. She had been thinking about the beam of light and remembered she had seen a flash of light before—back in Iowa when she was guided by the I Ching.

What once seemed like divine guidance, felt more and more like some evil Dr. No inhabiting her body. She could not believe that he—or they—had actually used her to talk to the guard. And such a burst of babble—put Volunteer Bob to shame. She eyed the brochure, which was still lying on the floor of the bus, and wondered whether or not to touch it. Not yet.

These Super 8 motels were billed as pet-friendly places, and this one didn't mind if she kept Schroeder in the room as long as she agreed to pay for any damages he might cause. Niki began the now-familiar ritual of moving things from the bus, including the cat box this time.

She was hungry, too, but couldn't think of eating another cold sandwich, or going back out after a shower. Then she realized that being in a "city" meant she could order a pizza and have it delivered while she showered.

While eating she glanced at the brochure, which she had gathered up with her other belongings. It read:

- The Very Large Array was completed in January, 1981.
- The cost of $78,578,000 (1972 dollars) is roughly $1 per taxpayer.
- The Visitor Center slide show describes radio astronomy and the VLA itself. It is the starting point for a self-guided walking tour that takes you around the central region of the VLA site.
- The walking tour will take you close to one of the 230-ton antennas.
- Be sure to bring your cameras, photographs are allowed.
- The VLA Visitor Center and walking tour are open from 8:30 a.m. until sunset every day of the year.

"Why did this cause the light beam?" Niki asked aloud. Then she remembered something Koteen said. He told her to always protect herself when dealing with the spirit world.

She lit a white candle, she had brought in, and touched the necklace, silently asking for protection. Instantly she felt safer, but she still wanted to know about the beam of light. "What is it?" she asked.

VALIS. The word formed in her head. That was the word the man in the TV said back at Red Rock Park. She grabbed her notebook to jot this down.

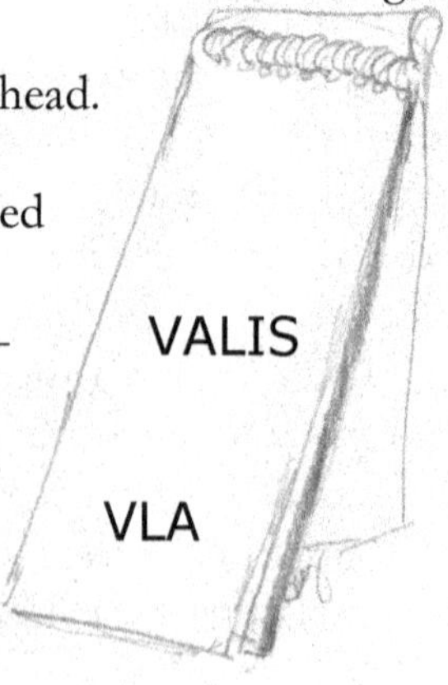

For the first time it became clear—it was an acronym, like the VLA, all capital letters. She wrote it that way. It was so obvious once she saw it. Both words had the same letters.

VALIS

VLA

Somehow VALIS was related to those radio telescopes. The crazy Dr. No entity must be some sort of scientist or—astrophysicist! It was starting to make sense.

She had been obsessed with Gribbin and because of her "gift" she was like an open channel. Some dead egghead wanted to use her to finish his science project. What was that crazy message that came through at the VLA? Something about proving radio signals are coming from Sirius. Niki scribbled that in her notebook.

Koteen was right, the soul-arc necklace was magical. Not only did it protect her, when she touched it, it did affect the spirits. They had responded.

Now is the time. Niki decided it was time to face her fears and find out if she was right. She found the incense and lit a stick. She wished she knew how to journey by herself, but all she had was the gourd rattle and no way of drumming. That was the key to getting into that altered state of mind.

The only way she knew of getting into anything like a trance state was through meditation. So she took the quilt-like spread off the bed, folded it a few times to make a cushion of it, and sat in a cross-legged lotus position on the floor.

With only light from the flickering candle, Niki focused on her breath, trying to observe and not change it.

She must have dozed off while meditating, because when she opened her eyes it was morning. Light was streaming in through the motel curtains and Schroeder was treading on her, ready for food. She was wrapped in the bedspread and still on the floor.

She had hazy memories of Koteen, like he had spoken to her—given her advice. Was it just a dream or something more? It felt like a different reality, a separate reality. Wasn't that the name of one of those Don Juan books, *Teachings of Don Juan*. She sat up, totally alert now. Niki vividly recalled a discussion about that book in one of her college religion classes. It was just like Koteen's Vision Quest.

In class they had discussed subtle energy, comparisons between Chinese medicine involving Chi—energy in the body—and how shamans of many native cultures used subtle energy for healing.

After feeding the cat, she took him out on the leash for a walk and continued thinking about shamanism. She wanted to read the Don Juan book. Surely in a city like Albuquerque it would be easy to find a bookstore. Niki stopped for a minute to admire the mountains, the Sandia Mountains. She remembered someone telling her they looked very different depending on the time of day. They were dark now, not the spectacular watermelon pink of the night before when the setting sun had reflected off them.

The Phil/Pike combo had been subdued since causing Niki's outburst of glossolalia at the VLA. The two had been given their final reprimand about overt, or even involuntary, interference. Phil would lose guardianship if he, or the two of them, stepped over the proverbial line again. Annihilation is not a laughing matter.

"Let the girl go on her compulsive book search," Phil shrewdly suggested to Pike. "We can subtly direct her to the right store and perhaps a book will happen to fall off a shelf, say *VALIS*."

The two, as one, nodded knowingly this time.

The yellow pages offered several options for used book stores, something Niki hadn't seen since her college days in Iowa City. Intriguing names, too: "Open Mind" called the OM Centre, the Brotherhood of Life, Blue Eagle, and Bird

Song Used Books, and all of them near the campus of the University of New Mexico.

Using directions from the motel clerk, she found her way to Central Avenue which apparently went for miles in either direction as part of old Highway 66. Niki headed east toward the mountains, and Harvard Avenue was one of the first side streets once she saw the college campus sprawling on her left.

Unlike University of Iowa, with its domed, former state house building, this campus was a collection of small adobe homes and single-story buildings. It would be interesting to study in a place with such cultural diversity. She hadn't seen much of that back in Iowa.

Niki had no intention of staying in Albuquerque. Taos and Chaco Canyon were calling her like a shaman's flute. She would load up on books and other supplies and then head north.

Both the OM Centre and Birdsong were in the Harvard Mall. Niki loved this funky little street which was lined with more of the adobe homes converted into restaurants, coffee shops, and bookstores. She could hardly wait to park the Westfalia and check them out. Some Rastafarian guys with dreadlocks gave her a thumbs up as she parked the micro bus on the street.

"Nice bus," one said. She was used to this by now. Everyone with a fantasy of living life on the road, from hippies to retired folks, wanted to look at it, talk about it, or even sit in it. Sometimes she let people check it out. Luckily these guys didn't ask.

A small chime on the door of the OM Centre tinkled as she entered. A wizened elfish man with wisps of white hair was arranging tarot cards and other magical objects in a glass display case. He asked if he could help her. Niki was instantly enchanted by the atmosphere of the small shop.

"I love your store," she said, looking at all the old books and odd objects. There were many shelves of Buddhist and religious books. "Those books about Don Juan—"

"Carlos Castaneda's books?" the man asked.

"That's it! Do you have any?"

"Actually, the place a few stores south, Birdsong Used Books, would be a better bet for the paperbacks."

"That's very kind of you," Niki thanked him and looked around a bit more. She saw an entire wall of little plastic cases with cassette tapes.

"I rent those by the week," the man explained. "Speakers on various religious practices, guided meditations, chanting, music. All kinds of spiritual things."

"Do you have an American Indian drumming tape by any chance?" Niki asked.

The man squinted and examined one of the shelves and then handed her a case. It was actually labeled "Shamanic Journey Tape: Double Drum Side 1, Single Drum Side 2."

"Wow! This is perfect. You said rent, but can I buy it? I'm just passing through Albuquerque."

"Well, I'll tell you what," the man offered. "While you go look for those Castaneda books, I'll dub you a copy for five dollars. Fair enough?"

"Very fair, thank you!" she replied. Niki liked the vibes of the store and the owner.

When she returned from Birdsong Books, she had three titles by Castaneda: the original *Teachings of Don Juan: A Yaqui Way of Knowledge, A Separate Reality, and Journey to Ixtlan.* "And, only a buck each. Thanks to you," she stopped realizing she didn't know the old man's name.

"I'm Rick Cramer," he said. "If you have a few dollars left to spend, I also found this brand new paperback, *The Way of the Shaman* by Michael Harner."

"Absolutely!" Niki practically grabbed the book from him. It was like an instruction manual for how to journey, full of techniques and detailed descriptions of accessing other realms and states of consciousness.

She left the store armed with the drumming tape and her shamanic guide books. What she didn't leave with was a copy of *VALIS* that her spirit guides had worked so diligently to knock off a shelf back at Birdsong.

She spent the afternoon in the mountains. Even though May days were getting warmer in Albuquerque, it was chilly at the higher altitude among the pines. It didn't faze Niki, who was used to the biting cold of Iowa winters. She found a spot in the sun, and read for hours while the cat played. She could hardly wait for sunset to try out her new-found journeying techniques.

When the time came, she folded the bed spread to make a long flat pad on the motel room floor. With the boombox from the van, the gourd rattle, the Kachina for protection, a white candle, and incense, she was ready. She sat cross-legged while she cleared her mind and prepared for the Vision Quest. Feeling anxious, she asked Koteen's hawk-spirit to meet her and guide her in the shamanic realm.

She lay down on the floor and punched the play button. It was amazing how the steady rhythm of the drumming brought back the feelings and sensations of being at Koteen's trailer. Niki could see his face so clearly, as if he was actually with her again.

I am with you. The words were a whisper on the wind, very different than the messages and the buzzing she had become accustomed to. She saw Koteen's face fade to a muted abstract image then transform again to a gossamer web then to the hawk. He was becoming the Dark Chanting Goshawk.

It wasn't scary or even strange, especially after reading about journeying. It was beautiful, like watching a movie.

Koteen, as a hawk, circled overhead. The landscape took on a muted, abstract quality. Niki was becoming part of the scene, instead of just watching. She was merging into a vortex of color, and pulsing energy.

The hawk circled
then swooped
and grabbed her
with its claws.

Even that felt natural,
not at all frightening.

Wind swooshed through her hair and against her face. They flew higher and higher until the ground was no longer visible.

Koteen communicated with her, in their altered state of consciousness, in the same way the spirits could. He assured her that as long as he was her guide, no harm could come to her. And that together they would find the ghost spirits and learn how and why they were connected to her mission.

Flying with Koteen in Goshawk form through the swirl of color created the same safe, peaceful feeling as the spiritual encounter with her dad. He conveyed that all experiences in the higher spirit realm have that quality. More insights came to her.

She *knew* that traveling to the lower world with power animals and totems would be different, and she also knew to keep her attention on the current feelings to maintain this feeling of freedom and bliss.

Ahead she saw an ancient stone building with arches and columns and recognized it from the temple dream with the flute music. They swooped down and through the main arch.

A pink haze surrounded her. She heard the flute music again, and smelled incense, but couldn't see anything but the haze. Then she realized she couldn't see herself either. There was nothing physical like arms or legs, yet she was aware of being in this place and could hear and see the colors. The hawk was gone, but she still felt Koteen's presence, as a warm light that enveloped her like a blanket. It was comforting and she felt safe.

See that light? He conveyed. She actually saw several lights, all of them soft and muted, but one stood out. Far off, she saw a blindingly beautiful golden light.

That is the Source. Our Great Spirit.

Niki thought about the smaller lights and instantly she knew those were the unresolved spirits, ones with unfinished business—the hungry ghosts, as Buddhists call them. Some will be reborn, others will merge with the Source light. She understood why these two spirits, her guides, were merged almost as one.

In this realm nothing was distinct. There were no clear boundaries or hard edges like in the physical realm. She sensed how matter evolves from the most ethereal, vaporous substance to a collection of molecules that swirl together until something or someone is formed. The most dense matter is rock or metal. It all made perfect sense from this perspective.

One of the muted lights moved toward her and as it did she saw it was actually a "double bubble," and within it was the flickering image of the man with the beard. Sometimes he looked different, wearing glasses and a shaved face.

It was the two of them—the "tutelary spirits" as they called themselves back at the VLA. Now it actually meant something. They were her mentors or guides, not evil at all. They didn't seem angry or demanding in this realm. She felt compassion and knew they needed help with their unfinished business.

For some reason they could not speak or convey anything to her now, but she sensed that Koteen's essence was communicating with them. She saw flickering images of the hawk, interspersed with glimpses of Koteen's face and long hair. The two men—especially the eyes of the man with the beard—were mostly a haze of light.

At some point she heard the cry of a hawk and then she was once again carried in its claws back through a swirl of stars and clouds and finally she could see the earth below. He conveyed information to her about the spirits and said when she returned to ordinary consciousness she would remember what she needed to about them. She also heard a very high pitched sound from a flute and fast drumming.

Niki wanted to open her eyes, but her eyelids seemed too heavy. She felt disoriented and weighted down. Finally, she saw flickering candlelight. Was she at Koteen's trailer? Memories slowly seeped in. The motel room. Her sense of smell was so acute. A musty smell of the blanket, faint cigarette smoke, mixed with incense.

"I'm in Albuquerque," Niki remembered. She didn't want to lose any of the sensations and quality of the journey she had just taken. It was so much more than a dream. I have to write about it, she thought. Every feeling and sensation and especially being with Koteen again, as a hawk and spirit. This was definitely the beginning of something important—life altering. She would never be alone again. She could journey to other realms, perhaps become a healer herself someday, or at least help others find peace. After all, that was her mission.

Niki wiped a tear from her eye. Koteen really was the Goshawk, her protector. The spirits were also trying to help her. For the first time in years, she felt safe.

∞

One cannot appreciate
the brilliance of the Light
without first knowing
the depths of darkness.
-- Taoist saying

15 Now and Zen

May 8, 1982, a Saturday morning

Interstate 25 North, toward the little town of Bernalillo, and then Highway 44 northwest, was the way to the famous Chaco Canyon. All roads might lead there metaphorically, but this was the actual route. Leaving Albuquerque, Niki admired the majestic Sandia Mountains again. She felt sad thinking she might not be back. She had spent several days there exploring Old Town, the oldest part of the city which dated back to the 1500s for the Spanish and even earlier for American Indians. Ten tribes live in and around Albuquerque, even more further north, she had learned. She would pass through several pueblos on the way to Chaco.

The mountains, the little adobe cafes and coffee shops had been perfect places to read "the Teachings" even if those were Yaqui Ways. She wondered if the Yaqui and the Yavapai had once been the same, but didn't have time to find a library and research that. It wasn't important for the series she was writing.

Niki had abandoned the generic travel log concept, and was focused on a three-part series on native culture. One segment would be on shamanic practices, what "white people" call medicine men and Hispanic New Mexicans call curanderos. Hispanics are fond of calling everyone Anglos, even Blacks, something Niki found curious. But this series would not get into all the odd colloquialisms she had encountering in the Southwest, that could be another series. For this one she would focus on healing practices, maybe call it "Beyond Medicine."

As she drove along Highway 44, she thought about the Castaneda teachings and all she had learned from Koteen. She could hardly wait to write and submit articles to Frank or even see if her AP contacts might pick them up, like they had her Gribbin story. Niki noticed the Coronado Monument as she passed by, but she was too anxious to get to Chaco Canyon to consider stopping.

This amused Phil. If she knew the role the Conquistadors had played in the demise of the native culture, she probably would have investigated that, he thought. *But what do I know? I couldn't even get her to look at my book when it was right under her feet.* Phil and the Bishop were tossing up hands—the universal expression for frustration.

"Let's go listen to *Parsifal* as performed at the original Bayreuth Festival," Phil suggested to his preacher pal. "I think it will be awhile before we're needed."

Still lost in thought about writing her series of articles, Niki turned right at San Ysidro. This was the road to Jemez Springs. She should have stayed on 44, but didn't realize this. When the scenery changed to the red rock, Niki felt excited. No wonder Koteen wanted me to see this—it looks just like Sedona.

The road to Jemez Springs was full of surprises. She passed a rock waterfall, and discovered there were hot springs. While looking for a place to have lunch, she made another discovery—the Jemez Mountain Zen Center. Niki couldn't believe her eyes. A Zen Center in Indian country? It was a sign. It had to be. She had to check it out.

The old wooden buildings were nestled in the pines along a creek running through the Jemez Mountains. Niki got out and knocked on a screen door which was badly in need of repair. No one came. Maybe it's abandoned, she thought, and decided to have a look around. It was deliciously peaceful and serene.

I could live here and never go back to Iowa. Niki opened the passenger door of the van to let Schroeder out to roam free in the wild flowers. When she turned around there was a young man wearing a dark red robe and sandals.

"Oh, hello," she said, startled. "I knocked a few minutes ago and no one answered. Is it alright to be here?"

"Usually we welcome visitors on the weekends," he hesitated, "but today is a holy day and we are in Zazen—meditating and fasting."

Niki felt her cheeks turning red. How embarrassing. Not only was it a Buddhist monastery, she was intruding on the holiest of all days.

"Oh my, it is May 8th, isn't it?" Niki asked, realizing it was the Day of Enlightenment. "I've been traveling and lost track of the days. I used to observe Zazen myself back in Iowa. I'm so sorry to intrude."

"You sit?" the young monk asked.

"Never formally. There were no Buddhist centers in Iowa." Niki felt uncomfortable knowing what an intrusion this was.

"Please accept my apology. I stumbled on to your center by accident. I was on my way to Chaco Canyon."

"There are no coincidences," he said and smiled knowingly. "It is auspicious that you found us on this day. Please, come with me."

Niki knew enough about Buddhist practices to know that no one would speak when they entered the meditation room, the Zendo. Through non-verbal means, a nod or gesture, the Zen Master would convey if Niki could sit with them.

As they approached the building with the large open room, the monk took off his shoes and Niki did the same. She was thankful her wool socks did not have holes.

Several men and only one other woman, with a shaved head, were sitting on small black pillows on the wooden floor. They were all in white robes. She felt so out of place in her street clothes. None of them even stirred.

The Master, an older-looking Asian man, glanced up and motioned them to sit using just one subtle downward finger movement. There was no way Niki could protest. Talk about "be here now." She was, and with no escape.

The young monk handed Niki a pillow. She managed to get herself into position, but wondered if hours of sitting in tight jeans might cut off the blood supply to her legs. She had thoughts of amputation, and noticed the Master giving her a stern glance.

After so many days of journeying and shamanic thoughts she knew how to be still. But total silence was odd. She longed for the drumming sound and to lie down. Her legs ached, and she wanted to scratch her back. Niki knew this was typical when one tried to become quiet. Becoming quiet and still was the purpose of Zen.

She tried to follow her breath and quiet her mind, but her legs ached and her stomach was rumbling. She had been thinking of lunch, not Zazen, when she stopped. "Thinking," she reminded herself. Thoughts come and go when meditating. You simply acknowledge thoughts and let them pass, like clouds in the mind. More thoughts came. Again she dismissed them. This is the nature of Zen. The mind and body struggle. If one can endure and get past the initial physical and mental turmoil, the experience can be truly transcendent.

To be at a Zendo for the Celebration of Enlightenment was an incredible blessing—like a catholic stumbling upon a sanctuary for Easter Sunday. 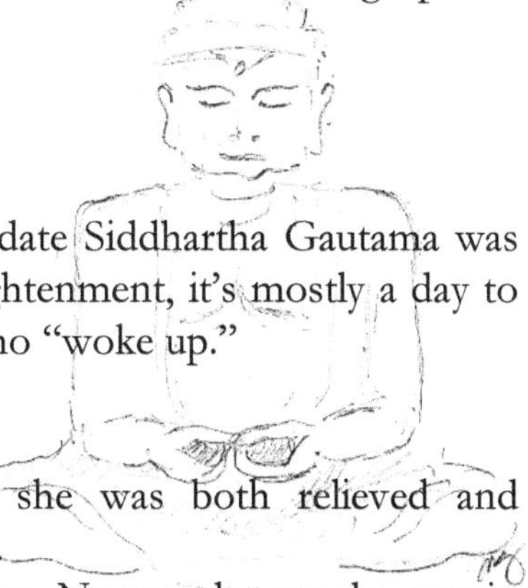
In some cultures, May 8 is observed as Buddha's Birthday, or the Day of Enlightenment. Since no one is certain of the date Siddhartha Gautama was born, or actually achieved enlightenment, it's mostly a day to meditate and honor the One who "woke up."

Niki sat and began to lose all sense of time and space.

When the gong sounded she was both relieved and pleased she had been able to sit.

Luckily it was a short session. No wonder monks remain silent and draw ensos, brush strokes of circles. They represent the moment, the one, where the beginning is the end. That's Zen.

She bowed to the Master and to the young monk whom she first met. When she got back to her van, Schroeder was curled up on the grass. He stretched too. Her legs, though sore, had survived. No amputations would be required. It was mid-afternoon and she was starving.

Extreme hunger reminded Niki of the story of a maiden who, in Gautama Buddha's life, offered the Buddha a bowl of porridge after he had been sitting for days, months, who knows how long. The bowl is attributed as a major link in his enlightenment.

It is said that the Buddha-to-be originally followed an extreme ascetic lifestyle. The way of hardship was a common practice in those times, and in India today. For Siddhartha, inadequate food and water caused his body to shrivel. It was so extreme, legend states, that he became indistinguishable from the bark of the Bodhi Tree that he had sat under.

Seeing the emaciated Siddhartha Gautama, a young girl offered him her bowl of porridge. Siddhartha realized that without food one can do nothing, and be of no service to others. He ate the food and refrained from further harming his own body. He lived, and of course, became the Buddha.

Niki had no lofty thoughts of becoming a Bodhisattva, she simply had to eat. She drove off hoping that the little community of Jemez Springs had a café or grocery store

.

∞

"Where's that damn modem?" Several hours later she was frantically tossing clothes out of the overhead storage bin of the van trying to locate the box where she put the extra computer parts.

"Ah, here it is," she said as she stood on a milk crate to pull it out of the far recess of the storage compartment.

Bringing her little Commodore computer and printer had proven to be a wise choice. Niki had been able to connect the keyboard to her ten inch black and white portable TV and could write in the van, and print, when she had electricity. But she needed a phone line to transmit data. Now, it seemed, she had the perfect opportunity.

Not only had she found something to eat at Jemez Springs, she found a perfect little hippie hostel.

The couple who ran it said she could stay for a week for twenty bucks. She could go back to the Zen Center or on to Chaco Canyon from this place, but best of all the guy was a geek too. He knew about gadgets and computer modems, and wanted to see her online set-up.

The topic had come up during her late lunch, when she asked if she could use their telephone to transmit an article back to Iowa.

Niki had a high-powered 1200-baud modem, not an acoustic coupler, but a true Hayes 1200-baud modem and she used it with an 800 number to connect to CompuServe or the AP wire at the *Courier*. It was much faster than the little 300 bps (bits per second) toy modem that came with the Commodore. All she needed was a phone line, and her room had that. For the demo, though, she stayed downstairs. Even though these two, Bill and Nancy, looked content as a couple, she wasn't about to have him in her room.

"Is it long distance from here to Albuquerque?" Niki asked Bill.

"I thought you had a toll free number to call," he said.

"I do, but when I was in Albuquerque I learned about some local computer bulletin board systems that are free. CompuServe costs by the minute. I just thought we might try one of these BBS things."

Bill smiled. "Well, to be honest, I know how to phone phreak."

"Are you serious?" Niki asked. "I've heard of phreaking but never knew exactly how it worked."

While Niki hooked-up her Commodore and modem to Bill and Nancy's television set, Bill dismantled the telephone hand set. He explained that some guys just whistle into the mouth-piece, but he had a special device that was guaranteed to emit the exact frequency to enable the long distance call.

The process was much more complicated than just dialing up CIS with her 800 number, but also a lot more fun. Not really legal, but they were only going to call a BBS. Niki just loved learning how to phreak and use the terminal program. When they saw the word CONNECT on the TV screen, it was as though they had hacked a bank.

"We're in!" Niki cheered and Bill clapped. Nancy had long ago lost interest in the tedious procedure, and Schroeder was sound asleep on the floor. Slowly more words came across the screen in a phosphorous glow.

ASK THE SWAMI. The Swami can foretell your future. **Enter your handle:** The cursor blinked waiting for a reply.

"Handle means an alias, I know that," Bill said, "but what is the Swami thing?"

Niki laughed. "It looked like the most interesting of the list of computer boards. I didn't care for 'FlyBoy' and the 'Wizard's Lair' would be all D&D, so I thought why not check out this one." While responding to Bill she had already started to enter her CB chat handle. The screen responded: ***Welcome ZenWoman!*** A menu of choices began to appear:

1) **Ask your question**
2) **Meet other Seekers**
3) **Buddhist and Hindu Resources**

"ZenWoman, huh?" Bill responded. "You're the only phreaking female, computer-hacking Buddhist I know." They laughed. "I'm going to let you enjoy your session with the Swami and check on Nancy."

This was great, with a living room to herself and a new online place to explore. Niki settled into the big arm chair and decided to try a question. She selected "1" and the screen slowly cleared and refreshed with a new line of text.

The Swami is ready to assist, it read. Enter your Question.

Niki thought for a moment, remembering it was a full moon that night—the important Wesak moon and Buddhist Day of Enlightenment. She typed:

"What about the Maitreya?"

Instantly the machine responded: "The Maitreya holds the key to your future."

"Do you have another question for the Swami? The menu choices were only: **Y**)es or **N**)o

Niki knew how that type of computer program worked. Whatever she had entered would have been the "key" to her future. The program simply took her subject and used it in the reply. She wanted to play along and entered "Y" for yes. The screen responded, "Continue."

To challenge the program she tried, "Why is the Maitreya the key?"

"The Maitreya is the source of your anxiety," it responded. Clever, she thought. It asked, "More?"

"Who is speaking to me?" she typed.

"The Swami speaks to you," followed by, "Do you wish to ask another question?" Niki was determined to think of something the program could not answer. "Where will I find the lost manuscript?"

"Where do you believe the manuscript is?" it asked.

As she suspected, it was a hacked version of a psychiatrist program that was making the rounds on CompuServe. Someone had modified it for this BBS. It was starting to bore her. Niki tried to get back to a main menu, but the program was in a loop and wouldn't let her out. She was trying every key combination she could think of short of just rebooting the machine. Just then more text began to appear:

"The Swami wants to chat with you." The screen had cleared, then displayed a special Chat Mode so the system operator (SysOp) could interact with the caller.

SysOp: Hello Zen Woman. Your questions are intriguing.
ZenWoman: So is your programming
SysOp: Are you a woman or just pretending?
ZenWoman: Are you a Swami or just pretending?
SysOp: Touché! <grin> I am a Baba, semi-Swami. You?
ZenWoman: I am woman, hear me roar!
SysOp: Delightful. Let's go voice!

"Going voice" simply meant picking up the receiver and actually talking, but this was something Niki wasn't sure how to do with the phreak connection Bill had established. She was glad, in a way, since she had no idea who was on the other end of this computer system.

ZenWoman: Sorry, can't tonight. Perhaps another time.

SysOp: Ah, hiding your male voice, after all.

Just then Bill walked in and glanced at the chat.

"I can set up a connection in your room, if you want to talk to the guy," he said.

"No, thanks," Niki responded, "at least not tonight. Maybe for a future call, but I'm exhausted now and just want to log off." She typed "next time. Bye for now" and let Bill disconnect without even waiting on the final word from the Swami.

They carried the computer and some of her other belongings upstairs to her room, and found a place for Schroeder. Nancy had freshened up her bed and put clean towels for her. As soon as Bill left, Niki collapsed. As she drifted off to sleep, she thought of how the Wesak Moon is an auspicious time for manifesting new beginnings.

The next morning, while flipping through her notebook and drinking coffee, Niki felt she had finally come to terms with her group of guides. Koteen was in the Shamanic realm to keep her two tutelary spirits in check. So, why not add a Swami to the mix? That would sound completely crazy to everyone back in Iowa, except Linda. Who cares, she thought. It's my adventure and I'm going to explore it all. With that, she decided to log back onto the Swami BBS and if he wanted to "go voice" she would.

Niki had no more than logged on and gotten to the main menu when the Swami interrupted her session.

SysOp: Thank you for calling back. Can you pick up now?

ZenWoman: Sure.

Niki used the procedure Bill set up so she could connect with the modem or use the phone. For a moment she still heard the squawk of the modem tones, but then a distinctive voice with thick accent came on the line, "Baba Dhyana here. Is this the ZenWoman?"

"Yes, it is."

"You win, my dear," the Swami said.

"I was certain you were a man. Men sometimes pretend to be women on the BBS to engage other men in conversations. How do you know so much about computers and online programs?"

"It's a hobby, but I also use computers at work. How does a semi-Swami know so much technology and speak fluent English?"

Baba Dhyana explained that he had worked at IBM for several years and decided to start his own online service.

"It's the wave of the future, my dear. Eventually, I believe I can charge for the service. Someday, everyone will use electronic mail and online services. Do you agree?"

"I don't know if everyone will use it. Computer hackers never pay for anything, so how would you make any money?"

"I'm a Swami, remember. I see the far future." Even though he was joking, there was a something about the man's voice that intrigued Niki. She asked, "Are you really a Baba? A spiritual Master?"

"In India I would not be a Baba. However, here in New Mexico where everyone hungers for spiritual nourishment, I am a Baba," the man laughed again, a deep, melodic sound that Niki found fascinating and mesmerizing. He continued, "I came to chat mode last night because you mentioned the Maitreya. Are you a follower?"

"I'm not sure how to answer that. Do you believe Maitreya is the future Buddha or the Christ?"

"Interesting question," Baba said. "We can find out in a few days."

"Few days?"

"Yes. May 14 is the Day of Declaration," the Baba said. Niki felt an ear buzz and instantly felt dizzy as though she might faint.

"ZenWoman, ZenWoman, are you there?"

"Yes, I'm still here," but she had no idea what to say.

"A group of Sikhs from my wife's spiritual community are going to Los Angeles. You would be welcome to join us."

"You don't even know me, and I don't know you, how could I possibly consider that?"

"Why don't you come to our Bodhi Tree café and we could all meet in person. Then you can decide," the Baba suggested.

"Bodhi Tree. Where is that?"

"Have you been to the college area in Albuquerque?"

"Actually, I have," Niki replied and her ear buzzed a bit.

Baba Dhyana proceeded to describe Harvard Mall again. What is the chance, Niki wondered, that she would be directed back to that same little street to a café that was between Birdsong Books and the OM Centre? She actually recalled seeing it set back from the street.

"Let me think about it, and I will respond later," Niki said. "I can send SysOp mail, right?"

"Yes, but we must meet tomorrow, Monday, since we are leaving Friday."

"Okay, I'll come to the café," Niki conceded, "but I'm out in Jemez Springs, so can we meet about two o'clock?"

"Perfect," the Baba agreed. "I'll have a pot of chai ready."

Since Niki had the long-distance line, she decided she would call back to Iowa. Not Frank, or Bruce, though, she needed the advice of a good friend. She would call Linda.

"Niki! I've been dying to hear from you," Linda sounded happy. "I want to hear everything! Every detail."

Niki provided a quick recap of her month of adventures, meeting Koteen, of course, topped the list.

"Oh la la," Linda was fantasizing, but Niki set that record straight quickly. Linda, who was into all things metaphysical, loved hearing about the shamanic journeying.

"I'm going to dig out those Castaneda books myself," she said. "I read them all back in the '60s. You weren't doing peyote, were you, hon?" Niki assured her no drugs were involved. That led into the ridiculous scene at the VLA in New Mexico, and how she ended up at a hippie hostel in Jemez Springs.

"I wish I was there. It sounds like fun," Linda exclaimed. "If anyone deserves a big-ass adventure, it's you."

"Well, that brings me to the current question," Niki said. "Remember how I thought I was heading for California to see Benjamin Crème and get an update on the appearance of the Maitreya? Well, with all these twists and turns, I kind of lost track of that until just now. I was using my computer equipment to check out some online services here in New Mexico. Remember when I showed you that CompuServe CB chat?" Linda was amazingly silent, so Niki asked, "Are you still there?"

"Yep, I'm here, but you know I don't understand that computer stuff."

"You don't have to, just that he's an electronic Swami. Anyway, I spoke with him on the phone just now. He and his wife are East Indians. They own a restaurant called the Bodhi Tree in Albuquerque. Linda, he wants me to go with a group of them to California—show up at his restaurant tomorrow to meet them and decide. What do you think?"

"Hon, it's more about what you think and it seems you're not sure or you wouldn't ask me."

"I could drive my VW. You know, follow them out to California, like a caravan. I haven't wanted to drive there alone. At least, I think I want to meet them tomorrow. It's a public place and we'd meet at two in the afternoon. That can't hurt. I'm curious about them now."

"Well, you're living on intuition now, sweetie, and all I can say is trust your gut. I'm so glad you called. Want me to pass on anything to the *Courier* guys?"

"Yes! Please tell Frank I've actually written some articles on American Indian culture and I will transmit them this week."

With that Niki said goodbye to her long-time friend Linda and then sobbed a bit. It was first time she had felt homesick since those crazy episodes in Kansas.

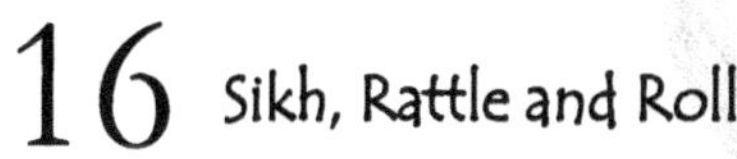

16 Sikh, Rattle and Roll

Niki felt nervous as she parked the van on Harvard Street, perhaps anxious is more accurate. While intrigued with the idea of meeting the smooth-talking East Indian soothsayer, her gut, as Linda called it, was acting up. Maybe the tutelary crew was causing it, but something was off.

She parked across the street and a few stores down from the Bodhi Tree so she could check it out. Seeing the OM Centre reminded her that she had not used the drumming tape since leaving Albuquerque. She promised herself she would, maybe even tonight. Maybe she could get insight on why this place bothered her.

It's a restaurant. Get a grip, she told herself as she locked the camper and began walking down the street. The place was inviting from the outside with its wooden A-frame storefront and frosted glass windows. A huge rendering of a Bodhi Tree was etched on the glass. Nice touch.

As she opened the door, Niki received a blast of sensory

input. Spices and incense combined with exotic tapestries and colorful artwork that seemed to vibrate to the heavy rhythm of drums and sitar music. Everything was dramatic, especially the man in the turban walking towards her.

"ZenWoman, it must be you," the man said with that rich, East Indian accent she recognized.

"What gave it away? Baba Dhyana?"

"My dear, you're even more spectacular than I could possibly have imagined." Niki felt embarrassed by his extreme exaggeration. No wonder they claim these guys can charm snakes.

"Do you have a first name, ZenWoman?"

For a moment, Niki considered saying it was Evelyn, knowing she could use her fake ID, but her intuition was to be honest. So she said, "It's Nicole."

"Nicole," Baba Dhyana emphasized the "oh" in her name rather dramatically, making Niki blush, then completed his triad of tributes by taking her right hand in both of his and studied her palm. He was actually rubbing her hand and pushing on her knuckles. It must have been obvious she was uncomfortable because he quickly explained, "In Ayurveda we study the hands and feet. I already know much about you from your hand."

"Really?" She wasn't sure she liked that, but it was too late now. Niki studied the man's smooth, dark face. He was certainly striking with his brilliant white teeth and jeweled turban. It created a mysterious allure. Not to mention his deep-set gray eyes, high cheekbones and cascading salt-and-pepper beard—a long, flowing stream that begged to be stroked. Very different from that of her spirit guide, whose coarse beard was cropped close to his chin and face. Baba certainly looked like a Swami, and his clothing completed the effect. He wore a heavily embroidered, multi-colored vest over an expensive looking gray silk shirt.

"You're pretty stunning yourself, Baba Dhyana!" They both laughed and Niki felt comfortable despite her unusual surroundings.

A slim woman with mocha skin and waist-length shiny black hair approached them. She was also dressed in a colorful, flowing silk garb.

"You must be Mrs. Baba," Niki said smiling. Everyone laughed again.

"Keriani," came a husky reply from a demure, petite lady. In an accent even thicker than her husband's she added, "We have prepared a feast in your honor."

"Oh my," Niki said overwhelmed as she was whisked to a table in the back of the restaurant. There was a large table covered in white silk, with hand-carved napkin rings, and many small silver bowls and trays of delicacies that Niki had no idea how to approach. What caught her eye was the ornate statue in the center of the table. As though reading her mind, Keriani said, "That is Vishnu,
Lord of the Dance."

"An incarnation of Shiva,"
Baba Dhyana added,
"He represents fertility and power."

The figure, which Niki thought was a woman, was apparently male. He was covered in snakes and dancing in a ring of fire with arms stretched outward and one leg in the air.

"It is a traditional Hindu statue," the Swami said. "Vishnu maintains the cosmic order through his energy and power."

"He certainly appears powerful," Niki said. "I would love to learn more about Hindu traditions." Niki envisioned yet another series of articles on Hindus in Albuquerque.

"You, dear, are the one with much to teach us.
You are in contact with Our Lord Shiva," Keriani said. The comment startled Niki.

"Why would you say that?"

Baba Dhyana quickly took over the conversation saying, "I am a Seer, remember? We have no doubt that you were sent to us. Before we have that discussion, we must enjoy the fine feast that Keriani and her sister have prepared."

Two young men, also in turbans, brought even more bowls to the table, along with a silver pot of chai tea. The room was thick with aromas and combined with the beat of the music, it was almost as intoxicating as Koteen's shamanic session.

There was a ritual before eating. They washed their hands in one of the little bowls, then shook off excess water, rather than drying them on towels. The part Niki liked was forming a triangle with both hands, fingers as the pinnacle and thumbs for the base. Holding your hand over the food in this manner was a way of blessing and purifying the meal. She was ready to dive in, even though she had no idea what she was eating.

The Baba and Keriani explained each dish and told her the names. Masoor dal, lentils, which Niki didn't think she would like, was delicious. So was saag paneer. She almost didn't try that one when they told her it was spinach, mustard leaves and Indian cheese. One of the best was the chicken masala, tender moist chicken in a yogurt and tomato cream sauce. But everything was surprisingly good. There was hardly anything, other than fish or something squishy, that she wouldn't try.

Keriani excused herself to attend to some customers in the front part of the restaurant. When she did, one of the server boys sat down.

"Nicole, this is our second son, Mani." Niki didn't know who was more alluring, the young man or his father. Mani was shy but with a sensual, brooding look. He was more fair complected than the Baba, but he had full lips and the same perfect white teeth. His eyes were very dark beneath long, full lashes. He kept them averted while his father talked about him. His turban was blue and simple in comparison to the complicated wrap with large jewel that the Baba wore.

"Mani is nineteen and will attend the University this fall," Baba Dhyana explained. "He aspires to become a journalist and could benefit from spending time with a mentor." Baba raised a brow as he regarded Niki. She blushed again and was thankful to see Keriani return to the table. The lovely East Indian lady exuded spirituality. It was obvious she was the stability of the family.

Keriani came to the table offering more chai, which had already become Niki's new favorite hot drink. It seemed like a cross between regular tea and coffee. The masala chai tea, Baba explained, was made by adding a variety of spices then served with steamed milk. Honey was optional. It satisfied the caffeine-craving spirits and Niki loved it.

The naan bread was similar to the tortillas she had been eating in New Mexico, only it was cooked without lard, so it was lighter and kind of puffy. The ultra thin pappadams, or pappas as the boys called them, were addictive. They were like snacks—crunchy rounds made of lentil flour.

Niki was not usually so interested in food. She had always been a light eater, but she had never experienced flavors like this before. She had grown up on mostly meat and potatoes, or stew, fairly bland fare.

She learned to dip and spread raita, a type of yogurt and cucumber, on everything. It was great for offsetting anything too spicy. Curry, she learned, was turmeric and cumin. Niki enjoyed tasting and learning about the food. It was great fun.

"We will close the restaurant at three," Baba Dhyana said, "that is the end of our usual lunch period. That will give us a chance for a private discussion over kheer and more chai." Kheer was a sweet rice pudding.

Niki, who did not want to be alone with the Baba, looked at Keriani, and asked, "Will you join us?" The soft-spoken lady dropped her head and put her hands together, as if in prayer, and said, "Yes. Let me bring my son Tagore in and I will sit and share chai with you."

As Keriani turned to leave, Baba explained that their oldest son was crippled and in a wheel chair. Apparently, he had been reading in a back room. Niki was thankful Baba had mentioned his condition, otherwise she might have yelped at what she saw.

The boy, who was actually older than Mani, was small. His limbs were gnarled and deformed. His skin was scarred, as if he had been badly burned. His eyes were mere slits. It was difficult to look at him. Niki could not imagine how he could read.

Keriani wheeled the boy toward Niki and introduced him. "This is our first son, Tagore."

"Ha-llo," he said slowly and with great effort. His voice was very deep.

Before she could say anything, Niki saw a flash of light. It was like the pink beam that shot into her eye at the VLA. She jerked involuntarily, to avoid the beam, and instantly realized how terrible this must have looked—as though she had recoiled or cringed at seeing the boy.

"My pleasure to meet you," Niki said, attempting to maintain her composure from the shock of the flash and the deformity of the boy. When Keriani wheeled Tagore away to his own table, Baba inquired, "Are you alright, Nicole?"

Niki was holding her head. A severe headache had come over her.

"I'm sorry, but just as Tagore came out," Niki explained. "I saw a flash of light and now my head is throbbing."

Keriani returned and it was apparent something was wrong. Niki was still rubbing her forehead. Baba repeated to his wife what Niki had conveyed about the light and her headache. Keriani instantly bowed her head again and put her hands together, prayerfully. She was whispering something—names, a prayer, but in Hindi or Sanskrit, not English. The Baba offered a loose translation for Niki.

"She believes you have been sent to us to heal Tagore. She is thanking Lord Krishna."

Niki was still in too much pain to protest or even react to his comment. Something strange *was* happening. The Baba said he had something that would alleviate the pain. He left for a moment then returned with a small brown glass vial. It was filled with tiny pellets. He shook out three into the lid of the tiny vial and instructed Niki to dump them under her tongue but not to swallow them. Within a few minutes, her headache subsided.

Niki picked up the bottle labeled *Lycopodium*. "What is that?"

"A homeopathic remedy we use in India. Very different from Western medicine. It acts upon the root cause," Baba explained.

Niki, who felt considerably better, asked Baba Dhyana, "What do you think caused the sudden headache?"

"Cosmic awareness," he said matter-of-factly.

"Why would you say that?"

"That is why I asked you to come here today. I believe you have insights that you are striving to understand. Can you deny this?" Baba Dhyana asked knowingly.

Niki was trying to remember exactly what questions she had typed in the computer that could reveal this to him. Meanwhile, Keriani continued making prayerful motions and chanting under her breath.

It was all too much—intoxicating aromas, the atmosphere, the crippled boy and the light that had flashed again. Who knows, Baba Dhyana may have slipped something into the food or that vial to weaken her defenses.

A tear ran down Niki's cheek. Keriani rose from her seat to give Niki a hug.

"It's been going on for a couple of months now," Niki confessed. "I've heard things and seen strange lights." Keriani looked up and in English said, "Thank you, Shiva, Krishna."

The Indian couple wouldn't take no for an answer. They insisted she come home with them rather than drive all the way to Jemez Springs. They were so concerned about Niki, they decided to close the restaurant for the evening, which made it even more difficult to say no.

Niki would not have been so trusting without Keriani's presence. Baba Dhyana was charming, but sly, and Niki still had no idea how he knew about her "awareness" as he called it. She had only entered Maitreya into his BBS program. Something was off, not right. She knew she should remain alert, but she also trusted Keriani completely.

They even suggested she leave her VW van on Harvard, but that was out of the question. Schroeder was in there. She had expected to stay only a couple of hours at the restaurant. So she insisted she follow them. It took awhile for them to load Tagore into their station wagon, and during that time she almost changed her mind. Again, following them to their house she had thoughts of veering off to I-25 and going back to the hostel. But she was tired, and still felt strange. The long drive probably wasn't a good idea.

The Dhyana home was just as colorful and unusual as the café. Icons, more embroidered wall hangings and shrines filled the house. The air was thick with incense and perfumed candles. The furniture was worn, but comfortable. Every inch of space seemed occupied with something—piles of books, clothing, Indian rugs and artifacts of all types. Beads and silk scarves hung from doorways.

Keriani took Niki into a special room the family used for prayer and meditation.

There was no furniture, only large pillows on top of many rugs on the floor.

"You may lie here and rest," Keriani suggested, then left Niki in the room. Beautiful gold-leafed paintings of various Hindu gods and goddesses adorned the walls. There was a shrine on top of a long, low wooden table. A white gauze scarf that looked like a Buddhist khata, covered the table top. Candles, wood carvings, gold statues and other Hindu icons and art were displayed. A large, ancient looking leather-bound book was lying near the shrine. Sitar music played in the background. The room was warm, and soon lulled her to sleep.

Niki woke to the sound of a bell or chime. The beautiful dark-haired woman was offering her a cup of chai.

"How long did I sleep?" Niki asked.

"A couple of hours," Keriani replied. "Have some chai and then we talk." She bowed and left the room.

A few minutes later the couple entered the room together, bowing again and gesturing to the shrine and icons. Niki felt a bit uncomfortable about sleeping in their prayer room. She also wondered what all had infiltrated her subconscious, since she was obviously so susceptible to ethereal influences.

"We're very curious," the Baba said, "why you ask of our Lord Maitreya. How do you know of the Cosmic Christ?"

"I didn't say Cosmic Christ, but I have been a Buddhist for many years."

"In Iowa?"

"I never said I was from Iowa." Niki wondered if she had back at the Bodhi Tree.

"Your vehicle plates."

"But I could have bought that bus anywhere."

"My dear," the Baba said, "you have a Midwest dialect."

Niki could not argue with that. "Are you aware of MIU, Maharishi International University there?" she asked.

"In fact, I do know of it," Swami-Baba said, a Cheshire grin revealing his iridescent white teeth.

"I have been to the fair fields."

His remark made Niki laugh out loud. The Maharishi had called Fairfield, a small town just a few miles from Ottumwa, the fair fields of Iowa when she covered MIU's original dedication ceremony. "Okay, so why would I not ask about the Maitreya. I've been exposed to the highest concentration of transcendental meditators on the planet."

Niki noticed Keriani making prayerful gestures again and felt she should remain calm and peaceful in her prayer room. Keriani seemed to read her thoughts and bowed her head slightly to Niki then asked, "What can you tell us of the lights and sounds around you?"

"Around me?" What an interesting way to phrase that, she thought. "You mean what happened when I saw your son, Tagore, and also at the VLA site?" Keriani nodded and Niki continued, "a flash of light hit me in the forehead. It happened before in Iowa, too."

The Indian woman bowed her head, touched her beads and began softly chanting. Baba Dhyana said, "She believes your third eye has been activated, making you a seer of sorts."

Baba Dhyana reached over to the altar and picked up a small gold box. It contained a thick, dark substance which smelled like extremely potent pot. Baba began packing it into an ornate gold pipe.

"Hashish," he said. Niki's eyes grew wide.

"In India, all spiritual discussions and auspicious occasions include a pipe of hashish. This is such an occasion."

Niki started to protest, but Keriani shook her head indicating it might be inappropriate to refuse. At the same time, something stirred within Niki. She got the sense her spirit friends might enjoy this. Baba lit the pipe and then handed it to Niki, who took a tiny puff. After a couple of rounds with the hashish pipe, Niki's defenses were down and the tutelary spirits were ready to reveal themselves.

Tagore is a permutation of Divine Spirit. Words were spewing uncontrollably from Niki's mouth. Keriani, of course, was praying, Baba looked intrigued, and Niki was stunned.

"What about Tagore?" Baba asked.

Mandir Ashram, Tagore is part of the Logia.

"The Logos?" Baba Dhyana looked perplexed.

"*Logos, Christos, Krishna—all are divine permutations,*" the words came out of Niki involuntarily. At that point Keriani keeled over, fainted. Baba Dhyana began rubbing his wife's arms to revive her. The shock of the scene seemed to bring Niki back to normal consciousness. When Keriani came to, she began to sob and spoke rapid Punjabi or Hindi or a combination of both.

"She is convinced now that you are in contact with Lord Krishna or perhaps even Sanat Kumara, one of Brahma's sons. Some call him the Logos, or Ancient of Days," Baba explained.

At some point the couple left to go to bed, and Niki must have dozed off from the hashish and stress of the events. Now she was alone in the room and it felt that from every wall, some Hindu icon was watching her. She stood up and stretched, then realized she desperately needed the restroom.

Niki tiptoed quietly out of the prayer room in search of their bathroom. The sight of smeared eye make-up and messy hair in the mirror confirmed she had to get out of here. She splashed a little water on her face and smoothed her wild locks, the best she could. On a scrap of paper she wrote a note and stuck it on their bathroom mirror:

Thank you for dinner. I'll log on to the BBS soon. Niki

∞

17 Dogon Doctors? R U Sirius?

Days passed and Niki did not log onto the Swami BBS. She knew the persuasive Baba would convince her to go to L.A. and for some inexplicable reason, she did not want to go—almost couldn't go. It made no sense. The timing would have been perfect. Her stay at the hostel would have been up. More importantly, when Niki left Iowa she was convinced that her mission—writing a peace treatise—centered on finding Benjamin Crème and the appearance of the Maitreya.

Logically, everything indicated she should attend the Day of Declaration event. Her inward communication was the same as Crème had described. No doubt he would speak of peace, perhaps the exact message she needed for her treatise, and now she even had a Swami guide and his lovely wife to escort her. It all seemed perfect, yet not.

There was only one thing to do. She had to find Koteen in the shamanic realm. His guidance was the only thing she could rely on.

What follows is a private entry from Niki's journal. The one she bought while traveling and began keeping just before she met Koteen:

May 13, 1982

I prepared the same way as usual for the journey—lit a white candle, placed blankets on the floor in my room, put the tape in my boombox and even danced around shaking the rattle, asking for protection and clarity.

I specifically asked for—summoned the hawk—to guide me, per the shamanic teachings. I wanted Koteen's help to figure out what to do next. As the drumming sounds took effect, I felt a lot of activity around my forehead. I couldn't stop thinking about Keriani saying my Third Eye had been activated. Is that true? I asked silently.

Almost immediately it felt as though I was swept into a tornado. I was swirling up and up into the Higher Realm. I saw the hawk fly past, but I was moving too fast. He tried to grab me with his beak, but I was gone, miles high. I sensed I might be in trouble but there was nothing I could do to stop myself. I was swirling out of control.

Suddenly everything stopped. I felt calm and everything was still and quiet. I don't recall hearing the drumming or any sound at all—just total silence. I sensed I was in "the eye of the storm." That term actually came into my mind. I was lying on the floor, but thought I should open my eyes, so I did. I couldn't have imagined what I would see.

There were three wispy, transparent figures in the room. One was on my left, another in the far corner of the room (by the door that led to the hall), and the third was hovering in the air over my legs. I wanted to scream but I couldn't.

I knew these ethereal entities were pure energy. I also knew I was not in a shamanic trance, because I could feel my finger nails digging into the palm of my right hand. The beings were translucent, filmy; more like vapor. *Not beings.* That thought came into my mind. "Not beings, not physical." They seemed pleased that I could understand their thoughts. They conveyed that they wanted to help me, not harm me. In fact, they could heal me.

We are Celestials. I understood this meant they were not ETs, not extraterrestrials. Celestial. An important distinction. They were pure energy and when I became anxious, I could sense their confusion.

Why are you afraid of us? They seemed totally surprised by my fear.

We are healers. We can help you.

Healing. I wondered what type of healing—mental? Had I finally flipped out and created Celestial counselors?

Physical healing, they corrected me. *We can adjust your spine and internal organs.*

That was such a shocking idea that I immediately sat straight up in sheer panic. In fact, I jumped up and ran out of the room.

That was the end of the notes as written in the journal. Niki was thankful that she had not encountered the hostel managers when she ran out of her room. They would have thought she'd seen a ghost.

Now, that's funny, Niki typed into her computer. The idea of seeing a ghost felt comforting after everything I've been through. She was typing up notes from her journal and other scribbling in her reporter notebook.

For some reason she felt she had to maintain an accurate account, almost an official record, of what was happening. She didn't know why, and couldn't explain it, any more than she could explain not going to Los Angeles to see Crème. It just seemed very important.

I've thought that since the first ear-buzz back in Iowa, she typed. Now with more Koteen encounters, the shamanic quests, and especially this odd experience with the Celestials, it seems critical to record the events. I can't risk losing the sensations of these experiences. I have to document all this.

It had taken a few days to summon up the courage to even write about it. There was something totally unnerving about Celestial "surgeons" wanting to tamper with her body. She had grown accustomed to spirits and shamans and even a Swami messing with her mind, but to think that an unseen force might actually be able to alter her physical organs was intolerable. Niki wanted to jump out of her own skin.

As she typed the notes and thoughts, new insights came. It was almost like automatic writing, especially when she typed on the computer keyboard.

This is a Transmission. That is what she heard in her mind. It was similar to what happened with the *I Ching* just before she left Iowa, only this was even more like taking dictation. Thought-messages flooded her mind. Incredible ideas and information came so rapidly she could barely keep pace, and she was a fast typist.

Niki understood the transmission process would be less threatening than any other form of communication. Seeing Celestials, even those sent to help her, was too frightening and disturbing. Just as guardian spirits were prohibited from manifesting, Celestials should not be invasive. Since Niki was a journalist, they indicated she could assimilate this type of communication; being a translator, an amanuensis of sorts—like taking dictation.

"Who is conveying this?" Niki actually asked aloud.

Consider it the Collective, came the response-thought. It was so clear. Sometimes entire ideas flashed through her mind and she had to summarize, but other times distinct phrases, like that, came to her.

If ever there was a time, she thought, now is the time for clarity. She could get to the bottom of all of it—why Nag Hammadi, the Maitreya, the peace treatise—everything!

Niki felt excited and no longer cared or worried about missing the L.A. trip. This was obviously just what she had been waiting for and why she needed to stay behind.

∞

Celestials? Phil wondered why they had not contacted him to clear up his endless speculation about VALIS and "what is" when he was alive.

"Maybe they did and you were just too dense to receive it, Phil," Pike laughed like the old days. A full-belly laugh.

Too dense. Both Pike and the Big Guy found that funny.

Phil did not.

May 18, 1982

Five days passed. Niki asked the hostel owners to let her renew her stay, since she had no place to go. They agreed, but said she couldn't stay much longer.

For now she told Bill she was using the phone connection for her "work" and just needed another week. It was work, of sorts. Staying allowed her to sit and type in a comfortable room using their electrical connection for her computer, and also gave her the option of logging back onto the BBS. She would do that soon, to see if the Dhyana family had returned from L.A.

Even with these new ways of "connecting" she still wanted to hear their thoughts about seeing Benjamin Crème, and what he had to say about the Maitreya's appearance. Not to mention, one of her transmitted messages warned "do not neglect Tagore."

18 a Midsummer's Mess

By the time preparations were underway for the Summer Solstice gathering at the Bodhi Tree, Niki had settled into a rhythm of typing her transmissions and spending time with the Dhyanas. She had moved to a sleazy motel near the café that was managed by friends of the Baba. But it was awful; not very clean, and too many bugs. She had to find a better place to live if she was going to remain in Albuquerque. For now, at least Schroeder had a supply of mice for food and entertainment.

Niki and Baba Dhyana sat at the Bodhi Tree enjoying a leisurely afternoon cup of chai, when a woman breezed in, making a red-carpet-award-show-worthy entrance as if she owned the place. Niki's psychic antennae instantly perked up. The Baba stood up and greeted the woman with his usual charm and debonair manner.

"Dora, dear," Baba basically gushed, "you must join us next week for the Solstice party. Have you met Nicole?" He graciously gestured toward Niki, who feigned a smile. Dora gave only a cursory glance and equally fake smile at Niki and then locked back on her target, the dashing turbaned one.

"Wouldn't miss it for the world," she replied and fluttered around for a few more minutes before asking, "and where is our dear Keriani?" The Baba excused himself and took Dora by the elbow, escorting her toward the back of the restaurant.

Isadora Kalbfleisch was known to everyone as Dora K, due to the complication of pronouncing her last name. Loosely translated it meant cold flesh. Niki thought that was a scream. Even funnier, she thought of her as the Dork. The woman had an entourage of UFO groupies who followed her around, waiting for her to utter something profound—like the latest instructions from Ashtar Command. Despite Niki's own odd insights, she found this peculiar.

Dora was a withering middle-aged woman who wore a short, bobbed brunette wig to hide her thin, graying hair. Her skin was as thin as tissue paper and was beginning to sag around her face and neck. Her long peaked face featured high cheekbones and a small turned-up nose. Too much eye make-up, rouge and painted pursed lips make her look like a skinny, dried-up Cupie doll.

"I don't like that woman," Niki said when Baba Dhyana returned. "Why did you invite her to the Solstice Gathering?"

Baba arched his right eyebrow beneath the turban.

"Her followers include many of the merchants from here on my street. Mr. Cramer who you admire so much, and the lovely Lena Moore who manages our neighborhood bazaar."

"Bizarre, is more like it, I'm sure."

"Now, now. Such talk is unbecoming of one who is in contact with our Lord and Master. Keriani thinks so highly of both of you. I believe you will like Lena. I'll introduce you to her and the others at the Solstice Gathering."

"Okay, but why would they follow the Dork?" Niki's new pet name for her.

"They need Dora, my dear."

"Need her? Why?" Niki asked.

"She is powerful and confident. My dear, not everyone is as self-reliant as you. They look to her for guidance and of course, her channeling of the Brotherhood."

"Powerful?" Niki couldn't get past that word, and didn't really hear anything else he said. "How did you meet her?" she asked as she sipped her chai.

Baba pulled out his leather pouch and began hand rolling a cigarette, supposedly of fine Turkish tobacco. He offered it to Niki who shook her head no.

"She, too, learned of my online BBS, and like you, she is in contact with the spirit world. I have read her channelings, and they appear authentic," he said taking a long drag from the thin cigarette. "Who am I to judge what is received from the other dimensions? There is room for many perspectives." Baba exhaled a small smoke ring as he inhaled Niki with his eyes.

Niki maintained the connection gazing back, directly into those dark portals of his soul and said, "I think she's a fake." She paused and added, "But I appreciate your point."

"Perhaps after the gathering, you will become the leader."

"Leader of what?" she asked. "Her Ashtar Command? No thanks. I've got my hands full with my own sources."

Niki had never told Baba, or Keriani, the whole story of how Koteen saw the co-mingled spirits in the Vision Quest, or that she continued to do some shamanic traveling of her own. And she had not revealed anything about her mission to write a peace treatise. If Baba and company knew all that they might build a shrine, or at least an altar, to her.

These thoughts made her smile. She didn't have to tell everyone her life story. And, if the Baba was such a Swami, he should know it all anyway.

"My dear, what are you thinking about?" Baba asked. "You've been gazing off for several minutes."

"I was just thinking about the messages and information I received while you were in L.A. Insights on discernment, and what's authentic—really real." She paused and again looked directly into the Baba's eyes. "I know one thing for sure—Dora is not."

Baba Dhyana leaned forward and in a hushed voice asked, "Do you have it with you? The recent transmission? I would love to see it."

"I'm sure you would," Niki laughed. "Not yet, Baba. You and I will have to come to terms first." She tossed back her waves of hair as Baba repositioned himself in the wicker chair puffing on his thin hand-rolled cigarette. Again, a single eyebrow arched. "What do you have in mind?" he asked.

Niki had been bluffing, but her ploy worked. Baba was reacting and appeared apprehensive. Now, more than ever, she suspected he could not be trusted.

"I can't reveal anything more until after the Solstice."

Baba Dhyana might have planned the Solstice event, but when Niki arrived at the Bodhi Tree, just before 7 o'clock on the evening of June 21, she found Keriani clearly in charge of the small gathering on Harvard Mall. Several neighboring store keepers had strung small, white twinkling lights in the shrubs and small curbside trees, at Keriani's request. The sun had not yet set, but Niki could see how charming it would become by twilight when the official festivities would begin.

Keriani had covered the round patio tables with crisp white linen and placed a candle in the center of each one. A larger rectangular table was also draped in white linen, outlined with greenery. It featured an ornately carved wooden centerpiece incorporating a three-tiered candle holder. Small figurines of the now-familiar Krishna, Vishnu and Shiva watched over the East Indian buffet.

Keriani, Mani, and some other helpers busily arranged the spicy, aromatic delights under the watchful eye of Tagore. He was the first to see Niki arrive, and tried to call to her. Within moments, Baba rushed up in his typical flamboyant manner, turbaned, bejeweled and sporting a new white Nehru jacket. On cue he began gushing over Niki and whisked her off to meet Dora's entourage of paranormal protégés.

"Niki, my dear, let me introduce you to Lena Moore." Baba bowed and gestured to a young woman about Niki's age. Lena extended her hand and surprised Niki with a firm, confident hand shake. She also made direct, intense contact with her translucent blue eyes. Lena had straight, chin-length dishwater blonde hair, which slightly cupped under at the ends, but mostly swung back and forth keeping time with her rhythmic motions.

"My pleasure," Lena offered. To Niki's surprise, Lena had a deep authoritative and well-modulated voice to match the handshake. "I'm from the Health Garden, just around the corner."

"You work there?" Niki inquired, forgetting or perhaps never really hearing Baba's earlier account of her.

"Actually, I manage it. It's a lot of work, but I enjoy it."

"Impressive," Niki said with a nod of approval.

"More importantly," Baba cut in, "Lena is in contact with Monka, the technical leader of the Space Brothers."

Niki's smile took a kamikaze dive. "Ashtar?" was all she could muster. Lena didn't flinch.

"An interdimensional entity, not a little green man," Lena clarified as if that made it perfectly normal.

"So, how did you come into contact with… um, sorry, what was the name again?"

"Monka. The Space Brothers have been monitoring Earth changes since the 1940s." Lena stated matter-of-factly.

"And, how does he—it—communicate with you?"

"Telepathically," Lena replied without missing a beat.

Given Niki's proclivity for co-mingled ethereal entities and a shamanic-hawk boyfriend, she really had no reason to be judgmental. What amazed Niki was how Lena seemed perfectly comfortable making such fantastic claims. Baba wasted no time mentioning Niki's predicament.

"Niki, dear, aren't you in contact with the Brotherhood?"

Physically backing up from both of them to create distance, Niki responded. "I really don't know for sure what's happening with me, but I don't think it's spacemen."

"Well, my understanding from the transmissions I have received," Lena began, "is that the Space Brothers *are* part of the Brotherhood of Light. The transmissions are the language of Light. Baba Dhyana told me you are receiving them too. Is that true?"

Transmissions! Language of Light. Lena sure knew the lingo. Baba has put her up to this, Niki suspected.

"Lena, if you could excuse us for just a moment." Niki took his arm and said, "We promised Keriani to help set up those…" She had stopped as soon as they were out of ear shot and began the interrogation. "How much did you tell her? She's using terms I received." Niki's green eyes flared and her face flushed with color making her resemble the brightly colored deities on the Hindu wall hangings.

"Very little, my dear," Baba said looking surprised. "I may have mentioned transmissions, but no details."

"Baba, I'm trying to figure out what's authentic and what's being manipulated. And, as of now the jury is still out on you, Lena and that, that awful Dora." Niki was visibly shaking and fighting to hold back tears. She stomped off toward her van with an overwhelming craving for a cigarette.

When she glanced back, Baba was still watching her. She slowly turned and sheepishly walked back towards him.

Baba pulled out his pouch of tobacco and began rolling a cigarette. When he was done he handed the thin perfectly hand-rolled smoke to Niki. "Turkish tobacco, nothing more, I assure you. It might calm your nerves."

Niki took a puff and handed it back. She started to speak, but Baba interrupted.

"I did not compromise your privacy or reveal the nature of your messages. I simply told Lena that you two have much in common and should meet."

"Why did she say that I was in contact with the Space Brothers?"

"My dear, the night you stayed at our home your source revealed that Tagore is imprinted by the Logos— the Ancient of Days. In our beliefs, the Maitreya is the Lord of all. And, as you, or rather your source confirmed, all of these entities are the same. Divine permutations, I believe was the term." Baba took a long, slow drag from the cigarette, waiting for Niki's reaction.

"So, Baba, you believe that Lena and Dora's Ashtar aliens are the same as Maitreya or Krishna? Niki reached for Baba's cigarette but it was gone.

"People perceive their religious experiences differently. Some see the Blessed Virgin Mary, others see Krishna or hear transmissions as you have. Another envisions an angel or a Space Brother. We all have our filters." He arched his brow and shrugged.

Niki recalled saying something similar to Bruce, in what seemed a lifetime ago.

∞

19 Chaco Time

The Health Garden was ahead of its time. With just a bit more work it could have easily been the most popular place in the University area. The location was ideal—easy walking distance from the campus.

Lena had created just the right blend of home-made food, teas, and juice drinks, long before most people were health conscious. There was even a special section for vendors to set up booths and provide anything from shoulder and back massages, to tarot card readings, or demonstrations of herbal remedies. The concept was terrific, but the building was run down, in need of paint and repair. The kitchen was clean, but the furniture in the dining area was shabby. As a result, there were too many street people and loiterers, and not enough paying customers.

Lena had asked Niki to stop by for lunch so they could continue their discussion of their mutual experiences. She wanted to see the transmissions. Niki still had no idea why she was keeping such a formal record of them, but she had them organized, both electronically and in print-outs, by date.

Niki ordered a frozen juice drink and read through the most recent transmissions wondering if she really should share them. It wasn't like her journalistic writing or the type of language she used when writing newspaper or free-lance articles.

In fact, Niki didn't think of them as her writing at all. She hadn't written them. She just typed what she heard and received in her mind. As she read the messages, she was still amazed at the insights and revelations.

Most intriguing was the continuity of the work. Regardless of how much time elapsed between sessions, the messages always flowed and picked up just where they left off, further validating that "time does not exist," at least in the realm of her unseen entities.

"Sorry I couldn't get over here sooner," Lena apologized as she sat down at Niki's table. "We had a busy lunch rush today. How are you?" Lena said, and appeared ready to give Niki all her attention now.

"No problem," Niki assured her. "I'm not on a schedule these days."

"That's right. You're not working, are you? How do you manage, if you don't mind me asking?"

"Well, I'm kind of on sabbatical," Niki explained. "I will return to my job in Iowa this fall."

"I sure wish I could take some time off," Lena sighed. "I usually work twelve-hour days. I have trouble making enough to hire people, and then sometimes they rip me off." Lena looked exhausted. Niki thought of making some suggestions about sprucing up the place, then decided against it.

"I'm sure the restaurant business is very demanding," she offered instead.

"At least I can take a break now, and I'm dying to see some of your transmissions. May I?" Lena asked, eyeing the stack of papers.

"Sure. I still don't know what to think of them, but I guess you know what I mean." Niki hoped that was true, but there was no response. Lena was already reading, and in no time appeared deeply absorbed in the material, pausing only to offer an occasional "wow" or "that's incredible."

Niki sipped her drink and watched Lena's changing facial expressions as she read the material. At one point, Lena stopped and said, "This is quantum theory, the same ideas Monka has been teaching us. Especially this statement about photons and light being neither wave nor particle matter. It's the technology they use on the ship."

"What ship?" Niki asked.

"The mother ship uses photon power," Lena said, still skimming over Niki's pile of papers.

"Why do they need a ship if they aren't in physical form?"

"They're in another dimension, but they still have light bodies made of photons instead of molecular matter like us," Lena assured her. Niki wanted to challenge that point, since the Celestials had been clear about not having bodies. Before she could Lena revealed, "The Celestial Fleet returned to earth orbit on June 2."

"You learned that from Monka?" Niki asked.

"He's the Technical Master of Ashtar Command," Lena told her, apparently noticing Niki's peculiar expression. "I guess it sounds crazy to you, right?"

Niki wanted to say totally insane, but in view of her own bizarre experiences, how could she? "I'm still uncomfortable with all of this, but you seem reconciled to the process; that someone named Monka, a Space Brother, is teaching you about photons and quantum physics?"

"How else would I know or understand this stuff?" Lena asked. "I see similar references in your transmissions. Where is it coming from?"

"I don't know. That's why I keep asking. I've been told Universal Consciousness or VALIS, the Vast Active Living Intelligence System."

"Yes, but what about the Celestials? I read the part where they told you they could heal you. You know they are from Sirius, right?"

"What?"

"The Celestials are the ancestors, the Original Ones, of the Dogon tribe in Africa. You know, the alien astronauts who taught the Egyptians how to build pyramids and created those huge runways and drawings in Nazca, Peru."

Niki was speechless.

"You are such a newbie," Lena laughed. "Read *Chariots of the Gods?* or *the Sirius Mystery*. You'll see."

"I have read Von Daniken, but I don't think it confirms anything. He asked a lot of questions. Even the title of his book is a question," Niki said recalling discussions of that book in the same class where she learned of Gribbin.

Niki had reluctantly come to the Health Garden thinking Lena would be too kooky to take seriously. Instead, here was someone who understood exactly what she was experiencing. She liked Lena, and Baba was right, we each have our own perceptions and filters. After so many years of suppressing and trying to downplay her special abilities, it seemed everyone around her was aware of other dimensions and realities. Was she trading in scientific reasoning for magical thinking?

If Phil had a body and a cup of coffee, he would have spit it all over Bishop Pike. That's really rich, he thought. "Honey, that ship has sailed." The dynamic duo had refrained from further overt intrusion or commentary. They had, however, been insinuating a few concepts into the transmissions.

They were not the sole source of the messages. Niki was a clear channel, a finely tuned receiver for every entity that wanted to transmit: Sirian Celestials, shamanic spirits—ghost sickness, Koteen called it. That gave Phil a soul shiver. He and Pike had started it, but she had other kindred spirits now—allies on both sides of the veil, something he had not achieved in life. He had felt so alone in his quest for truth.

∞

July 2, 1982

Niki wanted to do something special for her 28th birthday. She had been spending a lot of time with Lena and was actually enjoying it. So, she went to the Health Garden near closing time on Friday night. Niki drank an herbal tea while she waited for Lena to finish up. As the two women were leaving Niki said, "My birthday is coming up and I've been thinking about going to Chaco Canyon. Would you want to go up there?"

"Chaco is one of my favorite places. I love the Grand Kiva. Have you been in it?" Lena asked, but before Niki could answer continued, "What day do you want to go? When is your birthday?"

"It's a week from Sunday, July 11. That's why I thought it might work."

"That would be fun! We can do a moonlight ceremony in the Kiva." Lena added, "But even sooner, can we go to your motel and try asking some questions on your computer?" She paused, "I was thinking maybe Monka would come through. I don't write down insights I receive, other than a few notes. I'm always worried that Chuck will find them."

"Chuck? I thought you said you were seeing a guy named Jake."

"My ex. During the divorce, he threatened to tell the judge I was incompetent to keep my daughter because I talked to space aliens. After that I never put anything else in writing, not even notes. I would love to try your computer and see what happens."

"Sure, we can try." Niki had no idea that decision would mark such a significant turning point in her quest.

∞

July 11, 1982

"Does this thing have air conditioning?" Lena asked as she fanned herself. It was high Noon and the hot summer sun was unbearable.

"At least it's not humid," Niki offered.

"Yeah, I know, dry heat. But when it's over a hundred, you can forget that theory." Lena replied.

Niki recalled a cold, bleak day back in Iowa when Bruce asked if the Z had a heater. Now she was in the desert, but New Mexico not Egypt. This time Lena was in the passenger seat, and Schroeder was back in Corrales at Lena's house. The two women had a tent, sleeping bags and all the gear to camp out at Chaco Canyon.

"Lena, what was that book, the one about Sirius?" Niki asked. "That one's not by Von Daniken, is it?"

"No, I can't remember the guy's name—oh Temple, duh!" she laughed at the irony. "He did extensive research, probably because of Von Daniken's questions."

"Does he mention the Celestials and link them to Sirius?"

"I can't remember. We can find a copy for you when we get back," Lena said pulling out some granola and trail mix for them. "Maybe we'll get our own answers tonight in the Kiva."

"What do you think will happen?" Niki wondered aloud. "Do you really think we'll see a UFO? I hear there are still lots of sightings in northern New Mexico."

"I hope so." Lena said, "I'd go in a heartbeat if I got the chance. Would you?"

"With them?" Niki had to think about that. "I used to say I would, but now I'm not so sure." She thought of how anxious she felt when she saw the Celestials.

"Oh, I'd give anything to see Monka," Lena was practically drooling. "I envision him wearing a helmet with an insignia on it." Lena had tilted her head back and closed her eyes. "He looks human, with white hair and blue eyes."

"Human?" Niki reacted. "If the Space Brothers are Celestials, they're not human or physical at all. They're pure energy. Light beings. Photons, remember?"

Lena responded, but Niki didn't hear her. For the first time in a month, she felt her ear buzzing. Before she could stop herself she blurted, *Ecstatic union with the macro-isomorphic vortex. Not human.*

Lena stopped whatever she was saying. Her mouth hung open as she stared at Niki.

Find the Tractates. The Cryptica Scriptura, Niki, actually the Voice coming from her, said.

"Who is speaking to us?" Lena asked.

Dico per spiritum sanctum. (I speak via the Holy Spirit.) With that, Niki pulled the van to the side of the road. She was holding her head and rocking back and forth in the driver's seat. "My head. I've got a splitting headache," she said.

"I have an aspirin," Lena offered digging frantically in her bag.

Despite the sweltering heat, Niki felt chilled and curled up on the Westfalia's small sofa. She took the aspirin, and within minutes fell asleep. Lena got in the driver's seat and continued on toward Chaco. She could only drive about ten miles per hour over the deeply rutted, washboard road. Even with all the shaking and noise, Niki slept.

"Niki, wake up," Lena said excitedly. "Look. It's the Grand Kiva."

Niki felt totally disoriented, as if she had been drugged. When she finally focused her eyes and sat up, she saw ruins before her.

"Nag Hammadi?" she asked.

"No, silly. Chaco," Lena said. "We're here."

"Chaco?" Niki asked as if it was a foreign language. Niki had no recollection of where she was. Her mind was full of strange images—foreign-looking men digging in the sand; dusty, musty smells that all seemed hauntingly familiar. When she looked around and saw the interior of the van her pulse quickened.

"What is this? Who are you?"

"Stop joking," Lena said. "You're scaring me."

"Who are you?" Niki asked again wide-eyed.

"Niki, what is the matter with you?"

"Why are you calling me Niki?"

"Because you *are* Niki Perceval. I am Lena Moore. What is going on with you?"

Nothing the strange woman said made any sense to...

"My name is James," a voice said. "I came here to study the dig. We were lost. Where is Diane?"

"Who is Diane?" Lena asked.

"My wife."

Lena had no idea how to handle that. Clearly one of the spirits had taken control of Niki, but despite all her "training" with Dora K, Lena was at a total loss for what to do.

"Okay, James. Something has happened," Lena said. "I'll try to help. Where were you when you got lost?"

"In the wadi, near the dig site. Where am I now?"

"What year is it?" Lena asked.

"Year?" the voice from Niki sounded indignant. "1969, of course. Where am I? Where is Diane?"

1969! Lena felt scared and decided she better try harder to get Niki back.

"Niki. NIKI!" she yelled hoping to jolt her companion back to reality.

"Help me. Please help me," the voice was very weak this time. Lena shook Niki hard.

"Niki. It's Lena. Can you hear me."

Lena saw something change in Niki's eyes. Niki slumped against the van's sofa cushion then twitched, or kind of jerked. A minute or so later, she opened her eyes.

"Are we here?" Niki asked, stretching and getting up from the van sofa. "Did I sleep a long time?"

Lena said nothing, just stared in disbelief.

"Lena, what's the matter with you?" Niki asked. "You look like you saw a ghost."

"You don't know what just happened?"

"No, I was sleeping. What?"

"Someone was speaking through you."

"Oh yeah?" Niki rubbed her forehead, which still hurt a bit. "I was dreaming of a place in Egypt. At first, it was like biblical times with monks writing and working. Then it changed to ruins. It was very vivid and realistic."

"Do you remember anyone named James or Diane?"

"No. Why?"

"While you were dreaming, James was talking through you."

"What did he say?" Niki didn't seem too alarmed that a disembodied voice had spoken through her.

"It wasn't biblical times," Lena said. "He said it was 1969 and he was lost."

"1969?" For a moment Niki thought it must have just been one of those chaotic dreams where times and locations are all superimposed, but then her ear buzzed. Thoughts of Egypt, Sumeria, and Persian stargazers flooded her mind.

"I've got it, Lena!" she said. "I know why the Egyptians and other cultures were building those mysterious monoliths. They were used for transmitting back to their homeland. I actually saw the Nommo, the three-eyed sea creatures that evolved into the Dogon people. They did come from Sirius!" Niki was saying things that previously she would have only typed, and a bit skeptically, during a transmission session.

"Now I get it. James is the older man I've heard. The one I've called a rabbi. He wants me to know that lost Zadokite fragments will explain everything—the mysterious missing Q, the Ancient of Days—it's their historical record."

Lena just listened, wide-eyed as a Nommo. Niki recalled earlier thoughts about a scientist and rabbi who were unable to finish their work. Ideas kept crashing down. The guys were cut off somehow—

"It's so obvious now. It was two guys. They were killed, or died together. That is why they are tangled up in the after-life," she exclaimed. "Why didn't I see this sooner? Perhaps an archeologist and a theologian, on a real mission. A dig. They kept trying to get me to understand about their mission. It makes perfect sense."

Sort of, Phil thought and could sense Pike's agreement. Niki Perceval was closer than either of them had been to digging up the Truth. She was right about the importance of the Zadokite findings, and the mysterious "Q", that Christians have called the source material.

Phil could see that one person couldn't solve the entire puzzle. Omniscient as he was, there was always something left to ponder about the Unknowable. Dogon!

∞

PART THREE - The Truth Shall Set You Free!

"It isn't senseless drive,
or brute instinct that keeps us restless and dissatisfied.
It's the highest goal of man—
the need to know, and grow and advance…
find new things, new experiences…
to break out of mindless monotony…
to keep moving on."

Solar Lottery
-- Philip K. Dick

20 Sedona Regained

"I was abducted and taken to their ship," Lena said. "So I know for a fact that Ashtar Command exists."

The girls were sitting in the big open living room of Lena Moore's house in Corrales, sipping herbal tea. Niki felt like a prisoner, with no choice but to listen to these absurd stories. After the trip to Chaco, Lena had convinced her to move in for awhile and stay with her. It made sense, instead of spending so much money staying at the sleazy motel.

The sprawling old adobe home was in Corrales, a quaint rural community located just a few miles north of Albuquerque. It had been a hippie settlement in the late 1960s, and evolved into a Taos-type artisan community by 1982. The adobe stucco house, a few dilapidated out buildings, and many huge cottonwood trees sat on five acres of land. It all belonged to Jake.

Jay "Jake" Christiansen was Lena's on-again, off-again lover. Niki had not met him since he was in California.

Lena called him a "lead scout" for a new technology company that might locate in the Albuquerque area, and said he was making a lot of trips back and forth. He wouldn't be back again until September.

For all Niki knew he could be hiding from Lena, who seemed to be getting crazier by the hour. But it was free room and board, and Lena only wanted one thing in exchange. She wanted Niki to tune in to the cosmic forces whenever the Mother ship was close by.

It seemed like fun at first, and given Niki's dwindling financial resources, had saved her from an early return to the *Courier.* It also gave Schroeder a place to roam and get back to his alley cat ways. Niki was already feeling some anxiety about how and when she could leave.

"When did all this happen, Lena? I thought you wanted to go on a ship, and meet Monka, but—"

"I wasn't going to tell you because I know you think it sounds crazy, but I was impregnated by one of the greys," Lena confessed. "It was Monka and the Space Brothers that saved me. That's why I feel such a connection to them."

Lena could tell fantastic tales, such as this one, the way other women could whip up a batch of chocolate chip cookies.

"You're right," Niki replied, "that does sound crazy." For the first time in weeks she felt an intense craving for a cigarette. "I realize that anything is possible, especially given my experiences. But are you saying that you had sex with an alien?"

"It wasn't like sex," Lena explained. "Greys don't have sex organs like ours. It was some kind of injection."

"What happened to the baby?" Niki asked, afraid to make eye contact with Lena the Lunatic.

"The Space Brothers caused me to have a miscarriage. That was when I first knew about Monka," Lena wiped her eye. "I didn't *see* him, but he communicated what had happened. They saved me."

Niki slouched deep into the couch and wished she could hide there. The story was a slight improvement over the previous mental picture of Lena and a bug-eyed gray alien going at it. "How often do they communicate with you? The Space Brothers, I mean."

"There hasn't been much communication. After Chuck got the injunction and took my daughter Luci, I've been running the health store for Jake and trying to prove I'm a fit mother."

Niki was tempted to tell her that any talk of alien miscarriages would almost assure she would never see little Luci again, but thought it best to stay out of that business.

"You know, Nik, I've been thinking that maybe we need to go to Sedona," Lena suggested. "There are powerful vortexes there and I believe it may be like an Earth-base for Ashtar. I've wanted to go back."

"Sedona!," Niki said sitting up. "I didn't know that you had spent time in Sedona. Did I tell you that I went through there before I settled here in Albuquerque?"

"That's probably why you receive such a strong signal from Sirius. Ashtar uses the underground electromagnetic ley lines in Sedona to amplify their transmission signals. I bet it has something to do with Valis also."

"Like what?" Niki wondered.

"Well, why did you go there? I'm sure you were guided there so the signals could be strengthened," Lena insisted. "Don't you think it's odd that we've both been there and we both receive information from Sirius?"

Lena had made a quantum leap that Niki wasn't sure she followed. "I went because I met an American Indian guy in Flagstaff who said he could take me on a tour. He took me to Boynton Canyon—"

Lena interrupted. "Boynton Canyon is *the* most powerful vortex there. I'm sure it was no coincidence that he appeared and took you there. He was sent by your guides."

Niki was tempted to describe what she had learned during the shamanic Vision Quest, but feared a tsunami of wackiness would ensue, so she shrugged and just said, "probably."

"A guide! A physical guide. Nik, these things don't just happen. It's fate, meant to be. We have to go to Sedona!"

With Lena convinced that Niki had been guided to her and Sedona, there was no way to stop the inevitable. Actually, Niki liked the idea. After all, she might see Koteen again.

"When do you want to go?" Niki asked. Anticipating the answer, in unison they squealed, "the full moon."

∞

The next full moon was August 4th, a Wednesday. The girls started gathering and packing camping gear days ahead, and left early on a Sunday to make sure they got a perfect camp site by a stream.

"See, isn't this much better?" Lena said, tapping the air conditioning vent on the dash of her near-new 1980 Subaru wagon as they barreled down I-40 West flying past Gallup and toward Flagstaff.

"Your bus is cool, but not cool enough for August heat," Lena smiled at her play on words. "And, did you know the Subaru logo is the same as the Pleiadian star badge? I found out…"

Niki was thinking of Koteen, and wondering if they would stop at the same truck stop, where she first met him. She missed the entire story about the seven sister star cluster.

The camping gear was packed in the back of the wagon and once again Schroeder was back at Lena's with one of her employees who was house-sitting.

Niki had the copy of *The Sirius Mystery* on her lap. Lena bought it for her as a birthday gift after she had spewed the Nommo info at Chaco. Niki was amazed that it was written by an English scholar and member of the Royal Astronomical Society, like Gribbin. Odder still, it did theorize about, and describe, ancient aliens from Sirius.

The author, Robert Temple, claimed Earth was visited by an advanced race in 4500 BC. Babylonians, Egyptians and an obscure tribal group known as the Dogons, and that all had the same astronomical knowledge that they couldn't possibly have known without such intervention. The most profound claim for Niki was his conclusion that a form of interstellar telepathy between Earth and Sirius had been established. Mystics and shamans have been "tuning into that channel" ever since.

"I can feel it, can't you?" Lena asked getting excited.

"The interstellar connection?" Niki asked.

"I meant the pull of the vortices, but interstellar sounds good, too."

Lena wanted to stop for lunch at a place in Flagstaff called Black Bart's. It was supposedly famous, but looked like a seedy old saloon. It was a saloon and steakhouse. Bart had been a Wild West stagecoach robber. They had made good time, arriving there before noon. Lena also wanted to get to the canyon by early afternoon, so they didn't loiter long at Bart's big old barn. They had steak sandwiches to provide protein and energy for an afternoon of hiking and camping.

They were back on the road in less than an hour, heading south on Highway 89 toward Sedona and the descent into Oak Creek Canyon. The familiar red rock walls of the canyon became more dramatic with each twist and turn.

"Now, you feel something, don't you?" Lena asked.

"I think I do," Niki replied, swooning a bit. It could have been the change in altitude, or one of several electro-magnetic vortexes found in Sedona.

"I think we should hike into Boynton Canyon and camp there tonight. It will be incredible."

"Sure." Niki did not protest. "Do you know how to get into the Canyon?"

"Are you kidding?" Lena winked at Niki, "I practically lived back there a couple of years ago. We can't take any of the four-wheeling short cuts, but I can get us in through Dry Creek Road."

Soon some of the famous, spectacular Sedona red rock formations came into view. Niki had missed most of this last time taking Koteen's short-cut. Six miles on washboard road, similar to the drive into Chaco Canyon, took more than thirty minutes. Eventually a dirt parking lot came into view, and sure enough, there was a sign that read: Boynton Canyon Trail #47.

"This is it!" Lena cheered and clapped her hands. "Let's get our back packs together."

The girls took bottles of water, bed rolls on light aluminum frames, flash lights, and as much food as they could cram into the back packs.

"It will get chilly tonight, so bring your jacket." Lena tied hers around her waist, and so did Niki, who already felt loaded down. She was still contemplating an umbrella. Lena had already started toward the trail. "Are you coming?" she called back to Niki. Even though it was over 70 degrees and picture perfect, the sky was full of billowy cumulous clouds. Niki thought that far off, to the west, some looked darker.

"Do you think it will rain? Look at the sky."

"C'mon," Lena yelled. "It always looks like that."

Niki grabbed an umbrella anyway. She could use it as a walking stick. She slammed down the trunk and hurried to catch up with Lena.

The first couple of miles were fairly easy—dirt paths, slight inclines, and only occasional rocks blocking their way. At some point the path gave way to mostly rocks and a much steeper incline. Then, just as had happened on the hike with Koteen, they approached a ridge that meant climbing a very steep rock face. The weight of the back pack made it much harder to maintain her balance. After a half-hour of this, they found a ledge where they could rest and drink water.

"Are we going to the ruins?" Niki asked.

"What ruins?"

"The Anasazi ruins," Niki replied, surprised that Lena didn't know about them. "The rock wall with caves and glyph drawings. I saw them with Koteen."

"Wow, they must be sacred Indian grounds," Lena said, intrigued. "Do you think you could find them?"

"Maybe, once we start hiking, if I see anything familiar."

Soon they were on a precipitous rock ledge, and Niki's fear of heights got to her.

"I can't do this," Niki protested. "Not with this back-pack."

"Sure you can. Just don't look down." Lena was in the lead and just continued forging ahead.

"No, I'm serious." Niki had stopped and was clinging to the rock wall for dear life.

"Nik, look, just around the edge of this rock wall will be a new level. Come on."

"Lena, you do it, then tell me how far it is and what's over there." Niki felt angry and stupid for allowing herself to be in such a predicament. She should have remembered how scared she was when Koteen had her crawling along these ledges. But he could have saved her. Now she had the extra weight, plus the umbrella dangling from the frame of the backpack, where she had hooked it. There was no way she could see herself making it around that ledge. Niki heard rocks sliding and a moan from Lena.

"What's happened?" Niki called out.

"I twisted my ankle," Lena yelled back. Her voice wasn't too far away. "There's a big opening around here if you can just get to it."

Niki felt a strong sense to turn back, but she didn't have keys to Lena's car and wouldn't be able to get help. She wasn't sure she could find the car anyway. There didn't seem to be any other option. She mustered every ounce of courage and inched her way along the sheer drop-off. The loose rock was the worst part. Every step was agony as she clung to the rock face.

After several minutes, that felt more like an hour, she made it to the opening—just a wide spot on the ledge, they couldn't stay there. Once she stopped shaking, Niki checked out Lena's ankle. It wasn't swelling. They needed to rest and assess their options. Just removing the backpack was a huge relief. They ate some of Lena's nature bars and contemplated their next move.

Niki could see that they would either have to continue crawling along a rock ledge or attempt to descend into the canyon

"Look. See that place below?" Lena was pointing to a flat open area about 50 feet down. "We can drop the bags and climb down there."

"You think you can climb down?" Niki asked.

"Here watch." Lena tossed her back pack and clambered down favoring her right ankle. With no other choice, Niki tossed her pack, then the umbrella, and somehow got down the rocky ledge with only a minor scrape.

Once on solid ground, Niki dug into her pack for some ointment and bandages. She doctored her scrapes and wrapped Lena's ankle, then repacked her bag. The umbrella became Lena's cane. They continued to explore and search for a campsite.

By late afternoon they finally reached the bottom of the canyon and found a shady spot close to the creek. It was the ideal spot they had hoped to find.

"Thank god," Niki said. "I'm totally exhausted." She dropped the backpack and collapsed on the grass. "I sure hope there's an easy way out of here tomorrow," she added, rolling over on her back. That was when she saw the dark clouds straight overhead. "Oh no, Lena, look at that."

After seeing the clouds, Lena stopped rubbing her ankle and looked worried too. "We'll have to ask Monka to keep us safe. The only other option is to start climbing back out now."

Neither of them could imagine that. And, the sun was long hidden from view by the huge rock walls of Boynton Canyon. So the girls rolled out their sleeping bags on the aluminum mats, and didn't even bother to put up the tiny tent Lena had packed. They rested and ate snacks Lena had brought from the Health Garden.

"Let's visualize the clouds clearing out," Lena said. "In fact, we should do a ceremony and ask for protection."

Niki had gotten up and in the fading light tried to survey the area, just in case they needed an escape route. She could hear Lena beginning to chant. Then she heard what sounded like a drum. When she got back to Lena, a campfire was in full blaze and it was much darker. Niki heard the sound again, and knew it was not a drum.

"Lena, that's thunder!"

"Didn't Monka say they would activate the ley lines?"

Niki ignored her, more concerned with the flashing sky. In Iowa they called it heat lightning—flashes that lit up the sky instead of bolts. Each of these flashes illuminated the entire canyon.

"See, that's the ships. Remember when we stood in that field out by my house and Monka flashed messages at us?"

Niki actually did recall the incident. On that night, it had seemed as though their questions were answered with each progressive flash. It had been like a laser light show. She could only hope it would remain as harmless tonight, but her intuition told her otherwise. Niki wanted to run, but there was no place to take cover. Moments later, a dangerous looking bolt followed by a loud cracking sound hit much too close to the canyon. Sprinkles of rain followed.

At first it was just a light rain and Lena reached for the umbrella.

"No," Niki warned. "An umbrella is like a lightning rod, attracting it to us." Soon the rain was a torrent, giving them no choice but to huddle together on one makeshift bed and use the other mat as a canopy to fend off the downpour. The heavy rain completely drowned out the fire.

"It will stop soon, I'm sure," Lena said, reminding Niki she had been in Sedona during storms before.

"But you weren't on the canyon floor," Niki said, already suspecting that the creek was overflowing. They were getting soaked and she felt water seeping up from below.

"We have to move," Niki said. "Now!"

In unison they stood up. The next tremendous flash of lightning confirmed Niki's fears. She could see water rushing toward them from what had been a small creek.

"Shit, Lena, it's a flash flood." There was no arguing about it now. The situation was bad. They were in a canyon and the water was rising fast.

"We have to get to higher ground right now," Niki insisted. They grabbed a few essential items, and abandoned the soaked bedding.

"Get your flash-light," Niki yelled as she pawed through the bag for her own.

Running in the direction she had found earlier, Niki wriggled into the backpack and tied her nylon jacket over her head for protection. Lena was still using the umbrella as a cane and had trouble keeping up with Niki who was already scrambling up a rock ledge.

"Be careful," she called back to Lena. Her favorite hiking boots felt sloshy and she had no idea where she had stepped. Niki certainly didn't want to twist her own ankle on the rocks. "Can you make it up this ledge?" she called to Lena, waving her flashlight to keep the path illuminated.

Something scurried past, and Niki almost dropped the light. Some sort of animal. This was going to be awful getting out of here. Lena was shining her light around, too, trying to find the best way to join Niki. They finally found a path and scratched and climbed their way up a slope and away from the rising water.

"This doesn't look or feel like the way we came in. What if we're just going deeper into the canyon?" Lena asked.

"It's the only way we have for now," Niki said, glad that the downpour had let up. They had been climbing out for at least an hour.

"I've got to rest my ankle," Lena said. They both dropped their packs, which were not as heavy without the bedding.

Niki wanted a drink, but could not find her canteen.

"Here, use mine," Lena offered. "Just remember, that's all we have now." As Niki gulped a couple of swallows, she felt the familiar ear buzzing sensation. She silently vowed to listen more carefully and help the spirits, if they would just get her and Lena out of this predicament.

Help is on the way, she heard very clearly in her mind.

When they came to a ridge where there were two paths, Niki closed her eyes and felt guided to the right.

"This way, Lena. I feel certain it's this way." Niki took the lead and within a few minutes there was a path to follow.

"Why didn't you use your guides earlier?" Lena asked.

"As I recall, we were following yours," Niki said without missing a beat. "Isn't that how we got into the whole mess?" Lena had no response to that.

The path was muddy, but it was more distinct than some they had been on. Niki simply had to believe the spirits were guiding them to safety. Within a few more yards she saw a clearing, and that led to a gravel road.

"Thank you!" she cheered.

"This isn't where my car is parked," Lena worried.

"At least we're on a road." Niki closed her eyes and tried to sense what to do next. "To the left now," she said. "I feel this will lead us to someone or something."

They walked in silence along the gravel road for about half a mile.

"Could I please have one more sip of water," Niki asked. She knew the half-bottle was all they had, so she took a single sip and offered it back to Lena who did the same.

Both were covered in mud, still soaked all the way through, and had been hiking for nearly two hours since they left the canyon floor. That meant they had been hiking at least six hours since early afternoon. Niki felt it in every muscle, too. At times she didn't think she could take one more step.

It must be about eight by now, Niki thought, but couldn't see her mud-caked watch. She wanted to just sit down on the road and have a good cry. Just then, she saw a light.

"Do you see that?" she asked Lena.

"It's moving toward us," Lena said. Then more excitedly, she added. "It's a vehicle!"

"Help. Here! HELP!" they both screamed and waved their lights wildly.

The jeep approached flashing a blinding search light. The vehicle stopped and a uniformed man jumped out.

"Looks like you girls are in trouble," the man said. Niki didn't care if he was a cop or ranger, she was just glad to see someone with a badge and more importantly, a vehicle.

"We've been walking for hours. Can we please get in?" Niki could hardly wait for a warm place to sit and rest.

"We can't find my car," Lena added.

"Hop in," the man said. "I'm Tom with the park service." He helped the girls into the back of the vehicle then asked, "Where did you park?"

"Boynton Canyon trail head #47. In the lot," Lena told him.

Niki's teeth were chattering and she was shivering. "I felt hot awhile ago," she explained.

"Signs of hypothermia," Ranger Tom said, looking at them through his rearview mirror. "You girls probably need medical attention. How long were you in the storm?"

"We were in the canyon when it started," Niki told him adding, "Lena hurt her ankle and then our camp site was flooded."

"Bad flooding down there," the ranger nodded. "Worst in ten years. You were lucky to get out. We've got volunteers helping us with search and rescue. We think there might be more folks still down there."

Niki wiped the mud from her watch. It was nearly ten.

"I had no idea it was so late!" she gasped. The rain had started around six pm. Four hours of hell, she thought.

"You girls are a long way from your car. You came out the other side. I'm going to take you over to our temporary emergency relief center first. You can get cleaned up and see if you need any first aid. Then I can get you back to your car."

Niki was dazed, maybe in a mild medical shock, as they pulled into the information center where the park service had set up the emergency aid services. The ranger helped them in. Lena went first, because of her ankle, and Niki, after finding a restroom, sat in a waiting area. Soon someone asked if she would like water. The voice sounded familiar. When she glanced up she thought it must be a vision.

"Woman from Iowa? One who soars-like-an-eagle? Is it you?" It was Koteen! "What on earth happened to you?" he asked.

Even though she was muddy and messy, she didn't care. She grabbed him and he did not resist. They hugged and she clung to him for several minutes. Through her sobs she tried to explain.

"We got caught in a flash flood in the canyon. What are you doing here?" she asked, and then took several gulps from his canteen of water.

"I always volunteer for search and rescue missions since I have my jeep and know my way around," he said. "Didn't I warn you about this type of thing? Flash flooding? A few other flatlanders are trapped here, too." Flatlander. He had called her that last time. Hearing it made her smile.

"Yes, you did warn me," Niki said, and looked around for Lena. "Where's the woman who was with me?"

"She's getting treated for her ankle," Koteen said. He sat down beside Niki and took a long look at her, starting with her muddy hiking shoes and ending with her dirty face. His eyes locked on hers. "Are you injured?"

"Just my pride, I think. I'm freezing cold. We were in a real mess, though. Lost, wading in mud and water in the dark. It was very scary," she concluded. She couldn't take her eyes off him. Koteen patted her shoulder.

"Let me get a warm blanket and then find a paramedic."

Niki was still shivering, and the blanket felt divine. Soon, a paramedic confirmed she had mild hypothermia. She was also bruised and had a few lacerations, but nothing serious.

"You girls got off lucky," the medic told her. "Your friend just has a sprain and a few cuts. You'll both be fine."

Lena hobbled out with her ankle wrapped and Niki introduced her to Koteen.

"So you're the guide," Lena said shaking his hand. "We could have used your help in the canyon." Niki was thankful that Lena didn't launch into any strange talk of aliens.

"I'm sure you two would like a washroom," Koteen pointed the way for them. "After that, I'll take you back to your van. Where is it?"

Niki explained it was Lena's car parked at the trail head.

"Why don't I just take you two straight to the motel. It's late and I want to make sure you get settled into a room," Koteen said. "A hot shower will help you warm up. I'm staying there myself tonight, so I can take you to your car in the morning."

It didn't take much convincing. They were filthy, hungry and exhausted. It had been a long day, to say the least.

A light knock on the motel room door woke Niki from a dead sleep. "Who is it?" she asked. The motel clock read 5:40.

Niki was disoriented and groggy—not even sure if it was day or night.

"Rescue service." She knew that familiar husky voice. She jumped up then realized she had nothing on. Her muddy clothes were in a heap on the floor, so she grabbed a towel—a big, starchy motel towel, wrapped it around her and opened the door. There he was, Koteen, handsome as ever, in the pre-dawn hint of light. His high cheekbones, long sleek black hair pulled back, and riveting dark eyes.

God, those eyes that could see right into her soul, she thought. He looked over Niki's shoulder to make sure she was alone. Then without saying a word, he simply enveloped her in his muscular arms. In less than a minute they were on the bed.

He massaged her shoulders and back. It felt heavenly. Her body ached from the strenuous canyon climbing ordeal. Koteen's gentle, skilled hands elicited moans of pleasure from every touch.

"I cannot tell you how fantastic that feels," she said. He put his finger over her lips, to indicate no talking. She bit at it playfully, but felt a longing that could not be denied. Koteen turned her over on her back and began kissing her deeply and passionately. Soon they were entwined, finally as one. Their lovemaking was even more rapturous than their flights through the shamanic realm.

"Well," Niki said once she had returned to planet earth from this rather lengthy trip to the outer reaches of the solar system, "that's quite a rescue service you provide."

"So, tell me, what brought you back to Sedona?" Koteen asked, gently running his finger around her face and neck.

"Honestly?"

"Let me guess," he replied. "You tried to find the Anasazi site, got lost in the canyon, and then the rain came."

"I should have paid more attention to the sky," Niki touched the soul-arc necklace from Koteen and began to cry.

"I didn't mean to upset you," Koteen said pulling her close and holding her tightly. Her sobs became more intense. After a few minutes she regained her composure.

Niki pulled back and looked into Koteen's eyes. "I've been through hell since I last saw you," she said. "Since the journey where you met me, you can't imagine the things that have happened."

"Why didn't you summon the hawk spirit again?"

"I tried," she wiped tear tracks from her face. "Remember, when you couldn't catch me. When I traveled too far and fast?"

"I called to you," he said. "That's when I named you Soars-like-an-Eagle."

"It felt so familiar when you said it tonight," Niki smiled and touched his face. "Do you know about the Celestials who claim they can heal me? Have you heard of them?"

"Maybe. I might have heard the elders use that term. What happened?"

"It's hard to explain," Niki tried anyway. "I've been so confused. All the drumming and journeying, it's mind-altering. And I smoked some hashish, too. Everything became like a blur. Hindu rituals, Celestials, then the 'tutelary' spirits began sending transmissions," Niki said rubbing her forehead and temples. "So many things, all at once." She put her head against his bare chest again. He was a medicine man.

"I'm living with Lena, you know the woman here at the motel. She's kind of nuts. She believes she communicates with space aliens."

Koteen raised an eyebrow. Niki didn't have to be psychic to know what he was thinking.

"I know," she said. "I hear spirits and travel with you in the shamanic realm, but somehow that seems different than claiming you've been impregnated by aliens."

"She said that?"

"And more." Niki was touching Koteen's smooth, firm chest and wanted to stay there in the motel with him forever.

"I miss Iowa, yet I don't really want to go back there. I felt close to you, but then I was alone again. Usually I'm fine, but sometimes…" her voice trailed off.

They looked deeply into each other's eyes and Koteen held her close. The sun was rising, but there was time for one more close encounter before they had to leave paradise and find Lena.

Niki didn't want to know about the arranged marriage, what their encounter meant, or if she would even see him again. All that mattered was that she felt a deep connection to this Yavapai shaman and always would.

"Flow, my tears, fall from
your springs!
Exiled forever, let me mourn;
Where night's black bird her sad infamy sings,
There let me live forlorn."
-- *Lachrimae pavane* 1596

21 Shine On, Harvest Moon

What a mess, Niki thought as she rushed around the old adobe house trying to make it presentable for the Equinox gathering. You would think Lena would make some effort to clean the place considering that Jake was coming home and it was his house. Niki didn't mind helping, though. It was the least she could do since she was staying there for free. The adobe had such potential, she thought. Brick floors, lots of light pouring in from skylights and large exposed wood beams. It needed more loving care, and new furniture.

It was September 22, the Fall Equinox already. It had been over a month, almost two, since she had been with Koteen. They maintained a connection in the spirit realm, along with the two tutelary spirits, or spheres of fused luminosity, as her guides had recently referred to themselves.

In one of her recent journeys with Koteen, in his hawk form, he conveyed that these kind of fused spirits are really nagual—a term she recalled from the Castaneda books. These future shamans, in spirit form, make it possible for earth-born shamans to move between worlds.

Even with all this insight about other dimensions and realms, Niki still had no idea exactly what she was supposed to write. Her leave of absence would run out in a couple of months. She had to figure out what to do next.

She hoped the evening gathering would bring further insight. Important breakthroughs seemed to happen on the Equinox or Solstice. All of the Harvard Mall merchants would be there—Baba Dhyana and Keriani, Rick from the OM Centre, and Acer might bring his new pagan girlfriend, Morwyn. Of course, Dora K and her entourage would arrive in force. And finally, she would meet Jake.

The weather was mid 70s, and with no rain predicted, so Niki had decided to set up the tables and chairs on the back porch and patio. There was a long table where food could be arranged buffet style. She was arranging chairs and smaller tables when she heard the first sounds of someone arriving. It was Baba and Keriani loaded with trays of delectable looking East Indian cuisine.

"Nicole, my dear, we have missed you," Baba said as he gave her a kiss on the cheek.

"Yes, dear, why have you not come to see us?" Keriani asked, bowing her head. Niki helped, taking one of their food trays out to the patio. She had been reclusive since the flash flood at Sedona and her subsequent reunion with Koteen. She suspected Lena would tell their whole harrowing adventure in excruciating detail tonight for Jake and the others, so she had no interest in explaining it now.

"Oh, I've been writing—"

Before she could finish Baba interrupted.

"New insights from our Lord?"

Niki decided not to disclose anything about her recent shamanic journeys or cosmic transmissions.

"No, working on an assignment from my editor," she said, thinking she really did have to contact Frank about her leave status. Baba looked disappointed.

"Nothing new on the manuscript or Tractates?"

The question jolted Niki. She was surprised that Baba recalled that term. There was something almost sinister in his facial expression. Niki sensed he was hiding something, but what?

"No, nothing new," she said then excused herself to help other arriving guests.

It was actually Dora K and her gaggle of gals arriving. Niki couldn't even remember their names. They were like sheep to the slaughter in her mind. She could almost hear "bah" and "meh" as they waddled in with their jugs of sun tea and fancy hors d'oeuvres.

"Where's Lena?" Dora asked literally looking down her upturned nose at Niki. She was nearly six feet tall and thin enough to disappear if she turned sideways. I wish she would, turn and just vanish, Niki thought. "She left from the Health Garden to pick up Jake at the airport," Niki answered. "You've met him before, haven't you?"

"Oh yes," one of Dora's older groupies replied for her. "He's divine."

Niki looked at her watch. It was nearly six fifteen now.

"They'll be here anytime, with Rick, too."

"Rick, from the bookstore?" one of the matronly mob asked.

Before Niki could respond, someone announced that Lena and company had arrived.

Lena was helping Rick out of the back seat of her wagon when Niki glanced out the window. He had a cane and looked more skeletal and frail than when she last saw him at the OM Centre. She didn't see Jake, who was apparently retrieving his bags out of the far back part of the wagon.

Niki was in the midst of the crowd, hugging Lena and welcoming Rick when Jake first entered the house. She could hardly take her eyes off him. It wasn't just his appearance. He exuded an energy field so intense she could almost see it. There was definitely something special about this guy.

His presence was overwhelming. He was a large, masculine man, yet gentle-looking. Kind. That's what she sensed. He was about forty with thick salt and pepper hair over a well-tanned, weathered face. But it was a powerful, positive energy that affected Niki the most.

As Lena introduced them, Jake smiled and extended a big, hand to Niki that totally enveloped hers. The energy passing between them was so pronounced she felt certain that everyone, especially Lena, could feel it.

"Thank you for staying here and helping Lena with the house." His words rang with a deep, melodious tone. Niki felt mesmerized.

"Jake, it's wonderful to finally meet you." They had clasped hands longer than a customary shake. Niki broke the bond feeling awkward with this sudden surge of familiarity and excused herself saying she needed to check the food. She immediately stepped outside and lit a cigarette—something she had not done since Sedona.

"How on earth am I going to handle this?" she wondered. It felt like she had met her own cross-bonded Nagual—a combination of Koteen's special energy in a Gribbin-type guy.

Well, whatever it is, nothing is going to come of it, she vowed to herself. There was no way she was going to allow herself to be part of some sordid love triangle—that was for sure.

Niki startled when she realized Baba Dhyana had come out to join her for a smoke. As he expertly rolled a thin brown cigarette of pure Indian tobacco, he commented, "Quite a good looking man, that Jake. Don't you agree."

Niki felt her face flush again. It wasn't her imagination, Baba really did want to cause trouble. She had always sensed it. Niki looked Baba straight in the eye, took a drag off her cigarette, and said, "Very handsome indeed. And how about that hypnotist from the OM Center? Rachel, is it?" Baba's reaction to the buxom brunette had not escaped Niki either.

"Very lovely," he smiled, aware that they were now back on equal footing.

"I think we should get back to the group," Niki said, tossing away her cigarette filter. She went back inside with total resolve that Jay Christiansen, or Jake as Lena called him, was off limits.

The house and back porch oozed with atmosphere now. Nag Champa incense wafted through the air, blending with aromas from an array of exotic dishes. Jake was piling food on a plate and glanced up just as Niki was passing by.

"Say, I'm anxious to hear about your adventure coming out here from Iowa," he said. "Lena can't say enough about you and your many experiences."

Niki straightened her necklace, touching the soul-arc as if to draw strength from Koteen.

"Yes, it's been pretty incredible," she said. "I wouldn't really know where to start."

Lena walked up with the well-endowed Rachel to discuss doing a past life regression. Niki tossed her head back smoothing her wild hair away from her freckled face. She could sense Jake's reaction to the scene and the women. Not lust, more like humor, mixed with a bit of frustration as Rachel described one of Lena's regression sessions. It was odd, since she was used to tuning into the dead, not the living.

"I've heard that story," Jake said under his breath, and directed Niki away from the buffet table. "I'd rather hear yours. You're a reporter?"

"I work for a newspaper back in Iowa," Niki confirmed. "But I didn't come here on assignment." She hesitated. "I'm sure Lena told you that."

"The space brothers beckoned you to Roswell, our Land of Enchantment, right?" Jake's eyes twinkled.

Niki shook her head. "No, please don't confuse me with Dora," she said with a sarcastic edge. Jake looked relieved. "But I have heard things," she continued. "Messages with names that sound religious—Nag Hammadi, Maitreya, and then dreams about scrolls and missing manuscripts." Seeing Jake's glassy-eyed look, she shifted gears. "As a reporter, it was natural for me to keep detailed notes and records of what was happening. It became like a mystery that I had to solve. Various clues seemed to lead me here." She still felt embarrassed. "Does that make any sense?"

"I guess, but I've become jaded with all the space alien talk that goes on around here. But Nag Hammadi scrolls and missing texts—that's intriguing. I've dabbled in a variety of religions myself," he told her. "Taoism, Buddhism, Sufism, the mystical branch of Islam. So, I'd be interested in looking at some of your notes, if you wouldn't mind."

"Sure," Niki responded. Just then one of Dora's cult called out from the patio, "Hey, you two, break it up. We're about to start group meditation now."

"Guess we better join in," Jake winked. "Maybe tomorrow I can have a look at those notes."

Niki and Jake walked outside, where the others were forming a circle. Baba gave Niki a big Cheshire-cat grin which she ignored. Dora asked everyone to join hands for the meditation. Jake stepped in next to Lena and motioned for Niki to do the same. He reached for Niki's hand. His touch sent a tingle up her arm. That is definitely trouble, she worried to herself, then tried to dismiss such thoughts and focus on the meditation.

During the time it lasted, Niki felt especially calm, as if everything would soon come together. In fact, she heard the words, *he will help* in her head. Certainly, they meant Jake.

Actually, the Phil/Pike pair had not been monitoring the Equinox event in Corrales. It was the first International Day of Peace on Earth, slightly more significant. The duo thought someone at the gathering would know and mention it. *Your appointment will be yesterday*, Phil conveyed and chuckled at his joke (the title of one of his lesser known stories.) He saw that Niki was about to be hypnotized, another useful opportunity.

Rachel approached Niki as the meditation ended, ready to do the regression session.

"Now?" Niki asked.

"Yes, you're among friends," the hypno-therapist wannabe said. "I sense that you are especially relaxed right now. I'm sure it would be successful." Niki had reservations about Rachel's abilities, but the others encouraged her to do it.

Lena offered to find Niki's tape recorder, but Niki preferred to do that herself and make sure it had a blank tape. When she returned, Lena and Rachel had prepared a place for her to lie on the floor. Soft music was playing, the electric lights were off, and candle light set the mood. Most of the others had gone outside or in other rooms, to give them privacy, but Keriani had asked to stay and sat cross-legged close to Niki's head. That was comforting. Niki was lying flat on a mat Lena had rolled out.

Rachel began speaking in a hushed voice.

"Niki, you will completely relax. Every muscle in your body will enter a deep peaceful rest. You are already relaxing, and releasing all tension from your hips and lower back. Take a deep breath and exhale slowly. Feel any tension or tightness draining down your arms, through your hands, and out of your finger tips."

Rachel continued like this for several minutes until Niki did feel completely relaxed and at ease. She could feel her body going limp. Her eyes were closed. In the distance, it seemed, Rachel continued speaking in a soft, even tone.

"You will not go to sleep, you will simply enter an alpha state of heightened mental awareness. Your mind is alert but your body is totally relaxed. Is that true, Niki?"

Niki could barely nod agreement. She was drifting far away.

"As I count backwards," Rachel said, "you will relax even further. By the time I get to one, you will be in the alpha state." She paused and then counted very slowly. "Six… five, relax deeper; four, your mind is very alert; three, you feel totally and completely relaxed now; two, you are approaching the alpha state; one, you are now in the alpha state. You will remain deeply relaxed until I snap my fingers. However, you will see things like a movie in your mind's eye and tell us what you are viewing. Do you understand and agree?"

Again, Niki barely nodded her head. Her eyes fluttered, like someone in the REM dream state.

"What do you see?" Rachel prompted.

A deep voice came from Niki, much deeper than her usual speaking voice. Lena, Rachel and Keriani all looked at each other in amazement.

"I'm on the floor. The pink light is surrounding me. I can't get up."

"You don't have to get up. Just relax," Rachel said in her most soothing voice. "What do you see around you?"

"Pink light. I'm scared," the deep voice pleaded. "I'm alone and I can't get up."

"No, you're not alone," Rachel said. Keriani wanted to touch Niki, but the hypnotist shook her head indicating "no" and said, "We're still here with you."

"I'm blind, I can't see," the deep voice sounded frantic. "Who's here? Doris, is that you?"

Rachel looked at Lena with a puzzled look, and then asked Niki. "Where are you?"

"In the condo. On Quartz. Call an ambulance."

Rachel whispered to Lena, "I've never had anything like this happen. I better bring her back." Just before Rachel snapped her fingers the voice from Niki again pleaded, "I can't move. I'm trapped in the beam of light."

Rachel snapped her fingers. Niki slowly opened her eyes. It took her a minute or so to focus. She saw concerned looks from those nearby.

"What happened?" Niki asked.

"You don't remember anything?" Lena said.

"I remember feeling trapped and scared, like I couldn't get up."

"And, the deep voice. Who was that? Do you know?" Rachel asked.

"Was it the same voice you heard at Chaco?" Niki asked Lena.

"No I don't think so." Lena started to explain about the Chaco experience. "She felt trapped then, but in a cave in Egypt. She said her name was James." Rachel and Keriani listened intently. "She thought the Chaco ruins were in Egypt and said it was 1969. This time she said a condo of Quartz? Is that what she said?" Lena asked.

Jake appeared in the room in time to hear Lena telling Niki, "you said something about being trapped in the light."

Niki spontaneously broke out in tears. Keriani scooped her into her arms. Jake stepped in to take control.

"I don't think it's good to experiment with hypnosis," he said to Lena. To Niki he asked, "Are you okay now?"

She had stopped sobbing and had picked up the small tape recorder. It was still recording. Niki punched the stop button and wanted to rewind, but decided that should wait until she was alone in her room. "I'm better now," she said. "I'd like a glass of water, please."

One of the women got her a glass. But rumors had begun to ripple amongst the crowd. Someone said, "Jake had to break up the regression session." The tension was enough to break up the entire gathering. Dora and her followers were the first to leave. Baba and Keriani offered to take Rachel home. Before they left, Keriani sat by Niki and patted her hand and chanted a Hindi blessing.

Rachel still looked confused. "I hope everything turns out okay for you, Niki," she said and left with the Dhyanas.

Jake had to be exhausted from a long day of traveling and the odd events. He said, "I'll see you tomorrow. Will you be able to sleep?"

"Sure," Niki laughed. "I'm tired and believe me, I'm used to this type of thing by now."

Lena walked Niki to her bedroom to make sure she was settled. "Well, I thought it was incredible," she said. "I don't know why Jake got all freaked out and drove everyone away."

"He was tired from traveling, I'm sure," Niki said. "Try to see his point of view. It looks pretty crazy." She gave Lena a hug. "Will you leave early tomorrow?"

"Yeah, I have to open at the restaurant, so I'll be out of here at the crack of dawn. Jake will be here, though."

Niki couldn't wait to hit the pillow. The last thing she heard was arguing coming from Jake and Lena's room.

∞

"The clarity with which I can hear...depends on the wind.
It blows in from the desert to the east and north—
I receive the communications better, I've been taking notes.
Look at this... a stack of papers, about a hundred sheets."

-- Phil on Valis, in *Radio Free Albemuth*

22 Finding Phil

The smell of freshly brewed coffee woke Niki. It was a little after eight-thirty, according to her alarm clock. She threw on a pair of jeans, T-shirt, and brushed her wild, wavy hair. A splash of water here and there would have to do for now. She wanted coffee.

It wasn't until she stepped into the kitchen and saw the big, handsome hunk of a man sitting there reading the newspaper that she remembered she was alone in the house with Jake.

"Mind if I join you for a cup?" she asked, wishing she had taken time to shower.

"Niki! How are you feeling this morning?" Jake asked. He looked even better in the light of day, his cleft chin more visible, his gray eyes were expressive and intense, and his hair was full and fluffy. She was self-conscious of her ragged mop and ruffled it up, probably making it worse.

"I feel great. I just wanted a quick cup of coffee before I cleaned up."

"You look fine," he said and poured a cup of coffee for her. "In fact, you look rested. I was pretty concerned about you last night."

"Thanks," she said for the coffee. "I'm sure that must have been one bizarre scene, especially if you're not used to the goings on around here." Niki added cream and sugar.

"What exactly has been going on? Apparently this isn't the first time you've gone into some kind of trance. You mentioned something about what happened at Chaco, with you and Lena." Jake raised an eyebrow and waited for her reply.

"There's a lot of weird stuff happening," Niki blushed thinking about Lena's alleged alien miscarriage. "I don't like getting in the middle of it, though. Why don't you tell me how much you know about her cosmic transmissions and the Space Brothers. You mentioned that last night."

"I know that Lena met you at the summer Solstice party. I left for L.A. a few days after that. Since then I've just gotten bits and pieces of things. I'm not too clear about these 'transmissions' or episodes like last night."

"I couldn't help but hear you and Lena arguing. The last thing I want is to cause any trouble. I only came here because Lena insisted. I can be out of here—"

"We weren't arguing about you being here," Jake interrupted, "so put that out of your head. You're welcome to stay as long as you want."

"I need to hear that tape," Niki sighed. "I don't even know exactly what happened yet. In fact, I think I'll take a shower and then listen to it." She got up to rinse out her cup and felt Jake's eyes upon her again. She turned quickly and looked back at him. "Will you still be here or are you leaving?" she asked.

"I'm just going to hang out and do some yard work," he said. "I'll be around if you need anything."

As Niki headed for the shower, she wondered why he was living with Lena if he thought the cosmic stuff was crazy. More to the point, how did she get into this mess herself? How was she going to get out of it?

By the time she finished drying her hair it was about ten o'clock. She sat on her bed listening to the tape recorder. It was hard to believe that the deep voice she heard had come out of her mouth. No wonder everyone was so concerned, she thought. She scribbled a few notes:

-- trapped in a beam of light
-- asking for Doris and Tim
-- Quartz condo

As Niki wrote the last note, she heard *in California*. She repeated it. "In California?"

Santa Ana. Surely, Jake would have an atlas or someway to verify that there is such a place. She might even have a map in the van, she realized.

"Who was trapped in the light? You?" she asked.

Philip.

Niki sensed that was all she would receive. She knew how difficult it was for them to communicate. The transcribing, or automatic writing, she did on her computer seemed easier. Even that, she knew, was subject to her own interpretation of what she was "hearing" and sensing.

She gathered up her notes, journals and folder of typed pages and went back to the kitchen. Jake wasn't there.

She poured another cup of coffee and sat down at the table with all the materials. In her notebook, on a clean page, she drew a line down the center and labeled one side "James" and the other "Philip." Maybe she could discern which clues went into each column.

She suspected the religious terms belonged on the James side and the scientific notes would get logged to Philip. It wasn't always clear cut. *I Ching* definitely felt like Philip, but smoking seemed associated with James.

She was almost finished with the process when Jake walked in.

"What's this?" his voice startled Niki back to reality.

"Oh, I'm sorry," she said realizing she had papers strewn all over the big dining room table.

"I got this idea to categorize all my notes."

It took three full-size pages of notebook paper just to list all the terms and messages she had received over the past five months.

"So, tell me about all of this," Jake seemed genuinely interested as he joined her at the table. She noticed green stains on his hands from working in the yard.

Niki tried to explain her method of attributing certain clues to Philip and others to James. "I've run into difficulty because the two are merged, or cross-bonded somehow in a vortex, so at times I really can't tell which is which."

"Come again?" Jake said. "I'm sorry but I'm not following this very well."

Niki laughed, suspecting she sounded as crazy as Lena. "I'll start with the most recent developments. Maybe that will help," she said. "When I listened to the tape just now, I understood that last night in the regression, or trance as you called it, I was channeling someone named Philip," she paused for a reaction.

"Channeling is when a spirit speaks through you, right?" Jake asked. "Lena has described that to me. It happens to you?"

"Well, here's the thing," Niki decided she was going to reveal her secret. "I haven't even said this to Lena, but it's become so obvious I can't really hide it anymore. I'm kind of psychic. Not a practicing one like Rachel the Regressionist or Dora K, but it runs in my family. I had a fortune telling aunt, who was a bit of a charlatan, but my mom always suspected I was a true sensitive, as she called it. When I was about five years old, she actually had me tested for ESP, Extra Sensory Perception, as they used to call it."

"You read minds?" Jake laughed, a bit nervously.

"Sometimes." It was her turn to wink and watch Jake turn a bit crimson on the ears. "No, I don't read minds. I just get occasional flashes or insights. But something kicked it into high gear in March, and that's what I've been trying to sort out."

"Okay, I think I'm following now." Jake had put on a pair of reading glasses and was sitting very close to Niki as they reviewed the notes. She was keenly aware of his presence, his aura and energy, but also the musky smell of sweat and cut grass.

"It was at the VLA near Socorro when I really got a blast of the technical Philip voice," Niki said explaining the VLA notes. "That was the first time he actually spoke through me. Something about how the radio telescopes could be used to detect Valis—"

"What did you just say?" Jake interrupted.

"Valis? That's what he calls the vortex. I'm not sure how to spell it," she said. "VALIS. I've been writing it in all caps. It's short for the Vast Active Living—"

"Intelligence System," Jake finished her sentence.

"How did you know that?" Niki was stunned.

"It's Philip K. Dick. You know that, right?"

"No. Who's Philip K. Dick?"

"You've been writing Philip."

"Yeah, but that's all I knew. James and Philip. What do you know about VALIS?"

Jake grabbed the note pad from Niki. It was all there in her notes: a bearded man, in his 50's, wants me to "re-collect" the information. VALIS—a vortex of intelligence, a supra-temporal field. A flux of living information. And an exact quote from PKD:

"VALIS is a perturbation in the reality field characterized by quasi-consciousness, purpose, intelligence, growth and… coherence."

"Niki, this stuff is straight out of Phil Dick's novel *VALIS*. C'mon you or Lena must have copied some of that."

"No, I swear. I heard these phrases at the VLA and even said them at the Dhyana's house. Who is he?"

Jake told her to hang on while he went to another room. When he returned he laid a paperback book on the table.

Niki just stared at the cover. After hearing the term so many times, it seemed impossible. A science fiction novel?

Suddenly, she felt violently ill. She tossed the book back to Jake and ran for the bathroom. He could hear her retching and getting sick.

"Niki. What's wrong? Jake called out from the hallway. He waited a few minutes then called to her again.

"I'm not sure," a weak voice came back. "Just a minute." Niki was slumped on the bathroom floor. She felt like every ounce of energy was drained from her.

Phil felt guilty. He had caused her "ghost sickness" as Koteen called it. This time from his extreme joy over finally being discovered. The anti-matter thing, again—really bad effects on the living.

You dense-particle people have no idea—I mean *no idea*—how nearly impossible it is to convey messages from one dimension to another. If it was easy, everyone would be aware of us and the living would know everything that goes on here. It takes extreme concentration and determination on the part of a shade—I kind of like the idea of being a hip shade—and a very unique human to tune in to our wave length. Of course, it can also adversely affect the brain and nervous system. Look what happened to me.

At least ten minutes passed with no further response. Jake said, "Niki, if you can't come out, I'm coming in to get you."

No reply.

The door was not locked. He found Niki passed out on the bathroom floor, clammy and vampire pale. Frantically, he began tugging on her arms trying to get her to at least sit up. She was like a wet rag. There's an idea, he thought, as he got one and placed it on her forehead. He also slapped her face lightly.

"Niki. Can you hear me?" Slowly she seemed to be coming around. "Say something if you can hear me."

"Okay," in a faint whisper was all she could muster. Jake scooped her up and carried Niki to her bedroom, placing her on the bed.

"Should I call emergency?" Jake paced frantically.

"No, it's happened before," Niki said, still dizzy and light-headed. "Could I have some juice?"

By the time he came back, color was returning to her face and she was sitting up. Niki gulped the glass of juice and then began to feel embarrassed.

"Remember what I told you, about being a sensitive," she said. "Well this goes with the territory. I've gotten sick before when powerful energy or vibrations affected me. Learning about Philip—I think he prefers to be called Phil—was a huge blast of energy!"

"If I didn't know so much about Phil, and yes his friends did call him that, I would think you were totally crazy. But this actually makes sense, on some level."

Jake realized they were still sitting on the bed, and quickly stood up. Niki sensed he was uncomfortable.

"I think you should eat something," he said. "I'll make some soup and sandwiches."

"Good, I'm starving," Niki also got up, slowly. "I'll splash some water on my face and meet you in the kitchen."

"No. I want to make sure you're alright." Jake watched as Niki moved slowly to the bathroom and waited until she emerged. He insisted on helping her to the kitchen. It felt comfortable, though, like she had known him a long time.

Jake had gathered up all the notes and papers and put them in a stack on the dining room table. Lying on top of the stack was the *VALIS* book.

"May I please look at it while you're fixing the food?"

"Only if you're sure you can handle it," he smiled and handed her the book. "Seriously, you've never seen it before?"

"Never. I swear." Niki noticed the publication date. "It's new—published less than a year ago."

"Yes, and controversial, too," Jake noted while heating the pot of soup. "As a reporter, seems like you would have heard about his death. It was sudden, and shocked the science-fiction world."

"I've never really read sci-fi," Niki confessed.

"Obviously, if you call it that," Jake smiled. "This book is controversial because it's not really science fiction—more of a spiritual quest. Phil's fictional search to answer questions that always dogged him."

"Unfinished business?" Niki asked. "That's what I sensed and heard over and over. He had unfinished business."

"He sure did," Jake said turning down the heat so the pot didn't boil. "He died of a stroke while writing his final work, his alleged masterpiece."

That really got her attention. "What was that about, do you know?"

"Oh, we heard different plots, but kind of a Dantean theme and it dealt with an alien race of shamans who communicated only with light and sound."

"Alien shamans! Unbelievable." Niki said. She thought of Koteen, her intense interest in Castaneda and the vision quest—even Lena—all the signs had been there.

Jake placed a bowl of green chile chicken soup in front of her and half a turkey sandwich.

"If you want more, there's plenty," he said pouring her a glass of sun tea.

Niki couldn't get over the comment about alien shamans.

"Not Sirius?" she asked.

"I am serious," Jake said. "In his final books, Phil wrote the craziest stuff you can imagine."

"No, I mean were the alien shamans from Sirius—the star Sirius?"

"I think so, now that you mention it."

Niki leaned forward, her head in her hands.

"Are you getting sick? Is it the soup?" Jake asked.

"No, the soup is delicious. It's what you're telling me. My head feels like it might explode any second."

"You should lie down and rest. I think it is too much all at once."

Jake helped her back to her bedroom, then left saying, "Just call out for me, if you get sick or need anything."

A few hours later…

"I hope you don't mind, but while you were resting I read the rest of those notes you made this morning. The last thing you wrote was 'The key to understanding VALIS is in the Tractates.' Then you added, 'Someone will help locate the manuscripts.' Let me show you something." Jake picked up the copy of *VALIS* and flipped to the end of the book. There was an Appendix entitled *Tractates Cryptica Scriptura.*

"I can't believe it. I just cannot believe this," Niki said. "These are the Tractates they wanted me to read? Sci-fi stuff?"

"In the case of Philip K. Dick it's always more than just sci-fi stuff," Jake chuckled. "Phil had unusual experiences when he was alive, heavy on the metaphysical themes. He was one of the first writers to incorporate such ideas within science-fiction." Jake paused, looking at Niki. "Maybe I am 'the someone' who is supposed to help you find the manuscripts."

Niki didn't know what to say. Jake continued.

"Back in the late 60s, I was a huge PKD fan. Phil was producing novel after novel, each one more mind-boggling than the one before. He saw the computer revolution coming, artificial intelligence, and things we still haven't figured out. He wrote something like ten novels in less than two years. Back then it was considered junk—pulp fiction, and Phil was the Prince of Pulp."

Niki was hanging on his every word.

"In the early novels," Jake recalled, "Phil loaded the plots with anti-war politics, too. The Vietnam war was raging, the Cold War was still a menace, we were in the thick of the civil rights movement, and then Richard Nixon was elected president. It was shocking. A grim time for the liberal Berkeley crowd that Phil represented.

"We all thought the establishment was oppressive and figured Nixon would create a police state, raid our houses for no reason, other than to confiscate our grass. It's not even a drug. We couldn't grow our own plants, for Christ sake, and still can't thanks to those bastards." Jake was getting really wound up now.

"It was a mess. Civil rights? We had no rights! And then the race riots began. For someone like Phil, who wrote about this stuff, it was easy to feel paranoid. The nation was completely polarized over drugs and war." Jake realized he was really rambling now, but he wanted to set the stage for what happened in 1971.

"You were a baby then, probably didn't really understand what was going on."

"In '71? I was sixteen," Niki said. "but I understood what a big mess the war was, and I hated Nixon."

"Well, see, I'm ten years older than you. I was twenty-six, and just graduating from UNM. It took me awhile because I kept dropping out and coming back," he explained. "Anyway, I decided I would do my part to combat any thoughts of Nixon getting re-elected in '72.

"I wrote to Philip Dick. I suggested he go on the college tour circuit to preach the gospel of individual rights, liberty, pursuit of happiness; you know, the whole personal freedom thing. I really pleaded in the letter and told him it was his manifest destiny to fight the Man in the High Castle.

"*The Man in the High Castle* was one of his most famous books. I'm not sure if the man was 'The Man' or maybe it was someone reclusive, like Salinger. Regardless, my passion must have struck a chord, because he agreed to come to UNM."

"No kidding? He came to Albuquerque?"

"He did. Of course, I had to raise money to pay for his expenses. His agent told us we had to raise two grand, and that was a lot of money in 1971."

"It's a lot of money now," Niki added, clapping her hands and getting excited, "So what happened?"

"I got a committee together to help me," Jake recalled, "but in the end I think we only raised about $800— about 150 people showed up. Like I said, he was just a cult figure back then, but he came anyway.

"That was one of the highlights of my college years. It triggered a series of political fund-raising rallies at campuses around the country. Other students wanted Tim Leary, or someone high profile. But for me, the best part was that I got to smoke weed with PKD afterwards and rap about his books, philosophy and—"

Jake stopped suddenly. His expression changed and he looked strangely at Niki.

"I'm remembering something Phil said about Bishop Pike."

"Bishop Pike, that name sounds familiar to me," Niki tried to recall where she had heard it. Her ear buzzed.

"James-Philip!" she said aloud.

It hit them both at the same time.

"You're thinking the James in your notes is James Pike!" Jake exclaimed.

"My mom had a book about Bishop Pike, too, I think. Isn't he the one who communicated from a trance? Or maybe that was Edgar Cayce. Anyway, go on."

"It all really fits," Jake was really into the story now. "I even remember Phil telling about a book he was writing on James Pike. Let me see if I can remember any details." He paused to think. "Okay, something about how Phil met Pike after the Bishop's son died—actually, committed suicide."

"Wait, a Catholic Bishop and he had a son?" Niki asked.

"No, he wasn't Catholic. He was Episcopalian. Married more than once, actually," Jake clarified, "Anyway, his teenage son killed himself, and Bishop Pike was convinced that James Junior was trying to contact him from beyond."

Jake stopped again trying to recall the time frame. "This was earlier, maybe mid '60s. Somehow the Bishop contacted Phil, thinking he must know about communicating with dead people, because of his books like *Ubik* and *Three Stigmata.* I remember Phil saying, 'Hell, I was just a science fiction writer. I made up all that stuff.' Meaning he knew nothing about séances or mediums."

"Jake, I hate to interrupt you, but this is almost too much to grasp all at once," Niki said, her head reeling.

"Okay, just let me finish this one last point, now that I remembered it. The upshot was this: Phil developed a friendship with James Pike. They stayed in communication. Then, in 1969, I think, Bishop Pike was killed. This is the most important part, Niki. Phil claimed that Pike made some critical discoveries while in—"

"Nag Hammadi?" she interrupted, again.

"Well, close. I think he was near Jerusalem, but he was trying to tie together several sites where ancient scrolls had been found. Something like that." Jake paused and seemed to be recollecting the events.

"Oh, here's the clincher. Phil had received a telegram from Pike saying he wanted Phil to collaborate on a book when he got back. Only Pike never came back. He died in Israel."

"Died? Was he killed?"

"No one really knows for sure. The weirdest part is that Phil told me he thought the Bishop was communicating with him, you know, from the other side."

"That is unfinished business," Niki said again. "Both of them had unfinished business."

"Phil was raving like a lunatic that night about messages he was receiving, religious insights, material for the book," Jake said. "You know all that happened in early 1971. Then his place was broken into that fall and apparently all the notes and manuscript he was working on were stolen."

Phil finally felt like he had arrived in heaven. All the signs and codes were paying off. Now that Niki had *VALIS* in her hands and Jake to help her figure it out, he could take a well deserved break from his exhausting guide duties. Phil eyed a big fluffy cloud and before he could give another thought to probabilities and outcomes… zzzzzzzz!

23 the Screaming Woman Incident

Niki was too excited to sleep Thursday night. She stayed up reading *VALIS* until just before dawn. When she finally fell asleep, her head was so full of information from Jake and the book, she dreamed that she had a conversation with Phil. Did she? Who knows, but it certainly was vivid.

"That's it then," Niki said to the man in the dream. "The manuscript and notes are in California, right?

Yes!

"I'm not only communicating with a dead science fiction author, but you are merged with the dead Bishop?"

Yes!

"You died on March 2 of this year? Unexpectedly? Trapped in a beam of light from VALIS?"

Yes!

"And now I need to learn more about Bishop Pike? Or just find your manuscript?"

Both!

"For a writer, you sure don't say much," Niki still wished she could get more details.

Can't...

"You didn't seem to have a problem talking through me at the VLA or in front of Baba Dhyana," she said. "How is it that you can cause me to blurt a bunch of techno-babble, yet can't answer simple questions about where I'm supposed to go and how it relates to *my* mission?"

There was no response to that. In fact, she was awake now and having problems recalling exactly what Phil did or didn't say in the dream. She threw off the sheet and blanket and stomped to the bathroom. As shower water poured over her, Niki wondered how she could be sure what was real. In the regression session and just now, it seemed important to go to California and research Bishop Pike.

Niki tiptoed out of her room in case Lena, or even Jake, was nearby. She didn't see signs of either of them. Was she obligated to leave a note? She did, just in case:

> Off to the library and maybe some bookstores. See you later!

Niki rushed into the main downtown public library, like the old days when she was on deadline. How many people rush into libraries like breaking news is waiting there in the musty old volumes, she wondered. She was too excited to use the card catalogue. She ran up to the reference desk.

The man working the desk reminded Niki of Stephen Hawking (before he was confined to the wheelchair.) The librarian had some type of disability, perhaps cerebral palsy, but appeared to compensate for his physical limitations with brain power.

"Bishop James Pike," Niki said breathlessly. "Do you have any books on Bishop Pike?"

The librarian looked at Niki with his dark, deep set eyes and kind of chuckled.

"Slow down," said a raspy voice. "Let's take a look." He limped over to the card file. Niki felt guilty for not doing this herself. In less than a minute the librarian said, "There's something in biography called *The Death and Life of Bishop Pike*. He pointed to the biography section, smiled and dryly added, "Look under P."

"Thanks," Niki said sheepishly and then hurried off to the stacks. Within a few minutes she found it. Well, who would know his wife had written the biography, she thought. It was filed under Pike, Diane Kennedy Pike. Niki took the book and sat down at one of the study tables. There it was right on the inside cover: "Some material used in this book is from *The Other Side* by James A. Pike with Diane Kennedy, copyright © 1968."

Niki hurried back to the librarian. "I'm sorry to bother you again, but what about a book called *The Other Side* actually written by Bishop Pike?"

The man looked over the top of his glasses at Niki. "Shall I show you how to use the card catalogue?" Again, he limped around the desk.

"I know how to use it, but I didn't see any reference to that book, and it's really important."

The librarian checked the catalog, turned and said, "You didn't see it because we don't have that one."

"And I don't have a library card, but I really need to check out this biography."

The librarian handed her a form and asked to see her driver's license.

"Iowa?" he said. "Just visiting?"

"No, well, kind of," she said realizing she would have to make a decision soon about her leave of absence. Niki sighed. "I'm a reporter."

"You are supposed to have a valid New Mexico license to check out materials—" he began but must have seen the disappointment on Niki's face. "I'll make an exception this time."

"Oh, thank you! Thank you very much." Niki left with the book, anxious to read what the Bishop's young wife had written about Pike's death, but she also wanted the book that Pike had written about his son's suicide.

Driving north on Fourth Street back to Corrales, Niki noticed a strange little bookstore called Ethel's Exchange. It looked shabby and rundown, yet for some inexplicable reason Niki decided to stop anyway.

She parked the van and walked up. The glass window was dirty. Near the front door a couple of derelicts were gawking at girly magazines. Inside, books were piled from floor to ceiling with no apparent rhyme nor reason to location. A man and woman behind the counter, the owners or managers she guessed, were arguing. The woman was heavyset and looked very ill, hooked to an oxygen tank, yet barking commands to a scroungy-looking man working the cash register. Niki had nearly turned to leave when the man noticed her and slurred, "Can I help you?"

Niki drew a deep breath, wondering how anyone could possibly find anything here, and said. "You probably don't have it, but I'm trying to find a book by Bishop James Pike," she paused. "It's called *The Other Side.*"

At that moment a woman in the back of the store screamed out. The creepy counter man hurried to the back of the store. Niki was certain someone had been attacked by one of the perverts, or perhaps murdered back there. Again, she almost ran out the door, but curiosity kept her there. Niki glanced down the aisle where the man with the greasy blonde hair had dashed toward the screaming woman.

A middle-aged woman was all Niki saw. She looked okay, other than her face. She was pale with a horrified expression. Then trembling, she raised her hand.

"This book?" the woman asked, holding up a paperback.

"I'll be damned," the store clerk said as he scratched his dirty blonde head. He took the book and waved it toward Niki, who gingerly approached the two of them.

In large, bold letters the cover read: *The Other Side.* It was by James A. Pike. It was Niki's turn to suppress a yelp.

"Yes, that's exactly what I was looking for. Are you buying it?"

"No. I don't want anything to do with it." The wide-eyed woman hurried down the aisle and out of the store.

The clerk handed the book to Niki and she saw it was sub-titled: *My Experiences with Psychic Phenomena.* Niki couldn't help but laugh and so did the near-toothless clerk.

"How much?" Niki asked, just wanting to leave the filthy, smelly store.

"Normally fifty cents," he said. As Niki reached into her pocket for change, he smiled. "After that, it's on the house." He snorted and slapped his knee. Niki thanked him and as she was leaving she heard him telling the woman with the oxygen tank, "Ethel, it was a sign. Hillerman told me a story once about how the Dineh Blessing Way—"

Niki kind of wanted to hear what he was saying, but not bad enough to loiter with the perverts at the front of the store. She did make a mental note to investigate Hillerman, who she knew was an Albuquerque writer, and to hose off the paperback with Lysol before she read it.

> "I appeared in the form of an Eagle on the Tree of Knowledge, the primal knowing that arises in the pure light, that I might teach them and awaken them out of the depth of sleep."
> --the Apocyphon of John, 23. 25-30

24 Mission Improbable

"Jake, for the past couple of days I've done nothing but pore over VALIS and the Bishop Pike books. I'm convinced that James Pike and Philip Dick are morphed together, cross-bonded, I think they called it. I still don't really know why I'm the one to solve their unfinished business, but I need that book, the one you said Phil was writing about Pike. Which one is that?"

"To be honest I can't remember," Jake responded. Once again they were drinking coffee in the kitchen while Lena was working at the restaurant. "I remember feeling disappointed with *VALIS*—"

"I did too, at first," Niki interrupted. "I had trouble with ideas like an irrational creator or the in-breaking of coherence into our universe. But early this morning I got a glimpse of what Phil means. We are evolving—the Collective, our higher consciousness—away from chaos and cruelty, toward order, harmony, and ultimately peace. Does that make sense?"

"Yep, you sound like you've read *VALIS*," Jake said, with a slight eye roll. "You should see my friend Acer at Birdsong. He would know what books are published, and when Phil died. I can call him, if you want."

"Would you, please? I really need the one Phil wrote about Bishop Pike. I'm sure that's the missing piece of the puzzle." Niki paused and then asked, "Could we go there? Talk to him in person?"

Jake looked up the number of Birdsong, got Acer on the line and after a few pleasantries said, "Say, what's the name of that last book by Philip K. Dick?" Jake was making a face while listening on the phone.

"Oh yeah? And you have it, right?" He listened again and said, "both of them. We'll come on over then, and ask you a few questions, if that's okay."

Niki was anxious to know what both meant.

"Two books were just published this year. *Divine Invasion* and *The Transmigration of Timothy Archer*. That's the one—"

"*Divine Invasion*," Niki repeated. "I know I heard that term back in Iowa and on the road."

"Well, come on, let's go," Jake said. "I've got a few more days before I have to go back to California. Let's see what ol' Acer has to say." He smiled. "We'll take my Jeep."

As they parked on Harvard Mall, Niki felt guilty that she hadn't seen or called Baba or Keriani, or visited Tagore at the Bodhi Tree. Maybe she could convince Jake to stop in and have a cup of chai, especially with Tagore. Lena was just around the corner, at the Health Garden, so they'd better go there, too.

Acer and Jake shook hands and seemed really happy to see each other. They looked like two guys who ate Alice's wonderland cake and had grown too large for the little low-ceiling adobe house that was converted to a bookstore. Acer was considerably taller than Jake, who was six feet himself.

Acer looked like the hippie version of an NBA star with his long, thin beard and thinning, wiry hair to match. He towered over Niki like a giant. A friendly giant, though, he smiled and seemed to enjoy discussing the late Philip K. Dick.

"Well, first of all Phil had a stroke in February," he told them. "Then he had one or maybe two heart attacks in the hospital and died on March second, this year."

"March! Do you know where he died?" Niki asked.

"California. I think Orange County," he thought. "I could probably find the town, if you need that."

"Maybe later, but tell me about these latest books. Just a quick overview for starters, if you don't mind," Niki asked.

"Well, the final ones all deal with metaphysical issues, but not as overtly as *VALIS,* in my opinion, which is also pretty autobiographical. You read that one, right?"

"Yes, which one tells the story of Bishop Pike? I mean, the account of what happened when he died in the desert?"

"*Transmigration* is actually about Pike, thinly veiled—very thinly. The bishop is Timothy Archer."

That got Niki's adrenaline going, but before she could get too excited Acer continued, "But it's not the story Phil told us the night he was here." He looked at Jake. "You told her about that, right?"

"As much as I could remember. I knew he was working with Bishop Pike on a project, but then the Bishop died. What do you remember about that?" Jake prompted Acer.

"Well, you know that manuscript was stolen, right?" Acer said.

"How do you know that?" Niki questioned.

"Phil made a huge deal out of the break-in," Acer said. "There was a spread in *Rolling Stone* magazine. I'm sure I could find a copy of that article for you to read. His house was ransacked, his safe blown, apparently for the manuscript. Phil went berserk. That's what finally put him over the edge, I think. He tried to kill himself, and was never the same after that."

"And now he's dead." Niki couldn't get over what she was hearing. "Why is everyone sure about the stroke? He could have been poisoned or someone could have slipped him some drug to induce a stroke or heart attack."

"Phil would just love that," Acer chuckled. "If he could be at the center of an obscure murder mystery, nothing would please him more. He always thought someone was after him. He'd be the first to suggest he was murdered. I just never heard anyone speculate that his death was suspicious."

"Of course not," Niki said. Her head was pounding, her heart racing. She grabbed her head, holding her ears. "It's so obvious. *They were after both of us*!" She clasped her hand to her mouth, but it was too late. Acer was looking at her, clearly confused. Jake intervened.

"Look, man, we really appreciate your help," he said as he made some code-type gesture to Acer. "Niki hasn't been feeling well. You know, Lena and your Harvard neighbors have really been affecting her. We should probably leave. If you can track down copies of those books, I'll stop and grab them."

Jake hustled Niki out the door before a full blown James-Philip episode could manifest.

"What was that about?" he asked.

"I need a cigarette." Niki's hands were trembling. "I know what's going on. I gotta have a smoke—right now." She was so desperate she bummed one off a college kid, lit up and then practically screamed to Jake. "It's Pike!"

"What does that mean?"

"I have to read those last two books by Phil, but I feel certain most of the clues came from Pike. You know Nag Hammadi—it was Pike that wanted to go there. Someone named James spoke through me in Chaco Canyon, definitely

Pike. Seeing Rome, dreams of the temples, scrolls, even this damn smoking." She tossed the butt to the curb. "I never smoked or even thought of smoking until all this started in March. I read in one of those books that Pike was a chain smoker. Phil didn't smoke."

"He did snuff," Jake said. "Okay, let's just say you're right. What does it change? You've said they are bound together anyway, almost like one in the spirit realm. And, Phil died in March. Pike has been dead for what, twelve years. The break-in was over ten years ago."

A big shadow cast by giant Acer caused Niki to look up. He was holding a copy of the *Transmigration* book.

"It's brand new," Acer said to Jake, "but I owe you one for getting the man here in the first place. That's why I set up shop, you know—to keep everyone reading science-fiction." He handed the book to Niki.

Niki thanked Acer profusely and could hardly wait to start reading.

"You can start at the Health Garden," Jake reminded her that they needed to check on Lena.

"Oh yeah, Lena," she laughed. They walked around the corner and into the midst of a lunch frenzy. Jake went off to help Lena and Niki found a corner spot to begin her journey into Phil's final fiction.

She hardly knew when Jake brought water, and some herbal tea, but the aroma of the soup brought her back to this realm.

"How is it?" he asked.

"I haven't tried it yet, but it smells divine," Niki said, blowing on a hot spoonful.

"The book, I meant."

"Oh, I've only read about thirty pages, but it's kind of cynical, not what I expected from Phil." It felt odd saying it like she knew him, but after all she had been living with him for several months—him and Pike. That made her smile.

Niki tasted the soup, savoring the flavor of wild rice, seasonings and big chunks of chicken and veggies.

"Mmm. Almost as good as that stew you made the other day."

"Who do you think taught Lena how to cook?" he quipped.

"Really? She never told me that," Niki responded. "How long have you two been together?"

"A couple of years. She was going through the divorce from Chuck when we met. Did she tell you about Chuck?"

"Yeah, briefly on the trip to Chaco. How he took her to court for custody of their daughter. He sounded like a real asshole."

"Lena needed a way to make a living. So I helped her lease this building and fronted some money to start this place since she was so crazy about health food and vitamins. I think organic foods and health consciousness will increase in the coming years. Good investment for me, too."

Jake had a talent for spotting trends well in advance of mainstream thinking, according to Lena and it seemed so. He was on the forefront of technology and involved in some big money deal to bring a microprocessor plant to Albuquerque. Niki knew that everything would use computers in the future, so that certainly would be a boon to the state and probably Jake, too. Not to mention he knew all about her spirit guys. Brains, looks, and he cooks, Niki laughed to herself, then remembered her vow. No getting involved. He's taken, and by a friend.

∞

A day or so later after Niki had finished *The Transmigration of Timothy Archer*, she was sharing morning coffee again with Jake.

"Did you finish the book?" he asked.

"Yes, it was pretty freaky. It was really about how Pike, Bishop Archer in the book, was obsessed with the afterlife and may have come back through the son of his mistress." She paused wondering if she should tell Jake about her own insights on the Zadokite material, her vision on the trip to Chaco. That trip had been with Lena and discussing it with Jake seemed awkward. So she simply said, "I'm fairly certain the Zadok sect mentioned in there is the key to unlocking the entire mystery. But I don't think anohki means mushroom. I'm pretty sure there's more to it. Why would Phil write something so misleading?"

"Why do you think?" Jake winked. "If the Zadokite scrolls had anything to do with the break-in or Pike's heretical revelations, I'm sure Phil would have been too paranoid to write about it."

"You're right, but he did make the claim that the scroll proved Jesus was a Buddhist. Do you remember that?"

"I remember Edgar Barefoot was based on Allan Watts."

"Really? Is that how people in California thought of Watts? To me he was an authority on Buddhism, not a goofy guru."

"Who knows what was rolling around in Phil's head—" Jake paused. "I remember seeing Watts on Pier Nine in San Francisco. He looked like a guru. You think Baba Dhyana is goofy?" he finished, smiling.

"Kind of," Niki smiled back. "Speaking of kooks, I had an insight when Pike, I mean Tim—actually Phil who wrote it—tried to explain moksha in the novel. It means release or liberation. Dora the Kook probably twisted that term into Monka and then influenced Lena to believe that was the name of whoever she was hearing or channeling, or getting transmissions from."

"You haven't spoken much about Lena lately," Jake said. Niki blushed.

"Well, things have been a little strained. It started before you came back. After the fiasco in Sedona, we just slowly began to drift. I'm sure she wants me to leave so you two can be alone."

"Actually, I'm the one leaving. I've got to head back to California next week, early October. So, maybe you girls can work things out then."

"Where in California?" Niki asked.

"San Jose."

"Is that near San Rafael, or Santa Ana?"

"Well, those two places are light years apart," Jake said. "San Rafael is part of the Bay Area near San Francisco. Santa Ana is in southern California, SoCal as the natives call it—Orange County. Why?"

"I was always supposed to go back to California and find the manuscript," she said. "You know, that's what all the messages and prodding was about in the first place."

"And?" Jake raised an eyebrow.

Niki felt uncomfortable enough, but it seemed as though Jake was enjoying making her explain her idea. She got up to get more coffee and began with her back toward him.

"I thought maybe I could go with you or follow you out there. Like you said, it seems they led me to you. I don't have much time left now to solve this puzzle." She poured Jake coffee and looked at his expression. He was smiling.

"C'mon. It is obvious, isn't it? Niki smiled back. "You're going to California. I'm hitching a ride and getting a guide." They laughed.

"Lena would come with us?" Jake raised a brow.

"Sure, if she can. I would just appreciate your help getting around California. It might be a nice vacation for her."

"Lena won't be able to take the time off," Jake said. "She's been working twelve hour days because she doesn't have enough help. In fact, I've been going there to help with the lunch rush. And, if she can't go, I don't think she would want us traveling alone together."

"Well, I have to go," Niki said. "I don't have much time left on my leave. I'm supposed to be back in Iowa in a few weeks. She realized she needed to call and beg Frank for another month, or some type of extension.

"Okay," Jake said. "Suppose we meet somewhere. That wouldn't be leaving town together. But, where would we even start, investigating, I mean?"

"I want to start at the cop shop in San Rafael, where the break-in happened, and find that police report."

∞

Tuesday, September 28

Niki left a day earlier than Jake and asked Lena to keep an eye on Schroeder. She wasn't sure if they would take her van or leave it in the little town of Bernalillo, either way she couldn't contend with the cat once they were in California. She slept in the van that night and cleaned up in a public rest area. She met Jake at a funky little restaurant called *The Range* at seven Wednesday morning.

"I haven't done anything this spontaneous in years," Jake said as he gave Niki a quick hug. "It feels kind of exciting, like an adventure."

"It *is* an adventure," Niki proclaimed. On Jake's advice they ordered Huevos Rancheros—eggs and beans on flour tortillas smothered in red and green chile. He assured her that one day the little hide-away would be famous, a real tourist attraction. Mr. Corporate Businessman was always right, too, it seemed. He predicted a coming computer craze, health food and the whole holistic health movement. Niki, of course, loved talking tech with him, as well as picking his brain about Phil and Pike. She saw no harm in him helping her solve the mystery. They could have a platonic, friendly relationship. After all, he wasn't married to Lena.

They left Jake's Scout in Bernalillo and took Niki's van, so they had room for food, refreshments, and supplies, and could also take turns sleeping in the back to make good time getting to the Bay Area.

Any route they took would take about twenty-four hours by the time they made pit stops for gas, coffee and other necessities. The Westfalia bus could not be pushed much above sixty miles per hour, and anything above fifty-five was unbearably noisy.

Niki wanted the first shift to Kingman, Arizona since she was familiar with I-40 and driving her van. She estimated she could make that in about eight hours. But it actually took longer, even though she had blown past the Arizona border, and painted desert. Jake wanted a longer break at Flagstaff.

"We need to make some decisions," he had said as they gobbled up hot truck stop food and examined the map. Niki couldn't help but think she might see Koteen there, but didn't. Jake drove to Kingman to give her a break.

"We'll be going through the Mojave Desert at night. That's good and bad," he explained. "It will be cooler, but there's only a couple of places to stop for gas and supplies. I hope this old van is in good mechanical condition."

Niki thought to herself, so do I.

"It's been through a lot since Iowa," she warned, and then worried for the next couple hundred miles. They loaded up with hot coffee to go, more chocolate, and motor oil.

Jake hadn't driven to San Francisco in years. He could get cheap plane tickets on his corporate account. The idea of traveling in a VW bus was better than the actual hard-riding, noisy, air-cooled contraption. All they could do was listen to music and drink coffee to stay awake. It was too tiring to constantly yell over the loud road noise.

They made it safely to Barstow and took a much needed rest room and gas break, got more junk food and coffee. There was more desert to cross until they reached a little fork in the road called Mojave.

There was nothing there but a terrain change. They began a long climb toward Bakersfield. It was nearly two a.m. when they finally arrived and found a 24-hour truck stop. Niki felt a huge relief to be done with that part of the trip. She was very sleepy, even though Jake had driven the last six hours. He suggested she rest for a bit then she might drive part of the way on I-5 toward Sacramento. After that he said the route would get too complicated.

Jake took 99 North through Fresno and Modesto. His goal was reaching his efficiency apartment in San Jose by morning where they could clean up before heading up Highway One toward San Fran and San Rafael.

"Can we stop near the bridge for breakfast?" Niki was excited about seeing the Golden Gate Bridge and the famous park which had a history of a carnival atmosphere dating back to the depression era.

"Yeah, that's where the term panhandling came from," Jake explained. "The Panhandle and Golden Gate Park merge there. It became a hippie refuge in the 60s. We could either go toward North Beach and stop at City Lights or I could show you The Haight."

"You mean Haight-Ashbury? Really? I definitely want to see that."

"I lived there, just off the intersection, in 1967. No trouble finding a coffee shop, I guarantee you."

Before they got to the Haight, they passed through the famous Mission District. This provided some unexpected comic relief. Jake was explaining how the area first became a commercial refuge after the 1906 earthquake, but evolved into a punk rock night club zone. Niki felt her ear buzz and recalled her dream of the teenagers with the funny colored hair and clothes. Before she could tell Jake about the dream, she blurted, *you should see it now with the 'dot commer' lofts.*

"What?" Jake asked.

"No idea," Niki said, then added, "something about Phil liked it better with the hookers and speed." Jake understood that and laughed.

When they got to the Haight, every building had at least two bay windows, even though you couldn't see the actual bay from them. As promised, there were lots of fun looking coffee shops. They picked one. Jake was happy to be out of the noisy Westfalia and walking in his old haunt. He pointed to one of the buildings.

"I lived up there on the third floor. We used to get free food and entertainment, thanks to the Diggers, a radical street threatre group that promoted the Free Society concept."

Until now, Niki had been more interested in seeing the bay or the ocean, but was fascinated as Jake gave a firsthand perspective of the peace and flower power movement.

"I should have realized how important San Francisco would be to a peace treatise," she told him. "But we really do need to get that police report of the San Rafael break-in."

Their waitress must have overheard Niki speculating about the Marin County Sheriff's Office.

"It's on Civic Center Drive in San Rafael," the waitress told them. "I used to live near there. You can not miss the

Center. Looks like a space station—built by that famous Lloyd Wright guy."

"Space station?" Niki said to Jake as the waitress walked away. "Let's go."

"This sure has brought back memories for me," Jake said, driving away from the City toward Oakland. "Look at the Bay Bridge."

"It's bringing back memories for Phil too, I think. I've had non-stop ear-buzzing since the waitress mentioned the Civic Center."

It was true. You could not miss the futuristic Marin County Civic Center. It was a huge complex with a bluish dome that looked like a flying saucer. The outside was nothing compared to the curved multi-level interior and huge sky lights. No wonder Phil liked living nearby, Niki thought.

Niki found a building directory that indicated microfilm records were on the second floor. She and Jake took the escalator. They were greeted by a frail, ancient woman at an information desk. "Can I help you, dear?"

"I hope so. I'm trying to track down a police report on a break-in that happened several years ago. I don't know the exact address, but I know the date. It was November 17, 1971."

"That's over ten years ago," the wizened woman stated the obvious. "Was it your family, honey?"

"No," Niki said. "Does that matter?"

"Well, records that old would be over here on the microfiche," she said. "We'll start with the date. Do you know how to use these things?" The woman hobbled over to a desk with a microfilm reader and started digging around in a cabinet that housed the film reels.

"Yes, I can use it if you can find the reel for me."

"Well, I'm lookin'," she replied. Niki turned to wink at Jake, but he appeared to be dozing in a lobby chair.

The skeletal hand produced a reel dated November, 1971.

Niki thanked the woman and deftly put it on the machine and started spinning through the report files.

"You're pretty good at that," the woman wheezed.

"I've had some practice," Niki smiled. Maybe she should not have admitted that. It might have been better to seem helpless. Too late now. She continued to whirl through the film until she got close to the date, then slowed down so she could view the records frame by frame.

She began with early morning hours of November 17, since she had no idea what time of day the incident happened. She soon realized Phil might not have reported the incident until later, maybe even the next day or two. This could take forever, she worried.

She continued the painfully slow process and just when she was about to give up, there it was! The call wasn't made until November 25, Thanksgiving. Niki felt that was intentional on Phil's part. The report stated:

Officers called to 707 Hacienda Way. Subject wanted to report home safe was "blasted open a few days ago," but afraid to call authorities. Said important papers missing along with a gun and his stereo. Placed value around $600. Subject refused to identify himself. Claimed he was under surveillance, possible phone tap. No verification of that. Officer check of Marin County Recorder's Office shows residence owned by Philip K. Dick. Final report filed: 11-27-71

Niki looked up, and waved to the woman, who again took some time shuffling over to the microfilm area.

"Can I print this file?"

"You found it? Good for you, honey," she said. "We charge fifty cents per page."

"No problem, but how do I do that?"

"It's coin operated. You must have the exact change," the elderly aide had probably said this a thousand times.

With a couple of quarters she finally had the report. It had taken nearly an hour, but well worth it. Jake had found his own coin-operated machine and was finishing off a Coke when she waved the piece of paper.

Niki felt lots of flashes and familiar feelings as they cruised along Mission Avenue. She could hardly wait to get to Hacienda Way. Jake was driving and seemed to know where to go thanks to a street map he found while she was in the Sheriff's Office. Niki was simply soaking up the vibes.

"I still don't understand what you hope to find at the house."

"I just want to try and pick up some type of psychic trail or clue," Niki offered. "I feel it's here, somewhere here in San Rafael."

"The manuscript? Phil thought it had been destroyed, or at least that's what I recall," Jake said rubbing his forehead.

"I know, but what did he say about the conspiracy? The Church, right? He thought the Church was suppressing the info. I keep thinking about the telegram, the urgent telegram from Pike. It's too ironic he sent that and then just died."

"You just read all those books on Pike. There's really nothing to support that he was killed. Oh, here's Vendola and then—"

He didn't have to tell her the next turn. She saw the sign: Hacienda Way. He pulled up and stopped in front of 707. It looked so middle class, with white lattice fencing covering up most of the front of the house, nothing like she expected. Even so, it was a homecoming for Phil. She could feel his reaction. This was just what she had hoped might happen.

"Jake, I want to drive now. I need to drive this route, leaving Phil's house," Niki said, hopping into the driver's seat.

"You don't want to get out, and look around?" Jake asked as he got in on the other side of the van.

Niki didn't even respond. She pulled away from the curb the way Phil must have done hundreds of times when he lived here. It was like automatic pilot. West on Hacienda Way to Vendola, then another left onto La Pasada Way. The route was all residential—nice homes for a struggling science-fiction author, she thought. Then she came to a major street—San Pedro Road. Niki had just turned onto San Pedro when something caught her eye, a billboard with huge red letters that read: **Lost your way?**

Smaller black lettering read: Fellowship services Sunday mornings, 9 and 11 am. Wednesday evenings, 7 pm.
St. Paul's Episcopal Church, 1123 Court Street, San Rafael.

"Look! Episcopal," Niki pointed at the billboard. "It's a sign!"

"Yes, I see that it's a sign. Don't you think you might be reading a bit too much into this one, though? There are a lot of Episcopalian churches in California."

"I have to check it out." Niki swerved into a convenience store and asked directions to Court Street.

"It's only three miles from here," she announced getting back into the van, then whipped around the neighborhood like a local.

"See, Court Street is right here, actually a left turn, and the church is—" Just then the church came into view. Niki pulled into the parking lot.

"We're just going to walk in?" Jake asked. "There's a restaurant just over there." He pointed. "Let's have coffee, use their washroom, and decide what you want to say."

Niki agreed. They walked across to Bob's, home of the Big Boy Burger. Jake ordered one. Niki got a chef salad and iced tea. She couldn't take her eyes off the church.

"I'm getting some kind of vibe. There's definitely a connection of some sort. I just know it."

"Like what?" Jake asked with his mouth full.

"I don't know, but something." Niki kept a vigilant watch on the building, barely touching her food. Then a man emerged. Niki could see it was a priest.

"You finish up here," she jumped up. "I'm going over there."

Before Jake could protest she was out the door and crossing the street. The priest was getting into an older model Chevy Impala when Niki stopped him.

"Sir, could I have a word with you, please?" Niki shouted from several feet away.

The priest looked up, surprised, as Niki approached him.

"I've come all the way from Albuquerque, and before that from Iowa," she told him. "That's my van parked in your lot. I'm a reporter and I'm working on a biographical piece on the late Bishop Pike. Do you happen to know of him?"

"Know of him? He was a dear friend. I celebrated Holy Eucharist at his memorial service. Who sent you to me?" the priest asked.

"It's a long story. Would you have time now or later today when I could visit with you?" Niki held her breath hoping he would agree.

"I'm leaving for an appointment now, but I'll be back by four o'clock. I could meet with you then at the rectory."

"That would be perfect. Thank you so much. My name is Nicole Perceval. Would you mind if my associate joined us? He's over at the diner."

"That's fine. I'm Father Robert Goddard."

Niki shook his hand and said, "Thank you, again. I am truly looking forward to it."

Jake was standing outside the diner watching as the priest drove off. Niki waved him over.

"I was right. That was Father Goddard. He was actually a friend of Pike's and he agreed to meet with us at four."

"What did you tell him?"

"That I'm a reporter doing a bio of the late Bishop and you are my associate."

∞

Niki and Jake were right on time for the appointment. Father Goddard opened the door of the rectory and invited them in.

"Would you care for some tea?" he asked.

"I'd love some," Niki responded.

Jake nodded yes as well.

The priest showed them into a comfortable sitting room with large over-stuffed chairs, a sofa and coffee table. Niki and Jake sat on the sofa. Father Goddard relaxed into one of the chairs facing them.

"Now, how can I be of help to you?" he asked.

Niki took a deep breath and began. "As I mentioned, I'm working on a piece about the late Bishop Pike. I've read his book *The Other Side* and the biography written by his wife, but I still have some questions." Niki judged the man to be in his late 40's. So, he must have been around thirty-five when Pike died.

"Tell me again who referred you to me," the priest asked as he sipped his tea.

"My editor," she said, fingers crossed behind her back. "Would you mind if I taped this, just for my use later, rather than taking detailed notes?"

"I guess not, but what kind of information do you need?"

"I'm interested in his final work and findings at the Nag Hammadi site, particularly the Zadokite fragments. Did he share any thoughts on that with you before he left for Egypt?"

The priest tensed up and even Jake jerked a bit at her blunt beginning.

"You must know the Church opposed his explorations into the gnostic aspects of Christianity," he responded tersely.

"I have a general idea, but I'd like to hear your explanation of why those texts are so controversial."

Father Goddard settled deeper in his chair. "To over simplify, gnosis means direct knowledge. Those scrolls and texts dealt with direct revelations as opposed to traditional intercession required by Catholic and our Episcopal beliefs."

"I read some of the Nag Hammadi translation back in Iowa. Have you read any of the material? Is that allowed?" Niki asked.

"The texts which are referred to as the Nag Hammadi Library, which I imagine you reviewed, were discovered in 1945 at a site known as the Chenoboskion Monastery. Some fifty scrolls were found along with other fragments. With the new English translations, the material is fairly accessible."

The priest paused for a sip of tea then continued, "When Bishop Pike first took an interest in the discovery, the texts had not yet been authenticated. They were very controversial and generally dismissed as heretical. But it wasn't just those texts. Bishop Pike had ideas about tying together many lost scrolls and fragments from Syria and Israel." Goddard paused again. "The Bishop had already endured a great deal of public humiliation, being referred to as a heretic over the incident with his son's suicide. Do you know what I'm referring to?"

"His attempts to communicate with his dead son?"

The priest nodded. "In the mid 1960s there was an effort in California to translate texts. It was called something like the Coptic Gnostic Library Project. Bishop Pike fought to be assigned to that project, but the Church refused. Instead, a man by the name of James Robinson was selected and he eventually published the texts in English."

"That's the material I reviewed in Iowa."

Jake looked impressed. Father Goddard simply nodded. "His books are in university and public libraries now," the priest said. "In the late 60s the project was still obscure and, as I've said, controversial within the Church.

"Bishop Pike did not heed the Archbishop's advice. After the bad publicity over his son and his heresy trial, he went on his own to Israel to investigate translations and findings.

"James was convinced the Church would censor material and he wanted to translate important texts firsthand. As you know, he did not make it back from that trip. He died in the desert."

So far the priest had only rehashed known facts and had not added any real personal insight. Niki was determined to do more digging herself.

"I don't mean to put you on the spot, but do you have any reason to think there was foul play?"

Father Goddard folded his hands in his lap.

"There was some speculation like that," he said, appearing to be deep in thought. "I cannot understand how a man as intelligent and street-wise as Bishop Pike could allow himself to go wandering in the Judean wilderness in 120 degree heat without so much as a flask of water. They said he and his wife had only a couple of soft drinks with them. That made no sense," Father Goddard said, shaking his head.

"Not to me either," Niki offered and Jake nodded agreement.

"However, that issue was reviewed extensively at the time of his death. His young wife, Diane—incidentally, I officiated at their marriage—insisted the car broke down and they were caught off guard," the priest explained.

"So, you knew her, also?"

"Not really. I was just out of seminary in Los Angeles.

"I admired Bishop Pike's expertise on canon law. To be honest, no one else would have solemnized their vows. It was the Bishop's third marriage, I believe."

"I guess I'm asking if you have any reason to think it was a set-up. Could the car have been tampered with?"

"Of course it's possible," Father Goddard replied, then asked Niki a question. "Have you found something indicating it might have been intentional?"

She hesitated and looked at Jake. He spoke for the first time. "A certain author friend of the Bishop's believed that it was more than an accident."

"Are you referring to Philip Dick?" the priest asked.

"Did you know him?" Niki gasped in surprise.

"Bishop Pike knew him. They were close friends. Didn't I read that he died recently?"

"Yes, and to be honest that's why I'm investigating both deaths," Niki confessed. "Both men were working on the same controversial issue, and both died. Did you know that Pike sent Philip Dick a telegram from Israel?"

Goddard did not respond immediately, but gestured that he wanted the tape recorder turned off.

After Niki punched the stop button, the priest asked, "How do you know that?"

Jake spoke up again. "I had an opportunity to speak with Phil in person a couple of years after Pike died. He told me about the urgent telegram that the Bishop sent requesting his help on writing a book. Phil described a book he was working on at that time. It contained a lot of information about Pike's discoveries—"

Niki interrupted, "That manuscript was allegedly stolen during a break-in at Phil's home in 1971. I just read the police report this morning. That stolen manuscript may be the only way to really know what Bishop Pike learned on his trip."

"I have something that may be of interest to you." Father Goddard stood up and excused himself. While he was gone Niki and Jake exchanged looks confirming the session was going well.

The priest returned with a large manila envelope, which he handed to Niki. The post mark read November 11, 1971.

The envelope had no return address. The label was handwritten, addressed to Father Goddard at the church.

"This came from Philip K. Dick."

"This date—that's just a week before the break-in," Niki said pointing to the postmark. "What is it?"

"Open it," the clergyman suggested.

The envelope was not sealed, just closed with the metal twist on the back. Niki gasped—thought she might faint—when she saw the contents. It was the manuscript. Original typed pages, not a carbon or photocopy.

"It wasn't stolen? It was here?" she asked.

"Philip Dick contacted me a few months after Jim died." Niki took note of the more casual references and familiar tone Father Goddard was using as he described this.

"If you recall," the priest continued, "I said I spoke at the memorial service. I met the author there, briefly. He knew I was a friend of the Bishop. So he came to see me one day. I was in Santa Monica at that time, not here. He said he was working on a book, an account of Pike's quest for the Holy Grail—the truth about the Gospels. We chatted for a few minutes. He said when the manuscript was done, he might like for me to read it and comment on the accuracy of the theological references. Months passed, nothing came of it and I forgot about it. More than a year later, I received this envelope with a letter.

"I must admit, I didn't know what to make of the contents. It doesn't appear to be a novel, and as you have seen, the pages are originals."

Niki's hand trembled as she reached in and pulled out the folded letter. Jake rose out of his chair to look over Niki's shoulder as she unfolded and began to read the correspondence from Philip K. Dick:

> November 10, 1971
>
> Dear Honorable Father Goddard,
>
> I apologize for such an extended delay in sending you this material. My wife, Nancy, left me just days after we spoke last year. It was a very difficult time, as you might imagine.
>
> I am sending these manuscript pages now because I feel certain my life is in danger. I have good reason to believe my phone is tapped, that I am being followed at times, and can only hope my mail has not been intercepted. I hope this envelope reaches you, and maybe I too shall arrive soon. I'm leaving for Vancouver in a few days. This is the original. I have a carbon copy.
>
> If you can find time, please review these findings, particularly those pertaining to the Zadokite document. I'd like your honest assessment on matters of theology. Did our mutual friend mention any of these findings to you?
>
> Please keep this manuscript until I call or come for it.
> DO NOT mail it back to me. With sincere thanks.
> Cordially,
> (hand signed) Philip K. Dick

Niki and Jake exchanged looks of amazement.

"He never contacted you, or tried to come back for it?" Niki asked.

"No. It's been in my file cabinet all this time."

Niki flipped through the manuscript, noting the title page simply said "TBD" (to be determined, she knew as a writer.) She could hardly wait to read it.

"I think I know what happened," Jake said. "The break-in occurred a week after Phil sent this letter. If the crooks were looking for his manuscript, they didn't get it. Phil knew it was safe with you." Jake glanced at the priest. "I don't believe he locked up a carbon copy at home. He may have given it to someone else, or maybe he took it with him to Vancouver. He never came back to the Bay Area. Phil was living in Orange County when he died."

"Did you know that his final book, just published a few months ago, was about a bishop?" Niki asked. "The Archer character was basically Pike, and his revelations."

"If that machine is still off," Father Goddard said, "and you promise not to quote me, I'll tell you a bit more about those revelations." Niki nodded and the priest continued.

"After James died, I was curious about his findings. The Bishop was passionate about the translations. I spoke with one of the translators and learned that the documents are not instructions for priests, nor are they Essene in origin. In other words, they are not part of the Dead Sea Scroll "find" at Qumran. The Zadokite, or Damascus documents, are at least a hundred years older than scrolls found at Qumran or Nag Hammadi. However they refer to the One Living Teacher."

"That's not controversial, if it means Jesus, right?"

"It's extremely controversial if the messages were written before Jesus Christ was born. The words 'One Teacher' could not refer to the Savior. Instead, it would support what Pike claimed: the Teacher is within us. The Church may have been founded on false texts, or at the very least, bad translations."

"That could be enough evidence to motivate someone to steal a manuscript, or maybe even kill, to suppress those facts, couldn't it?" Niki looked to Jake for confirmation.

Father Goddard looked down and said, "If the One Teacher is not Jesus Christ, then there really is no basis for the Church—Catholic nor protestant."

Neither Niki or Jake said a word. The priest looked at his watch and announced it was nearly five-thirty.

"I have a dinner engagement at six, so I'm afraid I must end this session."

"May I take this and read it tonight?" Niki asked.

"Keep it," he said. "I was only holding the envelope until the author came back for it. We know that won't happen." As he rose from his chair he added, "Tell me again how you knew to come see me?" This time a light in his eyes danced—the reflection of a stained glass window, or maybe something more.

Niki smiled back. "It was a sign."

"I thought so."

"The whole damn thing was in Latin and a
little tiny bit in Sanskrit,
and there's not much market for that."

-- PKD on LSD

25 Piercing the Veil

After driving over a thousand miles alone, dozing and dreaming at rest stops, Niki had plenty of time to ponder the material that had been stashed in the priest's file cabinet for years.

When she and Jake first left St Paul's Episcopal Church, Niki felt bad for the priest. "No wonder he didn't want to open the envelope. He suspected what Pike had found."

She had read parts of the manuscript to Jake in the van. The thoughts seemed too disjointed and bizarre, even for Phil.

"What is it? A novel or a theological dissertation? It's like the Exegesis or the Tractates, that really don't make sense," Jake said. He looked for a restaurant where he could relax and take a better look at the document.

After sitting for hours, eating, reading and discussing the document, they still hadn't finished the whole thing, so they headed to San Jose so Jake could get back to his apartment.

"Alien spores? Sacred Mushrooms? Plasmates? That's what he says Pike told him to write about?"

"Well, you just read *VALIS* and his last book. What about the Tractates Cryptica Scriptura? Or anokhi as sacred mushroom, and the body of Christ. He said the Zadokites were basically a drug cult."

"That was fiction," Niki said. "This is supposedly fact based on Pike's discoveries. This was going to be Phil's first non-fiction work! Was the Bishop really digging around in the desert looking for alien spores? I don't recall reading anything like that in the biographies I read on Pike."

"Well, a couple of things to remember," Jake said. "This was written in 1970 just after Pike died. Phil was upset. He and everyone around him were doing a lot of drugs, and his fourth marriage was breaking up. Kids were getting drafted and killed in the Vietnam War. So, if you think of that time, you can kind of understand the perception that anokhi was not only a mind-altering psilocybin, but also the Righteous Teacher of the Zadokite writings.

"Okay, but who would blow up Phil's safe to steal this?"

"That speculation has been going on for years," Jake said. "No matter how odd you think it is, the Church doesn't want anyone claiming God is a mushroom."

"Not God!" Phil and Pike rolled their Third Eye. The duo was exasperated trying to clairvoyantly clarify their findings to Niki on her long drive back to Albuquerque.

"Plasmatic spores from Sirius had landed in Sumeria," Pike proclaimed. But it was just too complicated to convey, especially with her driving.

"You gotta admit," Phil teeped to Pike, "it does sound pretty goofy. A crazed holy man down on his hands and knees, digging around in a wadi—a Jerusalem drainage ditch, looking for alien spores to prove his heretical hijinks. Do you still believe the Eucharist is partaking in magic mushrooms?"

"It was a medicinal, healing ceremony, Phil, you know that," the dead cleric scolded. He was not amused. "You should talk. Look at all the incomprehensible gibberish you wrote, with or without me, or drugs, in the name of science fiction."

Niki sensed a psychic disturbance—a bad vibe, you might say—but was too tired to analyze it. She still had another ten hours to drive.

Crossing the Mojave Desert, in the wee hours, she decided she really didn't need to rely on a twelve year old, second or third-hand manuscript when she had direct access to the guys who wrote it. She trusted her own transmissions, especially their combined insight, more than that mess. She glanced at the envelope on the seat beside her. Another buzz.

Gnosis is behind all religions. Jesus, the Buddha, Moses, Enoch, Krishna, Quetzalcoatl—were all gnostics who *knew* the truth about inner peace. That, she did jot down at a rest stop. Niki preferred to think of Jesus as a Sumerian Shaman rather than an alien spore. Although, Christianity with Phil's *Tractates Cryptica Scriptura* as the kerygma, and Pike's form of sacrament, does make for good science fiction.

Jake had stayed in San Jose as planned. He had to work and would fly back to Albuquerque a few days later.

Niki had left that night. It was easier to drive at night in the Westfalia. The noise and slipping clutch kept her awake and it was cooler. Even in late September, the Mojave was unbearably hot. Perhaps not as hot, however, as what she feared she might encounter when she pulled into Corrales.

The lights were on in the adobe house, even though it was almost two a.m. Niki was exhausted and had hoped Lena would be asleep. She desperately needed some herself, as well as time to sort out exactly what she could and couldn't say to

Lena. The last thing she wanted was a run-in when she was running on empty. Niki decided she would simply omit some facts, if necessary, as opposed to a bald-face lie—a technique she had learned from various men along the way.

"Back so soon?" Lena said, opening the door. Schroeder came bounding toward her. Niki scooped up the big old tomcat and nuzzled his neck. He purred appreciatively. She had no idea if Jake had called or spoken to Lena, nor if she was being sincere or sarcastic.

"I didn't want to impose any longer than necessary," Niki said cautiously. "Thanks for taking care of him. Why are you up at this hour?"

"Couldn't sleep. Jake's gone again. In fact, he should have given you his contact info in San Jose. Is that close to where you were?"

"Pretty close," Niki said as evenly as possible. "I was in San Rafael meeting with a priest."

"A priest? I want to hear all about it."

"Well, not right now. I'm wiped out. I just drove over a thousand miles in that bumpy, noisy van with no Schroeder for company." The cat was rubbing against and weaving between her legs.

"I'll help you with your stuff," Lena offered but Niki declined.

"That can wait, too. I just want to take a quick hot shower and dive in bed, if you don't mind."

In the shower Niki thought of things she had suppressed on the trip. Feelings, longings for someone like Jake, or Jay as she wanted to call him, and here she was in his house with a woman he had been sleeping with and living with for two years. It was too strange, nearly as strange as her whole kooky journey. She was so exhausted she nearly fell asleep in the shower. All she wanted was to crawl into bed. She didn't even remember Schroeder curling up beside her.

The next morning, Sunday, October 3

"You found that manuscript?" Lena asked. "How? Where is it?"

"Well, Jake helped me a lot," Niki told her as she sipped her coffee, thinking how often she had shared a cup with him at that very table. "He showed me all the novels by Philip K. Dick, and we talked to the bookstore owner, that tall guy Acer at Birdsong, who added even more. Pieces just started coming together."

"Are you saying your transmissions were from a dead science-fiction writer? That sounds ridiculous."

"More ridiculous than receiving signals from an invisible mother ship that hovers over New Mexico and uses the VLA to amplify Cosmic Transmissions to you and Dora?"

Lena's expression of disbelief dissolved to displeasure.

"What's happened to you?" Lena asked. "You have quite a collection of transmitted material yourself. Why do you always mock Dora and me, and make fun of Monka."

"I'm not trying to be mean, Lena, but I have to go back to the *Courier* in less than a month. What am I going to tell the guys at the paper? I channeled ancient aliens, sci-fi spirits, went on Vision Quests to other dimensions, and then found a manuscript that said Jesus was a mushroom? Do you have any idea how they are going to mock me?"

Before Lena could comment, Niki heard the high-pitched sound in her left ear. *The information must be re-collected.*

"I did re-collect it," she yelled out. "It was garbage."

"Okay, I hear you," Lena responded. "So what are you going to do with it?" Apparently Phil, Lena, and the Bishop were all on the same wavelength and the signal was crossed.

The story must be told. Niki heard and then passed out.

∞

"You keep getting sick. I'm taking you to Dominic," Lena said emphatically. "I should have insisted a long time ago. You have a serious energy imbalance from all this psychic activity. He does Reiki energy healing and body work. He can bring you back into balance."

Niki remembered that Jake had called Dominic a quack. In fact, that was one of the arguments she couldn't help but overhear one night. She recalled Jake's disgusted tone when he said, "The only energy he manipulates is sexual energy." Niki confessed to Lena she heard that.

"I don't care what Jake said. Dominic understands these things. He's an M.D. as well as a healer," Lena defended her friend and physician. "I'm calling him," she said and left to make the call before Niki could protest further. While she was out of the room, Niki closed her eyes and tried to discern if she should actually consent to seeing the guy, or just pick up her things and leave the Corrales house. Lena marched back into the room before Niki could consider either option.

"Dominic said he'd be glad to see you, today. No charge," she announced. "I told him you were traveling and didn't have much money right now. We should take both vehicles, in case you want to stay."

"What do you mean stay?" Niki asked.

"Well, if he offers, he has retreats. You should consider it. It's beautiful up in the mountains this time of year." Lena gave Niki directions in case they got separated and suggested they meet for a late lunch at the Bella Vista Restaurant.

"You'll love it. It's an old funky place on the Turquoise Trail, right there on North 14, close to Dominic's. You can't miss it. It's huge. The building was probably added on to about a hundred times."

Driving east on I-40 toward the Sandia Mountains reminded Niki of when she first drove in through the canyon. It seemed so long ago.

Why was Lena so insistent they see Dominic on Sunday? And, if she was so worried, why make Niki drive? Lena claimed it was because she had the day off and wanted to see Dominic anyway. It felt like she was pushing Niki out. Maybe Jake called and told her about the trip. Whatever the reason, it was best to get away for awhile.

Lena was right about the big restaurant. It probably had been a Wild West watering hole originally, but had evolved into a sprawling mish mash of single-story wood-frame rooms until now it was billed as the largest restaurant in New Mexico, seating over twelve hundred people. That explained the huge line they encountered outside. Even so, they got in fairly quickly. The place had a beautiful view, like its name. Niki was still reading the history of Bella Vista on the menu and soaking up the atmosphere, but Lena was back to her sales pitch.

"He's absolutely wonderful. I don't know why I didn't introduce you to him when we first discussed your ghost sickness and depleted energy from channeling."

Niki only half listened to Lena. She was intrigued with the mountain lifestyle and decided that exploring the Turquoise Trail and old mining communities could be fun. Getting out of Jake's house was a relief given her conflicted feelings. Lena was still yammering about Dominic, "He's divorced."

"I hope that's not what this is about, Lena. I'm not interested in meeting someone."

Thankfully, the big-as-the-building plates of fried chicken and battered fish with fries and coleslaw arrived. After eating Lena's health food for the past couple of months, it looked divine. They ate without much further discussion and left.

Dominic's healing centre consisted of a large A-frame nestled in the pines, with several out buildings that Lena called yurts. It was a serene setting, and the mountain air was refreshing. Before Niki had parked, Lena had jumped out of her Subaru and was running up the drive.

Soon, she returned with a squat, semi-bald, round man.

"Niki, this is my dear friend and fabulous healer, Dominic Vandante."

"I'm Nicole Perceval," she said holding out her hand. The man's energy felt calm, nothing ominous or lecherous. In fact, he was nothing at all like she expected, given Jake's comment about how he just wanted to get his hands on women.

"Nicole, I'm so happy to have you here at the Centre," Dominic said with a deep, smooth voice that matched his mocha skin. He had a definite South American accent that was different from the Spanish or Mexican sounds Niki had grown accustomed to in Albuquerque.

"Dominic is Mayan, from Guatemala," Lena interjected. He had a graying goatee, and wore round, wire-framed glasses tinted a dark maroon color.

Dominic waved to Lena as she drove off and then motioned toward a large wooden deck on the A-frame building.

"Such a beautiful day. Let us sit here and discuss what's been happening to you." The weather, his property and the view of the canyon were all perfect. Niki had not seen such a sea of green since leaving Iowa. They settled into a couple of white-washed wooden lawn chairs with big comfortable cushions. A young girl appeared with a tray of snacks and herbal tea.

"I sense you are uneasy, but I want to assure you that I am also a medical doctor. I practiced for fifteen years before opening this alternative health centre." Dominic's manner of speech was intriguing, a bit mysterious. She enjoyed listening to him as she sipped the tea.

"Lena explained that to me. How much did she tell you about my experiences?" Niki asked.

"Lena and I are friends and she did tell me of you. I had hoped to meet you at the Equinox gathering. Other commitments prevented that," he paused. "You also receive star transmissions, right?"

"I'm not sure about that," Niki hesitated. "I am certain I've heard messages from dead people—real people I've been able to identify."

"How do you know this for certain, as you say?"

Niki dreaded another long explanation of all that had happened. She quickly summarized the early experiences and then cut to the more recent developments.

"It was the term *VALIS*—Vast Active Living Intelligence System—that helped solve the mystery. Jake is the one who knew about Philip K. Dick. He had read his books, actually met him in the 1970s, and knew that he had died in March of this year."

"The religious terms, Maitreya, Moksha, Nag Hammadi. The sci-fi author was responsible for that, too?"

"It's complicated. Phil, the writer, and the late Bishop James Pike were friends.

"Bishop Pike was a controversial figure in the late 60s; a priest who believed he was communicating with his dead son. He contacted the sci-fi writer, Phil, and convinced him to attend séances. But then, the Bishop was charged with heresy for his public involvement in such matters. He didn't back down, though. He gave interviews on TV and was featured on the cover of *Time* magazine.

"Pike felt the Church was suppressing the gnostic roots of Christianity. His research proved that alleged mystical, so-called occult, powers were actually what Jesus practiced and preached."

Niki couldn't seem to stop talking. For some reason she felt compelled to explain everything she had just learned about the Zadokites to this man she hardly knew.

"The most amazing discovery is the Damascus document," she continued. "It dates to 200 B.C. yet contains some of the most famous words attributed to Jesus. The Bishop was on the verge of revealing even stranger findings that would call into question, if not invalidate, the concept of divinity. It was all related to the gnostic teachings."

"Gnostic, you say. What exactly does that mean?" Dominic asked.

"Gnosis means 'to know' through personal revelation. But apparently Pike believed there was much more to the Damascus and Zadokite findings." She paused, knowing she should not reveal anything about the mushroom cult.

"Let's just say Pike went there to get directly involved in the research."

"This is fascinating. Please, go on."

"So, he went to Israel in 1969, but never made it to Syria or Nag Hammadi, Egypt. He died, apparently digging around for answers." Niki raised a brow and laughed, knowing that he was digging for proof that the anokhi was a mushroom, but she did not reveal that. "Newspaper stories called it an accident, but Phil, the writer, believed he was set up to keep the truth from getting out." Niki was overly animated now and beginning to feel woozy.

"Here's the part that affects me. Phil believed that the dead Bishop was communicating with him from Beyond—'the Other Side'—prodding Phil to tell the story. Phil began having a series of strange experiences—visions, hearing messages, similar to what happens to me."

"Nicole, how do you know all of this?" Dominic interrupted.

"He wrote about it, in great detail. Not just fiction books, but in journals and notes. And, there was this non-fiction piece that would have exposed everything." She was actually beginning to slur her words. "It would've really rocked the Christian world, but that manuscript was stolen during a break-in at his house."

"It's a fascinating story, like a movie. But why is it making you sick? What is the personal impact on you?" It sounded more like "and jew" due to Dominic's accent.

"They're both dead now," Niki said, feeling very woozy. "Both Phil and Pike are dead and they communicate with me."

"So, you have two spirits inhabiting you, correct?"

"They're all merged and cross-bonded," Niki's eyes were beginning to roll back. "We're all in a vortex called VALIS—a big ole Vast Active Living—"

"Intelligence System," Dominic finished her sentence. He was looking at his notes and she had come full circle now. "Okay, I think I understand enough now to comment." He straightened up and placed his fingers on his temples as if he was drawing in cosmic information himself.

"The human body is a microcosm of the universe and contains magnetic and electrical fields. These fields create a grid structure around and through our bodies. This grid holds all memories, patterns and beliefs of this and all other lifetimes—past, present, and future. This also happens on a planetary level, just like what your writer called VALIS. You follow?"

"Kind of." Niki was struggling to focus. How could this Guatemalan guy know all this, she wondered.

"The grid is a living intelligence system," he continued. "So, when you say these entities are merged, it is entirely possible. They are somehow merged into your grid system, too, I think. This is why you feel sick or drained. They use your energy field to communicate."

"Really?" she slurred.

"If we clear your grid and align your body system—the emotional, mental, physical and spiritual bodies—this is what I call balancing. Once this takes place, I think your symptoms will cease."

"What happens to my guides?"

"They should be released to resolve their own karma."

The prospect of totally releasing her guides created new anxiety for Niki. "I'm not ready to give them up, not yet." Niki tried to stand up and stumbled. "I need some air."

"We will move slowly and you need to move slowly now." Dominic stood up. "Let me help you to your lodge so you can rest." He took her arm and steadied her. As they walked, Dominic did the talking.

"I use a combination of energy work, some regression therapy and sauna, and sometimes a native practice called a sweat lodge ceremony. Are you familiar with that?"

"Yes," Niki touched her soul-arc totem necklace and thought of Koteen. "I'm actually learning shamanic practice."

"You know that I am a Mayan shaman, right?"

"Really," Niki slurred again. "Lena never used that term."

"There's no coincidence. It's all part of the synchronicity of life. All things are inter-related," Dominic said, smiling. "Will you be comfortable here?" he asked as he pulled back the flap of a strange little hut. All she wanted was to lie down.

"Don't miss our full moon ceremony tonight," he said, pointing to another structure, his own round stone Kiva.

"Our Mayan tradition is based on moon cycles. Tonight's *Kay Nikte'* is actually a cleansing ceremony. It may help with your energy issues."

"Clear her energy grid my ass," Phil wanted to scream. The James-Philip duo wasn't about to "just go" without a fight. "Who does that guy think he is?" James added. They had respected the young hawk shaman, but this Mayan wise man was a wise guy. He had spiked her tea with some truth serum or potion and then mesmerized Niki. Phil felt it was time to intervene again, and fast. He had to do something.

The same young girl who brought tea earlier took over as Dominic left. She helped Niki into the yurt that she would share with two other women.

The building was a cross between a straw hut and a tipi, or wickiup as they called them out west. The design provides ventilation. The key feature is a ring opening at the top which also offers an opportunity to see the night sky.

The girl handed Niki a colorful Mayan wrap-around garb of hand-woven fabric and indicated she should wear it to the evening *Kay Nikte'* moon ceremony. Niki was about to pass out or collapse onto the cot, when she heard one last message. It was not from the girl. *Stay out of the Kiva tonight.*

The sun was setting when Niki woke up. Her head throbbed, like a hangover, but she recalled the warning.

Now what should she do? If she didn't go to the Kiva, or even if she passed out, Dominic would probably send someone to carry her to the ceremony to make sure she was cleansed of the "evil spirits."

As the sun dropped into the western horizon, Niki dashed out of the yurt and into the community room of the A-frame building, to use the restroom but also to hide out. When she finally peeked around the corner, she saw a familiar site. It was the turbaned one.

"Baba! How did you find me here?"

"My dear, you forget I am all seeing and knowing," he smiled, flashing those near-blinding pearly whites. "I went to the Health Garden for a cup of chai and Lena told me," he confessed. "You should have called if you were not feeling well. I could have suggested another homeopathic remedy. Did you follow through with the lycopodium?" Baba asked.

"No," Niki admitted. Actually, she had forgotten about the little pills Baba had given her. She hadn't taken seriously his alleged medical practice. "You know Dominic?"

"Oh yes. I knew him when he was allopathic. In fact, we discussed the merits of switching to a holistic practice."

"Allopathic? What's that?"

"Standard western AMA medicine. Pharmaceuticals. Drowning symptoms in drugs rather than curing the root cause as we do with homeopathy," Baba Dhyana elaborated.

"You're serious, that you were a healer in India?"

"I'm so hurt you would doubt me. Dominic got his ideas for the Centre after a session in our prayer room where we discussed alternative healing."

That meant after smoking hashish. Niki would have thought Baba was just bragging again, but a slight ear-buzz and tingle up her spine, caused her to pay more attention.

"Lena mentioned you might do a sweat lodge."

"That's up to Dominic," Niki said. "Whatever he has planned, it will have to happen soon. I'm supposed to leave in a couple of weeks to return to Iowa."

"Leave?" Baba was surprised. "My dear, even if you start the treatments today you won't be able to travel in two weeks."

"Why not? I just drove back from California—"

"I'd like to discuss your trip to California," Baba interjected. "Congratulations on finding the manuscript."

Niki almost returned a thank you, but stopped.

"How do you know I found it?" Niki paused. "Lena! She told you, didn't she? She sent you here! Why else would you be here? Did you help Dominic concoct that truth serum?"

Baba said nothing. If Lena knew about the manuscript, Niki thought, then she had been talking to Jake, because Niki had not revealed finding the manuscript, or anything about the Zadokite sect, to anyone. Did Baba say he just had chai with Lena at the Health Garden? She never works on Sunday. Something was wrong. Who were the real diablos muertos?

Niki definitely needed to do a ceremonial that night, but not in Dominic's Kiva. She needed to find Koteen and get advice on how to resolve the whole mess.

26 Showdown at the Sweat Lodge

Niki returned to her yurt without saying another word to Baba. With the *Kay Nikte'* cleansing ceremony well underway, it was a perfect opportunity for a shamanic journey. Everyone was in the Kiva. She had the yurt to herself as well as live drumming and chanting, which she could hear perfectly.

She moved her mat and blankets to the floor, silently asked for protection and guidance, and let the sounds carry her away.

As her inner vision focused, she saw the tree—the Tree of Life. She climbed and urgently summoned Koteen. In the midst of the swirl of colors and images, the hawk came into view, flew closer, then swooped down and carried her away.

Niki rode with the wind, through the clouds, beyond the stars, and to a place she would always share with this magical soul. In the cosmic realm, where light is language and sound heals, she was able to convey what had been happening. Not just her confusion and mental trappings in the maya—the illusion of time—but also being literally trapped at the healing center.

With the breath of the Great Spirit, Koteen blew away the cobwebs and remaining veils. Niki really could *see* as she had during the spiritual encounter with her dad. A shift in perspective can break open our eye, and allow us to truly see with new eyes. Peace and love are possible, and essential to save ourselves and Mother Earth, she realized.

In the shamanic realm the interconnection of everything is obvious. Animals, birds, and people are merged and of equal importance. The universe—All That Is—or VALIS as Phil called it, requires the infinitesimal photon for Light. Koteen as the Dark Chanting Goshawk was *more,* not less, than the Yavapai guide she met in Sedona. And, Niki finally evolved into what Koteen had seen from the beginning. She wasn't just a freckled-faced white woman; her inner spirit was Soars-like-an-Eagle and would no longer require a guide to navigate the celestial realms.

You are safe in the universe, now and always, she heard. Niki saw an image she would never forget. Many faces were shifting and pulsing in rhythm with the cosmic life force, the sound of eternity. Everyone who had played some role in her life: her mother, friends who had died, historical and religious figures, even pets, animals she had rescued, Pike, Phil, and finally her dad, who like Koteen whispered with the wind—*now is the time.*

As the drumming and the moon ceremony ended, Niki returned to ordinary consciousness from her journey and knew exactly what to do to get out of the Black Iron Prison.

∞

The next day, October 6, 1982

"*The Black Iron Prison*, Phil conveyed, "is when we feel trapped and the veil is covering reality. Maya, as the Hindus call it, and interesting that Guatemalans are called Mayans."

Niki had hooked up the computer in the community room, since the yurt had no electricity. She didn't need a phone line. She simply wanted to use the keyboard.

The automatic writing was coming fast and furious now. Apparently the electrons and crystal within the computer enabled, or at least amplified, the connection. Lena had been right about that. There was some scientific reason, at least. She relaxed, let her fingers hover over the keys, and Phil—or Pike or their Collective mind—did the rest.

Time is an illusion. It can be overcome.

"But how?" Niki asked and began to type furiously as the steps to breaking the Seal were clarified:

1) Recognize the world as karma
2) Anamnesis – person re-collects his true identity
3) Christ Consciousness floods the person's mind
4) Word is now experienced from Creator viewpoint
5) Time does not exist, only vast space
6) Bardo (Thodol) trip ends with rebirth or release
7) Second Coming or Assimilation into Divine: Salvation!

These were the steps reenacted by Jesus in his passion.

These steps, the method for resurrection, was explained over two thousand years ago in the Zadokite scroll.

The secret—*the key*—is that it is not a physical process. It's an inner journey. "The Journey of the Soul" it is called in the Gnostic Gospels. The Zadokite material depicts a sacred mythic rite *outside of time*, not an historical event.

Christ is now here

Niki typed, in bold letters, the message she heard in her mind and had once seen in a newspaper clip. With help from Phil and Pike, she realized the Maitreya had not resurrected in bodily form. It is not a physical event, nor referring to one person. It happens to each of us. It should have read:

Christ is now here: within each of us.

11:11

The cipher had a new meaning! When she finished typing, she thought, that really was some heavy shit, as Phil would have said.

"Is this what Bishop Pike learned in Egypt?" she asked.

"Yes! 'Christ', 'Holy Spirit', 'Father' and 'Godhead' represent various stages of this process. Find the *Keys of Enoch*."

"Keys of Enoch? What is that?" Niki asked, but the communication was fading. She sensed this was probably her last transmission. She had the manuscript and could research the Zadokite documents. But what are the Keys of Enoch, she wondered.

A few days later, Saturday, October 9

Mayan Zumpul-che Purification Sweat-bath Ceremony

The sweat bath would begin at sunset. But part of the ritual was constructing the lodge. Dominic had invited Baba Dhyana, Keriani, and Lena and asked them to arrive by four o'clock. It would take a couple of hours to build the small lodge.

Dominic and Niki had gathered materials earlier in the day. Now there were piles of branches, rocks and a tarp to cover the structure once it was built.

"We build a rough wickiup hut from these branches," Dominic explained, showing Baba how he wanted the lodge constructed. "It is made from willow saplings and mud."

The two men worked to form the skeleton support, which was similar to the design of the yurts only more temporary. Niki and Lena helped by holding and tying the support branches, and then filled in the gaps with smaller twigs and mud. This lodge would be covered with a tarp, rather than animal hide, Dominic had told them. By six o'clock they had the lodge in place.

"We are actually creating a womb from mother earth," he said. "Just as new life is formed in the mother's womb where it is warm, dark and wet, we simulate that with the building of the lodge.

"To prepare for the ceremony," Dominic said, "we start a small fire in the center of the lodge. The rocks and stones will become very hot. We will add sage to the fire for protection, and pour cool water on the rocks to create cleansing steam.

"When I close the flap over the door, that is when the ceremony begins. We sit in the dark and cleanse our soul.

"For this sweat we will concentrate on the spirits that have attached to Nicole, and attempt to release them. The purpose of the sweat lodge is to purify body and spirit, purge toxins," Dominic continued.

"Traditional Guatemalan sweats did not permit women to enter the lodge. The men would sit naked. Of course, a true lodge would not permit any 'pale face'—male or female. Since we are in mixed company, we will wear shorts or bathing suits." He glanced at the darkening sky, "We should change now and make our final preparations," he concluded.

As the sun set and illuminated the western sky, the group headed to the healing centre to change. Niki came back first wearing shorts, a tank top and a towel draped around her shoulders. The night air in the mountains was chilly, and it would have been very dark, but the full moon had peeked over one of the mountain ridges and was beginning to provide some illumination.

The lodge was built in a wooded area behind the A-frame. Baba, still in his turban, had on a pair of cut-off jeans. He was speaking quietly with Dominic, who also had changed to shorts. Lena was the last to come out in a one-piece bathing suit. She also had a large towel around her and was carrying a white candle and her turtle totem.

"Is it okay to bring these into the lodge?"

"Yes, if the objects are meaningful to you," Dominic said.

Niki touched her necklace, her only meaningful item. She knew Koteen would be there in spirit form, along with many others, and just smiled.

"We'll light the fire with a sage branch once we're inside. I think we should hold hands and invite the spirits to join us," Dominic suggested. The four stood in a circle, holding hands.

After a moment of silence, Dominic spoke in a foreign dialect, apparently Guatemalan or Mayan. Then he began to chant. Baba and Lena joined in. Niki continued to meditate, feeling sad about losing her spirit guides. What would it be like without them? She could not imagine it.

Niki felt Baba and Lena let go of her hands, and looked up. Dominic handed her a large oval rock and motioned for her to enter the lodge. She placed the rock in the fire, which was already heating up. Niki folded her towel and sat on it.

Then Lena entered with two smaller rocks, tossed them into the fire and sat beside Niki. Baba was next with three rocks. He added his rocks to the fire and sat across from her. Dominic was the last with the final two rocks, which made the eight Niki had requested. The lodge was already becoming hot even with the leather flap still open. Dominic added the sage to the fire. Heavy white smoke began to billow up. Finally he added a small container of water and a dramatic burst of steam rose up. He closed the flap to the lodge.

Within minutes the heat was almost unbearable. Niki could feel sweat breaking out all over her body. Dominic seemed oblivious, offering her a burning sage branch so she could smudge herself. The hut was so small and she was practically sitting on the edge of the fire. Niki closed her eyes, hoping she wouldn't pass out from the thick sage smoke and heat. Dominic chanted in the same mesmerizing rhythm of the drumming and Niki quickly began to swoon. A loud hiss of steam startled her and she opened her eyes.

For the first time, Niki could see them clearly—the Bishop with his glasses, and Phil with his broad forehead, beard, and penetrating eyes.

It was like seeing double. They *were* super-imposed, cross-bonded, as Phil had called it.

Just as Koteen suggested would happen, during the Lodge Ceremony the two began to separate. He had assured Niki the ceremony would help them as much as her.

She silently thanked Phil and James for all they had done to show her the Way. "Your business here is finally finished. You are free," she conveyed and could sense both elation and sorrow as their images began to fade. They left her with one final message: *The story must be told.*

"It will be," Niki assured them, and sobbed. She felt Lena touch her shoulder and say, "Let your tears flow." Then someone pulled open the flap to the lodge. A burst of cold air rushed in jolting Niki back to ordinary reality and creating a new cloud of steam.

With all the smoke, steam and tears, Niki could not see what was happening. She heard a deep unfamiliar voice, more like grunting sounds, some guttural language she had never heard. Then she was pulled from the lodge. Someone strong picked her up and carried her to safety. Even though her eyes refused to adjust to the bright moonlight, she didn't have to see him, she knew it was Jake.

"How did you get here?" Niki said choking and coughing.

"Shhh. Just breathe!" he said. An odd calm came over her. Even though she was shivering in the chilled night air it felt good. The coolness soothed her lungs and throat which had felt on fire. Finally, she could see again.

There was an old man standing over her. His face was brown and wrinkled like leather. He placed a thick woven blanket around Niki's shoulders and made a gesture—some sort of blessing.

Niki saw that Lena and the others had also been pulled from the lodge. She looked for Jake. He was with Lena, who looked terrified.

"Get dressed, all of you, then we talk," the old man spoke in broken English and shooed everyone toward the A-frame building. That was the raspy voice she heard as she was being rescued. Who is he? she wondered. She knew one thing, if she had been in the lodge much longer, her lungs might have exploded or burned out.

A few minutes later everyone had returned in warmer clothing, and Dominic pulled chairs into a circle on the deck. He introduced the old weathered man.

"This is my grandfather, Raphael. He's a curandero, a medicine man from Guatemala. It's his sweat lodge." At that point the hunched-over, wizened man straightened up and spoke with authority.

"She," Raphael said, pointing to Niki, "had ghost sickness."

"This one," he pointed to Baba Dhyana, "was misleading you. A trickster." Baba squirmed uncomfortably.

"Speak the truth now," the old man said, making a gesture at Baba Dhyana, who amazingly opened right up.

"I wanted the manuscript," Baba admitted. Keriani looked as though she might faint, and began her prayerful gestures. Niki was perplexed. "Why?" she asked Baba. "What did it mean to you?"

"I thought it was the Zadokite scroll," he confessed.

"It's the draft of a novel," Niki frowned. Even if that was a white lie, she was never going to reveal the bizarre material in that envelope. That would remain her secret.

"Leave the circle," Raphael ordered Baba, "and unwrap your head. You are no guru."

Keriani must have been in shock. She was frozen in place, as Baba walked away from the group, to his car, and left.

"The spirits are gone now. They are free," the curandero proclaimed, then turned his attention to Dominic.

"You should feel shame. You could have been a healer." He shook his head and then waved his thin hand at his grandson, as if shooing away a fly.

Dominic hung his head, but did not leave the circle.

Lena looked lost and confused.

"The sacred sweat bath is not a game," Raphael folded his arms and continued. "My grandson should know better.

"The Mayan people knew how to live on Mother Earth, and treat her with respect. Life is sacred. You will see how all things depend upon each other. You may trick one another, but soon you will learn you cannot trick nature. She will fight back. Dangerous times lie ahead," he warned.

Both Niki and Keriani bowed to the true healer.

"We can leave together," Niki whispered to Baba's wife. "I have my van. I'm done here."

Lena looked puzzled and said, "I don't understand what just happened."

"I'm not surprised," Niki replied. "Perhaps Dominic, or even Jake, can explain it to you. I think you all have your own unfinished business. I'm taking Keriani home now. I'll call and make arrangements to get Schroeder and the rest of my things in a few days." Niki gave a stern glance—almost a glower—at Jake. He looked wide-eyed and shrugged.

As Niki and Keriani walked to the van with their arms around each other, she heard the old Medicine Man say, "The sacred sweat bath always reveals *what is.*"

"The sun of the first day put the question
To the new manifestation of life—
Who are you? There was no answer.
Years passed by.
The sun of the last day
Uttered the question on the shore of the western sea,
Who are you! No answer came."
-- Rabindranath Tagore, 1938

27 the Final Key

A few days later, Jake came to the Bodhi Tree looking for Niki. He brought Schroeder, some of her clothes and other belongings. Keriani greeted him and offered him chai tea.

"Where is your husband?" Jake asked and sipped the hot drink.

"He has returned to India for now," she replied, making her usual prayerful gestures. "He will spend time in our Ashram and contemplate his actions. Look at Tagore. It's a miracle. He can walk and speak."

Niki entered the room with Tagore, who was walking, slowly and still unsteady, but out of his wheel chair. The young man was smiling.

"We were all healed that day," he said.

That brought tears to both women. Even Jake looked misty-eyed.

"It was a healing and purification ceremony," Niki confirmed.

"With Baba gone, are you okay?" Jake asked Keriani.

"Oh, yes. Mani is here to help. Nicole has been helping us, too. And, as you see, Tagore is growing stronger every day."

"Can this arrangement work for both of you, for awhile?" Jake directed his question to Niki this time.

"Yes, it is good for all of us," she confirmed. "I'm very comfortable and sleeping in the prayer room. I feel safe there."

Keriani whispered, "Om Namo Naryana." Repeating it several times until it was too faint to hear.

"With all respect, Keriani," Niki began, "I've wanted to know the meaning of that chant. Can you tell us?"

Keriani lowered her eyes and chin and placed her hands together in a prayerful position just below her lips.

"It is a prayer to Vishnu, the all pervading God—God of all gods, the Creator," she told them.

Tagore limped to the table. There truly was a special light in his eyes. "Bliss, bliss, bliss," he said.

"That is true," Keriani confirmed. "Bliss in English, or extreme joy."

Tagore pointed to Niki and said, "Bhakti bhava."

"He said two things," Keriani translated. "You have the light in you and now is the time."

"You're right Tagore. The time *is* now." Niki already knew that, but somehow Tagore saying it confirmed she could not return to Iowa. Her mission was here. "But Tagore, you are the one with the Light. Amazing blessings lie ahead for you. That I can predict."

Jake winked at Niki and stood up.

"Well, Ladies and Gentleman, I must return to San Jose and finish up some work there. I'll be back by the Solstice, though, and insist we meet at my house in Corrales for a final gathering."

He bowed to Keriani, shook hands with Tagore, and hugged Niki. She felt it was an especially close hug, and also detected an extra glint in his eye. Tagore said he had left a tip and note on the table. The note was in Sanskrit.

प्रेमास्तंभ्य
मस्ति

"Jake wrote in Sanskrit?"

The boy smiled and said, "He asked me to write it."

"What does it say?"

Keriani looked at the note and her eyes turned moist. She translated:

"Love is unstoppable."

Niki felt her heart leap, but logically she couldn't understand it. "Why would he do that?"

Keriani said, "Sometimes we must trust the universe and what is meant to be."

Koteen had told her she was safe in the Universe during their last shamanic exchange. For now, Niki would have to trust that she was making the right decision to stay in New Mexico and let the story unfold.

Niki enjoyed spending time with Keriani and the boys, and agreed to stay at least through the holidays, when Baba was supposed to return. After that? She would have to trust the U.C. to show the way.

When she wasn't helping at the restaurant, she spent most of her time researching the Zadokite material and organizing her notes about Phil and Bishop Pike.

Their story was incredible, but was it her mission? Was their unfinished business the basis for her peace treatise? Something was still missing, like an incomplete puzzle.

Speaking of puzzles, she received a package of mail from Frank. Inside was an envelope from Sussex. Niki looked at it, as if not sure what to do. Finally, she opened it. There was just one hand-written page on thin air mail paper:

Dearest Nicole,

Please accept my heartfelt apology that I did not ring you up about my change of heart on the March tenth event. It was all so sudden with the BBC contacting me. I hope you can forgive me. I have an important message for you—a tip that I hope will make up for my transgressions.

I met a Mexican scholar, well credentialed, who lives in San Francisco. He is working on a theory that I am certain will intrigue you. He claims he has decoded the Mayan Calendar and is certain that time as we know it will end in the year 2012. I do not think I should provide his name by post. If you ring me, I will tell you precisely how to contact him. In fact, we might meet in California again and I can introduce you to him. I hope to hear from you. The International number in Sussex is +44 xxxx xxxxxx

Yours,
JG
John R. Gribbin

Niki looked at the letter, Gribbin's signature, and the idea of chasing down another Mayan connection, with Gribbin, no less. All she could do was laugh.

∞

An important break-through did occur a day later.

On November 11, Niki stopped in at the Birdsong bookstore to go over some of her notes about Philip K. Dick with Acer. While talking to him, an odd thing happened.

Sunlight came in through the window in such a way that it illuminated a large white volume on a shelf behind him. It was so dramatic, she interrupted their discussion and asked Acer to turn around and look.

A ray, almost a beam of light, shone directly on one book. Acer reached up and pulled the white, leather bound volume from the shelf. Embossed in gold, the title read: ***The Keys of Enoch.***

"I absolutely must have that book," Niki said.

"Why am I not surprised?" Acer laughed. He asked about Jake and Niki explained that Jake was back in San Jose, but should be back for a Solstice gathering in December.

"I haven't seen Lena at the Health Garden, either," Acer said. "Someone else seems to be managing the place."

"I guess we'll find out next month. You'll be there, right?"

"With bells on, and with Morwyn, if we're invited."

Niki hugged the big, friendly guy and patted her white volume. She was ecstatic and convinced that she finally had the key to the mystery.

What she would see later, when she reviewed her notes again, was the **11:11** cipher that Phil and Pike had created to signal that all the materials had been re-collected.

Not only is the cipher in the Enoch book, as a symbol for Christ Consciousness, of course the ray of light hit the book at precisely 11:11 am on November 11, and the *Keys of Enoch* truly are the keys to the Zadok's theory of Enlightenment.

∞

28 the Truth Re-collected

When Niki called Frank to tell him she was staying in New Mexico, he was not happy about losing his favorite investigative reporter. But on some level he always knew she wouldn't be back.

"You're young, you have your whole life ahead of you," he said over the phone.

"Now is the time to take chances. When you get to be my age, all you think about is safety and retirement."

"Thanks, Frank. You've meant a lot to me and always will. I certainly appreciate everything. Hey, what about Bruce?"

"He's here. I'll let him tell you his news."

When Bruce came on the line, she laughed at hearing his high, energetic voice.

"Wow, Nik, you're really staying out there? Do you have a job?"

"Yeah, I do have a job, Bruce. It's a long-term project," Niki laughed to herself. "I'm fine. How are *you* doing?"

"I got married in September. We didn't know how to reach you to tell you. And, guess what?"

"You're having a baby, right?"

"No, we kept the kitten. It's a beautiful Burmese. We named him Buddha—Buddha the Burmese, just for you."

"Take good care of him, he's more special than you know. And, congratulations. I bet you have a rug rat or two by the time I come for a visit."

"Nope, no kids for awhile," Bruce insisted. "We're buying a house. And, you know Frank would take you back in a heartbeat if you get in trouble out there," he whispered.

After she hung up the phone, she smiled, remembering how badly she had wanted out of the *Courier*. Finally, she was free. She had also severed her last tie to her hometown, and now she was basically homeless. She couldn't stay at Keriani's much longer. That meant getting some kind of job, because writing a book wouldn't pay the bills. Tears welled up in her eyes. Sadly, there was no ear buzz to guide her.

A few days before the Solstice, she decided to call Jake in Corrales and see if he was back. As much as she wanted to see him, she dreaded facing Lena, Dominic, or any of the UFO groupies.

"Jake, it's Niki. Just wanted to see if we're on for Friday."

"Yes, definitely," he said. "I've been cleaning up a bit here."

"And Lena? How is she?"

Jake hesitated. "I don't know. She's not here."

"Where is she?"

"I'll explain all that when you're here. It will be a small gathering. Just come a little before sunset."

"Okay," she agreed. "No Dora dork or her gang, right?"
"No, none of them. I look forward to seeing you, Niki."

December 21, 1982

Driving to Jake's house for the Solstice gathering, Niki thought of what all she had to tell the group. Keriani would meet her there, and perhaps even Baba would surprise them. He was a *new guru,* according to Keriani, who had "seen the light" while in the ashram. She could hardly wait to share her story of finding the Enoch book and how it explained the transmissions and the Language of Light. Ashara, the name of Enoch's wife, was probably the source word for both ashram and Ashtar Command. Enochian aliens, Zadokites and Sumerian Shamans account for everything in the bible, she decided. And, of course, Sirian spores. Niki glanced at Schroeder and giggled.

She also wanted to discuss the letter from Gribbin. Even though she was done with doomsday, it would be fun to see if anyone else knew about the Mayan prophecy. Niki thought about Phil and Bishop Pike and wondered what they would have said about 2012.

Just like old times, she felt a bit of a buzz in her ear and knew what the peace treatise, 2012, Enochian light messages, and Dogon star people all had in common. It was right there in that final transmission from Phil. *It's an inner journey.* It's all about perception. It's up to us to find peace.

Heading north toward Corrales, the rose-colored rays of light illuminated the Sandia Mountains. "VALIS pink," Niki said aloud, and smiled. Some things never change.

Despite everything that had happened, the fact that she could laugh was a good sign. Otherwise she'd be totally mad by now. Put away in Mt. Pleasant, she thought. That's what they say back in Iowa, meaning the town with the state mental hospital.

Niki turned west again down the tree-lined road that led to Jake's property. She loved this little rural area more than any other place in New Mexico. The huge cottonwoods, even without their greenery, reminded her of Iowa. She noticed the postcard stuck in her visor, one that had been there since her first trip through Albuquerque. It looked almost exactly like Jake's place—an old adobe, nestled in the trees of the Rio Grande bosque, and perfectly framed by the watermelon pink mountains.

She pulled the van into Jake's big double driveway. Only his Scout was parked there. Niki thought she was running late, but apparently not. The driveway and paths were lined with luminarias—little bags with candles—usually reserved for Christmas Eve. A new chile ristra hung from one of the exposed vigas on the portal. Just like the postcard, Niki thought as she tapped the brass door knocker.

When the big wooden door swung open, there was Jake. He looked younger, and happier than she had ever seen him. He grabbed her in a bear hug. Over his shoulder, Niki could see that everything was clean and neat, and she even spied some new furniture.

"Jake, what's going on?"

"You like it?" he beamed with pride.

"I hardly recognize the place." She walked through the adobe house admiring all the changes. The brick floor was actually shiny. No piles of papers or books. A small piñon tree with a few ornaments and twinkling white lights stood where a broken shelf had been. The old ratty sofa was gone, replaced with a new Taos-style wood framed settee. The room glowed with candle light.

"An amazing transformation. Who's coming tonight?"

"You better sit down," Jake suggested. "And let me get you a glass of wine."

He poured Niki a glass of white Zinfandel and continued.

"Niki, listen. Lena's gone."

"Gone? Where is she?"

"She took off for Peru with Dominic. I guess that episode at the sweat lodge really affected both of them. They went to Machu-Pichu and plan to open a new healing centre there."

"Peru! What about his retreat? And the Health Garden—Lena just left that?"

"Well, like I told you, the Health Garden is really mine. Lena was managing it. I have an old friend running it now. Dominic's place was all leased land."

"So, how do you feel about that?"

"I think they belong together," Jake said. They both laughed, Niki a bit nervously. "What about tonight? I invited Keriani to meet me here. In fact, I thought Baba might show up. He's due back any time, for the holidays."

"They won't be here," Jake said. "I spoke to Keriani. No one else is coming here tonight."

Niki felt her face flush. She stood up and walked around the room again. She couldn't look at Jake just yet.

"Let me give you my update," she began. "I've been working on the book while staying at Keriani's, and doing research at Rick's OM Centre. It's amazing how many similarities there are among the gnostics, shamans, and Buddhists.

"Remember how I discovered moksha meant release from suffering? For Phil and Pike, their attachment—what kept them here—was their desire to complete their work. It's not ghosts that haunt us, it's finding peace."

"Insightful," Jake said.

"I miss them, though," Niki looked up mostly to hold back tears. "Do you believe Celestials and angels watch over us?"

"Well, space brother, avatar—is it really that different?" Jake asked. "I mean take a look at those blue people flying around in the Hindu art. Those could be angels or ancient aliens. Who are we to say?"

"Are you serious?" she asked.

"You mean the star?" He laughed. "Why not?" Jake sipped his wine and studied Niki. "You still haven't been able to explain the Dogon doctors."

"No, but that Enoch book helped me see that labels just create confusion. We're all seeking the same things; clarity and mostly peace."

Jake took another sip of wine and studied Niki. Then he got up and took Niki's hand.

"Come on, follow me," he said as he led her towards her favorite small study where he had first shown her the PKD books. The room was totally transformed.

The old milk crates and board book shelves were replaced with a brand new built-in work station with a big "L" shaped desktop area. There was a newly installed white-washed light fixture. It looked antique and hung low over the desk. All the PKD books were neatly arranged on one of the shelves. It was a perfect writing spot and Niki felt a little envious.

"It's wonderful, Jake," she tried to sound gracious. "What motivated you to do all this?"

"You. It's for you," he smiled.

"Me?"

"After all if you are going to stay in New Mexico, you need a quiet place to write."

"Here?" Niki looked at him confused, surprised, and with no idea what to say. Before she could even try, Jake took her into his arms and whispered, "Yes, Niki Perceval, here."

He pulled back and she could see and feel the love.

"We've both known since we first met." He looked deeply into her eyes, then took her face into his hands. As their lips met, it was the final piece of the puzzle falling into place.

Tears began to stream from the corners of her eyes.

A few minutes later he added, "I do have a suggestion about your book."

Niki tensed up, certain the magical spell was about to be broken.

"What?" she asked.

"Your working title, *Biomorphic Madness: Analysis of a Phenomenon,*" he said. "That's quite a mouthful. It doesn't sound like the right title for a peace treatise.

"And, what would you suggest?" Niki pulled back to see his face.

"How about *A Kindred Spirit,* in honor of Phil? After all, the "K" in his name is Kindred."

"Jake, that is genius. Perfect!" At that very moment Niki heard a buzzing sound and jerked. Could it be?

As if reading her mind, Jake pointed to the light fixture. The light was flickering. It buzzed again and then came on brightly. "Now that really was a sign!"

They hugged and laughed.

"Okay, speaking of names, I have a suggestion."

"What's that?" Jake asked.

"Maybe we should rename you, too."

He looked confused.

"Let's have a fresh start. I don't want to call you Jake. Your name is Jay Christiansen. I want to call you Jay."

"Well, it's not only the Solstice, you know. It's the second full moon of the month tonight," Jay said. "We only get a chance like this once in a blue moon. Let's go finish lighting those luminarias."

Jay put his arm around Niki and they walked out into a perfect twilight evening. Like Keriani, she bowed her head, put her hands together in a prayerful position and touched her forehead, lips and heart, silently giving thanks to everyone who had watched over her on her long, crazy journey.

In the end, it's doesn't really matter if there were ancient aliens, Zadokite zealots, pink info-firing beams or any of the other mysteries that Philip K. Dick spent a lifetime trying to resolve. No outer search can solve it. We can only find peace within. That is what Niki's dad was trying to convey.

Life is for living, not for endlessly speculating about the unknowable. Phil and Pike finally understood this, although they had to die to do it. Peace and love—that's what is really real, and what makes us human. The story is finally told.

The end? Hardly!

As Phil once said, "The real adventure is just beginning."

See this fleeting world as a **shooting star**—

"a bubble in a stream,
a flash of lightning in a summer cloud;
a flickering lamp, a phantom, a dream."

-- Buddha, from the Vajrachedika "Diamond" Sutra

The answer to the cipher was in your hand the whole time – in the papyrus on the back, and in Phil's final transmission.

The Gift of Peace

The next time you feel angry, or frustrated, just remember to ask yourself, "Who am I really hurting?" We only hurt ourselves with hate and dis-ease. How people act is their business. How we **re-act** is ours.

- Hatred does not hurt our enemy—it only hurts us.
- Bitterness is poison and can kill us.
- We don't own anyone or anything. We come into this world alone and we will leave alone. As John Lennon said, "the only thing we take with us is our soul."
- Letting go of hate and anger is the way to health and healing.
- Peace is an inner journey!

May peace guide the planets and love steer the stars!

Afterword: A final message from Phil

"I can say no more… I am a fictionalizing philosopher, not a novelist; my novel and story-writing ability is employed as a means to formulate my perception. The core of my writing is not art, but truth.

What I tell is the truth—I can do nothing to alleviate it, either by deed or exploration. Yet this seems somehow to help a certain kind of sensitive troubled person, for whom I speak. I think I understand the common ingredient in those whom my writing helps: they cannot or will not blunt their own intimations about the irrational, mysterious nature of reality…

My audience will always be limited to these people. It is bad news for them that, indeed, I am "slowly going crazy in Santa Ana, California," because this reinforces our mutual realization that no answer, no explanation of this mysterious reality is forthcoming.

Where this will ultimately go I can't say, but so far in all these years no one has come forth and answered the questions I have raised. This is disturbing. But, this may be the beginning of a new age of human thought—of new exploration. I may be the start of something promising: an early and incomplete explorer. It may not end with me."

-- Philip K. Dick, April, 1981
Excerpt from the Exegesis
Previously printed in a longer version in
Lawrence Sutin's "In Pursuit of Valis."

Acknowledgments, Credits and Thanks!

On March 2, 1982, Philip Kindred Dick reportedly died from a stroke. He is buried in Colorado next to his twin sister, Jane, who died as an infant. During his 53 years he wrote over forty novels and more than 100 short stories, many of which were frequently mentioned and described here, and thoroughly enjoyed. PKD also left behind his Exegesis—more than eight thousand pages of notes and journal entries where he struggled to make sense of his revelations, theological and philosophical insights.

Did he make contact with Nicole Perceval, or the author of this book, in his final quest for the Penultimate Truth? What is real? The truth is often stranger than fiction.

Paul Williams, who served as Literary Executor for Philip K. Dick's estate for many years, talked of publishing this story, just as he had many of his own books and one of Phil's early novels, *Confessions of A Crap Artist.* Unfortunately, by 2008 it was clear, due to Paul's health, that would not be possible. I hope he sees this book so he can know that the story was finally told.

Paul wrote this note after reading my first book proposal. Later he gave me the quote used on the back cover.

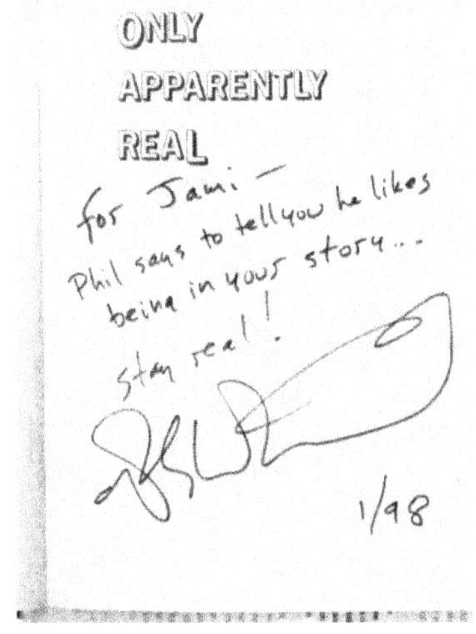

Blessings Paul,
on your own journey!

My Tree of Life includes friends—kindred spirits—and many people who inspired me, and played various roles in assuring the story was told. There is only space to name a few of the die-hards:

John Loyd and the **"core four"** who endured from first idea through the publication process. John, because he introduced me to Philip K. Dick, and **Brandy Turner**, author-to-be of the same Turner-Loyd Clan—Alphane Moon descendants—who spent many hours in "book talk."
Maureen "Mo" Riley was present when the plot hatched and has remained a loyal friend/grammatical coach/pinch-hitting editor and provided tireless moral support. Not to mention her famous "who said it had to be either/or" philosophy! You go, Mo!
Michael Garcia, true blue friend and self-proclaimed "#1 Fan."
Jonathan Cartland miraculously re-appeared at exactly the right time to re-collect everything! Thanks to him, CogDisCo, LLC, his fabulous cover design, and technical assistance, we got it published!

Kay Blanchette Garza, part-time proof reader/full-time friend, Word Wiz, and of course, keeper of the "skeletons."
Dennis Domrzalski, Editor and friend. We barely survived this!
Mary Gray (graymm@earthlink.net) Illustrator/artist who never questioned drawing odd sketches. She just did a wonderful job!
Marie Eleina Quintero, angel and promoter extraordinaire.
Rosendo Romero, the Ultimate Reader (at 82) y Amigo!
Rob O'Neil, PKD fan, researcher and friend.
Tessa B. Dick, Thank You for loaning me your husband ;)
And, my lil' bro, **Jeff Nichols**, who truly is a Kindred Spirit!

Again, my very special thanks to John R. Gribbin, E.C. Krupp, and Tom McKay for allowing me to fictionalize their roles in this story.

And, to previously mentioned **Paul Williams,** whose early support and encouragement, *PKD Society* newsletter, Rolling Stone article, his own account of *Only Apparently Real*, plus hours of personal comments and tours of California PKD-land, were truly invaluable.

Asa "Acer" Mullins still owns **Bird Song Used Books**, but it has moved from the famous 1980s "Harvard Mall" location to 1708 Central Ave Southeast in Albuquerque. Please patronize the store!

The OM Center is no more, but **Rick Cramer** remains spry at 92, and is teaching T'ai Chi Chih in Albuquerque! Baba of Bodhi Tree? No telling in what dimension I found him and his lovely family.

In a true phildickian moment, I learned of the first U.S. Philip K. Dick Festival just as this book was going to press. **David Hyde**, aka Lord Running Clam (another Alphane Moon descendant), provided a perfect venue for the Intergalactic Release of AKS!

Special thanks to **Gregg Rickman** and his *Philip K. Dick: The Last Testament.* His interview of 2-17-82 provided invaluable insight into Phil's final state of mind. I never met **Lawrence Sutin**, in the course of writing AKS, but my copy of *Divine Invasions: A Life of Philip K. Dick* is well worn. It was my PKD Bible. Ditto for Sutin's edit of the Exegesis: *In Pursuit of Valis.*

I spoke at length with **D. Scott Apel** a few times. His non-fiction *Dream Connection* (Impermanent Press) and my own experiences were eerily familiar. Thanks, Scott! Sadly, my PKD article(s) never appeared in ***Radio Free PKD***, which vanished while I was writing. But **Greg Lee** and Phil fan/SF author **Paul DiFilippo** provided early encouragement, and for that I was and am grateful.

Finally, the PKD Email Discussion List (pkd@jazzflavor.com), maintained by our pal **Cal Godot**, has been an ongoing source of inspiration since the mid 1990s. Check it out!

You might enjoy deciphering the code on the back of the novel and searching for mentions of PKD novel and short story titles scattered throughout my story. I urge you to buy and read Philip K. Dick novels and other books, poems, and songs mentioned in my story.

Thank you again to all the above, and anyone I forgot to mention!

Final Legal Disclaimer

I do not take credit for words or works I did not create. My use of any copyright material falls under Fair Use of copyright works as parody, commentary, or quotation. I happily give credit to the poets, lyricists, writers, and creators of the following:

High Flight - Poem by John Gillespie Magee (1941) adapted as song "On the Wings of a Dream" by John Denver (1982.)

St Peter's paraphrased quote by Robert Frost – "But I have promises to keep, and miles to go before I sleep."

A line from the song *Aquarius* by Gerome Ragni & James Rado © EMI was quoted by fictional reporter Niki Perceval in the *Courier* and author ej Morgan. Other brief song mentions: *American Pie* (McLean), *Already Gone* (Temchin/Strandlund), *Radar Love* (Kooymans/Hay), *Sunshine of your Love* (Clapton/Brown/Bruce), and *Vincent* aka Starry, Starry Night (McLean)

I Ching: Book of Changes quotes are from two versions of Richard Wilhelm's translations. His 1950 version, rendered in English by CF Baynes, and the pocket edition further simplified by WS Boardmen.

James M. Robinson, edition of *The Nag Hammadi Library* (New York: Harper and Row, 1977). Quotes from 1977 or the revised 1988 edition.

Robert Hutchings Goddard was an American physicist and inventor who is credited with creating and building the world's first liquid-fueled rocket. Father Robert Hoggard was an associate of Bishop James Pike, who may or may not have known about an alleged Zadokite mushroom cult.

The London Times and *Ottumwa Courier* are real newspapers. Niki Perceval (a fictional character) did not work at either, nor was the quote from Gribbin actually in or from the *Times*. He did say "I don't believe anything" on a BBC radio program in reference to faith versus scientific fact.

And last, but certainly not least, quotes from **Philip K. Dick's** novels, as well as comments about his ideas, are acknowledged. While only used fictionally here, I hope you are inspired to purchase and read his novels.

Author Info:

e j "jami" Morgan was born in Ottumwa, Iowa, but has lived the crazy, creative life in the Land of Enchantment since 1982.

"New Mexico is a great place for artists and writers," she says. "Of course, I *had* to stay near the VLA to receive those pink-beam transmissions from VALIS!"

More Sirius stuff:

Morgan was a television and radio broadcaster, news journalist, government geek, and helped Al Gore invent the Internet in the early 1990s (she says smiling ;) She created and ran (SysOp'd) one of the first personal computer hobbyist Bulletin Board Systems (BBS) in the United States in the early 1980s and hosted the first international online New Age Conference.

Morgan also published a small booklet called *Beyond the GodForce* © 1991 and plans to re-publish it before 2012, along with a multi-media, multi-dimensional "homeopape" version of AKS.

You can follow the book on Facebook or Twitter as AKSbook, or go to **AKSbook.com** for all the current developments, book events, eBooks and more. Thank you so much for your interest. May you find Peace and …

a Kindred Spirit!

www.ingramcontent.com/pod-product-compliance
Lightning Source LLC
Chambersburg PA
CBHW070802180626
46818CB00001B/60

* 9 7 8 0 9 8 2 7 6 1 9 0 8 *